Ken Coffman and Kristen Lolatte

Other books by Ken Coffman and Kristen Lolatte

The Reluctant Queen

Other books by Ken Coffman

Steel Waters
Alligator Alley (with Mark Bothum)
Twisted Shadow (with Mark Bothum)
Glen Wilson's Bad Medicine
Toxic Shock Syndrome
Immortality, LLC
Hartz String Theory
Endangered Species
Fairhaven
Mesh (with Adina Pelle)
The Sandcastles of Irakkistan
Fianchetto
Buffoon
Real World FPGA Design with Verilog

ISBN Print 978-1-949267-69-3
ISBN eBook 978-1-949267-70-9

STAIRWAY PRESS

APACHE JUNCTION

www.StairwayPress.com
1000 West Apache Trail Suite 126
Apache Junction, AZ 85120

Kristen's Dedication

For my Mancub: always follow your NorthStar.
For Maddy: always believe in magic.
For David who left us far too soon, and for Elizabeth who shines like a bright star leading us onward.

For all the warriors I know and love: don't ever stop.

Ken's Dedication

To fallen friends musical heroes: Armando "Chick" Corea and Allan Holdsworth

Credits

Cover Photograph by Wayne Fournier, www.thruthesoberlens.com
Cover Design by Guy Corp, www.GrafixCorp.com
Chapter icons by Brian Antoine Woods,
www.BrianAntoineWoods.webs.com...
and Olha Bondarenko (starting with Crystal Ball)
Cover Model: Madelyn Sweet

Fiona and Minnie—Lost in the Woods

IT WAS DARK and the angry stars had turned their backs on them. Minnie was tired and whiny.

"I was asleep and dreaming."

"I know, baby," Fiona said. "I'm sorry. I was dreaming too."

Minnie tripped on a root—Fiona was barely able to catch the little girl before she hit her head on a granite outcropping.

Minnie leaned against a tree and whispered, "I'm not moving until you tell me what we're doing here. I want to go home."

The word *home* hit Fiona hard. There was nothing more she wanted than to go *home*—to be with Sean and the Fachan and the warm, safe house in the clearing in the woods. Instead, they were stumbling around in the dark—and there were trolls around, she could hear them cursing the cold and stomping through the underbrush. She shuddered to think of what the trolls would do to them if they were found.

"Please, Minnie, keep your voice quiet and I will tell you." Stretching out her hands like a blind person in a strange room, she found a log to sit on. She pulled Minnie close and held her tight. "I was dreaming, but it wasn't a dream. It was more like—prophesy. Do you know that word?"

Impatient, Minnie raised her hands in frustration.

"I'm not six. I read."

"Of course," Fiona said as if to herself. "I'm sorry. I forget how smart you are sometimes." She took a deep breath and let it out slowly. "It wasn't a dream, it was what would happen if we stayed." She shivered. "Everything in flames. The house. The woods. Sean…"

After a few seconds of silence, Minnie whispered, "What about Sean?"

"Dead. Chopped to pieces. Boiled to stew. Eaten. It sounds silly, I know, but really, devoured with his bones tossed to the wolves. I can hear his bones crushed for their marrow. We're forced to watch, but worse, our mouths are pried open and…"

Weeping rivers, she buried her face in her hands.

Minnie patted Fiona's shoulder.

"We're not safe in these woods," the little girl said. "There are trolls everywhere."

"You're right, we're not safe, but Sean is. Understand?"

Minnie's shoulders slumped.

"We had to leave to protect Sean. He promised to protect me—to protect us, but we have to protect him instead."

"I saw it. The only way—and even this is not for sure—is to run away and hide. Get in the Bug and go as far as we can. And, there's something important, are you listening?" With everything in her, the waif listened. "No magic. If we use magic, we'll be found. Promise me. No spells. No incantations. No hexes or invocations. We must leave all that behind, or else. I need to hear you say it. Cross your heart and swear on your mother's soul."

"Not even something small, like…"

"None. Nothing. Zero. Do you swear?" To their left, there was a rustling. Fiona clasped her hand over Minnie's mouth. "Shush," she breathed quietly. "We can't let them find us."

After a few long seconds, the rustling moved away.

"I can find the Bug," Minnie whispered. She slid off Fiona's lap and tugged her hand. "This way."

Slowly, the sky grew perceptibly brighter. They followed a faint trail with the sound of their footsteps muffled in damp leaves. Trees. Marsh. Ditch. Road. Ahead, the Bug sat where the Faire people had pushed it to a turn-out. By the front tire, there was a spot blacker than the gloomy murk. Luna stood guard.

Fiona released Minnie's hand and raced to the car where she gathered the warm cat into her cold arms. Luna accepted the embrace for a few seconds, then slipped away to allow the trailing Minnie a few strokes before pawing at the dirty car's door.

"Yes," Fiona said. "You're right, we need to go now if not sooner—assuming the stupid car will start."

The stupid car seemed eager to go—the engine caught as soon as the key was turned.

Fiona thought about it for a moment.

The lost key that was in the car's ignition.

There was no time to ponder the mystery. In a Maine minute, they were settled in and rolling. Initially, the road led them north, but soon they turned to the west. An hour later, it occurred to Fiona to look. The fuel gauge hovered near empty.

"Baby, see if our stash is still hidden under the seat."

Minnie moved Luna aside and fished around. It took a few moments until she found the bundle tucked up in the seat's springs. Fiona breathed a sigh of relief. They would not get far if some passerby had found the emergency packet. There wasn't much cash in the cache—maybe two-hundred dollars or a little more—but it was much, much better than nothing.

"There are granola bars if you're hungry," Fiona said. Holding the packet on her lap, Minnie shrugged. "Yes, it's better to wait, I agree. We'll be a lot hungrier later."

Luna pawed at the packet.

Waiting was not part of his plan.

"If you eat your kibble now," Fiona said, "you'll have none for later." Luna turned his big yellow eyes on her. "Right. Later is later and now is now. Give him what he wants."

Minnie was already tearing open a packet of tuna-flavored treats. In a few seconds they were gone and once Luna realized that was all he was getting—and believed it—he groomed his whiskers and settled in for a nap while the rattling Bug ate mile after mile—rolling toward the west.

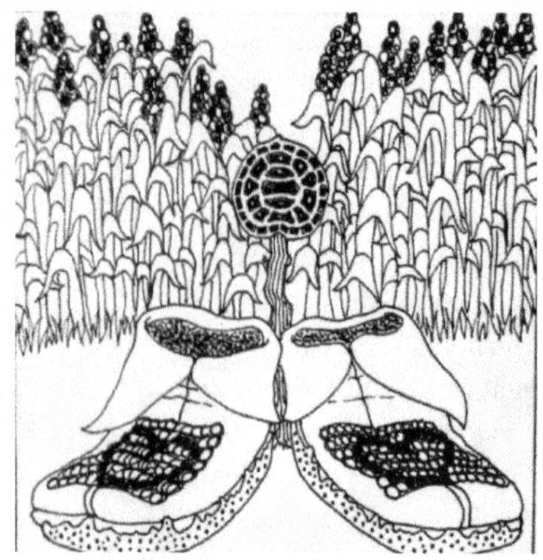

Fiona and Minnie—Corn Field

THE BUG SWERVED and Fiona struggled for control. The night was dark and dreary. It was not raining, but the clouds in the overcast sky were low and threatening. She pulled onto the soft shoulder, then turned off the engine and killed the lights.

"I can't keep my eyes open. I need to stop for a nap."

"Where are we?" Minnie said.

"I don't know. Iowa? One of the flat states."

Luna opened his eyes and looked out into the black night. He was unimpressed; he lowered his head and tucked it between his paws.

"No," Minnie said, "we can't stop here."

"I just need a rest my eyes for a minute."

Fiona lowered her forehead to the steering wheel and in a few seconds was unconscious. Minnie was fidgety. Before and behind, the road stretched straight ahead—she could only see a few feet, but the road stretched out forever in her imagination. The Spring corn was only three feet tall, but rustled as if rudely gossiping about the intruders. It was growing, she could feel it. Seeking the sun, the corn grew a couple of inches every day. The problem was not the corn, it could not help being what it was, feed and ethanol corn, not sweet corn for broiling and eating. The problem was what lived in the corn. Minnie, nervous, weaved and wound her fingers together and tried not to think about what slept in the darkness.

A mist rose from the field and surrounded the car. There was a little light, so Minnie could see her reflection in the side window. She looked pale and terrified, but tried to remain calm.

"This will soon be over," she whispered.

Her reflection was mixed with another; a thin, ghostly face superimposed on hers. Her heart leapt into her throat. Thin fingers scratched the glass and beckoned. The door wasn't locked—the lock did not work. If he wanted in, he would come in. She closed her eyes and hoped he would go away. When she reopened them, he was still there, waiting.

She would be murdered in a corn field—they would all be murdered. With a long, impatient fingernail like a claw, the man tapped on the window. She glanced at Fiona who remained unconscious. Minnie steeled her will and opened the door.

Outside, the wind tugged at the hem of her dress and she pressed it down with shaking hands. He wore muddy moccasins with multi-colored beads. She realized the beads were colorful kernels of dried corn. Slowly, she raised her eyes. The man unwound and towered over her. He was thin, impossibly thin, and wore green rags that fluttered in the wind. He had a longbow across his shoulder—along with a quiver of arrows.

"Kill me if you must, but please spare my, my—mother."

The man studied her—as if weighing and appraising her words. Nervous, Minnie was tongue-tied.

"No, she's not my mother, but she's all I have. My real mother, my first mother, my birth mother, she died. Fiona is taking care of me. She's my mother now."

The man laughed—it was a low-pitched, earthy chuckle.

"I am not here to harm you. I am here to protect you if I can." He gestured in a circle. "You should not stop here. It's not safe."

"Fiona could not drive anymore, she needs sleep. We've been driving for days."

The man studied her face.

"You are not the Corn Maiden or child of the Wheat. You are not the Bean Maiden. I'm married to the one and only Bean Maiden and I think I would know if I was married to you. So, mystery-girl, who are you?"

Minnie could hardly get the words out.

"I'm Minnie. Minerva. I'm no one."

"Minnie? That's not a good name for a young woman with your power. A fingerling fish can be a Minnie, not you. Now, in return, you must have my name. The Báxoje called me Oh-Da-Sthe-Deh, but they were tricksters and could hardly be trusted. I call myself Coranich, a singer of the fields, but never mind. Have you heard of the origin of the corn? A beautiful young woman evaded intruders by hiding in rushes by a stream. This lovely maiden wore a green cloak and had golden hair. After praying to stay hidden from the men who would desecrate her virtue, she turned into a cornstalk. So, be careful what you wish, do you follow? You might get what you ask for, not what you wanted. This is known, but is everything known also true? No, it's not. So, I will protect you, but there is something I want in return. From this day forward, if you eat an ear of corn, eat every kernel whether you want it or not. Do you understand? Eat all of it or none—leave nothing to waste. Look carefully at the cob and leave not even the smallest kernel. Do you promise? Do you swear?"

Minnie nodded.

"I swear."

The tall man cocked his head.

"It's coming. I will give you one gift—while you're in the corn, spin the totem once an hour and you will be safe. When you get to your new home, bury it with the seed inside—bury it where it will get sunlight. Understand?"

He handed her something wrapped in a long leaf. There was a rustle in the field. The man twirled and smoothly nocked an arrow.

Over his shoulder, he said, "How long does she need?"

Minnie was unsure.

"An hour or two?" she said.

The man grimaced.

"An hour, very well, but no longer. Don't worry, fish-girl, I will buy your hour. Then you drive, keep driving and don't forget the totem."

With that, he was gone. As quietly as she could, Minnie got back in the car. Inside, she unwrapped the leaf to reveal a stout twig stuffed into a tiny tortoise shell. She shook it gently—inside was a dried pea or stone.

No. Corn kernel.

It was a child's rattle. At the small sound, Fiona stirred and mumbled something incomprehensible, but did not awaken.

How long is an hour?

It can be a blink of an eye or it can stretch into a lifetime. For his warmth, Minnie pulled Luna onto her lap and shrank inside her jacket. It was cold and getting colder.

When it was time, Minnie shook the rattle. It was loud in the car. Fiona sat up straight and finger-combed her hair. She started the car.

"What do you have there?"

Minnie handed it over. Fiona examined it in the dim light.

"This is an odd thing. What else do you have stuffed away in your rucksack?"

Minnie shrugged.

"Nothing," she said. "Can we go?"

Fiona looked around.

"First I will go into the corn for a wee."

"No," Minnie said, "you can wait until the next town."

"Oh, I suppose. I hope it's not too far." She revved the engine and pulled out onto the road while Minnie fiddled with the heat controls. "I wish the heater worked better."

"Me too," Minnie said.

"Thanks for letting me sleep. I needed it bad. Hey, did I say anything? I had some crazy dreams."

"No, you didn't say anything at all."

"Good, that's good," Fiona said. "You're a child, I don't want to scare you with my bad dreams."

"Right, I'm only a child," Minnie said.

She gave the rattle a spin to hear its clatter.

As the car rolled forward through the fields, the sun slowly climbed the sky behind them.

Fiona and Minnie—the Continental Divide

THE BEETLE HAD a mind of its own; it stopped when it wanted to stop and went on when it wanted to go. Halfway through Colorado, Fiona had pulled into a gas station for a stretch and a pee in Golden. Ahead, the jagged mountains looked like an impenetrable wall—a wall no sane person would try to scale. The gas-sipping bug held enough fuel to easily make it to Grand Junction, but, after an hour of winding highway and being passed by pickup trucks and RVs, the car sputtered and threatened to stall before the Eisenhower Tunnel.

Georgetown.

Minnie and Luna were catnapping. Fiona pounded the heel of her hand on the steering wheel.

"No," she muttered. "This is nowhere."

It didn't matter, the car wanted a break. She pulled off the highway and steered into a convenience store where she prepaid for her gas. The tank accepted less than two gallons. Embarrassed, she went back in for change.

What a waste.

Outside, an old man stood at the back of her car holding a rusty toolbox; it was as if he had materialized from the cold, thin mountain air. With wispy hair ruffled by a breeze, his eyebrows were wild thatches. He stared from deep-set, suspicious eyes. Fiona had an immediate sense of him—one of the town's eccentrics. Lonely, a man who loved machines more than his fellow humans. With gnarled hands, he'd worked the silver mine—she felt that part of his soul was buried in a deep hole bored in the mountain.

It was a stupid question, but she asked it anyway.

"Where did you come from?"

"You got a couple thousand more vertical feet to go before you get to the Ike-Divide. You won't make it. You don't want the engine to lug, didn't you hear the nasty pinging? Pay attention to what your engine tells you or you'll be stuck under the stars freezing to death. You people don't stop no more—too busy, too much of a hurry."

You people. She instantly bristled. *What did he mean by that?*

She pressed her irritation aside.

"I don't have any money for repairs."

"Didn't say nothing about no money. Let the cat out—take the kid, go in and stay warm, I'll tune up the buggy. Get some coffee. Tastes like it was brewed from old rags in grease, but it will keep you going over the pass."

He dropped the toolbox.

"What are you going to do?"

"I already told ya. I'm going to look over things. Check the tension on the generator belt and retard the spark for the altitude. You can find someone in the Junction lowlands to set it back for you. Go on now, git got."

When Fiona opened the passenger door, Luna jumped out and was gone in a flash. She unfastened Minnie's seatbelt and lifted her out. Minnie was growing; she was no longer a wisp. Only by straining could Fiona lift her.

"Where are we?" Minnie said.

"Just a place to use the potty."

"I don't have to go."

"Well, you can go anyway. I'll buy you a hot chocolate."

"Put me down, I can walk."

Fiona wanted to lead Minnie around the front of the car, but Minnie caught a glimpse of the old man—already with his head buried in the rear engine compartment. Making curved parallel lines with her fingers trailing along the side of the mud-splattered bug, she walked back. The man sat on his toolbox cussing under his breath.

"Out here in the wild with points damned near shot to hell…"

"There's a storm brewing," Minnie said.

"Around here," he said with his face buried in the engine, "there's always a storm brewing."

"Does the ghost-man play every day?"

The old man reared back on his haunches and studied her face.

"Get on in where it's warm and get your choc'late."

"Don't act silly. I know you hear it." She waved her arm toward the mountains to the north. "It's a sad song."

The old man sighed and brushed hair off his forehead with the back of his hand.

"It's the Ghost of the Silver Plume—sawing away on the fiddle all day long. He don't ever stop."

"Fiddle is for the body—it makes you move. I know the difference, that thing echoing down the mountain is a violin. It makes you think and feel."

"You got a smart-butt mouth for such a little thing."

"I get tired of people assuming I'm stupid—or ignorant—because I'm young."

The old man tilted his head back and laughed.

"Me too," he said.

"Who'd you bury up in those hills?"

The old man's laughter died.

"Everyone," he said. "Everything." He shook off the mood. "I gotta finish this beetle-bug. Go on before I apply the palm of my hand to your hindquarters."

She turned to go. Through a plate glass window Fiona could be seen agonizing over expensive bags of trail mix snacks—weighing the money in her pocket against the weak nutrition.

"Hold on," he said.

He reached deep into an inside pocket of his grimy jacket, then held out a bundle wrapped in a scrap of cloth. She weighed it in her hands.

"Heavy," she said.

"As long as you got that in your back pocket, you won't ever be poor or hungry."

"Thanks," she said. "Can I show it to Fiona?"

"Show it to the devil for all I care, it's just dead metal. Now scoot," he replied before returning his attention to the engine. "Tell the big boss I'll be out of here in five."

When they came out, he was gone. Fiona cocked her head, thinking she faintly heard something echoing from the hillsides—a long, mournful musical note, but could easily have been something imagined. She checked the latch on the engine compartment. They were ready to go. She looked across the parking lot for Luna, but then noticed he was already inside.

"How..." she muttered, but decided to let it go.

Once they were settled in the car, she patted the dash.

Did the old man harvest some parts? Was that his game? Steal vintage Volkswagen pieces to sell in the Little Nickel?

She turned the key and the car started instantly. The engine seemed to be happy. Too happy. Fiona was irritated.

"Who owns whom?" she said.

"I got to use the restroom again," Minnie said while picking raisons from the bag of trail mix.

Fiona turned, but Minnie laughed at her.

"Just kidding," the little girl said. "The car will make it through the tunnel now, so go, already."

Somewhere in the middle of the cavernous 1.7 mile Eisenhower Tunnel, they crossed the Continental Divide and it was generally downhill from there to the Pacific Ocean.

They, the three of them, could feel it. Things were different.

Newer, fresher, rawer and wilder—more of a frontier than the old, civilized East. On the long downgrades, the little car ate miles.

Fiona intended to stay on I-70 to Grand Junction, but the bug slyly pulled to the north at a little town called Silverthorne. She didn't even perceive the route change until seeing a highway sign that said 9. Then she noticed additional clues—except briefly, she shouldn't be seeing the bears and the North Star: Ursa Major, Ursa Minor and the Polaris, but there they were, hovering in the sky like galactic billboards. Minnie, munching on trail mix, stared out through the side window.

"How did we get off the 70?" Fiona said.

"It's because the river flows north here."

Taking her eyes off the road, Fiona glanced at Minnie.

"I told you. No magic. We need to keep quiet and hide."

Minnie shrugged.

"I did nothing. Pull over if you can find a safe place."

"You said you didn't need a bathroom. If you needed to make water, you should have done it at Georgetown."

"Make water, that's a funny expression, isn't it? Like anyone could *make* water. Water just is; it doesn't need any making." She pointed at the road ahead. "There, that will work, pull over and give me ten minutes under the stars."

Fiona sighed. There was no need for battle; she'd never win an argument with a stubborn twelve-year-old. With a pang, she realized Minnie was no longer twelve—she'd turned 13-going-on-30 as the cliché goes. Fiona thought back to the days when she was thirteen—half a lifetime in the past. The teenage years were less than great for her—truth-be-told, they were a nightmare. Minnie seemed to be dealing with the physical and emotional changes much better than Fiona had.

A flash of guilt flowed through Fiona. After all Minnie had been through, how could Fiona deny her anything?

"Just a few minutes, okay? It's cold."

The car was barely stopped when Minnie burst out. Fiona

reached for the trail mix and shook the bag, examining the contents in the reflected headlights. Minnie liked the raisins, they were all gone. Fiona leaned her forehead on the steering wheel.

I'll just rest my eyes for a minute.

At the side of the road, a mountain goat trail switch backed to the rushing water of the Blue River. While debating the cost and benefit of making the descent, Minnie waved at midges swirling around her face. Thinking about their journey, she had an instant vision of what a life-in-hiding would be like; she'd be a crawly, slimy creature hiding under a rock. It would be safe in the darkness; hiding had that going for it, but hiding held no honor. Was everything in life a balance between being exposed and being safe?

There is power in stones. Trolls won't find me hiding like a worm.

The wind was bitter cold and the roadside gravel was frozen in chunks with gleaming ice—turning it into nature's temporary concrete. She shivered, but felt a heat from inside her core. Her hormonal body was changing. There was a new Minnie blooming, a Minnie who was no longer a child. She raised her arms and threw her head back. The Earth stopped spinning—it was iced in place like a still life painting. The stars stopped inching across the sky. The wind died.

I have the power to stop the world.

"You give yourself too much credit, young lady." The voice did not surprise her. She stood still, leaning back even further—stretching her arms out as far as they would go. The tips of her fingers tingled with electricity.

The voice continued.

"Do you think she'll embrace her destiny and make us a proper Queen?"

Minnie released the air from her lungs.

"She does not want to be Queen."

The response was deep laughter like an earthquake.

"And I don't want to be a boulder. Yet, when you look at me, what do you see?"

"I don't know, because I'm not looking."

"Is your arrogance unbounded? Does the world cease to exist when you're not looking?"

She laughed.

"Yes. Poof, it's gone like a will-o-wisp dream exposed to the morning sun."

"They said you are eloquent for such a tiny tendril of girl."

"Are you happy not moving and being stuck in one place?"

"Does it really seem like I'm not moving? One day I will roll into the river and change its course. But, beyond that, we're whirling around the sun and scooting through space at an unbelievable speed. How can you say I'm standing still?"

"Easy. You're standing still. You're not moving—you're stuck like a rusty nut on a discarded bolt." The boulder shifted and the gravel heaved. She bent her knees and rode out the Earth's movement. "Am I supposed to be impressed?"

More laughter.

"Maybe not." There was silence for a moment before the rumbly voice continued. "The mountains are strong and powerful. They will protect you from the army rising in the east, but not forever. You're a silly thing, but you'll remember that, won't you? The mountains give you time to prepare for battle, but nothing more. Just time. Time to grow your strength and get ready. Time that is infinite, but should not be wasted."

"What is happening to me? I feel different inside."

"I'm made of stone, what do you expect me to know about frivolous little flesh-and-blood girls? Go now, go on with your journey. The square city is waiting. Go before you freeze solid and join me."

With that, she was cold. The stars and the wind resumed their dance. She walked back to the car and climbed in. Fiona woke with a start.

"How long was I out?"

"I don't know. A minute, an hour or a year? Something like that. Let's go."

Fiona put the car in gear.

"Do you think we should go back to the main highway?"

"No, we always go forward, never backward, remember?"

"Okay, you're the boss," Fiona said.

After a few miles on the winding highway, Minnie spoke.

"Do you know anything about a square city?"

Fiona thought for a minute.

"Nope, no clue," she finally said.

"I guess we'll find out," Minnie said.

Fiona and Minnie—the Square City

WHEN THEY FINALLY reached I-80, the choices were east or west—which was no choice because they were not going back toward the east. Later, after they'd been driving nonstop for five hours, a sliver of moon hovered on the hazy horizon. Then, the bright lights of the city spread across the great basin valley like scattered costume jewels. After the long hours on the highway, the sight of civilization was welcome.

"What do you think, Minnie?" Fiona said. "Shall we take a rest here?"

Minnie shrugged. "We'll see, I guess."

As they descended, the city grid was obvious.

"Normal means at right angles," Minnie said.

Fiona glanced over. "What?"

"Nothing," Minnie replied.

"I like the look of it. With all the LDS, surely it's one of the safest cities in the world."

"Square places are not good for the soul."

"What do you mean?"

"Nothing."

They saw the lights of a motel. Fiona weighed the idea of sleeping in the car and decided they could afford a night of relative luxury and comfort. The car agreed and allowed them to pull in.

The lobby was plain, but functional. The night clerk was a huge, oval-shaped man with a face deformed by acne—both fresh outbreaks and old scars. He appeared to be Samoan or Polynesian. His nametag said Ahonui. His voice was high and thin, far from what was expected from such an immense man.

"Do you qualify for any discounts?" he said. "Triple-A or anything like that?"

"I hope I qualify for the nearly-broke-and-I'm-not-kidding discount."

"You can get the stay-for-free-if-you-help-clean-the-place discount. We're down a maid tomorrow. Do you have any experience with motel cleaning?"

Fiona shook her head.

"Not a whit," she said.

"You can help anyway. Just wipe the floors with the used towels and then haul them to the laundry room. You could stay around a while. This is a great place to live."

Her mind flashed on the image of what she might be mopping up with the soiled towels.

"It's certainly something to think about."

After taking the keycard, she walked back to the car where she saw Minnie talking to a husky lady. Fiona stopped and stared, but realized she was being impolite. In an instant, she became attuned to the area. A thin man, screaming about something, pounded on a motel door until the door opened a crack. He didn't go in, there was an exchange through the doorway and he walked on—fidgeting and looking over his shoulder. A man—watching—sat in an ancient Cadillac smoking a cigarette. All the sudden it hit her. Despite the bright lights of the temple just a few blocks away, this was an unsafe place. Standing by the pool with their arms thrown across the fence, three unblinking, predatory men watched.

With effort, Fiona made her feet move. Standing with

Minnie, the woman was not. Up close, the illusion fell apart. There was heavy powder on her chin which did not hide black stubble growing beneath. Her wig looked like it was made from shredded plastic and her satin gown was frayed and dirty. Inside, Fiona was torn. She wanted to be fair to people who embraced alternate lifestyles, but that did not mean being stupid. Anyone, even a priest or a president, could be dangerous.

"Who is your friend, Mmmin…"

At the last instant, Fiona held her tongue because she did not want to reveal Minnie's name.

"Miss Mavis," Minnie said. "She says I look skinny—she wants to buy me dinner. With ice cream and cake."

The trail mix was many miles gone. Fiona felt a twitch in her empty belly. A hot, comfort-meal sounded great. Meatloaf, mashed potatoes and gravy. Her mouth filled with saliva.

The woman held out her hand to shake. Fiona reached for it—it was limp, clammy and cold, like shaking a dead squid.

"I'm pleased to meet you, Mike."

The woman's eyes turned ugly.

"I'm crossed; call me Mavis when I use this gender expression. Do I know you? How did you get Mike?"

"Sorry, I didn't mean any offense. We could use a meal, that's for sure."

Minnie spoke, "We sure are hungry, aren't we?"

Mavis glanced at the little girl. Minnie's expression was neutral.

Mavis bristled. "I only have money for the two of us—the baby and me."

Minnie grinned. "I could bring back a box, right? We could bring mamma the leftovers?"

Behind Fiona, a car honked its horn—a long blast. She jumped, then realized they would not be spending the night at the motel. Around the lake, the salt flats stretched for endless empty miles. That's where they would sleep. Uncomfortable. Freezing.

"Jump back in the car."

Minnie smiled sweetly at Mavis.

"It was a pleasure to meet you."

Mavis reached out to grab the little girl's shoulders.

"No, you won't," Minnie said.

Mavis strained her powerful arms, but could not move. She opened her mouth, but could not speak.

Minnie opened the car door and slipped in. Cooperative, the bug started right away and in minutes they were back on I-80, headed west. It took many miles before Fiona felt like speaking.

"You enjoyed that, didn't you?"

"I told you the square city was not good for us."

Fiona was frustrated, but she didn't know what to say. Long miles elapsed in silence. Minnie pulled a paper sack from under the seat and rustled around in it. She handed Fiona half a tuna sandwich.

"Is this from…"

"No, not Mavis," Minnie said. "The old guy back in the mountains."

Fiona looked at the sandwich suspiciously, but it smelled heavenly. It was made with grainy, hand-cut slabs of home-baked bread.

There's nothing like near-starvation to whet the appetite.

She took a huge bite. Chopped pickles and onions were crisp and tingly on her tongue.

"Did he give us any…"

Minnie was ready. She twisted the top off a plastic bottle of water and handed it over. After eating the second half of her sandwich, Fiona felt almost cheerful.

"Look, back there, Mavis…"

"I know. Some people are good. Some are bad. It don't matter what they look like or how they choose to live."

"Okay. Fine. Did the mountain-coot give us any candy bars? That would be perfect. I could eat a monster Butterfinger and die happy."

Minnie opened the bag. "How does a Mounds bar sound?"

Fiona's soul soared. Under the bug's wheels, the long miles flew.

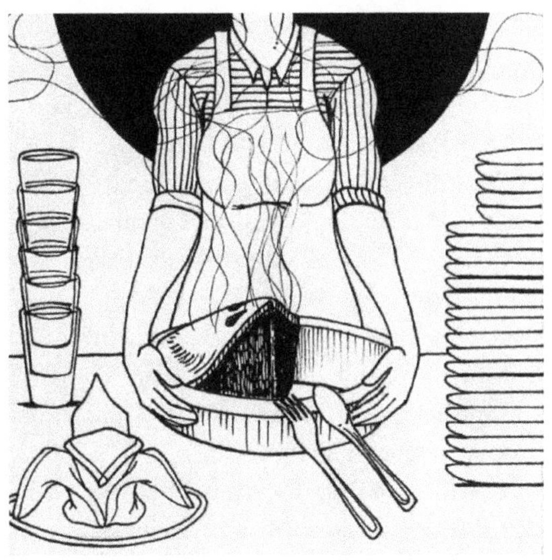

Fiona—Pie

THE DINER, CALLED *Mom's Pantry,* wasn't much to look at from the road—just a converted, post-war rambler-shack with a gravel parking lot, mildewed siding and a mossy, broke-back roof. The place would be razed when the budget for widening the highway was approved, so there was no justification for doing any upgrades. However, the highway improvement plan had been on the books for over a decade and there was no sign of immanent progress.

Through a grimy side window, Fiona saw a black, slinky shadow near her faded purple Bug—the VW looking like a junkyard relic under a sprawling oak tree. The cat, Luna, had something limp clamped in his jaws. Fiona frowned. She was not Luna's mother—Mother Nature was—and that mother could be cruel to the slow or the unfortunate. Feeling no need for a sad reminder of how tough the cold world could be, she shuddered and turned away from the window.

Her thoughts drifted back to her first encounter with this lonely place. The restaurant stood between the highway and Washington State's Skagit River in a forlorn, isolated spot. Her first glimpse of it was while dreary Pacific Northwest rain oozed from a spongy sky.

In the restaurant business, the three clichéd keys to success were location, location, location and this restaurant had none of the above. When she and Minnie had stopped, they were nearly broke and the Bug was running on gasoline fumes.

In the window, a Help Wanted sign had said: *You Pretend to Work and We'll Pretend to Pay You.*

Fiona hadn't understood Chef Chet; he didn't seem to care if they ever had any customers. He served the standard stuff: hot dogs, burgers and fries, but always had something special on the menu for those who knew enough to ask.

He was a stocky man of indiscernible heritage with black hair, olive skin and a roundish face. Was he Indonesian? Filipino? She relived their first conversation…

"'Bout to shut down for the night," he'd said. "Ain't had a customer for a couple of hours."

Minnie looked around the dilapidated room with wonder.

"The river is talking to me," she whispered to Fiona.

"Shush. No magic." To Chet, Fiona said, "I doubt you'll be impressed—I'm down to my last couple of dollars, so I can't afford a meal. I'm just wondering how far it is to the next gas station."

Chet had studied her with calm intensity.

"Couple miles down-river, but they are closed until seven in the morning. If you can make it another thirty miles, there's an all-night place."

Fiona sighed.

Another night sleeping in the Bug.

They were used to it by now, but that didn't mean they had to like it.

"Any tea, by chance?"

Chet grinned.

"I have Walini."

Fiona's insides lurched.

"What?" she said.

"If you prefer black-Lipton factory tea, I have that too."

"I don't believe you really have Walini."

Chet shrugged.

"With ginger or no?" he said.

As it turned out, along with the exotic Indonesian tea, he had sourdough bread and oyster stew that would be thrown out unless it was eaten. Resplendent with chopped potatoes, sweet onions and glorious shreds of salty oysters, it was the best meal they'd had in a month.

"These oysters are incredible," Fiona had said.

Chet beamed like a lantern.

"Kumamoto oysters from the farm down the highway a ways. Taylors. Someone once said eating a fresh oyster is like French-kissing the sea."

Chet also happened to have a room attached to the restaurant—and spare blankets stuffed in a closet. By the time the evening was over, Fiona had a job with no pay, but she didn't have to share the tips, if there were any—and she and Minnie had a place to hide.

Quiet Celtic instrumental music from Fiona's iPod floated from wall-mounted speakers.

Back in the microscopic kitchen, Chet wore his snow-white chef's mushroom hat tilted far back on his head while chopping leafy romaine for the evening's salad mix. Fiona nibbled from a bowl of steamed baby carrots and daydreamed about baking pies.

The California Red Haven yellow peaches Fiona had examined at the fruit and vegetable stand off Highway 20 were perfectly ripened, so that was a no-brainer, but what else? Baked pecans—they had plenty—those would go in, but was that all? She was trying to decide how adding pistachio paste would taste when the tinkle-bells over the door sang. Her heart sank when she saw Mr. Miller. She spoke quickly to preempt all hope.

"No pie today, Mr. Miller. Peach tomorrow, I swear."

Miller shook a gnarled finger in her face.

"I didn't just fall off the pumpkin truck, so don't try the funny stuff with me, young lady. I saw you baking yesterday. Where's the pie you promised?"

They weren't intentionally in the pie business because properly baking a pie was a lot of time-consuming work and who would bother when people who knew no different were happy with corn syrup-saturated assembly line pies from the frozen food section of the grocery store?

Fiona's mother had baked an endless stream of pies, day-in and day-out. Then, one slow day when sleet attacked the windows, Fiona craved the cozy smell of a pie baking in the kitchen, so she gathered ingredients from the restaurant pantry and baked a razzleberry pie with a tablespoon of chunky peanut butter and drizzled, bitter-chocolate sauce. She remembered the day very clearly.

A youngish urban couple dressed in spotless North Face rain gear had come in after parking their Range Rover. After eating buffalo burgers and beer-battered onion rings, the lady put a hand on Fiona's arm to stop her.

"What are you baking? It smells heavenly."

"Oh. I baked a pie, but it's not for sale."

Fiona looked through the slot where infrared lamps heated the meals waiting to be served and made eye contact with Chet. He made a cutting motion across his throat. They'd already talked about this; the remaining slices of pie were going home with him for his wife and daughters.

The male customer was impossibly handsome with curly sand-colored hair and sapphire-blue eyes. A diamond glittered in his ear and he wore a Greubel Forsey watch that looked like a random pile of gears encased in museum glass. One could buy a house for what that watch cost—and not a cheap house at that. From a gold money clip, he peeled off a hundred-dollar bill which he nonchalantly dropped on the table.

"We're very generous tippers," he said.

She searched their faces. There was nothing she hated more

than the rich and arrogant, but this couple was young and innocent and just wanted pie and were willing and able to pay for it. And, she could really use a hundred dollars for her get-out-of-town stash.

While considering, there was raucous giggling from two woods elves under the corner table, but Fiona ignored the pests. She picked up the greenback and waved it at Chet before stuffing it in her pocket.

"Pie it is," she said. "Coming right up."

The ice cream came from a family dairy a few miles away—they churned and sold it to the locals in five-gallon buckets. The young couple didn't ask, but once the pie had heated in the oven, it demanded heaping scoops.

"I've never tasted a better pie," the young lady said. "We'll tell all of our friends."

"No, please don't," Fiona said.

Her attention was dragged brusquely back to the present.

"You didn't eat all of it," Miller said, while pointing at the metal box where they stored the pies. "How much is left? I'm not leaving here empty-handed and don't try to charge me no full price, either. I'll be having a steep discount for my trouble."

Fiona was distracted. A vivid-blue Steller's jay stood on the windowsill, pecking. Chet had warned her.

Once you start feeding them, they'll come back and harass you relentlessly until you feed them again, every day per their schedule.

Like people and their damned pies, Fiona thought.

"Chet had some. He owns the place, so I never win an argument with him. There's half left."

"Chet didn't eat half," Mr. Miller said.

Fiona shrugged.

"I wanted to try it myself and see how it came out. Then Minnie stopped in. She was hungry."

"Show me," he said.

Fiona sighed and lifted the storage box lid. Inside, the pie looked pathetic—the remainder was closer to a third than half.

Happily, Mr. Miller was not the type to demand too much.

She lifted the picked-over pie out and placed it on the counter. He lifted the plastic wrap and captured a dollop on his finger which quickly found its way into his mouth.

"Sublime," he said.

In a minute, she had his twenty dollars tucked away in her apron pocket and Mr. Miller was gone.

She didn't know how her mother did it.

Every day, endless pies and always with a smile on her floury face.

Baking pies in a too-small oven was exhausting for Fiona and she could never seem to make enough of them. Outside, the jay pecked and squawked. It wanted the Wagner's sunflower seeds Fiona bought at the feed store in twenty-pound bags. While scooping the seeds, the doorbells chimed again.

"Pardon me, Miss," the customer said. "Do you have pie today?"

Fiona shook her head.

"Sorry," she said, "but we're completely, totally and inarguably out."

Minnie—River

LATELY, MINNIE FELT as if she would explode out of her petite body. Everyone treated her like a baby and she couldn't deny it—when she looked in the mirror, she saw what others saw: a waif, a tiny child, an urchin. If one more restaurant customer told her how cute she was, pinched her cheeks and brought out a brush to tame her tangled hair...

Minnie couldn't compartmentalize like Fiona—she couldn't shove roiling emotions into neat little internal boxes and close the door against them. She was a feeler, and an intense one at that. When seeing an expired animal lying beside the sinuous highway, she was pulled to it to know its life and feel its last moments as it was freed from the bonds of Earth.

She could walk through the forest and lay a hand on a tree and *know* its story, feel its joy at being touched by the sun and share its fear of lightning or the crosscut saw. She never picked flowers because they cried as they were ripped from the soil and torn away from their Mother Earth—from their families and homes. She didn't like neat and orderly things in rows and columns because nature's proper way is a mixed muddle.

Minnie did not like squares; they were inorganic—with lines too straight and corners too brutal and sharp. Malevolence bred in right angles—in these portals, evil things grew and bad spirits took form. No good could come of them and when the hard edges conjured dark spirits, then what? The collected darkness needed to be faced and excavated to remove the wickedness seeking root. This was something Fiona still needed to learn: there was no escape from destiny. A confrontation deferred would only be more dangerous when enemies were allowed to grow and gather strength. Minnie preferred facing things head on.

She also preferred circles with flowing, mesmerizing lines and no hidden places and shadows. Things in circles were expressed simply. What was, was. As time passed, she truly understood why Fiona thought it best to leave Sean's refuge. Fiona was the new Queen and Minnie was the long sought Princess and in the magic land, they kindled the flames of conflict, vengeance and vendetta. But Fiona was wrong about one thing. Hiding didn't end the war, it merely delayed the inevitable.

Deep inside, Minnie knew all this and understood what was at stake, but the pieces were not yet in place. In the outside world, the future swirled; but she yearned to be back home with Sean and Flix. She yearned for the sweet innocence she had when Sean first found her—when he rescued her and made her whole. But, as always, once you open a door, even if you close it quickly, things will never be the same and there is no choice but to keep moving forward. Crossing a threshold, you can never cross back without being a different person.

So it was for Minnie—innocence lost.

Behind the restaurant, a muddy trail weaved through dripping maple, ash and witch hazel brush. There, the green river flowed deep—a powerful force sweeping through a rock channel into a tabletop-flat pool. Mosquitoes descended in clouds, but Minnie knew a spell that made her invisible to them so she was rarely tapped for blood.

She didn't question the pull of nature, she flowed with it. On this day, a thick mist hovered over the cold water that was fresh from cascading from the looming mountains. It was a cool day but the mist felt like a blanket settling in and soothing her weary young mind.

"Minerva, come closer, we've been waiting for you..." said a watery voice.

Minnie stopped. Fiona cautioned her over and over to avoid big magic; they needed to lay low and draw no attention to themselves. Interacting with the magic world could open a portal and disclose their location to the Dark Prince. Minnie insisted he would soon know anyway, but Fiona wouldn't budge. It was a point of contention between them. Just this once...

"Minerva, be not afraid. I know how you miss Sean. Fiona does too, though she won't let it show. Come closer and dip your fingers in my river. Let me reach up and touch you. With one touch you will be able to see your enchanted, far-away home. You'll see what Sean and Flix are doing. The Fachan is hopping about pretending to help Sean in the garden. They miss you so. They ache for you and Fiona. Come and touch me with your delicate fingers and have a peek. Fiona doesn't have to know. It can be our secret..."

The river was a temptress—a misleader and a cheat. She might look innocent, but many had been pulled into her current to drown. She was not evil, but demanded respect for her power—she did not suffer fools with patience and kindness. Minnie stood on a boulder and studied the swirling water. An inviting strand of green moss waggled in the gentle current.

She looked around to make sure she was alone before pulling out the stubby troll sword hidden under her jacket. With its tip, she stirred the river water and considered.

There was no harm in dipping in one finger. She crouched and fanned her dress around her and reached out with one little finger.

"I wouldn't."

The voice didn't come from any particular direction. Minnie stood up on the boulder and looked around.

"Show yourself," she said.

Jagged, bright green leaves of Oregon Grape rustled. A

mountain elf barely a foot tall stood on the pebbly shoreline. His cape was the color of old moss and he carried a gnarly walking stick. A quiver of arrows was carried on his back and a longbow was strung over his shoulder.

She brandished her sword.

"I'm not supposed to talk to the forest people," Minnie said.

"Then don't."

"I don't see the harm in touching the river."

"The Mari-Morgan water spirit rules from the waterfall to the narrows; she'll drag you in if you aren't careful. You're not ready yet."

"I'm tired of being treated like a child. Who are you? How did you find me?"

"Linnaeus. A friend." He shrugged. "Without thinking about it, you used magic to dispel mosquitoes. We noticed."

"Just a minor spell from an old, forgotten book." The elf shrugged again. Minnie continued, "If you're truly a friend, then you'll understand. I'm trapped like a butterfly in a jar and I have to do something. Anything."

After placing the sword on the rock, she slipped off her jacket, then squatted on the boulder and unclasped her patent leather shoes. After removing her frilly socks, placed them on the shoes and reached out toward the icy water with her toes.

In a flash, the water reached up to pull her in.

The mountain elf was right—the water spirit was powerful in this part of the river. In an instant, Minnie left the domain of air and light and entered the cold world of water and moss and fish. It was okay. She spread her arms and let go. Everyone faced death sooner or later. She was ready. The water was brutally cold, but only for a few seconds. Then she was numb and disconnected as her eyes, ears and all the other nooks and crevices of her body were filled.

"Goodbye," she said with the last of the air in her lungs.

The Mari-Morgan was silvery and sleek with huge blue eyes and green hair. She was unhappy—it was better when the air creatures struggled and fought against the depth and current. Her face twisted with frustration and her eyes flared with arctic light.

"Be gone with you," the water spirit said.

In an instant, Minnie was back on the rock coughing and spitting. Shivering, she wrapped her arms around herself. Something had changed. Her cold flesh was different. Something new emanated from deep inside. Her hormonal cells stirred.

"Come warm yourself by the fire," the mountain elf said.

She turned. In a pocket of rocks and tangled roots, the elf had kindled a small fire no larger than a birthday candle.

"That fire wouldn't warm a field mouse," she said.

The elf laughed.

"Right you are," he said. "So stay out there and freeze."

He already had her shoes and socks—they were hanging on a branch. Sword in hand, she picked her way across the boulder and hopped to the shore. The closer she got to the little fire, the warmer she felt. Inside the protective cover of the nook, it was warm and the radiation from the licking flames tickled her skin.

"Take off your dress," Linnaeus said.

She crossed her arms across her chest.

"No."

He laughed.

"Suit yourself, but you'll get warm quicker if you hang up your dress to dry. I won't look."

"Turn around," she commanded.

He nodded, then complied. She pulled the dress over her head and stepped out of her panties.

Naked, she turned in circles to let the fire spirit soak into her bare, smoothness. She was different. Something was different. The flickery light caressed her skin and she glowed. As she faced the flame again, she saw Linnaeus staring at her.

Defiant, she raised her arms to cover herself.

"You said you wouldn't look..."

Linnaeus shrugged.

"Men lie about things like that," he said. "You're not beautiful."

"That's not very nice." Instantly smiling and defiant, she raised her hands and straightened her spine to stand boldly while running her hands through her hair and smoothing it across her shoulders. "Everyone comments on how pretty I am."

"Pretty, yes, but not beautiful. Not yet. Not for a month or two, then you will begin to be."

She reached for her dress—it was warm and dry.

"Oh, I hope so," she said, "I really do. I'm so ready to be beautiful. I'm ready for things to be different."

The elf shrugged.

"Be careful what you wish for. When your body changes, you might lose connection with the spirit world. It happens, almost always—it flows out of you with the blood."

"Fiona would be happy if that happened. She thinks we can bake pies and hide and both worlds will forget about us."

"If so, she'll be the Queen of Nothing. The Queen of Sadness and Despair. The Queen of Misery. It could happen, that's one of the many outcomes. When the sun rises from the East, don't you see it? A black spot—growing. It will eat the whole of the Sun unless she stops it."

Minnie tugged the hem of her dress around her knees.

"Tell me what I should do," she said.

He was gone. A breeze tugged at the underbrush and riffled her dress. She was alone. With a puff of creamy smoke, the wind killed the little fire and she was cold. She pulled on her jacket and retrieved the short sword. Standing by the river, she ran a thumb across its blade. It was blunt—troll magic sharpened it when it was raised in anger. There were canvas loops sewn inside her jacket—the sword slipped back in its place.

She walked back to the river and kneeled. Thoughtless, she dipped an idle finger. The Mari-Morgan was far downstream—ignoring her. She raised the finger and studied a drop of water gleaming in the waning sun. Tilting back her head, she let the drop fall on her tongue. It was crisp and cold and tangy with minerals. In an instant, it filled her from head to toe.

Tell me what to do...

Like ghosts in a graveyard, clouds of mosquitoes materialized.

She waved a hand to disperse them.

There are no answers here, not today.

The gathering gloom threatened her temper, but she waved the dark mood away with the mosquitoes. There was enough light to follow home—just barely if she didn't stop to listen to the owls and prowling foxes.

If I could trade the secret world for glamour and beauty, would I?

This is what she thought about while picking her way along the faint forest trail.

Trevir, the Black Faerie Prince—at Hawthorne Hill

THE THRONE WAS not much to look at. It was an orange, upholstery-covered armchair placed on a plywood platform held aloft by concrete blocks. Far overhead in shrouded fixtures, halogen lamps dangled on cables hanging from the cavernous ceiling. Panes of fractured glass had been covered with cut-up boxes—weak sunlight streamed through and left patches on the floor reminiscent of mouthfuls of missing teeth.

The sprawling brick building was born as the Hawthorne Hill Insane Asylum, but was converted after World War II into a factory making vacuum tube computers, but this was before transistors took over and mass-manufacturing moved to Asia.

Later, the building had stints as a screw-making shop and injection molding facility—it still reeked of burnt plastic and machine oil. The rural ruin had belonged to the Dark Prince's grandfather. The current legal ownership was fuzzy, but it didn't matter because no one cared. This remote area north of Boston was far from any highway and was hidden in trees and forgotten. The driveway was nearly a mile long, so the place was isolated and private. It might as well be on a different planet.

Trevir sipped sour wine from a plastic cup and wrinkled his nose at the odor of oily smoke drifting through the huge room.

"What are the trolls cooking now?" he said.

Troll Srenzo looked up from the book she was reading and shrugged. She sauntered to him and ran a dirty finger down the side of his face.

"Same as usual, I expect," she said. "Rat. Do you want me to check for you?"

Trevir scowled.

"No, I really don't care to know. I don't know why I asked." He looked around the factory floor at the rubbish and rusting machinery. "We have to move out of this hell-hole. Why can't we move to the Mandarin Oriental?"

From a tall goblet shaped like a heron, she poured blood-red wine into his plastic cup.

"Soon, my love," she said. "Soon."

Minnie—A New Friend

WHEN THE LIGHTS of the restaurant came into view through the trees, Minnie realized trouble was brewing. She was not supposed to be in the woods after the sun went down.

How will I explain why I am so late and why my hair has dried into a tangled mess?

She could say she slipped on a rock and fell into the river—which had the benefit of being partially true. Would that be enough? Probably not. Fiona was persistent and would ask endless questions.

I could say I was pulled under the water by a river spirit and took off my clothes while a forest elf lit a fire to dry me; then I'd suffer Fiona's wrath about secrets and using magic and blah, blah, blah.

Sigh.

It was a no-win situation. Maybe she could just slip in unnoticed and hope Fiona was preoccupied. With the lights of the restaurant in view, she stopped and doubled over with laughter at her little joke.

I hope Fiona is preoccupied—with her pies.

Recovering her composure, she walked on the final stretch of the muddy trail back to the restaurant. Lost in thought and talking with her hands, she was completely unaware of being followed. When she stopped focusing inward for a moment, she stopped in her tracks. The *thing* behind her stopped in its tracks as well. She turned to face her shadow, but there was nothing.

A voice in her head whispered.

There's never nothing.

Spruce trees. Blackberry brambles. A sliver of moon.

She touched the short sword under her jacket and stretched out her mind.

There was something, something small. She kneeled. At her feet was a small bundle of black and white fur. Skunk. It sat on its haunches—fat cat style.

"Hello there, little one. Are you following me?"

It cocked its head to the side as if listening and understanding. Minnie held out her hand. The skunk approached and sniffed her fingertips, and then nuzzled her hand.

Between her ears, she could hear Fiona scolding.

If that filthy creature sprays, we'll never rid ourselves of the stink. The restaurant will die.

As a small act of defiance, Minnie picked up the wee creature and cradled it like a newborn baby. The skunk crawled up her arm and nuzzled into her neck.

"Awww, I can't leave you out here to fend for yourself. You're like me, no family. Alone. No one. For whatever reason, you're outcast like me. Fiona will kill me for bringing you home but I don't care. We have Luna and now we'll have you. Hmmmm, but first a name. Let me look at you for a moment."

Minnie held the skunk at arm's length and studied it, then settled it on the ground. The skunklet waddled here and there, sniffing and rooting about. With thoughts drifting, Minnie tuned into the tiny animal's spirit and discovered it was a female. She wasn't supposed to use magic, but this was important—it would not do to use the wrong name. After what seemed like a very long time, Minnie uncovered it like a gemstone in mud.

Keela.

She recalled a vague sense of the Celtic name.

Beauty that only poetry can capture.

"Keela. That's fitting. Not everyone can see the beauty in a skunk, but I sure can. You are simply precious. What do you say, Keela? Shall we go home and face what will be?"

Keela turned and raised her tail.

"No, no, no, you don't need to go spraying anyone. Best to never squirt. If you do, that would be a surefire way to make us both into homeless orphans. It will be okay, I'll take care of you."

Minnie reached out her hands. Keela bounded.

You're staying whether Fiona and Chet like it or not. If Keela must go, so will I. No discussion.

Up to her elbows in suds, Fiona washed the diner's dishes. They were endless. Spoons, forks, knives, bowls, plates, serving platters, utensils, aluminum pots and black-iron frying pans. All the while, she looked nervously through the window as darkness raped and pillaged the day.

"Where *is* that girl?"

Earlier, she had felt a ripple in the air and knew Minnie had gone and gotten herself into something.

Why doesn't she listen? Why must she always do things her way? Does she not realize what's at stake? Our peace, our freedom…our lives. Sean's life. Why must she always argue? How am I supposed to rein her in when I'm not her mother? Good goddess, I'd give anything for some help.

All this and more swirled in her head. She put the last carving knife in the drainer when Chet approached with a gumbo spoon.

At the tired look on her face, he stopped.

"It can soak and wait for tomorrow," he said. "Or, I suppose I could wash it myself."

She sighed. "Hand it over."

It was coated with something like concrete or dried wood glue, but she managed to clean it proper. Holding it up so she could see her reflection, she studied her frazzled hair.

"You are an evil spirit."

The spoon did not know if Fiona was referring to him or to her image in his bowl, but either way it was okay, he decided to let it go.

She caught a glimpse of Minnie walking up the path—clutching something small.

"Oh, goodnight, what is she bringing home this time?"

Be open-minded, Fiona, no good comes of going into a conversation with stopped-up ears and a closed mind.

She tapped the spoon on a cutting board, but realized the tune in her head was something she heard at the Renaissance Faire, so she stopped. Ren Faires are unsafe.

Minnie is okay and returning home—that's the important thing for the moment. The rest would sort itself out. As long as we're hidden here in Nowheresville and far from trouble, it always will.

Unconsciously, she tapped the rhythm again while Minnie walked to her cubby room under the staircase. There, she held the rodent in front of her face. The image that appeared in her head was vivid: skunks are more like weasels than rodents. Keela showed off her carnivorous teeth.

Okay, sorry, Minnie thought. *Weasel it is.*

She let Keela hop to the floor. The salt-and-pepper bundle of fur walked around and sniffed everything, then found a tossed-aside towel in a corner and claimed it for her own. Like a dog, she burrowed in with just her black nose sticking out. She emitted a happy feeling: safe, warm and clearly at home. Giggling, Minnie walked over and stroked the top of Keela's head. Then she changed out of her rumpled clothes.

Time to face the Queen, I suppose.

Minnie stood for a moment watching Fiona stare out through the kitchen window—tapping on a cutting board with a giant metal spoon. Somehow, Minnie knew the song, a modern version of an Olde English folk song. She took a deep breath and sang in a clear soprano voice.

Bugle-Nosed Jack carved a goat with his beak

While Doodem Daddum played quoits with his dog
And Pussy Willy quaffed a pint in one draught.

"You have to stay out of my head," Fiona said. "I've told you a million times. No magic. It's not safe."

There was only one safe place Minnie knew and they had left it in the dark of night, running away like thieves. How Minnie longed for Sean and Flix and the Fachan. She dreamed of being back there, surrounded by magic, warmth and love. They didn't have a care in the world when they were there—they were out of harm's way. Well, not really. She knew the brat prince was looking for them—forever searching and scheming. He wouldn't give up until he found them. But, that wouldn't stop her from dreaming of home. Already, those days seemed far away—when she was younger and more innocent.

Fiona's hands were red and wrinkled from the soapy water. On tippee-toes, Minnie reached up on a shelf and pulled down a bottle of *Corn Huskers Lotion*, then motioned for Fiona to stretch out her hands. Fiona closed her eyes and drifted away while Minnie worked the lotion into her mother's aching fingers.

The peace and quiet—perhaps like the calm before a storm—felt like an oasis in the desert. They stayed this way until Fiona's hands were supple and pink. There was a hum and rhythm to the process and both Minnie and Fiona moved to its time and cadence like a well-practiced dance. When all was done, Minnie leaned over to hug Fiona around the neck.

"Well, goodnight."

"No you don't, hold it right there, young lady. Tell me about your day."

Here we go, thought Minnie.

"I took a walk down to the river and slipped on a rock in the water. After a bit of a struggle I climbed out and started a small fire to dry off a bit. Then I came home. The end, see you in the morning."

"The end, huh? You omitted the part about the river goddess grabbing you and spitting you out and the forest elf starting the magic fire to dry you off. It's okay to be naked in the woods, is it? And, what is it you carried home?"

"If you're so smart and knew what I did, why did you bother asking?"

"To see if you'd tell the truth, the whole truth."

"You assume I would lie so you need to check up on me?" Fiona stood still as a statue giving Minnie the eyebrow. Minnie hung her head and appeared to be on the verge of tears. "I'm sorry. I didn't mean to lie. I know how much the magic upsets you and I didn't mean to do any of it. You always get so angry with me and it's not always my fault, but you never believe me."

Was this preteen stage acting or was she being sincere?

Fiona reached out to hug Minnie and folded into her.

Sincere, Fiona decided.

Fiona remembered how much Minnie had been through and how much more she might still have to endure. The path to becoming a teenage girl was never an easy one and less so if you were a child of magic. Minnie had no real parents. She and Sean, Flix and the Fachan were all Minnie had; and they had to flee the safety of that world and go it alone. Fiona had to remind herself of all of this.

Go easy on the child, but not too easy.

"Tell me what you brought home with you."

Minnie pulled away and gave Fiona her most compelling, mischievous grin, one with an irresistibly sly twinkle in her eyes. She took Fiona by the hand and pulled her to the little bedroom where she opened the door and pointed to the corner. All Fiona could see was a little button nose sticking out from between the folds of the blanket. She looked at Minnie, and Minnie went "shhhhh" with her fingers up to her lips.

She tiptoed over and ran her finger over Keela's little head. The nose moved and was followed by a yawn. Fiona put her fingers over her mouth to cover a grin.

"Leave it to you to bring home a baby skunk, Minnie. What's her name?"

"Wait, what? I thought you'd be mad?"

"I am angry. Fuming like a wet wasp." Fiona couldn't do it, she smiled. "Teach her not to spray, okay? You'll need to keep her safe and figure out what she wants to eat. She's your familiar. She needs you and you need her. While I'll admit, it's rather different than any cat or dog, but it suits you. We don't choose our familiars, they choose us. So, my beautiful Minnie, what's her name?"

"Keela. I think she's an orphan like me."

Hearing the word *orphan* made Fiona's heart go heavy.

Yes, Minnie was an orphan and if Keela would comfort her and make her happy, then Keela would stay.

"Welcome, Keela. I hope we serve you well. You and Minnie have much to learn of each other and I've no doubt you will be with each other for many moons."

At that, Keela looked directly at Fiona and blinked her deep brown eyes.

Fiona sighed.

"I suppose I'd better break the news to Luna that he has a new sibling. As well, I'll try to catch Chet in a good mood and let him know."

She turned to leave the room.

Minnie called out to her back.

"Thank you, Fiona."

Fiona turned and winked, then headed out to call Luna.

"That went better than expected," Minnie said to Keela.

It had been a long day. Minnie curled up next to the skunklet and fell fast asleep.

Outside, Fiona was wrapped up in a blanket looking up at the stars. Orion cartwheeled on the horizon.

"Oh, Sean, where are you when I need you most? I don't know what I'm doing here. Am I right, am I wrong? Was I wrong to leave you? Why did all of this come to us? How I wish we were all still together. I miss you so."

Cold tears seeped down her face. A falling star flashed across the treetops while she quietly wept. She had to remain strong and hide her feelings away; she could never let Minnie see her like this. These displays were a sign of weakness and they couldn't afford any missteps. At all cost, Minnie must be kept safe.

Luna pranced up and dropped his prey at Fiona's feet—an unfortunate shrew. Fiona wrinkled her nose but patted Luna's head and doled out the obligatory praise. Luna missed Sean too, so if praise is what he wanted, praise is what he would get. Both Fiona and Minnie had their familiars; they were family.

"Luna, my handsome prince. We have a new house guest. Minnie brought home a skunklet named Keela. She's just a baby, an orphan like our precious Minnie. Be kind to her, or else. I didn't sense any magic or trickery about her, so I don't think she was sent to us with any ill intent. Nonetheless, she would benefit from your guidance. Are you up for the task?"

Luna looked up at her and puffed up. He missed his missions. Fiona stroked his head and cooed.

"That's my handsome warrior prince. Now, shall we go in for the night?"

Luna raced to the screen door.

"I'll take that as a *yes*."

Fiona followed.

Standing at the door, she looked up at the stars and moon one last time and whispered, "Goodnight, Sean."

Once inside, she shut the screen door firmly behind her.

Kelley Koeneg and the Drudgery of School

GOOD GAWD, HOW she hated walking through the schoolhouse doors every day. It was no good, the kids who didn't hate her felt sorry for her, and that was worse. Her dad served overseas in the Army and everyone knew they were poor. Her mom worked, but the jobs she found paid almost nothing, so there wasn't extra money for school clothes. Kelley did her best to mix things up, but there was only so much that could be done with her fundamentals: two pairs of thrift store jeans and five WalMart blouses. Today she wore Goodwill finery: a fake-leather skirt, black and white striped leggings, Doc Martens boots (well-worn comfy ones), a black, loose-fitting t-shirt with hoodie that said "transcend the bullsplatter." She wore heavy, black eye makeup and tussled, short red hair she dyed herself in a bathroom sink.

Pure pain. Complete monotony. Indoctrination and conformity. All the things her inner radical rebelled against. If you could look inside, you'd see Kelley standing with her hands on her hips, chin thrust upward in defiance and her feet stomping in a tantrum, leading a revolution against unfair psychological torture.

Logically, she knew she had to be in school. Her mother did the right things to encourage and cajole her. She'd heard the lecture too many times to count.

"We need to *try* to lead a normal life, Kelley..." and "...I know you don't agree, but school *is* important."

Ugh, blah, blah, blah, empty words that fell into her ears. They meant nothing, this mandate to *be normal*, *try to fit in* and *get a good education*.

Every morning, she thought of running away. From mopping the Frosty Freeze every other night, she had over a hundred dollars in cash stuffed in a sock in her underwear drawer. She could take a bus to anywhere and it would be better than here.

Education-shmeducation.

Honestly, it was either run away or open the veins in her wrists. Something had to give. She wore long sleeves to cover the wounds she made in the bathtub. She didn't cut herself deep, but the razor called to her. Like a roadmap, it was clear where her future would take her and it was not good. It would be different if she had one friend, just one. But, she didn't. She was too weird and no one liked her. Besides, school was for losers and she didn't want any friends who were losers.

What will my education buy me in the hard world?

"Pfft, nothing, that's what," she muttered to herself as she walked down the hall to her homeroom.

"Talking to yourself again, freak?"

The venomous words were spat at her by Lacey. It was such a cliché, Lacey was a cheerleader—all short skirt, long legs, perfect hair and boobs. It wasn't fair, at 14, she had boobs. All her other sins were nearly forgivable, but not that one. Boys slobbered over her, it was disgusting. Lacey flounced by; the hem of her skirt lifted and showed black skimmies skin-tight against her toned thighs.

She's such a show-off.

Kelley was strong, she had to be, but the relentless scorn

wore her down. For an instant, she believed everything the social girls said about her. It was like a black bear sitting on her chest and crushing her ribs. She could not breathe.

Would the other kids even notice if I died, here, on this spot?

She could hear the announcement for Janitor Rick over the intercom.

Clean up in the hallway outside the music room. Big mess, bring a mop.

She glanced to her left. There was a slight girl standing between lockers. The new girl.

Kelley was instantly angry. New, old, it didn't matter. In a short time, this tiny new girl would hate her and would be added to the long list of people Kelley wanted to see die writhing in pain. Kelley stopped and stared at the small girl—towering over her.

"What are you looking at, creep? Did you lose your way to kinky-garden?"

"Watch this," the little girl said.

She squished up her eyes and rolled her finger. Lacey tripped over her feet and sprawled in the hallway in front of her friends. Her MacBook skidded on the tile and slid along the hallway until one of the other cheerleaders stopped it with a high-top sneaker. After an instant of shock, Lacey bounced to her feet and did a graceful somersault, then jumped impossibly high in the air—stretching her arms and legs into an X.

"Go, Lions," she shouted.

Her friends laughed.

Kelley was suspicious.

"Who are you?"

Minnie shrugged.

"I'm new."

Kelley leaned forward and whispered.

"Did you do that?"

"It wanted to happen and I helped, that's all. Did you know we're going to be best friends?"

Kelley stepped back with crossed arms clutching her backpack across her chest in a defensive posture.

"I doubt that very much," she said. "Leave me alone."

The bell sounded.

Kelley turned and walked away.

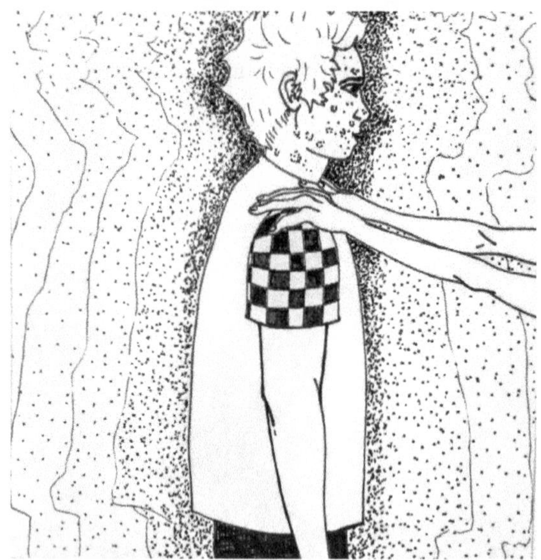

Kurt—Chess Champion

ONE GOOD THING about this rural, sports-oriented school was no one paid attention to Minnie. She was small for her age and not one of the "beautiful ones," so the horny boys left her alone. The popular girls took a look at her on day one and then looked the other way. The jocks didn't even think twice and the stoners, well, they were in their own world. This allowed Minnie to drift through school with no friction.

She moved through the halls like a ghost, unnoticed. She could dress her own way, say what she wanted and be who she wanted to be—and no one cared. The teachers weren't worried about the odd bird they had in their classes because Minnie was smart—she was quiet and did not draw attention while pulling solid B's in every subject.

She could do better, but why?

Minnie watched Kelley walk away. She knew what Kelley was feeling; she'd been picked on and bullied. The girl was strong, but lost at times. All around, some people were doing well, but generally, this rural town called Cement City was dying—she could smell it. There was a reason she was here. When the puzzle was examined at exactly the right angle, there would be a piece missing, a piece shaped like Minnie.

"Excuse me."

With her deep concentration disturbed, Minnie shook her head to clear her thoughts. She opened her eyes. Before her, the boy was older and a mess—a pudgy ginger with a constellation of freckles across his nose and wild, bushy hair that defied the brush. His face was like an open pit mine—it was the worst acne she had ever seen. His teeth were crooked. Smart though, his eyes were alert and penetrating.

"I'm Kurt. If you ever need help with your computer..." his voice trailed off. Minnie studied his face, but did not speak. "And you are...?"

"I'm the new girl." She reached out and put her hands on his shoulders. His bony shoulder blades molded to her palms. "In two years, you're going to be a prize."

"Uh, okay," he said.

He was needy, but not hopelessly. He wanted things that would come his way—and was smart enough that the gifts would not be taken for granted and wasted. With her mind, she reached out and tweaked him. Just a little nudge, that was all he needed. Everything inside him was nearly in alignment, but not quite. She pressed and then admired what she had done. He shook his head like something he could not understand had passed through the hallway. They were indoors. There was no breeze.

"Listen, do you want to join our chess club? If you don't know how to play, I will teach you—it's easy."

Minnie laughed.

"No, but thank you, I appreciate it."

He stepped back and hung his head like a sad puppy.

"Sorry, I didn't mean..."

I'm not supposed to do this.

Fiona was not right about everything. Minnie stiffened her spine and gave a big push—she gave it everything she had.

"I'll tell you who to ask," she said.

He looked puzzled, like the world was melting around him. "Who?"

"Kelley."

His expression collapsed.

"I already asked her. She told me to f-f-f, uh, pardon me for saying, 'F'. She told me to 'F'-off."

Minnie tilted her head back. From deep inside, the laugh came out. Kids rushing by to take their seats before the final bell looked her way, but she didn't care.

"Ask her again."

"Are you sure?"

Minnie doubled over. The scene was so incredibly funny, she could hardly speak.

"Yes, yes, I'm very sure," she managed. "Now scoot, we don't want late slips."

He walked away briskly, looking back at her over his shoulder. The puzzled expression on his face was priceless. Wiping her eyes, she scurried and found her U.S. History seat precisely as the final bell tolled.

Minnie and Lacey—Part One

MINNIE KNEW THE clock would do its job at its own pace whether she watched it or not, but could not help throwing a glance here and there. Like all the other students, she felt a thrill when the 3:00 bell finally rang and the regular school day was over. She streamed out the front door and walked toward the restaurant. She could take the bus, but, weather permitting, she preferred the long walk through the woods. A strident voice followed her.

"Hey half-pint, wait up!"

Really, is that the best insult Lacey could come up with?

"Are you ignoring me, pipsqueak?"

Oh c'mon. Lame ass short-of-stature insults were a thing of bygone days. If you're going to hurl an insult, make it a good one.

Minnie kept walking. She was nearly at the fringe of the evergreens. It had been a long, tiresome day at school and she just wanted the solitude of the forest to envelope her. But no, on this day, Lacey raced after her like an over-excited Chihuahua. Minnie kept on walking.

Eventually, as she knew would happen, Minnie felt Lacey's hand grab her shoulder.

Minnie stopped. She turned slowly around and looked directly up into Lacey's eyes.

"Can I help you with something?"

Lacey froze. She wasn't expecting this reaction. Lacey didn't chase and certainly didn't need anything from mysterious little girls. She might be ignored if someone wore headphones or was talking on their iPhone, but, when they were conscious of Lacey, they would stop and drop all that they were doing, apologize profusely and give her a consolatory hug. But not this one—not this little runt. She had the audacity to not care and what's worse, look her dead in the eye with defiance.

"Did you hear me calling after you?"

"Well, yes, but you never said my name. For all I know, you were bellowing like a lonely calf at some other pipsqueak."

Lacey looked down at her feet.

"You could have stopped or something."

"Why?"

Minnie's question hung in the space between them. It was an honest question, but one that would never earn an honest response. The tension between the two of them grew. Minnie enjoyed having the upper hand for once and could have stood there all day. However, she had a forest calling; she decided to make it easy on Lacey.

"Well, if there's nothing you need, I'd best be on my way. Have a great afternoon."

She turned to go. Lacey reached for her shoulder again.

"I'm not done with you," Lacey spat.

Those were fighting words and ones that Minnie didn't take kindly. She could smite Lacey where she stood, but magic should be her last resort. It would lead to questions and draw unnecessary attention to her and ugh, there would be Fiona's wrath to contend with. No, she'd have to play this one out for the time being.

"Then I will ask again, may I help you with something?"

"Why do you defend that freak all the time?"

"Who might that be?"

"You know who. That freak of a nature who cuts herself. The one who's all goth and anemic looking. Why do you pay any attention to her?"

"Why do you care, Lacey? You see her as a blotch, like a bloody scab on your perfect legs. What is it to you who I talk to and who I don't?"

"I don't, I don't care at all. It's just that—she just never talks to anyone and I want to know what she says to you. Does she talk about me?"

Ahhhhh, one of her cards revealed. Lacey was an attention whore. She wanted the galaxy and all of its planets to revolve around her. Anything less and she would have a tantrum.

"What's the matter, Lacey? Someone in your orbit isn't paying attention to you? They don't fall at your feet, so you conspire to have everyone ignore and be mean to them? Bully them to the point where they don't want to exist and prefer to be invisible to any and all? Is that your plan, Lacey? To create a perfect utopian world where everyone adores you?"

Where did that come from? What happened to the calm, sweet Minnie?

Even Minnie herself was shocked at what spewed from her mouth, but she liked it. She really liked it. She stared upward at the stunned Lacey and drew in power. She felt more words bubbling from her depths—felt truth flowing from Lacey and prepared to throw ugly words into her pretty face.

"You, you with your perfect hair and smile. Your blossoming body and beguiling nature. You keep this up and mark my words Lacey, you'll be pregnant before you leave high school. You know what you're doing. Turning all of the boys upside down whenever you prance by and smile. It's all a game to you. Is that how your father told you to act? Be pretty and sultry and you can have the world. Does your daddy ask you to parade around for him, show him what you're wearing to school and coach you how to act? Do your daddy's eyes linger a little too long when he looks at you? Is your mom the meek and dutiful housewife? Making dinner every night, keeping the house clean, putting on the 'perfect wife' act so you and your family can embody Americana? Does your mom turn a blind eye to what's going on?"

All the color left Lacey's face. She stood still. Stock still. Shock still. Even the birds hushed.

Minnie stood strong, then wilted.

Ashamed, she returned to herself. She had crawled into Lacey's skin and swum around underneath; she'd uncovered the deep, dark truth the pretty girl carried around with her day in and day out.

A small, scared voice was all Lacey could manage.

"How do you know?"

Minnie spoke quietly.

"I might be new and I might be small, but I'm not dumb. I observe. I watch. I listen. I take note. I'm not to be underestimated. Ignore me all you want, I'm fine with that. I don't need to be a part of your world. I choose to go where I go and I choose my friends carefully. I help those in need who can be helped. What do you choose, Lacey?"

Lacey looked down at her feet, then off to the forest. She felt a twinge deep within her; like a seed had sprouted. Pushing it away, she smirked and tossed back her hair. She loved her father's attention and would not trade it for anything.

"Please don't tell anyone."

"Why would I? It's not my story to tell."

"I'll be keeping an eye on you, Miss Minnie. This isn't over, not by a long shot."

Lacey turned to walk back to school. Inside she was shaking but she refused to let it be shown. She was Lacey after all, and Lacey always maintained perfect composure.

Nearly inaudible, Minnie mumbled.

"And I'll be watching you too, Lacey. Watching and learning."

With a short, backward step, Minnie was embraced by the forest.

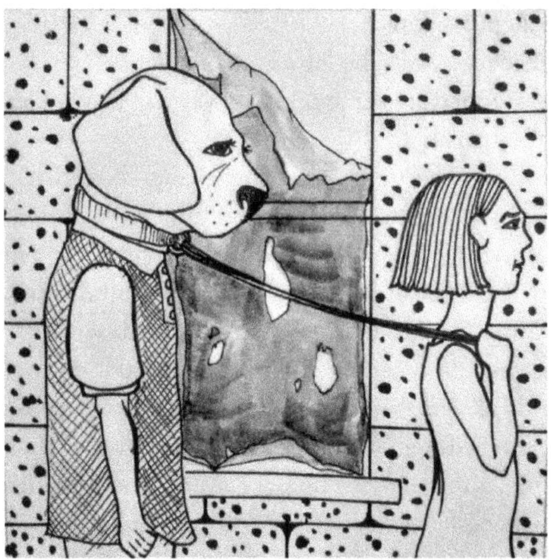

Minnie and Kurt

SHE WASN'T SUPPOSED to use magic; she'd almost made that promise to Fiona which she wanted to honor. But really, following a trail of sparkly breadcrumbs down a hallway in the school was hardly magic. It wasn't her fault no one else could see them. It wasn't her fault everyone else was tuned into clothes and music and sports and who was hooking up with whom. It wasn't her fault she was surrounded by such simple beings. How could she not follow the mysterious trail? In the preceding weeks, she'd heard a mysterious voice steering her footsteps and didn't respond. She'd ignored random blue-satin butterflies appearing from nowhere and begging her to follow. However, she had ignored enough. It was time for an adventure.

Kurt trailed behind like a lost puppy.

"Your English class isn't that way, Minnie, you'll be late-late-late."

Good goddess, why was this young man so tedious? Why is he following me?

Who was she kidding? He always followed her. Heaven forbid he do something on his own.

Minnie kept walking.

"Minnieeeeee, you'll be late," moaned Kurt.

Minnie stopped in her tracks. It was hard, but she lifted her eyes from the sparkly trail.

"Kurt, I love you dearly as a friend and all of that, but truly, you're driving me nuts. Come with me on a little detour or scamper off to your class. If you carry on with your whining, I'll take off my dirty sock and shove it in your mouth. You really must stop being afraid of absolutely everything in this world."

"I'd eat your dirty sock if you wanted me to."

"Honestly, Kurt, that's disgusting. What is wrong with you?"

Minnie turned her back to him and kept on walking. After a few moments, Kurt scurried and caught up. He walked beside her with eyes darting left and right. She felt a pang of pity—she knew what it was like to live in terror.

He's literally afraid of his own shadow.

And why not? His shadow was an unruly blob with sharp teeth and would bite just because it could.

Fiona will not be happy, but this is cruel. I have to fix this if I can.

Abruptly, Minnie stopped and took a grip on Kurt's collar to stop him too.

"Stop," she said. "Close your eyes."

"What? Why?"

"Do as I say and keep them closed until I tell you different."

He cocked his head like a curious puppy.

"Do it," she commanded, "and no peeking."

He pursed his lips a little as if he hoped she would kiss him. This made her smile.

Nope.

She whispered a request to the universe and then reached down to straighten his shadow. It was surprised and did not want to stay in its proper place, but she gritted her teeth, repeated the spell and tugged hard. It reluctantly assumed the unthreatening form it was supposed to.

"Behave yourself," she muttered.

"Me?" he said.

"Okay, open your eyes."

Up close, she studied his face. He looked around.

"Did you do something?"

She took a step to the side. His shadow stretched out in front of him—no longer a danger, it was now his slave as it should be.

"How do you feel?" she said.

"I don't feel anything different."

She knew this was untrue. He stood a fraction of an inch taller and he had lost a piece of his fear. It might take some time before he realized it, but boldness would take hold where fear declined.

Good.

She turned to carry on, half expecting the shimmering, sparkling breadcrumbs to be gone, but they were still there—leading the way. The trail took them down one hallway, then another. They found themselves in an older, mostly abandoned part of the school—they descended stone steps then followed another dimly lighted hallway. Then, down a few more steps and along yet another hallway.

They turned to the left, straight, then to the right. It felt as if they were going underground, yet there was still light streaming in through dusty windows.

Kurt's boldness faded.

"We shouldn't be here, Minnie. This is part of the original school. They shut it down when they built the new addition—they shut it down due to black mold and poor air quality." As if to reiterate his point, he coughed. "There are rats and spiders and dead things down here."

Minnie rolled her eyes and spoke quietly.

"You chose to come with, so stiffen that spine and man up. If you've come far enough then you're free to go back. No harm done. You might carry on with me, though, because I can feel it. We're almost there."

"Almost where?" whined Kurt.

Minnie refused to answer and just kept walking. Kurt, ever the faithful puppy, kept up as well.

Suddenly, Minnie stopped. The sparkly trail stopped in front of a closed door painted black with a window covered with frosted glass. Inside, the room was illuminated with diffused sunlight. Placing her hand on the old doorknob, she felt its cold smoothness. It had good energy. She explored what she felt. Life from times gone by: the lingering spirits of students, teachers and families, but there was something else.

A witch had blessed this room. A friendly one. A healer. Young. Wise beyond her years. Yes, this was a good place. This would be her retreat for the misfits.

Minnie slowly opened the door. The room exhaled as if it had been holding its breath for years and years. The air was musty, but not foul. Inside were old desks and chairs, and a big teacher's desk. Vines had somehow managed to creep in through the cracks near the windows. They climbed the outer edges, seeking rays of sunlight that streamed through cracked panes. There was a big blackboard that took up a whole wall, with chalk and erasers still standing their ground in the chalk tray. On side walls, there was an incongruous framed picture of a manly centaur with crossed arms and a smug expression.

"Curious," Minnie whispered.

There were various other school-related items scattered here and there, but nothing of overwhelming importance. Kurt hadn't uttered a single word since he stepped foot in the room; Minnie had nearly forgotten he was there.

She turned to him.

"Are you okay? You're quiet."

Kurt simply nodded.

Channeling an inner Alice-in-Wonderland she whispered, "Curious and curiouser."

After a careful inspection of the room, Minnie declared it "Theirs." She wanted to do a spell to protect it but decided against magic. First, hard work and cleanup. Instead, she cleared her mind, radiated positive thoughts and energy, blew a kiss and turned on her heels to go.

She walked by Kurt and said, "Ready? If we move quickly, we will be forgivably late."

That jolted him from his thoughts.

"Ready for what? What just happened?"

Minnie raised an eyebrow at him.

"We just found our sanctuary." She then looked at him quizzically. She sniffed the air. Sulfur. "Why, Kurt, did something else happen?"

He looked confused and far away. Looking at her glassy-eyed, he shook his head as if shaking cobwebs from his mind.

As he turned to go, he said "No, no, nothing at all."

Something clearly happened, though she knew not what.

How could something so important slip by me?

The empty room was sacred, it always had been, and was as protected as it could be.

Yet, something was there, watching.

A shiver ran up Minnie's spine, but she refused to grant it any power. If something was present (which she believed), there it would stay until it made itself known. For now, the two misfits would make their way back to class and concoct a plausible, mostly true excuse for being late so they would both come out of the day unscathed and with no pink slips for missing class.

It was Minnie after all, and in that school, Minnie could do no wrong.

Minnie and the Misfits

AS DAYS WENT by, Minnie and the misfits spent every unsupervised minute in their sanctuary. They spent hours cleaning, but did not overdo it—ancient dust and dirt were left as tribute in the corners.

"Dust is a monument to the march of time," Minnie proclaimed. "The old ghosts deserve their tribute, but not too much because filth is still filth."

Once the room was emptied, they painted. When the first roller of vivid paint touched a wall, Minnie grinned at the memory of how she had come by the paint.

Minnie made a point of visiting all the businesses in the small town. There was no specific reason, she was just curious about the local people and what they did. Off Main Street, there was a stub of street called Grand Avenue where a few shops were withering away and dying. If ever there was a street that was not *grand*, it was this one. In the middle of the block, between an abandoned sheet music store and a thrift shop was Bill's Paint Shop. The sign on the door was turned to OPEN, so she walked in as bold as a paying customer.

Inside, at the tinkle of the doorbells, the owner looked up from his folded newspaper and studied the little girl. He was a very small, hunched-over man, so small that Minnie was startled.

Troll?

No, just an impossibly small, gnarled old coot.

Minnie giggled and recited a snippet of poetry.

A gnarled old coot like a mulberry root.

He chewed the end of a pencil stub and returned to his study of the newspaper's crossword puzzle—Minnie was invisible again. She wandered the narrow aisles and examined the rollers, brushes and tins of paint thinner. Finally, after her inspection was complete, she had a choice. Exit or engage.

With faux courage, she walked to the counter.

"Excuse me?" she said. The man spat out a fleck of his pencil. "Pardon me, but do you treat all of your customers with such distain?"

"Distain," he said. "That's good. Six letters. What a hard-working paint shop proprietor should feel when a pesky little girl wastes his time." He wrote on the puzzle. "Thank you. Now you can go."

"You shouldn't prejudge people. I might be here to buy something."

The old man removed his glasses and rubbed his temples.

"You are not a customer. My customers wear overalls and are covered in paint splatters from hat crown to boot heel. You're not going to buy anything, you're here to get a donation for the tomboy soccer club or some damned thing. I already support boy's baseball and they clean me out with their endless need for new jerseys and groin protectors. So, I say good day to you."

He returned his attention to his puzzle. She hauled over a gallon can of paint and stood on it so she was at eye-height with him.

"I'll stay here and be annoying until you give me the respect I deserve."

"I am," he said.

"These paint-stirrers are free, maybe I could use a dozen or so." With a pair, she tapped rhythm on the counter. "We can use them as drumsticks."

The man sighed and folded up his newspaper.

"Okay, you win. What do you want?"

"I need paint. I don't care what color. I think you have some around no one will buy and you might as well give it to me."

The man studied the veneer of innocence on her face.

"You're a troublemaker, aren't you."

It wasn't a question, it was more like an accusation.

"No, I'm just a kid who needs paint you can't use and I know you have some."

She drummed on the counter.

He reached out and stopped the sticks.

"I have five gallons of summer peach. A customer ordered it. When the missus saw how it looked on a wall, she wisely decided on eggshell white instead. It's a decent-quality, oil-based paint, but only a colorblind midget would take it. On a wall, I'd call the color baby bottom, paddled pink."

"It sounds perfect," she said. "Now, shall we talk about your free delivery service?"

After the empty room was thoroughly painted and glowed pink like a sunrise, they brought in potted plants and pictures, art supplies and an old oscillating fan. Old books populated shelves and somehow a large, well-worn oriental rug made its way onto the floor. With four grunting lifters, they brought in a massive tube radio to play music, but were careful to keep the volume low to avoid detection. Word would get around soon enough, but they wanted to delay the inevitable.

On a gloomy Thursday, Minnie was there seeking solace. With her sketch pad, she unconsciously doodled with a charcoal pencil. She remembered the Thinn Man and how she had destroyed him—drawing what she saw, drawing what she felt.

Her friends thought her drawings were images from her fantasy-filled mind. Little did they know it was her factual past and her real reality.

Footsteps approached. Her back was to the door, but she was aware. She sent out her thoughts and scanned the energy.

"Mr. Danvers?"

In walked Mr. Danvers. He was an old hippie teacher at the school...*old* being relative to one as young as Minnie. He taught history and philosophy. He had a kind soul and spoke from the heart—words channeled through him as he stood in front of his classes, rocking on his heels with his eyes closed. He was one of Minnie's favorites, an ally. His classes were a safe place in a sea of teenage drama and politics. However, there was a weight on his soul; Minnie had picked up on it from the day she had met him. Today, his eyes were dark storms with clouds swirling like a tempest.

Minnie spoke with confidence, though she was worried that they would lose their sanctuary. Busy with her charcoal, she spoke with her back to him.

"Hello, Mr. Danvers. What are you doing here?"

"Hi, Minnie. How did you know it was me?"

"I sensed you," came out quicker than she could stop it.

Damn. Magic.

She speedily turned around.

"Oh, I mean, it was the shuffle in your step. It's distinctive and gives you away."

He gave her an appraising eyebrow and grinned.

"It's okay, Minnie. Your sensing secret is safe with me. So, this is where you and your cohorts hide out?"

Minnie conjured a blank expression.

"It's okay, Minnie. I won't say a word. You are safe down here. No one ever comes down to this end. If they do, the noises usually scare them away."

"Noises, what noises?"

"Interesting. You've heard no noises since you've been down here? No voices? Nothing flying around?"

"Nope."

"Hmm, you must have calmed the restless spirits then." He laughed. "I'm kidding, of course. There are no spirits, just dark old rooms and kids with hyperactive imaginations."

Danvers strolled around the room and nodded approvingly.

"You kids cleaned it up nice. You kept the integrity of the space but made it your own. Well played."

Minnie stared at him. She could feel a confession coming on. His secret reached out, unwilling to be held inside.

"Forgive me for repeating myself, but why are you here, Mr. Danvers?"

He let a heavy sigh escape, then looked out the window and drifted far away.

"When I started teaching, I was young and idealistic. I wanted to save every student that walked through my classroom door. I didn't think I could change the world, but I thought it was worth trying. Then my marriage failed. I was too much for her; maybe I was too much for myself. Inside, I went to dark places which carried over to my class. I tried to keep it out, but it seeped in. One day, one of my troubled kids pushed me too far. He'd been annoying me like a relentless gnat buzzing around my ears. He gave me no peace. My inner voice was shut off or I would've recognized his attitude as a call for attention, a cry for help. I caught him cheating on a test. With an apology, I could have overlooked it—it was minor in the grand scheme of things. But I couldn't. I didn't. I failed him—I failed him in more ways than his grade. The big red "F" I imposed on him was the last straw, his last straw. His cry for help fell on my deaf ears. He went home and never returned—he hung himself that night. His mother had passed out from doing too many tranquilizers. When she came around, it was later in the morning. The school had left her a message wondering if Joshua would be in that day because he'd not been on the bus. She figured he was out fooling around somewhere, as usual. She opened his door and that's when she saw him. Hanging there, from a beam in his room. He had pinned his test paper to his shirt. On it he had written 'I'm sorry I failed you Mr. Danvers. I'm sorry I failed you momma. I'm sorry.' They say hindsight is 20/20. If I'd only known. Minnie, you don't know how many days I've gone back and replayed that day in my head. If only I'd done this or that, if only I'd not been so wrapped up in my own darkness; too many days and nights of 'if only's'. So, there it is, Minnie. That's why you see the trouble in my eyes. On that day, I took a vow to never get so lost in myself again that I let anyone fall through the cracks. That day changed me, Minnie."

Danvers let out a big sigh, and the room sighed with him. Minnie didn't know what to say. She didn't know what to do.

"Why me, Mr. Danvers? Why tell me?"

"Because you need to know, Minnie. You need to know you have an ally in this school and I will always have your back. You need to know the power you wield is strong. You keep the darkness away but one day soon it will come to call again. When it does, we'll all be here for you. Just know that, okay?"

Minnie nodded.

Mr. Danvers walked by her and he seemed a little lighter. He glanced down at her charcoal drawing of the Thinn Man.

"You draw from experience, Minnie. Like your drawing, the darkness won't win. Also..."

"Yes, Mr. Danvers?"

He grinned.

"Make sure you're not late for class; the bell rings soon."

And with that, Danvers left the room and walked back down the hall.

Minnie looked down at her drawing and whispered, "None of you will ever win." She heard an evil laugh on the wind, but she paid no attention to it. She knew who it was but she was stronger.

"No, darkness won't win, not then, not now, not ever."

Minnie closed her sketchbook and headed off to float in the sea of teenage drama. Behind, in the sanctuary, the smell of sulfur returned.

Minnie and Kelley

SPRAWLED ACROSS THEIR old, spring-sprung couch in the sanctuary, Minnie nibbled a dry soda cracker and tried to keep her eyes open so she could read Stine's *Blind Date*.

He thought she looked a little like Alice in Wonderland, except for the purple lips.

Failing, she daydreamed about sunlight bathing a giant oak tree in a faraway meadow when the door opened a crack, then shut.

"It's okay, come in," Minnie said.

Nothing.

After a moment, she commanded, "I know you're there. Enter!"

The door eased open. It was Kelley. She wore a short denim skirt—with a thin trickle of blood from her outer thigh showing on her white stockings. Dropping the book, Minnie rotated her body and sat upright on the sofa.

"You've been cutting..."

"No," Kelley said. "I haven't."

"Don't lie to me. Ever." Minnie pushed a pile of toppling pile books to the side to make room. "Sit here with me; I'm going to help you."

"I came here to be alone."

"No, you didn't. Sit."

Hesitantly, Kelley obeyed. Minnie straightened her spine so her eyes were on level with Kelley's.

"Hold out your hands, palms down."

"Hypnosis does not work on me," Kelley said.

"I didn't say anything about hypnosis. I don't know anything about hypnosis. Relax and close your eyes."

She held out her tiny hands, palms up and wiggled them until Kelley sighed and gave in, placing her coarser hands on top of Minnie's delicate ones.

"You'll pinch me if I close my eyes."

"Wherever did you get such an idea? No, forget it, I don't want to know. Keep your eyes open." Maintaining eye-contact, she rotated her head slightly. "How do you like my butterfly?"

"That's not a butterfly, it's a blue hair ribbon—a ribbon you're too old for, by the way. It makes you look like you're six."

Minnie sighed.

Kelley was too wound up to relax. This would take a little help from the alternate world. She was not supposed to open the door, but a little now and then could not hurt.

Right? Minnie thought.

As much as she could, she took all the edges from her voice.

"Pay attention and look more closely. You can tell the difference between a butterfly and a ribbon—even if it's a blue-ribbon butterfly."

"I told you, this won't work on me."

To distract from the gesture she made with her left hand, Minnie reached out with her right hand and pinched Kelley's shoulder.

"Sometimes you get pinched when your eyes are open."

"I don't like that."

Minnie sighed.

This will not be easy.

"I am going to tell you a great story, the best story you ever heard. Once there was a cat, a magic cat named Luna…"

"If the story has a cat in it, there's no way it will be the best story I ever heard. Cats are brainless and gross."

"Shut up and pay attention. Focus on my words with everything you have—I command it."

"You're not my boss." As Minnie expected, the contrary Kelley relaxed a little. She held out her hands and Minnie raised hers too. "Okay, what about your stupid cat?"

"Luna had a pet mouse named Steve. Steve was always causing trouble. He wouldn't stay out of the soda crackers. In fact, they couldn't keep any soda crackers anywhere in the house unless they were hidden in a metal box. It had to be metal, because Steve chewed through plastic like it was a sport. He was a champion chewer. If chewing plastic was an Olympic event, no other mouse in the whole world would have a chance. So, whenever you wanted crackers, you had to take the metal box down from a high shelf. To get to the shelf, you had to get the stepladder out of the closet. The closet was down a long hallway. On the wall, if you're tall, you can see a picture a young girl with a doll. The doll is holding a ball. The ball is like the Earth, it holds the all. The all is safe and warm and everything is soft on the ball. The ladder is almost too short; you stand on your tippy-toes and reach-reach-reach. When you bring down the metal box and put it on the counter, inside, there are no crackers. There is nothing."

Kelley's eyes fluttered.

"Did you know you have a butterfly in your hair?" she said.

"Never mind that," Minnie said, "your hands are getting light. In fact, if I don't hold them down, they will drift away like blue-ribbon butterflies."

She flipped her hands so they rested lightly on top of Kelley's.

"Kelly, I want you to pay attention, what I am saying is very important. You are a miracle. Your mother, in her whole life only ovulates five-hundred times. You are one of those five-hundred."

Kelley spoke slowly with a dreamy voice.

"Mr. Goldenburg talked about ovulation in our Health and

Wellness class, it was disgusting."

Minnie shook her head with irritation, but pushed it away.

"Yes, you're right, the miracle of life is disgusting, so disgusting we should pretend it does not exist and forget that without it, we would not be here."

"No, that's not right."

Okay, that's better, Minnie thought.

"But that's not the biggest miracle. Your father creates billions and billions of the swimmers..."

"You mean..."

"Yes, that's what I mean, questing, single-minded swimmers who only want one thing. Billions and billions and only one won. If the winner was a microsecond slower, the zinc flash would have signaled someone completely different from you."

"The flash is not light..."

"I know, never mind. No, okay, focus on that, there is no light, light doesn't exist. Zinc doesn't exist. Swimmers don't exist. Your mother does not exist. You don't exist. There are no crackers in the box."

"No, wait, I do exist, I am."

Right, why are you so contrary, even deep, deep inside?

"No, you don't exist. You are nothing, not even a dream within a dream. Nothing matters. Everything is an illusion. And, you will cut and keep cutting, you'll cut until there is no blood left in your body, cut until everything flows down the drain in your bath, until your life flows out like water, until there is nothing left and you are nothing."

"No..."

"This is my command. When I let your hands go, they will float into the light and you will be burned, burned worse than ever before, worse than you could even imagine. The only thing that can stop the burning is my voice. When I offer you a cracker, the burning will stop, do you believe me?"

"No."

Good.

Minnie lifted her hands. Slowly, Kelley's hands rose in the air and her face began to contort in pain.

From the end table by the sofa, Minnie picked up a cracker and snapped her fingers.

"Uh...," Kelley said.

"Have a cracker," Minnie said.

"Okay."

Kelley looked at the saltine cracker as if she'd never seen one before.

"Don't eat it."

Kelley scowled.

"I will if I want."

She took a nibble.

"How is it?"

Kelley shoved the rest in her mouth. Gently, Minnie reached out to pluck a crumb off the corner of her mouth.

"It's good. I didn't know a simple cracker could be so good."

"If you appreciate the small things life gives you, then you deserve the grand things that will happen."

"Whatever. I told you that hypnotism would not work."

"And, as always, you were right. You're always right."

Kelley glanced at her plastic watch.

"Crap, I have to go. I didn't know it was so late."

She got up and walked to the door, where she stopped and looked back at Minnie.

"I feel lighter. You did something."

"Come back, sit down and we'll talk through it."

Kelley shook her head.

"No, I have to go." Still, she hesitated. "You're a tricky one, aren't you?"

Minnie rotated on the couch to lie down, then reached over to pick up her splayed book.

"No, not me, never," she mumbled.

She smiled at him, bright purple lips on her pale face.

The Turning Point for Minnie

WHEN YOU GROW up in a small, rural town, there's really not all that much to do. When you move in from away, it seems as if there's even less. Then an outsider comes into the folds of quiet and whispers and is looked upon as an oddity, an aberration, an unwanted harbinger of change. You must earn your way in, it is not a given. Perhaps that's as it should be, but perhaps not.

When you're young, there's no going into bars or getting a fake ID to drink. Everyone knows who you are, when you were born and where. Who your mama is, and your pa's bad habits. Cement City had a decrepit roller rink, but in these modern days, who wants to go skating around in circles on a polished wooden floor while assaulted by music from a bygone age? Maybe some people do, but certainly not iPhone teenagers. When you're in a small town you turn outward. When you're surrounded by nature, that's where you go because you feel that's all you have.

Mugwumps.

That's what the local teens created. These were parties held regularly in a field far off the beaten path. No one can pin down who came up with the term "mugwump." It certainly didn't pertain to the political term of the Republican Party activists who bolted from the Republican Party back in 1884. While these teens were independent in spirit, they were not all on the same page when it came to politics. More than likely, it was a term dropped into a conversation where it rolled around in their mouths in a most pleasing way. A few drinks in, some puffs from the pipe, a raucous laugh and some pats on the back for the inventiveness of a term and the mugwump officially came to be.

To be sure, the local police knew about them, but they left the kids alone. They did no harm and they were enclosed by the forest. One road in, one road out. Once upon a time the police were sent in to retrieve an errant teen whose presence was requested at home. They came in, found the teen, turned around and left. If they saw anything, they turned a blind eye. They knew what they had once done as teens and this was far more tame than that era. Kids around a bonfire being kids; that's all they saw.

There was a small pond in this mugwump land. Sometimes swimming was to be had, but only during the day. At night it seemed to take on an eerie glow. All sorts of stories had popped up of drownings of yore, or mysterious mists and noises, but nothing concrete. Nonetheless, when the teens gathered, it was an unspoken pact that no matter what, you'd not enter the water after dusk. You could be near it, gaze into it, throw stones into it, barf chunks or even pee into it, but don't go in, not even a toe. Besides, the water was always cold at night, far colder than it should have been. That was part of the mystery.

The land had been somewhat cleared by the pioneers. A town was planned, but did not come to be. Now it was mugwump territory surrounded by trees and open to the night sky. There was an old fire pit where many a bonfire left its charcoal impression up the earth. Often times people would spend the night in their cars, in sleeping bags or under blankets. There was drinking and smoking to be had, at times acid made its appearance as well. There was always music and good cheer; sometimes high school drama played out on this stage as well. Hook-ups and break-ups a-plenty, arguments and make-ups, laughs and cries; it all could be found here at the mugwump. The microcosm of high school life, all on display in a field under the stars.

It was to one of these events that Minnie would find herself. Just a few days before, Evan had approached her in the school hall.

Evan.

He reminded Minnie of Kurt Cobain; grunge with a touch of goth. He was a brooding, misunderstood poet who possessed a soul deep as a bottomless well. His hair was dark as a raven's wing, with piercing blue eyes that went right through Minnie whenever he spoke to her. Eyes the color of blue ice, with the tiniest hint of faraway starlight. When he spoke, his words were like liquid, raining down over Minnie, flowing into all of her cracks and broken places, filling her up and making her feel whole. He made her feel warm. Things stirred in her, things she wasn't sure she was ready for, things she didn't fully understand.

However, she instinctively knew that when she called, Evan would come to her side. He was older than she was and he felt like a protector. Why he chose Minnie was beyond her comprehension, but choose her he did. Maybe it was the magic that coursed through her, magic that could be detected by only a few. Perhaps it was that she was an outcast and he was just as unknown. Maybe it was secrets hidden within the depths of himself, secrets that even he didn't know, but over time Minnie would help bring them to light. Maybe his role was to bear witness to what would come down the road; what would be coming all too soon.

On this day, Evan approached Minnie at her locker.

"Hey."

"Hey, yourself."

"There's gonna be a mugwump Friday night. Do you think Fiona will let you go?"

"She might, though I'm not sure she knows much about them. I could fill her in though, and keep it low key."

"Feel free to bring some of the misfits with you too."

"I'm not sure they'd be into it but I'll definitely ask. Thanks!

You'll be there, right?" Minnie blushed as the words came flying from her mouth quicker than she could stop them. "I mean, um, I hope you'll be there. I don't really know any of the older crowd except for you."

"Yeah, of course I'll be there. Don't worry, they know you're cool and no one will bother you. I've got your back." As he walked behind her to get to class, he ran his hand across the small of her back and said quietly, "I'll always have your back Minnie, always."

He stared into her eyes as the words poured like a gentle waterfall from his mouth.

Minnie was entranced.

She smiled and simply said, "I know you will, and I'm counting on it."

Evan walked on down the hall to class, turned around once to give her that all knowing smile, and continued on his way. Minnie felt the stir and a slight breeze wafted by. She thought she heard a voice on the wind but she couldn't make out the words. She flapped her hand in front of her face to dispel the air; she wanted to simply be in this moment.

When Minnie met the misfits for lunch she brought up the mugwump. She announced that she was going (though in truth she didn't know if Fiona would let her), and she asked who wanted to go with her.

As expected, Kurt piped up first.

"I doubt my parents would let me go. Plus it will be dark and probably cold. Why would you want to go and hang out with a bunch of delinquents in the middle of the woods anyways?"

"Good thing I'm not offended by you, Kurt. We're all delinquents in some way, so I look at it as hanging out with kindred souls. As for it being dark, well duh, it's at night. And cold, last time I checked, bonfires give out heat."

Kurt looked down. He knew it was his fear talking. One day he'd rise above that, but today was not that day.

"Sorry," he said with downcast eyes.

Minnie put her hand on his.

"It's okay. Just sometimes think before you speak?"

So, Kurt was out. Max wanted nothing to do with it.

"Too many humans in one place for me," she said.

Minnie knew that to be true. She understood that too many humans depleted Max.

Raven, Marcus and Angel were in. They decided to meet up at the Real Scoop ice cream shop and then walk from there. It would be a mile or two, but they might be able to hitch a ride with someone along the way.

Now to convince Fiona and then check back in with Evan.

When she got home from school she plopped her backpack in her room and nuzzled Keela on the nose. Keela rolled over to expose her belly.

"Ohhhh, so it's a belly rub you want, huh? Well then, a belly rub is what you will have."

Keela trilled and smiled. Minnie pulled out green grapes from her pocket and gave them to her little skunklet. Keela grinned and hungrily chewed her way through the pile.

Minnie strolled into the kitchen where Fiona was just pulling a pie out of the oven. It smelled absolutely heavenly. Chet was busy at the grill. A few regulars sat at the counter. Perfect timing, Fiona was a bit preoccupied.

"Hey, there. How was school?"

"It was good, mundane as always, filled with keyboard exercises about quick brown foxes and lazy dogs, random facts about butterflies and moths we're supposed to memorize in case of emergency, useless equations about squares and right triangles and whitewashed history."

Fiona stopped briefly to give Minnie the once-over. It was an energetic scan. Minnie had come to expect these daily check-ins, so she made sure to clear her energy before she even got within a mile of Fiona and the restaurant.

"You have something to ask?" Fiona said.

"Friday night, is it okay if I go to the mugwump with Raven, Angel and Marcus?"

"I thought those were for older kids?" Fiona said with a

quizzical look in her eyes.

"All kids go now and again, Fiona. Evan asked me today. You know him, he'll look out for me. Besides, after what we've been through, I'm pretty sure I can handle a high school mugwump if it got out of hand."

With a twinge of stubborn resistance, Fiona accepted the fact that Minnie was right. The waif was growing up and she was strong and independent and fearless. She was vastly different from scared-cat Fiona. She sighed.

"Yes, you may go. Guess you won't be my little girl forever, huh? Promise me you'll be safe and you'll remember the rule?"

The rule.

No magic.

"Of course I remember the rule. Thanks, Fiona."

Minnie gave her a giant hug. How Fiona loved those hugs. She couldn't ever get enough of them. Teenage years were tough on everyone. She'd take what she could get from Minnie.

Friday night came, as did Raven, Angel and Marcus. Chet fixed them a quick sausage scramble with fiery peppercorns while Fiona ran down her obligatory list of "what to do if…" scenarios. The kids listened dutifully while kicking each other under the counter. Minnie kissed Fiona and Chet "bye" and the misfits left to begin their walk. Once they were out of earshot, Chet put his arm around Fiona's shoulders.

"There, there, momma. They're good kids. It's time for them to spread their wings a bit. They'll be fine."

Fiona poked his expansive belly. She knew they'd be fine, but all the same, she hoped Minnie would remember the rule about magic. In recent times, a shift was happening, she could feel it. She could taste it on the air, barely perceptible, but it was there. *The Voice* cycled through her iPod at that very moment. The haunting, faerie voice of Eimer Quinn filled her ears and momentarily transported her to Sean. Fiona did not believe in coincidences. She stood lost in the song with a faraway look in her eyes.

"Listen, my child," you say to me
"I am the voice of your history
Be not afraid, come follow me
Answer my call, and I'll set you free."

"I am the voice in the wind and the pouring rain
I am the voice of your hunger and pain
I am the voice that always is calling you
I am the voice, I will remain."

"I am the voice in the fields when the summer's gone
The dance of the leaves when the autumn winds blow
Ne'er do I sleep throughout all the cold winter long
I am the force that in springtime will grow."

"I am the voice of the past that will always be
Filled with my sorrow and blood in my fields
I am the voice of the future, bring me your peace
Bring me your peace, and my wounds, they will heal."

"I am the voice in the wind and the pouring rain
I am the voice of your hunger and pain
I am the voice that always is calling you
I am the voice."[1]

Chet still had his arm around her shoulders. Good thing or Fiona might have fallen over. The moment of melancholy passed.

"Pie," she said.

"Get busy or I'll fire your idle butt," Chet said.

The misfits waited at the Real Scoop for a few minutes before Evan showed up. Minnie had told him their plan and he happily offered to pick them up. In his car, Raven, being classic Raven tried to sit up front. She found Evan sexy as hell and wanted to get

[1] *The Voice*, Brendan Graham

into his pants. Despite being a teenaged guy, Evan wasn't interested. He knew he could have any girl at moment's notice, but he wasn't like that. He was aware of his appeal, his power, but he preferred to be a lone wolf.

"Why do I need that stress?" he would often say to Minnie.

Though Minnie felt she would gladly relieve his stress, she understood. So, Minnie sat up front and the rest sat in the back. As they drove they sang along to the radio and talked.

"When do you need to be home?"

"I told Fiona I'd be home by midnight-ish."

"Fair enough." He raised his voice to address the others in the car. "I'll bring you all back to Minnie's place by midnight."

As they got closer to the mugwump they could hear the music and see the kids setting up the bonfire.

"Oh, good, they haven't started yet. Rumor has it they have an outhouse to go on the top. It will be a chore to get it up there but it will be worth it."

Evan parked his car and they all got out. The smell of pines was intoxicating. The dirt was fresh and the grass was damp. The stars were out and the moon was beginning to rise. Full moon coming. Of course. Why hadn't Minnie realized that? No wonder there was a mugwump tonight...one must always howl by a fire under a full moon. The energy was palpable—it could be seen and felt as it wafted in waves.

As Minnie took in the scene, she saw Jude. Jude was one who played with fire. He was of medium height and on the slender side. He had jet black hair and gorgeous dark eyes. His eyelashes. Why did boys always get the eyelashes that girls craved and tried to create with mascara? Fire was his friend. He was a fire eater. He and fire communed and understood each other completely. Some would say that he tamed the fire; but Jude would say that he became one with the fire.

"Nothing in this world can be tamed, only understood," is how he would say it.

Raven had wandered off to prowl to see who she could have for the evening. She was hungry and sex was on her mind and on her menu. Full moon power. Nothing would stop her and Minnie knew that there would be more than one willing boy to succumb to her charms.

Jude called to Evan and he wandered off. Minnie, Angel and Marcus stood on the edge taking it all in.

"Where to?" asked Minnie.

"Well, I don't know. How's about we just help stack wood onto the bonfire and go from there?" suggested Marcus.

"Seems reasonable," said Minnie.

They wandered off in the direction of the wood pile and started hauling timbers and branches onto the newly formed mound. It would take some time but eventually it all made its way to the pyre. Now the task at hand would be the outhouse. By this time, testosterone was running high so the boys told the girls to "step aside", so step aside they did.

Minnie could see that it was cumbersome and slow going, so she slowly backed up from the masses. She began to twirl her fingers in front of her, generating tiny sparkles. Luckily all eyes were transfixed on the task at hand, so no one seemed to notice the incantation and sparks coming. Suddenly the outhouse seemed that much lighter and the boys were easily able to get it to the top. Beating their chests like a bunch of apes they felt triumphant.

Minnie shook her head, "Humans..." she mumbled while walking back to the gathering.

Jude lit his torch and ran the perimeter of the mound. As he ran he spoke to the fire, asking it to begin the blaze. The torch agreed and began to dance upon the timbers. Soon it was all ablaze. Jude began his fire dance and soon others joined in. If Minnie hadn't known better, she'd have thought it was some sort of pagan ritual. A few other fire eaters joined in with their hoops and torches, but none matched the talent and beauty of Jude. Music played and cheap beer and Boones Farm wine were passed around. The smell of fresh herb hovered in the air and laughter could be heard. Mugwumps...the rural solution to boredom.

Time marched on as it always does. The full moon rose over the treetops and the howling began. In the distance, the coyotes answered, which of course made the kids howl that much more. Minnie was sure that the creatures were laughing at the humans, amused with their antics. Every once in a while Minnie would walk by someone and play some magical trick on them. Their drink suddenly spilled, someone walked up and kissed someone as if they had no choice in the matter, someone else erupted in singing and blamed it on too much wine.

"No harm done…" Minnie would whisper to herself.

"No harm done, but it helps me find you dear, sweet, Minnie," came a voice on the wind. She knew that voice all too well. "I see you tampering with these humans. Humans, what are they anyway? So much time and effort wasted on them, and for what? They've done nothing but destroy this world. This very Earth upon which we depend is dying under their very feet. Hope lies in the young ones? Look at them, Minnie. Do you place your hope in them? Join with me, Minnie. Together we can rule this world and make it what we want. They will bow down to us in fear. Bring your band of misfits too. We have room for them in our court. You can't run forever, Minnie. I'll come for you and Fiona."

Just like that the voice was gone. Minnie refused to show any emotion. She stood steely in resolve. She had grown cocky, used magic and now the door was open. Soon Evan found her—he could feel her radiating from a hundred feet away.

"Are you okay, Minnie?"

"Yeah, I'm fine. Thanks for inviting me. This place is great. I had no idea it was like this."

"Seems as if Raven got what she wanted," chuckled Evan.

Both he and Minnie watched her walking confidently out of the edge of the woods, while her lover of the moment stumbled out, looking lost and confused. They both laughed at the scene.

"Guess it's time to go, huh? I don't want Fiona mad at me for getting you home late after your first mugwump."

"Good point. If I want to come to another one, if I'm invited to another one that is, I want Fiona to say it's okay," chirped Minnie.

Evan put his hand on the small of her back again.

"You'll definitely be at more of these with me," he said, as he smiled down at her. That smile of his made her heart beat faster every time. Minnie was glad it was dark so he wouldn't see her blushing.

They all climbed into Evan's car, smelling of woodsmoke, wine and cheap beer. Neither Minnie or Evan partook of anything but the others sure did. Not too much, but enough to catch a buzz. Evan dropped them off at 11:45 and drove off waving. Raven, Angel and Marcus hugged Minnie and walked toward their homes. Minnie noted that they were stumbling a bit and she quickly said a protection spell and sent it floating over them. They would be safe and no one would get in trouble.

Minnie went inside and sat on the bed next to Fiona. She had been waiting up reading and was relieved that Minnie came in.

"Did you have fun?"

"Yah, it was really fun. There was a huge bonfire with an outhouse burning on top. Jude ate fire and there was music and dancing and laughing and…" her voice trailed off.

She wasn't sure she should divulge everything.

"Minnie, no need to hide it. I was young once too. Let me guess, pot, beer and wine too?"

Minnie just nodded.

"Did you have any?" asked Fiona.

"No," said Minnie.

"You're growing up, honey. I will understand if you experiment. I may not like it but I promise you I'll understand. Just be honest and always tell me, okay? And, there are things you should avoid, not even a taste. Do you know what I mean? Meth, speed, coke, heroin. The new stuff. Fentanyl and Black Death. Those things are evil, distilled."

Minnie hugged Fiona. She was glad that she wasn't able to read her thoughts. If she wanted to chalk her anxiety up to drugs and alcohol and being young, that was just fine with Minnie. She couldn't bring herself to tell Fiona that she opened the door a crack and the King had spoken to her.

Minnie said her good nights and went to her pile of pillows. Keela snuggled up next to her. Minnie lay on her back fiddling her fingers in a circling fashion, singing along to the music that played quietly.

Great Spirit by Nahko and Medicine for the People had become a favorite of hers of late. It spoke to something deep within her, something that could no longer be denied or kept hidden. Her power was coming to the surface. She knew Fiona felt it too. The time was coming when they could no longer hide, no longer deny what needed to be done.

So which wolf will you feed
One makes you strong, one makes you weak
And those who know and those who seek
Amidst the chaos, find your peace
I know which wolf I'll feed
I know which wolf I'll feed

Far away to the East, the troll King was awake and watching. As Minnie drifted into sleep, she fed the flames of her inner fire.

"I know which wolf I feed, Fiona. I will not feed fear. I will feed strength. We can try to hide, but the time is coming, Mother. We must be ready."

Keela climbed onto Minnie's chest and snuggled in for the night. Minnie spread a blanket over the both of them.

"You'll be safe, Keela. No one will harm you."

In the dark the King listened.

The door was open. He simply had to wait...

Minnie's Undergarment

AFTER A LONG day at school, Minnie walked into her cubby-room and tossed her backpack onto her bed. She bent down to check in on Keela and fed her some grapes. She let out a sigh.

"Oh, Keela. Be thankful that you're a skunklet and not a human. I swear, high school drama can be so nauseating at times."

Keela looked up at her human with knowing eyes and nuzzled her leg. Minnie ran her hand down Keela's back and scratched her head. Smiling down at her familiar, she watched the precious animal devour the grapes. When the last one was gone, she bent down and nuzzled Keela head-to-head. Keela always made Minnie forget the troubles of her mundane teenage world. In no time she'd forgotten all about her day and felt ready to face an uncomfortable subject with Fiona.

"I'll be back, little one. Then you can help with my English homework."

Minnie walked into the back kitchen where Fiona fussed over the three pies that barely fit into the old oven. Minnie was assaulted with an odd mix of smells swirling around back there: pastries baking, Chet's greasy staples burbling in hot oil and aromatic seafood thrown in for good measure. It made Minnie smile and shake her head with wonder. She couldn't immediately place the odor coming from the pies.

Fiona turned as soon as Minnie entered. She looked positively giddy as she crouched before the little girl.

"Chet is a genius, you'll never guess what he found." She offered Minnie a strip of translucent golden glass that glittered in the kitchen light. "You simply must try this."

Minnie was skeptical.

"What is it?"

As if to show it was safe, Fiona took a nibble.

"M*anisan pala,*" she said. "A nutmeg sweet imported from the Banda Islands in Indonesia." Observing Minnie's confusion, she continued, "The Spice Islands, silly."

Minnie took the strip of candy and took an exploratory bite.

She shrugged.

"Yes, it's good. Thanks."

Fiona giggled.

"Did you know they smoke ground nutmeg seeds in India—with clay pipes? You have to be careful, because it will give you the most vivid nightmares. What's the difference between poison and the most incredible and exotic flavor? The dosage, of course. Did that sound like Doctor Seuss? When you taste my acorn squash pie, your face will melt."

Perhaps mother inhaled too much of the nutmeg fumes.

"You talk about my melting face like it's a good thing. Forget all that, Mom, I need to talk to you about something."

Fiona turned to look at the pies in the oven.

"Great, perfect, fantastic, let's talk," she said.

Minnie tilted her head toward Chet and twitched her eyebrows.

Leaning close to Fiona, she whispered, "We need to talk somewhere more private."

"Go ahead, Minnie, I need to babysit the pies, they will ruin if they bake a millisecond too long."

It took a few moments for Fiona to catch on.

"Uh, wait, what?" A brief instant of panic flashed through Fiona's eyes. She looked Minnie up and down. "No, please, you're too young for any of the *private* talks. There's still time, lots of time."

"This won't be so bad, mom. You can do it."

Fiona closed her eyes and took a deep breath to compose herself. Her low voice was a monotone.

"That's right, yes, I can do this. I must."

They walked from the kitchen to their cramped sitting room. Minnie decided to get right to the point.

"We're going shopping and you're buying me a brassiere."

Fiona was puzzled. She examined the tiny Minnie carefully.

"A what? Why? You are far from needing any…uh…support." Relieved, she straightened her spine and threw back her shoulders. "That was a close call. I was right, there is time." She tossed a quick thanks to the Goddess upstairs. "I have time to gather my strength and get ready. For now, I have to get back to supervising the pies."

She patted Minnie's shoulder and turned to walk away.

"Mom, listen. I have a problem on cold days. The boys are noticing my…nubs. And, sometimes, when my dress rubs on my chest, the material is thin. It stirs something in me. We need to do something about this."

Fiona turned and studied Minnie's face. A long moment passed while, slowly, insight replaced confusion.

"Oh, I'm sorry. I should be more observant. Whether I like it or not, you're growing up, sweetheart. You're entering a new phase of being human. We can handle this, it's a beautiful thing."

Minnie made a face and rolled her eyes.

"Mom, please, don't compare me with a blossoming flower, that's such a horrible cliché."

The analogy exploded in Fiona's mind.

"Right, that's it; you're blooming like a flower. A fresh and wonderful flower."

Minnie groaned.

"What is wrong with me? Chet mentioned something the

other day. I should pay attention to things around here. I have no skills as a mother."

"Gaaaack! Chet said something?"

Minnie instinctively crossed her arms over her chest.

As if on cue, Chet peeked around the corner with his chef's hat tilted at a jaunty pitch.

"Once upon a time, I had sisters that were your age."

Minnie turned ten shades of red. Then, in a flash, embarrassment changed to anger. She stood up.

"Okay, here I am. Look at me. Talk about me."

Unconsciously, her hands rotated as if spinning a ball. Something ugly began to take shape.

Fiona crouched and placed her hands on Minnie's shoulders.

"Minnie, listen, we love you—with everything we have, we love you."

Minnie looked at her hands and what they were doing as if they were alien things that belonged to someone else. Quickly, her anger dissolved into nothing.

"It's okay," she said.

It took another hour of tending the aromatic squash pies before Fiona was free to go. In the VW, Fiona was in an odd mood, feeling reflective and philosophical as she adjusted to a new reality.

She put her hand on Minnie's shoulder.

"You'll be fine, just fine," she said.

Minnie and Fiona pulled up to the Target department store in a strip mall. Though it was early in the evening, it was already dark and the wind and rain battered the little car. Minnie huddled in her fluffy down jacket—wearing it like a tortoise wears its shell.

"I don't like stores like this, they have no character...no soul. Can't we go to the thrift shop like we usually do?"

Fiona considered the idea.

"The thrift shop is good for shoes and hats, but underwear? We'll go if you really think so, but getting something new that fits makes more sense, doesn't it? Your call."

Minnie stared at the store's glowing red target. Instead of answering, she got out of the car and started walking across the parking lot. Fiona hurried to catch up, but, feeling something reaching for her, stopped and looked around. Years before, it seemed like she was born in a parking lot like this on a similar wet and stormy night. Instantly, she felt empty and weightless. She felt a pull toward her home—her home thousands of miles away that didn't exist anymore, except as cold ashes. Something rolled across the parking lot, making a distinct wake in a large puddle. It hit her foot and stopped. She leaned down to pick it up.

It was a copper penny, an old one. In the dim light, she could see the date…the year she was born. With a glimpse of memory from a million years back, she remembered helping a woman with dropped change. She looked for the owner. There was no one near.

Okay, she thought as she dropped the penny in her pocket.

Walking through the automated doors with a no-nonsense stride, Minnie marched to the center section of the store where endless manikins wore bras in bright colors, boring colors, spandex, lace and cotton. They all looked foreign and horrible.

Why did women voluntarily confine and enslave themselves in these horrid contraptions anyways?

A young man stood by a display of scarves…watching. She reached out to him and recoiled. There was something roaring in his veins, something artificial and ugly. Rail thin, his hair was stringy and his skin was yellow and loose, like he was lost in threadbare drapery. His racing heart was barely working; he didn't have much time left on this Earth. Instinctively, she knew what he was doing—hovering around the Juniors' Intimate section of the store like a jackal waiting by a waterhole for an unwary kitten. Filled with a hunger that would never be satiated, he licked his yellow teeth and watched out for witnesses.

He did not want the children for himself; there was a man who paid $500 in cash for each child he delivered to a van by the bus station. The man was not the customer; he was an agent for someone else. Who, in turn, was probably an agent for someone else.

What did they do with the children?

He didn't know and didn't want to know.

All he cared about was what filled his glass pipe when he got the cash. This was not his town, he was from far away, back east. Once a child was nabbed, and he scored, he moved along to a new town hundreds of miles down the freeway—with a rendezvous at another bus station that was like all the other bus stations.

The man smiled. It was not pretty.

"Come outside and I'll give you ice cream and a puppy, your choice. They're cute." Sensing that he was missing his target, he tried again. "Or a cigarette, maybe you'd like that better. Or, I have pills that will make you forget all your problems."

Inside, Minnie bared her teeth and snarled. Images filled her mind as she thought of all of the ways Mother Nature gave her creatures protection. Thorns, quills, needles, fangs and claws. In his own way, he was a victim too—she was ashamed of her reaction. She held out her hands in supplication.

"You don't deserve to be around people. Go to the woods where you will be by yourself. Alone. Away."

Confusion washed across his face—which dissolved. There was nearly nothing between his skin and his skull. Looking over his shoulder and moving on reluctant legs, he walked toward the store's exit signs.

She knew it was a death sentence—his feeble heart would not carry him through a single night in the woods. Instantly, she tried to take the curse back, but it was too late.

Fiona tapped her shoulder and disrupted Minnie's trance.

"So," said Fiona, "what kind do you think you want? Here's a pretty pink one." Minnie turned to look at the sketchy fabric Fiona proffered. Fiona was puzzled by the look on Minnie's face—a mix of pleading and savagery. "Are you okay, little one?"

Minnie shook off her anger and guilt.

"Nope, looks itchy. Besides, you know I'm no huge fan of pink."

Fiona pulled another from the middle of a display.

"How's about this one? It's not lacy, but smooth and comes in all sorts of colors."

Minnie let out a sigh.

"It will show through all my shirts."

In despair, Minnie raised her eyes and looked around to see if anyone was enjoying her torture. She spotted Kelley from school—who appeared to be gathering courage to shoplift something she couldn't afford to buy.

"Mom, go find some towels or iPhone accessories or something while I look at every little thing. It would be better for me to do this on my own."

Fiona was not paying attention.

"How's about you look around a bit on your own, honey? When you find something you like, we can go to the fitting room and try them on. I will help you decide once you narrow the choices."

What did I just say?

"Excellent idea," muttered Minnie.

She walked around and around and felt like she was going in circles; which in fact she was. Nothing appealed to her, but knowing how she looked to Chet, she had to find something. She caught Kelley's furtive eye and waved.

Put that blouse down and come talk to me.

Kelley met her halfway, but was suspicious.

"You want me?" she said.

"I need some bras and I don't know what I'm doing."

Kelley looked Minnie up and down and shrugged.

"This puzzle is not so hard to figure. Let's look at the workout clothes."

In the Gym section, Minnie felt like she could breathe again. Instantly, a palm tree display caught her eye. Coconuts are like breasts. Or, in Minnie's case, shaped like Clementine oranges. Very small Clementines. Regardless, this was what she was looking for—garments that would do the job without calling extra attention. And, they would automatically fit so she wouldn't have to try them on.

Even better.

Kelley had wandered off and fingered a satiny black jacket.

"You like that?" Minnie said.

"Yeah, but I could never afford it. Mom has to flirt with the landlord to make the rent. We're poor."

"Put it in with my stuff."

"Your mom will have a fit. She'll bust a gut. She'll come unglued."

"She's been doing well with the pies and tips. She won't even notice. It will be okay."

Kelley shrugged.

"I won't be able to pay you back, so this is like a gift, right?"

"It's not *like* a gift, it *is* a gift. Don't argue. And scoot before Fiona sees you and asks a thousand and one questions."

When they were finally back in the car, they both let out a sigh.

"Well, that wasn't so bad, was it?" asked Fiona.

"No, I guess not. Sometimes I wish I was still little though. Back when it was just you, Sean and I—and I didn't have to worry about this growing-up nonsense."

She turned and looked wistfully out through the VW's window into the dark night.

At the mention of Sean's name, Fiona felt a tug on her heart. How she longed to be back in their magical house in the woods with Flix and the Fachan; with the enchanted gardens and magical library. To be in the arms of her Sean, safe and loved. She rested her hand on Minnie's arm.

"Everyday, I have the same wish too, honey. We'll get back there someday. I promise."

Minnie turned to Fiona and looked directly into her eyes.

"When?"

"I don't know, honey. When it's time, I guess."

They drove the rest of the way home in silence. Both pondered when it would be time and longing for that time to be now—but also knowing that it's darkest before the light.

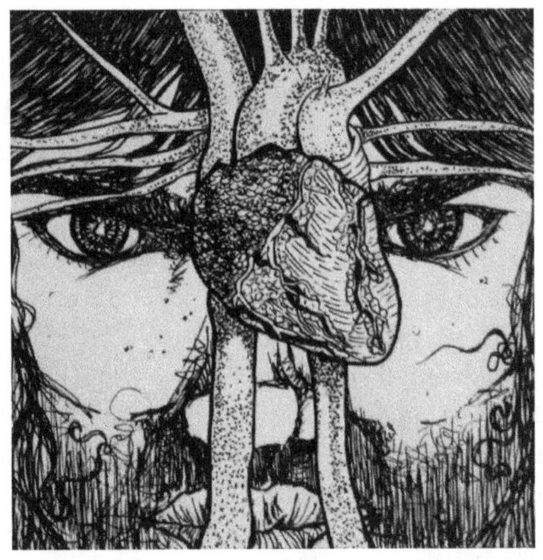

The Yellow Man and the Black Faerie Prince

AFTER LEAVING THE Target department store, the yellow man walked across the parking lot and tripped into a gulley. He was instantly soaking wet and freezing.

"Help," he croaked. "Help me."

Thousands of miles to the East, Trevir, the Black Faerie Prince, stirred and woke. Naked, he got out of bed. Sleeping next to him, Troll Srenzo stirred, but did not wake. She was beautiful in her own way—stubby and thick at the waist. She had red lips over sharp fangs—fangs she used to nibble on him hard enough to draw a little blood, but cause no permanent damage. He wanted her, but this was not the right moment. On the factory's main floor, the trolls kept a fire burning in a metal barrel; he walked through the abandoned machinery toward it. It was cold; he waved his hands in the flames and warmed them. Staring into the flames, he projected outward.

"Who calls for my help?"

"It's me."

"Ah, the yellow man. You seem to be having difficulty."

"It was a little girl. She did something to me, now I'm alone. It's cold and I need a hit. Please."

Trevir liked the way the flames felt on his hands. He kept them far enough away to avoid scorching, but only barely.

There's nothing like heat when the world is cold.

"Are you there?"

"Oh, I'm here," Trevir said. "Don't worry about that, my man. Tell me about this girl."

"Uh, could I have something first?"

Trevir considered the request. The man's heart was like tissue paper. With one solid jolt, he would expire.

"One question first. Was this girl a cute little blonde with pin curls and blue eyes, like I asked for?"

The yellow man was confused.

"No, she had dark hair and dark eyes. She did something. You said you would protect me."

Trevir laughed.

"I will give you exactly what you want."

He pushed, not much—it didn't take much. The yellow man's heart twitched and fell into pieces. Cold and alone, he died.

Thinking about a tiny, raven-haired girl with dark, bottomless eyes, Trevir walked back to his bed. Troll Srenzo would be unhappy to be disturbed from her peaceful slumber, but she would serve him.

In the end, everyone would serve him.

Looking down at his mate, he clenched his fists.

Not today and not tomorrow, but soon, everyone will honor me.

He pushed the troll onto her back and waited. She opened and closed her eyes a few times and then stared up at him with unveiled hostility.

He liked her best when she was angry.

"Now, m'Lord?"

He tilted his head back and raised his fists above his head.

"Yes, now," he said.

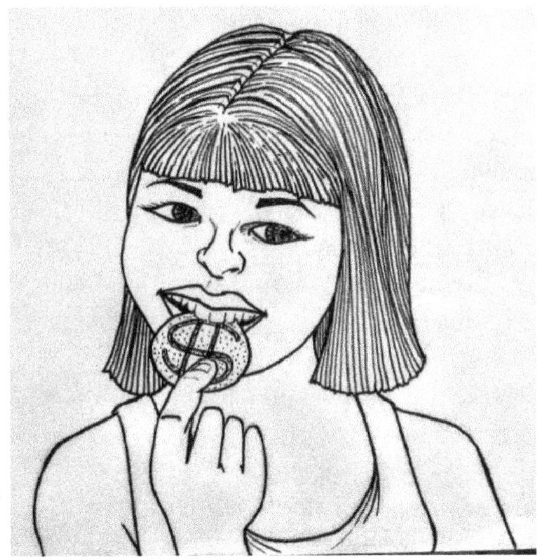

Payment Rendered

LOST IN THOUGHT with books weighing heavily in her backpack, Minnie trudged on the sidewalk toward the school's front doors. There, she was waylaid by Kelley.

"Hey, Minnie, come over to my house today after school."

"Uh—why?" Minnie asked with THAT look on her face.

"Oh, c'mon. You haven't been over in ages. I can do up your hair and we can hang out and stuff."

"*Do* my hair? Did you just hear yourself, Kelley? Do I LOOK like I EVER *do* my hair?"

"That's the point, Minnie. You never *do* your hair. You never *do* anything. You're one of those natural beauties who makes us all green with envy. When you finally come into your own you're going to be drop-dead gorgeous. But until then, lemme do your hair. I'll braid it or something and it will stay in for like a week. Easy-peasy. Low maintenance. Then you really won't need to *do* anything to your hair for days. C'mon. It will be fun."

Minnie sighed. Kelley was NOT taking *no* for an answer.

"Fun isn't the word I would use, but okay, I'll come over. But just for a bit. I have to help Fiona and Chet today. They're short staffed and need my help."

"Even MORE of a reason to get a little pampering. You work so hard Minnie...at school, at home. You're always helping people and gawd knows you saved me. One afternoon of pampering and hanging out won't kill you. Don't chicken out. I'll meet you by your locker after school, okay?"

Without waiting for a response, she gave Minnie a quick hug and skipped off to class.

Minnie whispered to herself.

"I suppose it will make Kelley happy—and goodness knows she can use extra cheer now that the cutting phase of her life is behind her."

She resigned herself to the fact that she'd be having a girly afternoon and went on to class.

Soon enough, the end of the day came. As promised, Kelley stood by Minnie's locker. She could barely contain her excitement.

"Okay, let's go," she squealed.

"Whaaaaat are you so excited about?" Minnie said. "It's ME, remember; not some lost-and-found puppy."

"I know, silly. It's just, I haven't had anyone over in so long and now that everything has changed it's just, I don't know, it's just different. Life, you know? I promise, it will be fun."

Minnie and Kelley walked home. Usually a driver picked up Kelley but she had so much energy she felt the walk would do her good. As soon as they walked through the door, Kelley yelled.

"Mom, we're home. I brought the Minnie with me."

Her mom came running from the kitchen. Smiling from ear to ear, she had flour splattered on her face.

"Minnie. What a wonderful surprise—I've not seen you in ages. You girls go put your stuff away and then come on into the kitchen. Can you smell them? I made a fresh batch of snickerdoodles—a perfect after-school snack for growing girls."

Minnie could smell them and her stomach growled in approval. The girls dashed up to Kelley's room, dropped their stuff and came right back down. In minutes, they were sitting in the kitchen eating cookies and talking a mile-a-minute. Minnie felt as if she was in a wholesome episode of *Leave it to Beaver*, but she enjoyed it nonetheless.

After a bit, Kelley said, "You stay here Minnie. I'll run upstairs to get everything all set up, okay?"

"Set up? What are you going to DO to me?"

Kelley giggled.

"Who knows? But I need my stuff all out and ready. Sit tight, I won't be long."

Kelley's mom smiled and spoke quietly.

"You know Kelley. Once she gets an idea in her head, there's no stopping her."

"Oh, I know that all TOO well," said Minnie. "I'm here, aren't I?"

Minnie had a sudden realization. All this was planned. This moment was a set up. She studied Kelley's mom.

Something was up and was about to be revealed.

"Minnie, I can't thank you enough for all you've done with Kelley. For Kelley. For me. You stopped what could have led to disaster. You gave her hope and courage. She's no longer a victim—she's back to being my strong and spirited young daughter. I can't thank you enough."

She reached across the counter and put her hands on top of Minnie's before continuing.

"I won't ask how. It's a miracle. It doesn't matter how it happened."

"It's nothing," Minnie said. "I'm glad I was there when it happened, but I didn't do anything. It was all Kelley, in Kelley, ready to sprout. Kelley is awesome."

"Nothing, huh? Right. Regardless, I'd like to pay something for what you did for her—and for me."

Minnie choked on a cookie crumb dusted with cinnamon.

"Pay me?"

"Yes, Minnie. It's the least we can do. Please don't say *no*. You have no idea how much we spent on talk therapy—therapy that did nothing. In desperation, we were headed toward the mood-altering drugs—you know what I am talking about. The mental poisons. Valium, Halcion, Klonepin, Xanax, Ativan. I'm not saying these drugs can't help, but only as a last resort, when everything seems lost. Please, Minnie."

"That's very kind of you but I really didn't do anything worthy of being paid."

Minnie's mind flashed to her little bedroom. In a drawer behind her socks was a wad of cash. It seemed like a lot and Minnie was embarrassed. People gave her money and she tried to press it away, but sometimes—for their sake—she felt the need to respect people and let them make their gestures.

"I'm really not sure how I would ever explain money to Fiona. Thank you for the offer."

"Minnie, I truly must do something. The impact you've had on us is huge, something I can't even put into words. Please, Minnie, let me do something."

Minnie thought for a moment.

"You know, there IS something. Chet's diner. It's in need of a lot of help. Like it needs kitchen upgrades and painting and sprucing up. He's always talking about it but he never has the time or money to do it. Instead of paying me, would you consider—I don't know, something like an anonymous donation to his business?"

She came around and lifted Minnie off the floor and hugged her.

"YOUUUUUU are such a love. Yes, Minnie. That's a fabulous idea. I'll start working on it right away. Hmmmm, maybe instead of just a check, I can arrange for one of our contractors to go over, meet with Chet and they can work up what he wants done. Totally custom. Others will toss in a few dollars. Brilliant idea, Minnie."

As if on cue, Kelley called from upstairs.

"No dawdling. Time for your makeover."

It *was* on cue.

They set this whole thing up.

Kelley's mom beamed.

"Our secret, Minnie. After, let me know how Chet likes it all, okay?"

Minnie smiled like a toddler in a candy store. It felt good to help people. Kelley's mom was happier than she'd ever seen her and Chet would be awestruck, Fiona would be giddy and Kelley was thrilled to play makeover queen.

For once, for a very brief moment, everything felt all right.

Minnie and Lacey—Part Two

LACEY WAS FILLED with pride, over-filled. The hallways buzzed with the news of her victory—it was the first time a Sophomore had ever won an election as class president. It was a long campaign, one that had started in her Freshman year with her work on the student council.

As a Freshman, she did not run and was not elected to the council, but she attached herself to nerdy Chad Wilson, the elected secretary, and attended all the meetings, even filling in for him a few times when his schedule was over-booked. She was everywhere—participating in pep rallies, bake sales and collecting warm clothes and canned goods for the poor and helping teachers organize field trips.

She studied hard and helped the teachers maintain order in the classroom by scolding and cajoling. Even the delinquents, hoods and outcasts responded to the carrot and stick of her smiles and scowls. She shut down the class clowns, poked the drowsy and shamed the secret cell phone texters into paying attention, or at least pretending to. She had a clique, an inner circle, of course she did, but she also moved around and ate lunch with different groups, even the close-knit Hispanic and Asian clusters, the spazzes, the geeks, the table-gamers and other hopeless cases.

Her father helped. Over and over he lectured her on the importance of networking and smiling to broadcast her expensive dental work. Her dad was wealthy, mainly from owning Cement City's largest insurance agency (seven employees, including a pretty blonde front desk admin who seemed overly ever-present to Lacey), but he dabbled in real estate and owned the print shop. The print shop helped, she had twenty poster designs and her dad had hundreds printed. They were everywhere—and were quickly replaced when they were damaged or torn down.

He would collect her into his arms and hold her so tightly that she could hardly breathe.

"Name recognition is the key to winning," he said. His eyes were fixed on the ascending hem of her skirt. "Most people don't think, they just pick a familiar name to get the chore of voting over as quickly and painlessly as possible."

She worshipped her father. He had been a high school football star and the years (and hour-long sessions in their garage gym) had been kind. He was handsome, his belly only protruded a little over his belt and his hairline had receded only a little. She mixed his Bacardi-and-Cokes strong—the way he liked them—and acted young and innocent in a manner that pleased him.

Her victory was his victory—he had already called on her cell phone to congratulate her and promise a celebration dinner in the big city, just the two of them. It would be a late night, so they would stay over at the casino hotel. He promised her a special surprise, but she'd already found it in his desk: fake identification so she could drink and gamble. In her slinky new dress and high heels, it would be a night to remember—she looked forward to it with every cell of her body.

The second-place contestant was senior Ralph Campbell. His posters were misprinted and had to be remade, which cost him a week of exposure. She asked her dad about the problem, but he just winked at her.

"Stuff happens," he said with a knowing grin.

"Keep it simple," her father had said when he helped with her slogan. She asked if she really needed a stupid slogan—he looked at her as if she was a simpleton. "Lacey Gets It Done!" he suggested. "Everything we print will have the slogan and it will get etched into the kid's psyche. We'll do stickers, pencils and rubber stamps. Do you think you can find someone who will accept a free tattoo? You walk around and be sweet, we'll get a Lacey Army to spread the good word—we don't want you to get a reputation for being self-centered and conceited. When you're giving speeches, tell them what you are going to tell them, tell them, then tell them what you told them. Don't assume everyone is as smart as you, they aren't. Promise them something for nothing, that's a sure-fire winner."

He put his index finger on her kneecap and let it gently rest there.

"What do the kids want? An extra half-hour at lunch? Moving the Prom from the gym to a fancy hotel ballroom? I'll sponsor it, then write it off as a business—promotional—expense. Free donuts on Fridays? Pick a message and stick with it. Paint your opponent with a simple-minded nickname, but nothing too harsh."

With his finger, he lightly sketched a figure on her knee. An electrical wave ran up her spine and her body filled with hormonal heat. She squirmed on his lap.

He continued speaking with a dreamy voice.

"How about Radio-Friendly Ralph? Does that indicate he's plain vanilla and boring? Whenever you refer to him, keep it light, and once people know the nickname, shorten it to RF-Ralph. Don't say anything bad about him, let your posse do the heavy-lifting and dirty work—we won't go negative unless it looks like the race will be close."

And so, she won with 288 votes. Ralph was a popular kid, he got 105 votes. Running into him at the corkboard displaying the results, she kissed his cheek and congratulated him on running a spirited campaign and asked for his help in ruling the student body. He blushed with honor at the request and agreed to help her.

Good, he can do all the work, she thought.

However, there was something that bothered her.

Minnie did not run a campaign—she wasn't even on the ballot and she came in third place with 38 write-in votes.

How did that happen?

She asked around and someone said Minnie was reading a book in the library. This turned out to be true. Lacey towered over the slouching Minnie.

"Whatcha' reading?"

Minnie, deep in the story, did not respond.

Lacy plucked the book and looked it over.

"*Let's Get Invisible!* Stine? I've heard of him. Isn't he for little kids?"

Minnie shrugged.

"I'm a little kid—and in my Stine phase, I guess."

She recited three phrases.

He has to win at everything. If he comes in second place, he kicks the furniture. You know the type.

"Cute," Lacey said. She dropped the book on Minnie's lap. "The election results were posted."

Minnie searched for her place in the book.

"I'm sure you won. Congratulations."

"Thank you. R-F ran a good campaign, but my team was able to eke out a victory."

Minnie snorted.

"It helps if your daddy owns the print shop. Have you ever thought about it? Eke is a funny word. Olde English. It means making a small supply of something go farther or last longer. Small supply, like your talent or my patience with this conversation." She immediately regretted the snarkiness. "Sorry, that was uncalled for."

"Half the time, I don't have a clue what you're talking about. There's a reason I'm here. Aren't you curious?"

Minnie smiled.

"No, not really."

"You got 38 votes."

Minnie looked up, surprised.

"Really? Okay, that's nice. I didn't vote, but don't worry, if I did, I would have voted for you."

Lacey could not help herself; she increased her internal count from 288 to 289. It felt good.

"How did you do it?"

Minnie frowned and bit her bottom lip.

"I didn't do it. I didn't do anything." She set her book aside. "Look, let's put aside any artificial competition and decide to be friends."

Lacey pondered.

"That seems awfully simple-minded."

"Maybe not as simple as it seems. What do you say? Maybe I can help you, or not, what do you have to lose?" As Lacey's face scrunched up in concentration, Minnie continued, "Don't overthink this. Friends or enemies? What does your gut tell you?"

Lacey's initial reaction was to slap Minnie across the face, hard, and then run away. But, she stifled the pointless impulse. Why, she could not say.

"Okay," Lacey held out her pinky.

Minnie raised hers and they intertwined.

"BFF?" Minnie said, laughing.

"Let's not get too far ahead of ourselves," Lacey said. "We're not exchanging MP3s or sweaters or finishing each other's..."

"...sentences," Minnie interjected.

"Exactly," Lacey said. "Look, I have to go and do whatever it is President-elects do."

"And I have to go back to being invisible."

"Don't forget—come to the cafeteria for your free donut."

Minnie casually waved her off.

"I'll come down when I finish this book."

Feeling inexplicably light as air, Lacey flounced off.

Kurt and Minnie—The Night the Magic Died

KURT WALKED INTO the Sanctuary.

He muttered, "Someone must have forgotten to turn off the music. Don't they know that's one of the rules?"

He shook his head while reaching for the power button, but then stepped back and cocked his head to listen to the new song that started.

Trouble—it will find you
No matter where you go
No matter if you're fast
No matter if you're slow

He recognized the song.

Trouble is a Friend.

He knew of the pretty Australian singer, Lenka, from a YouTube interview. Not being a fan of the mechanical, synthesized drums, he reached out to shut off the song, but the dreamy voice captured him and he stood, entranced and swaying to the beat. Fashioning himself as a serious music critic, he thought, *her voice is sickly sweet and there's not much harmonic substance, but the bouncy tune is catchy*. Drifting to the music, he wandered to the chair near the windows, plopped himself down and gazed out through the frosted glass at the world.

So don't be alarmed
If he takes you by the arm
I won't let him win
But I'm a sucker for his charm
Trouble is a friend, trouble is a friend of mine…

When the song ended, it was odd, but nothing followed, the wireless speaker went quiet—which suited his mood. He reflected on how his life had changed and kept changing.

There was an old Kurt, and an emerging new one. If you ever wanted to know what distilled fear and insecurity looked like, all you had to do was look at the old Kurt.

He was one of six children; one of the older ones. His parents were still married and presented themselves like the nuclear family of the 1950's *Leave it to Beaver*. Affluent. Suffocating. Rigid. No room for a boy to be different. Favoring his older, more athletic son, his father referred to Kurt as *Stupid*, or sometimes *Ugly*.

"Hey, Stupid, don't sit there like an ugly, useless lump of flesh, pass the peas."

Kurt shook his head. It was as if someone had actually said that in the quiet room. Looking inward, he observed himself for a reaction, but the remembered words did not trouble him. His father had failed at sports and projected his unfilled needs onto Kurt's brother, Karl. It made sense that his weakling, introverted, nerdy, bookworm son would attract his criticism. It was something they would grow out of.

Maybe.

Regardless, it was the way things were. It did not make sense to struggle against things that are the way they want to be. It's better to tack with the wind to find the best path, not fight it.

His mother didn't hurl insults, but she was equally negative in her own way. Consumed and conditioned by a strict Catholic upbringing, she never rocked the boat. She maintained order in the household and would plaster on a false smile should company come to call. Everyone had their place and everything was always where it should be. Don't believe it? Put a dirty shoe on a sofa and see what happens.

In this home, there was no room for creativity and no margin for error. Kurt's greatest fear had been stepping out of line. He hated to be alone; though he felt alone in his house when surrounded by his family. A bubble of fear grew around him from a young age and he never shed it. Fear of being abandoned, fear of being alone, fear of not fitting in, fear of seeking and not receiving approval. Emotions were for sissies, so no expression was allowed. Any unveiling of the soul would draw a response like "Good God, boy-child, act like a man, for goodness sake!"

Fear. That's what he knew. His deep brown eyes had held a whirlpool of fear. Under the covers of his bed, he read self-help books and listened to podcasts; gleaning all he could to help make himself feel normal. His fear had made him needy. His fear had isolated him. His fear and failure to let go reigned his life.

But that was in the past. Something had happened and he felt alive—and more alive every day.

I used to be afraid of my shadow.

This was literally true. Seeing his shadow had been one of his many phobias. There were creepy, evil things in the dark regions where his body blocked the sunlight. But, now, he could feel it, he was sprouting. Growing. He'd even gathered his courage and asked Kelley to join the Two Kings Chess Club. He rejoiced when she did not say no. He assumed she would shut him down, humiliate him with an insult and leave him hiding tears in a bathroom stall. Vividly, he remembered what she said.

"This is an idea I will have to consider carefully before rejecting."

Her words seemed stiff and formal, and could be interpreted

to mean she could possibly accept sometime in the future.

Score!

While thinking of chess, he reflected on an error he'd made in his last game and what he should do next time. His game was changing and improving. Instead of habitually playing defense, he would sometimes attack—to the surprise of the boys he usually played with. His high school chess club ranking was improving.

Fear still lived inside him, but in a ball in his gut that got smaller every day.

A liquid voice came from nowhere.

"You are afraid of everything, Kurt, but I can help you."

Kurt looked back at the speaker, but it was quiet and inert. This voice was not a whisper or an illusion; it was real in the room, deep, menacing and filled with authority. The only thing Kurt had going was his intellect. If he was going mad, he had nothing to cling to. The fear-ball in his belly rotated and grew warm.

"Who is speaking?" Kurt's voice wavered. He shook his head. "Pfft, whatever."

"Don't 'whatever' me, boy. I can help you if you're not too much of a pussy."

"I'm no pussy. Besides, that's not a nice word. Show yourself, or are you just in my head?"

"I'm in your head and all around. I can smell your fear from across the many miles. But I can help you, Kurt. I can make it so you're never afraid. Minnie and the other misfits will be in awe of you, of your power and prowess. You'd like that, wouldn't you, Kurt? You'd like to be seen differently than you are now. You'd like to be respected. You'd like to stand up to your parents? You'd like to walk down a hallway and boldly look the bullies in the eye, instead of running for the dark corners like a cockroach. Yessssss, you'd like that. You'd like the girls to fall at your feet and serve your secret needs. I know you would. I hear your heart beating faster. Your palms are sweating and you're wondering if this is really happening. Trust me, Kurt, it is. Let me in and I'll solve all of your problems."

Kurt was frozen—he could not move. His eyes darted madly about the room, but he was the only one there. Instinctively, he looked up at the painting of the Centaur hanging on the wall. He looked into its eyes.

That's where the voice was coming from.

"Okay, I found you. You're in the painting. Whomever planted a microphone and a camera up there can stop. Game over. I found you out. I'm not so dumb after all. Come on out."

"Nice try, Kurt. You may have found where I am at the moment, but this is no joke. Do you want my help or would you prefer to stay as your sniveling self? I'll give you a minute to decide. After 60 seconds my deal is off the table. 60…59…58…57…"

"STOP COUNTING. I can't think when you're counting."

The voice laughed maniacally.

"…50…49…48…"

Kurt couldn't think. He couldn't see. He closed his eyes and his world began to spin. Drums beat in his ears. He smelled something like sulfur, only sweeter. He fumbled his fingers like he'd seen Minnie do when she thought no one was looking.

"Yes, yes, that's right, Kurt. Copy what Minnie does. Knock-knock, let me in. Open the portal. Let me see through your eyes, see where you are. Let me empower you and take away your fear…."

Minnie looked around.

Where was that troublesome boy?

It wasn't like Kurt to be late, let alone skip a class.

"Lordy, skip a class," muttered Minnie to herself. "Never in a million years would he do that."

Still, there was his empty seat and it was now fifteen minutes into English Lit. She sent her mind out to scan the school and found nothing.

Wait, she was being blocked.

Blocked?

Who would dare to block her? Who could if they dared?

Automatically and naturally, she could read people's thoughts, especially those of the misfits. Kurt was blocking her thoughts; he was keeping her out. On purpose.

"When did he learn how to do that?" Minnie asked herself.

Annoyance nibbled at her, but she focused on where she was and what she was doing. Her class was reading and discussing *1984* by George Orwell. Most of the class couldn't see how that "story" was being played out on the human stage today.

"Humans…always in denial of everything, even when it's in plain sight," said Minnie under her breath.

Normally, Minnie stayed as quiet as she could and tried to avoid any attention.

"What was that, Minnie?" asked the teacher. "Do you have something to contribute? We'd all love to hear your thoughts and have you join our conversation about this book."

Thus began a raucous conversation about life and The Matrix and what was real. Before long, everyone in the class had joined in and the teacher was pleased.

"Best class we've had yet," she proclaimed.

Thankfully, the time passed quickly and the bell rang. Minnie had the next period free and decided to head for the Sanctuary. Her hackles were up and she had goosebumps on her arms—she knew something in the world was not right. Unnoticed, she was able to get to the stub of hallway with the abandoned door and slip through. All during the long walk down and around to get to the Sanctuary, her feeling of dread and impending doom increased. She did not like this feeling. Life should be sunlight and flowers, particularly for the young. Each step was harder to take, but she forced herself onward.

When she reached the Sanctuary door knob, it was hot. Burning hot. Inside, it sounded like elephants were stampeding. Standing back, she waved her hands and said a small spell and the knob cooled down immediately. She quietly opened the door and put her hand over her mouth so as not to gasp.

Papers were flying while Kurt ran up walls and jumped around on tables and desks. He had a wild look and his shirt was off. He had deep scratches across his back and chest. He wasn't aware of what he was doing. It looked like a mix of craziness and bliss; but Minnie thought momentarily that those emotions were very close to being one and the same. She stood lingering near the doorway, just watching. Sulfur. She smelled sulfur, rotting flesh, death and decay.

The Black Faerie Prince, thought Minnie. *Now the King.*

At that moment, Kurt turned to look directly at Minnie.

"Well, well, well, if it isn't the beautiful princess Minnie. Have you come to join me?"

It was Kurt's squeaky voice, Kurt's skinny body, but not his words.

"Get out of him, Trevir," said Minnie sternly.

"Whatever are you talking about, my beloved? Kurt and I are one. He asked for this. With your help, he opened the portal himself. Now, now, now, don't look so shocked. He's a watcher, this one. He's been watching you, Minnie. You've been careless. You've been weaving spells. Tsk, tsk, tsk. For one as powerful as you, how could you be so careless? Humans, Minnie, will always disappoint. Don't you know that by now? Oh, but of course you do. Look at your poor mother. She couldn't save herself and you couldn't save her."

Minnie steeled her will and presented a controlled composure—she knew she dared not to show any emotion Trevir could use against her.

"Leave my mother out of this, Trevir."

"Mother? I've heard you call Fiona that. What do you think that means to your mother? Your *real* mother? You're a nasty daughter to abandon the woman who brought you into the world in blood and tears. Treacherous Minnie, that's what she thinks. Faithless Minnie. Minnie the betrayer. She hates what you have become."

For an instant, Minnie believed it, believed every word of it. She wanted to think her mother would want her daughter to seize joy wherever and however she could, but how could she know?

Kurt slipped off the wall and slowly sauntered closer. As he walked toward her, Minnie studied him. Trevir was in full possession of Kurt's body, mind and spirit. In an instant, she knew it. To forcibly remove the Faerie Prince would mean Kurt's death. She had to play his game. Trevir had to leave of his own accord.

He came closer to Minnie as if to kiss her. Minnie turned away. Kurt put his hand on Minnie's cheek and turned her face back to his. He bent closer to her and slowly closed his eyes.

"Kissing Kurt would be like a romantic kiss with a brother," she whispered. "And that's disgusting."

Mood broken, that gave Minnie the chance to back away. She headed for the couch. Kurt floated after her with his feet barely touching the ground.

"I like what you've done with the place, Princess. But you know, the castle, our castle will be much better. You'll have everything you desire. Finery and food aplenty. Your misfits, even Sean and the Fachan will be there. Fiona will have to die, that's a sad truth, but that's a worthy exchange. You'll have the world groveling at your feet and all your other friends will be safe. Protected. Alive. All you have to do is join with me, Minnie. Fear me, respect me, love me. Join forces and we can balance this heinous world. Dark and light, good and evil, we will bring order out of chaos. Take my hand and we start today. Right now."

"I'm afraid I have homework to do today—a History paper to write, English Literature to read and then there's Algebra. Terribly sorry but today won't work for me. Not today. Nor any other day."

"Baaaaah! You're becoming too human, Miss Minerva. You're getting caught up in should's and have-to's. Come with me where there are no boundaries and we can do as we please. We can be what we want to be. You can bear me a lineage of powerful offspring."

"What? Are you kidding? Sex is disgusting. And with you? I'd die first."

Kurt tore about the room in a whirlwind.

There was no winning this one over. Not today.

Trevir grew weary of the back and forth. He was unaccustomed to appearing nice and logical. The trolls weren't like this; it was all "Yes, Master" or "No, Master" or "How would you like it best, Master?"

And if they didn't? Into the melting pot with them. His energy began to wane, as well as his patience. Projecting across the Rocky Mountains took energy—the barrier sapped his strength.

"I'm done with you Princessssss. You can have Kurt back. Take his sniveling, scaredy-cat ass from my sight. But know this; I know where you are. There's no more hiding. The portal is open and I can enter freely. I see all and know all. It will be best to join me freely, Minnie. Join me and no one else will be hurt."

With that, there was a hiss and Kurt fell to the ground. Minnie saw smoke go into the Centaur painting and heard Trevir's parting omen, "I will appear in your depressing little town. The mountains will not protect you, that you can count on."

Kurt fluttered his eyes. Minnie ran and put his head on her lap.

"Wha—what happened?"

"Shhhhh, don't talk, Kurt. Let me get you some water."

Kurt looked wild-eyed and terrified.

"No, don't move, Minnie. My shirt, where's my shirt? What are these scratches? Why are they burning?? It feels like they're festering. Minnie, what's going on?"

Minnie said an incantation to reduce his anxiety. Kurt closed his eyes and his breathing slowed. The incantation worked, but it solidified the link between her and the King-Prince. Minnie realized, despite her denial, that Fiona was right. Using magic made them a target.

In her mind she called for Mr. Danvers.

"I need you, Mr. Danvers. I'm in the Sanctuary with Kurt. It's bad. Really bad. Please come."

In what felt like an eternity, Mr. Danvers finally stepped through the door. He stood stock still. He took in the scene. For a moment, he thought Kurt was dead.

Minnie read his thoughts, shook her head and said, "He's resting."

Danvers walked closer, saw the scratches and noted that they were turning black. He felt Kurt's forehead and said, "He feels hot. We need to get him to a hospital."

"But how do we explain what happened?" She motioned to the scratches. "How do we explain all this?"

"I don't have any answers, Minnie. But you know as well as I do that he needs help, medical help. Can we move him?"

"Yes, I think so."

"Okay, let's at least get his shirt on. We'll carry him down the hall, away from here." He glanced at his watch. "It's between periods, the hallways will be vacant. You went looking for him and found him in the hall, passed out on the floor. That's all you know. Can you sell that story?"

Minnie nodded. Humans wouldn't understand what happened. It had to be this way. They had to lie.

Minnie and Mr. Danvers got Kurt dressed and carried him down the hall. They staged his body and backpack in such a way as to make it look like he passed out. Minnie sat down and put his head back on her lap. Kurt still hadn't moved but he was breathing and seemed at peace.

"Are you ready? I'm going to call 9-1-1. I'll say you saw me and called me over and I know nothing more than what you told me. Are we on the same page, Minnie?"

Minnie nodded again.

"You have my word, Mr. Danvers."

At the Urgent Care facility, Kurt rested comfortably. He was in a private room, hooked up to drip tubes and a ventilator. His wounds had been treated and covered. No one could explain the black scratches covering his body like runes. His mother wondered if he'd been playing with an Ouija board—she'd seen a movie and knew they were a portal to dark regions. His father told her that was all nonsense, but he had no better explanation for the markings.

In the dim light, displays glowed and hummed while monitors looked after his heart rate. There was no indication of brain swelling. They'd run all sorts of tests, but the doctors could not explain his condition. For all they knew, one minute he was alive and well in school and the next he was in a coma.

Minnie knew how and why. She knew it was her fault. Despite what Mr. Danvers said, this was wholly and entirely her fault. She opened the portal. Fiona warned her and tried to make her promise, but she still did it, often without a thought.

She used magic and set the stage for Trevir to emerge.

And now, now Trevir knew where they were. Fiona. Chet. Luna. Keela. Lacey, Kelley and the rest of the Misfits. The school. Trevir now had access to it all.

Kurt's parents went to meet with the doctors.

"Is it okay if I sit with Kurt for a few more minutes?"

Kurt's mother was distracted.

"Yes, yes, of course, whatever, sure." She bent over to kiss Minnie's forehead. "If only we had a daughter like you instead of the irreverent Kurt. Him and his books. He defies God and this is what happens."

Minnie's heart sank. His parents would not protect him.

It wasn't your God, or any other god, it was me.

She took Kurt's hand. It felt cold, like a dead fish. She traced a finger on the IV line—it felt foreign and mechanical. It made Minnie shudder.

"I'm so sorry, Kurt. I never should have used magic. Fiona was right. This is all my fault. I caused this. I will fix this, Kurt. I will fix this. Trevir won't win. You'll be safe. Come back to us."

She squeezed his hand and he squeezed back, though maybe it was just her imagination.

Mr. Danvers waited in the reception area.

"I'll drive you home, kiddo. It's been a long day. What will you tell Fiona?"

"Nothing. I'll tell her I stayed late to work on a paper and that you offered to drive me home. Is that okay?"

"Yes, of course. It's not too late. Hopefully she won't be

worried. But Minnie, you should at least mention to her what happened. She'll hear about it sooner than later anyway."

Minnie was stoic.

"I'll tell her the story. The same one I told the Principal. The same one I told the ambulance people. The same one I told the doctors and Kurt's parents."

Mr. Danvers did not push any farther. They walked to the car in a silence that carried on during the short drive to the restaurant.

They pulled up and Minnie thanked him for the ride.

He squeezed her hand, looked in her eyes and said, "It will be okay, Minnie. You're not in this alone."

Minnie forced a small smile in return and said, "Thank you. It will be okay; I'll see to that."

I'm not alone? I wish.

Minnie closed the car door. As she walked toward the restaurant, she closed the door to magic.

"No more. Do you hear me, NO MORE!"

This was not enough. She stood under the drizzly sky and raised her hands. From the tip of her toes to the top of her head, she aligned all of her forces.

"No magic," she whispered, but with force, all the force she could manage.

The trees rustled in compliance and the birds grew quiet. It was as if she was in the eye of a storm; all eerie silence with the world holding its breath. Under her feet, a pebble gleamed. She leaned over to pick it up, it shined like a diamond.

Not even the smallest thing.

The moon hid its face behind a cloud.

"No more," she swore.

The words echoed in the hillsides, then died. She was small and her power was not fully formed, but still, her energy was immense. In a circle, no, a sphere ten miles around her, the magic died. She dropped the pebble and kicked gravel over it.

It's done.

She walked in, threw down her bag and snuggled with Keela.

Keela sensed darkness and nuzzled her human. Familiars didn't ask questions, they simply knew. When Fiona walked by, she saw Minnie snuggled up with Keela.

Keela looked up into Fiona's eyes.

"Ahh, one of the bad days, huh, little one? We'll let our princess sleep. Watch over her."

Fiona covered them up with a blanket, kissed Minnie on the forehead and put down green grapes for Keela.

Covered with flour, she stepped outside to get fresh air and heard a soft whisper.

"I see you, Fiona."

Her arm hairs stood up. She knew the voice but refused to acknowledge it on any level. She shook her head and looked up at the rising moon. Luna pranced up and rubbed against Fiona's leg. She picked him up and he nuzzled her neck. He too looked up at the moon, gazed at it and looked back to his mistress. A lone owl let out a nighttime cry, a warning perhaps, or a call for his family.

"Shall we go inside, Luna? Our princess seems to have had quite a day, she and Keela are already bedded down for the night. Let's get you a snack and I'll finish cleaning up in the kitchen."

She stared out into the quiet darkness. Something was different.

"If it's all the same to you, I don't think you should be outside tonight."

Luna nuzzled in agreement and they both went inside.

It had been a very long day indeed.

Black Death

THOUSANDS OF MILES to the East, Trevir lifted his head from the flames and looked around. Troll Srenzo, dressed in leather with chains dangling from her belt stood near, surrounded by trolls, hundreds of them.

"I'm suspicious of things that are too good to be true."

He walked to his plywood throne. Troll Srenzo offered him a cup filled with blood-red, syrupy wine. He took a sip, then dropped it on the factory's concrete floor—the cup shattered and wine splashed in all directions.

"This is a new day. Unless I am mistaken, little Minnie abdicated her power, opened the door and threw out a welcome mat. A red carpet invitation. Of course, we still need to get there, but get there we will. I didn't have to do anything, she gave me her life—and the fake Queen's life—for free. This is the best thing that has ever happened. We need to celebrate."

Troll Srenzo whispered in his ear. His mood instantly soured and his face turned red with rage.

"We have other business to attend to on a glorious day like

this?"

He reached to a sheath alongside his makeshift throne and slowly drew out his long sword. The razor edge gleamed with malice. It was thirsty. Troll Srenzo lowered her head. If he cared to have her head, he could slice it off with no effort.

He pressed his foul mood aside.

"Let's have a look at this *business*," he said.

With Troll Srenzo and the other trolls trailing behind, he walked through the factory brandishing his sword. He stopped to look at the vats where thousands of gallons of Windowpane were being formulated. The fumes were strong, but Trevir did not care—there were no health and safety rules in his factory. In fact, the less safe it was, the more he liked it. A careless troll or two in the vats added to the flavor.

With his entourage following, he kept on walking out of the building, across abandoned railroad tracks with rusting machinery and into an adjoining building. There, they found trolls lolling, but they immediately snapped to attention. There was a figure tied to a chair with a black sack covering his head.

"I will see his eyes now," Trevir said.

A troll pulled off the sack and tossed it aside. Trevir crouched and made a gesture. Troll Srenzo lifted the man's head by his long; oily hair. He was missing some teeth and blood dripped down his face. His clothing was formal, a tuxedo and bowtie, but filthy, torn and ragged.

"Hello, Mister Gott," Trevir said.

"You..."

Trevir leaned closer and turned his head so the man could speak into his ear.

"...don't know who you are messing with."

Trevir tilted his head back and laughed.

"That's it? What could be your last words and all you can manage is a weak line from a bad movie? Besides, it's not true, I know exactly who you are. We made an offer, you declined. With you out of the way, we'll make the same offer to the disposable creep who steps up into your role. No, not the same offer, a lesser one. You won't be around, so you won't care. That must hurt most of all."

Trevir, walked in a circle with his sword raised to the sky.

"You made a fortune from Meth, Methamphetamine. Nasty stuff, that, though I suppose what the losers get out of it is understandable. Neurotransmitters creating a sense of euphoria that lasts eight or ten hours. A ravenous sexual appetite and temporary alertness. When you're hopeless and stupid, even the briefest glimpse of heaven is worth it, even if it costs your life. What's a life anyway? For most, it's a short and brutal thing. Meth is a great tonic for depression, not that I would know, but I hear things. You had the trade locked up in DC, Baltimore, Philly, Newark, the City, and Bean Town."

He stopped and kneeled in front of Gott.

"Then I come along with something better, much, much better. Black Death. Not the crystal meth of yesterday, this is a much different world. You won't believe what people will do to get this stuff, once they try it. They will steal, kill, anything. When they can't get the money for a fresh dose, they die. It's perfect. Do you read the papers? Does it seem like the world is falling apart? Like you might be murdered for ten bucks in your wallet? Like no one is safe, anywhere?"

Trevir scowled.

"He's falling asleep. Give him a little."

Troll Srenzo put a gas mask on their captive and motioned. A troll turned a valve and gave Gott a shot. It worked. Gott raised his head. His voice was stronger and easy to understand.

"I'd take a little more."

Trevir laughed.

"That's what they all say. I'm glad you're back with us, because I'm going to tell you what is next. Have you heard of alkaline hydrolysis? High pressure, elevated temperature and potassium hydroxide—there will be nothing left of you but bones. We dry the bones, grind them up and poof, it's like you never existed. And, you'll like this part, we mix your liquefied body in with the Black Death, so my customers will be smoking you and enjoying the hell out of it. Delicious, right?"

Gott's bright eyes swept around the room.

"I'm ready to accept your offer," he said.

"What kind of man would I be? Yesterday, when I said my offer was final and expired when I left the room, it's important to honor that, don't you think? You didn't get to the top of the trade by lying all the time, did you?"

The captive pleaded.

"Please."

"Now you're insulting me."

Trevor stood and placed his sword against Gott's chest.

"I'm almost angry enough to finish you right now, but that's not good enough. I want to imagine how it feels when the fluid runs into the chamber and your flesh starts melting. You'll be immortal, we'll put the audio up on the internet for the tweakers to enjoy."

Trevir stood.

"Take him," he commanded.

They watched as the trolls cut the bindings and hauled Gott away. Trevir handed his sword to a troll to take back to his throne, then walked out of the building and stood, facing west in the cold space between the buildings.

I'm coming for you, fake-Queen and fraud-Princess.

From behind him, Troll Srenzo reached around and loosened his belt.

"You know me too well," Trevir said.

Enjoying the moment, he raised his face to the sky, closed his eyes and let the mist fall on his overheated skin.

Jimmy and the Pisstols

MINNIE SWORE OFF magic and there was no going back. She felt more human than ever and hated every moment of it. But, there was no choice.

Walking around the hallways she could still hear everyone's thoughts. She couldn't turn that off—it seemed to be a part of her inner fabric, built into her very being. She walked by a cluster of girls in the hallway. They were huddled around Simone's locker.

"Did you see what she was wearing today? It was gawd-awful. I mean, like I know it's hip to transition from being a boy to a girl but puhlease, someone needs to give her some lessons in makeup and hair!"

Annette piped up.

"I'll befriend her and then not only will we get the inside scoop but we'll make her look just faaaabulous."

"Agreed. We can't have her walking around looking like a homeless former reality-TV star. How will she ever get a boyfriend? Okay, Annette, get on that A-S-A-P, like today, even.

Makes me shudder to think that she'll go through the rest of the day dressed like, like, like she only shops during Dress-For-Less bargain day."

The circle disbanded and they went off to their respective classes.

Minnie shook her head.

Who cares if she is a he, or he is a she? Who cares what people are wearing or how? Why can't people flow along with what is? Nooooo, they have to stick their noses in—not for the betterment of the person, but to be nosy and to say they helped out of the goodness of their putrid, drama-filled hearts. Ugh, it makes me sick.

Lost in thought about the idiocy of this place, she managed to get to Algebra class without encountering anyone else. How could people be so self-absorbed about mundane issues? How could they when someone good like Kurt lay in a hospital bed, hooked up to machines and floating between this world and the next.

He's the lucky one, escaping all of this.

Minnie opened her book and focused on the teacher. Mr. Payne. Wayne Payne. He went by his middle name, Hugh, but everyone called him Wayne the Pain—all the way back to the first grade.

"Class, today we're beginning a unit on simplifying algebraic expressions using *properties*. We'll be talking about topics such as the order of operations and commutative, associative, identity and distributive properties. We'll begin with a preassessment exam to figure out what you already know and what you need to master in these interesting and useful topics."

Ah, the black and whiteness of Math. Math didn't argue, it simply was. It was A or B. It didn't change. It wasn't emotional. It. Simply. Existed. That's what I need right now.

As she waited to receive her preassessment grade, the hulking boy sitting next to her leaned over.

"Hey, Missy, do you have a lighter?"

Minnie turned to him and whispered, "What?"

His hair was spiky and he wore a trace of black eye makeup. On the inside of his wrist, there was a smeared, sewing needle tattoo of the "A" anarchy symbol, a sloppy, bedroom, stole-one-of-Dad's-beers-and-had-a-brainfart job.

She knew his name, Jeffrey Johnson.

His father worked for the electrical utility company and drove a truck with a cherry picker on the back. She liked his dad; she'd seen him rescue a cat once. The cat didn't really need rescuing, it was perfectly capable of descending if it wanted, but the owner, an elderly, blue-haired woman with a forest of hair on her chin, was panicking and having heart palpitations.

Impatient, Jeffrey continued, "What, no English? I asked if you have a light. A simple yes or no is the appropriate response. I don't suppose you do, though, you're too vanilla, clean-cut and proper."

"You have no idea about me, but you're right, I don't have a lighter. What's the name of your punk band?"

"We're trying to decide between *The Bloodclots* or *Jimmy and the Pisstols*—that's with two S's, like taking a piss, see? The lead singer is Jimmy and his dad used to be in a band and still has the van and a P-A system. Racks, stacks and sticks. Get it? Racks of amps, stacks of speakers and microphone stands, which we call sticks."

Minnie sighed. Yes, she got it. She stifled an impulse to start a fire and ignite his greasy jeans.

But, no magic.

She understood the natural forces of teenage rebellion, but why did people copy what they saw in a magazine advertising campaign?

You're not really rebelling if you simply exchange one set of cultural clichés for another.

Her fingers itched to rub together and kindle an open flame, but she resisted. Then she remembered a book of matches she had stuffed in her book bag. Trying to stay quiet, she fished out the matches and handed them over.

"Thanks," he said.

"You're welcome," she mouthed.

The teacher caught the transaction.

"Notes? You're passing notes? That's quaint, I thought you all just sent text messages and exchanged panda-bear emojis now."

With a cruel edge to his voice, Mr. Payne continued, "Perhaps, Mr. Johnson, you'd like to come up to the front of the class and read the note?"

Jeffrey took his time getting up and sauntering to the front of the class. The shiny chains on his boots and belt rattled. He cleared his throat and looked around the room before speaking.

"*Bill's Paint Shop. We MATCH your paint.* The match is in all caps, for promotional emphasis. Get it? Matchbook? Paint matching? That's what passes for marketing around Hicksville. Not that it matters since it's the only paint shop in town."

A scowl crossed Mr. Payne's face. He held out his hand and Jeffrey passed over the matches. He glanced at the matchbook to verify what Jeffrey said—that there was no hand-written note. He opened his mouth to speak, but couldn't think of anything to say, so he impatiently gestured Jeffrey back to his seat. Jeffrey held out his hand for the return of the matches, but Mr. Payne pointedly refused.

With a voice dripping with sarcasm, Jeffrey said, "It's okay, you can keep them for your crack pipe."

The class tittered and Mr. Payne was grouchy for the rest of the class session.

As expected, Minnie got an 86% on the preassessment test—a solid B and not an outlier compared to the rest of the class. She could have done better, but did not care to. The class seemed to last years and the whole time, while praying for the bell, Minnie wondered what possible use Algebra could be in real life.

The lunch hour came after class. She thought of slipping away to the Sanctuary, but she felt no desire. What was the point? That room was full of magic and she'd sworn off every last bit of it. The other misfits missed her and figured she hadn't been there because it was too soon. Knowing she was hurting, they gave her space. They didn't grasp the real reason—that it was her fault Kurt was in a coma and might never wake. They didn't know it was her who led Trevir to their world. They didn't know the danger for each and every one of them.

Craving the outdoors, Minnie wandered across the parking lot and sat under a tree, taking in fresh air and trying to exile sad thoughts from her head. She drank bottled water and munched grapes, cheese and crackers. From far away, she looked on as kids huddled in groups gorged on bologna sandwiches, frozen-food pizzas and other school lunch absurdities. Couples were scattered here and there. Clusters of popular girls sat in a circle talking about dreamy boys. Some were barely eating and were sitting "just so."

She tuned into their thoughts.

"God, I gained like two pounds last week. It might be because of my period but I'm taking no chances. I'm sticking to water and apples this week. I need to drop that weight. Otherwise, how will I fit into the cute clothes I just bought?"

"Oh, you think you have problems? I felt my thighs touch the other day. My THIGHS! I can't have my thighs touching and be expected to perform on the Squad. Oh, hell no! I don't want anyone picking me up and making comments about my thunder thighs. I'm all about the water and the treadmill."

"I looked in the mirror and what did I see? A muffin top oozing over my belt. Ugh, it was so trailer park—so all-in two kids, a flip phone and sixpack of cheap beer."

Minnie stopped listening.

Really?

Weight and appearance were THAT important? What was wrong with 'Thin enough to be healthy, fat enough to be happy?' But, who was she kidding? Even in this small town, it mattered. Who was dating whom, who wore what brand, who was the best at this, that or the other trivial thing. Minnie didn't belong here, she belonged with Fiona and Sean in their enchanted world; not here drowning in the dismal drudgery of human existence.

She leaned her head against the tree and closed her eyes for a few moments—feeling the warmth of the tree, the energy it gave to her and the kinship it shared with her. The tree spoke to her.

"There, there, Minnie. We all know magic is banished and

we're leaving. But, please know, we still love you and always will. Part of what you need to learn is what it means to be fully human. The world needs you, dear sweet Princess, all of you, alive and healthy. Rest easy. Breathe in the fresh air. We're with you and always will be."

Minnie felt a tear roll down her cheek. It all seemed so dark; she felt so small and helpless. There was nothing she could do but be human for now. She must endure a world without magic. All around, the enchantment of the world was leaving, drifting away, dissipating. It left a hole in her gut, a gaping chasm, but there was no choice.

There was no other way to keep her friends, her family, her town, her world, safe.

Lacey's Night to Remember—Part One

STUDYING HER FLANK in the bathroom mirror, Lacey smoothed her dress and turned to the left and right. The dress was perfect; it flowed over and hugged her slim figure. She realized that after years of wishing her breasts were bigger, they were big enough. She'd feel sloppy if they got any bigger. She raised her eyes to the heavens.

Enough. Stop now.

He mother had bought the bra and brought it home from a trip to the Victoria's Secret store at the mall, but Lacey knew her father had really made the choice. It was lacy and sheer, more revealing than nakedness. More padding would help hide the shapes the bra emphasized—she thought about stuffing in tissues to smooth things out. Her father, shouting from downstairs, interrupted her train of thought.

"Baby! I'm sure you're perfect. The limo is waiting, dear."

There was time for one last check of the lipstick, blush and eye shadow. She fluffed her hair and adjusted the floppy, blood-red ribbons over her ears. As self-critical as any teenage girl, she accepted the reality that she looked like an angel. Like a sunflower at the peak of the growing season, she would never look better. It was thrilling and depressing at the same time. Deep inside, her mother, a tired and broken mouse, lived in her. Looking into the mirror, her mother's mottled skin and etched lines appeared and her bright eyes faded into despair. Her shiny hair drooped and fell lifeless to her shoulders. It was a nightmare. Lacey shook her head and pinched herself.

Snap out of it, girl.

Careful because she was not fully accustomed to the spiky heels, she gripped the banister and walked gingerly down the stairs. Watching, her father patted his chest.

"My Lord, girl, be careful, you could stop a man's heart." He turned to her mother. "What a marvelous creature we created."

Her mother glanced up, but quickly returned her gaze to her drink. She drank, everyone knew it, but not so often and so openly. Her sewing room had a lock, but Lacey had seen her mom's private freezer filled with bottles of Ketel One Oranje which she poured over ice in tall glasses and consumed constantly.

Eating her alive, her father's gaze lingered where she wished his eyes would not go.

He took her hand and escorted her to the door and turned.

"We're off, dear."

Her mother mumbled and dismissed them by waving the back of her hand.

"What was that, mother?" Lacey said.

"Let's go," her dad said.

Unsteadily, her mother stood and navigated the few steps between them. Reeking of vodka, she put her hands on Lacey's shoulders and whispered into her ear.

"Be careful, dear."

"Thanks, Mom. I will."

Outside, the white limousine glimmered under the streetlight. The driver held the door open. Gripping her hand tightly, her father escorted her, watching carefully as her dress hiked up as she was seated. Before her father had his fill of the image, the driver pushed the door closed and got an angry stare.

"Let's get you in the other side, sir," the driver said.

Her father clenched his teeth and held back an ugly insult.

"Right," he said.

As the limo pulled smoothly away from the curb, her father grinned at her and ran a thick finger along the outside of her leg—from thigh to knee.

"This will be a night of many surprises," he said. "What would you like to drink? I bought the full limo package. Brandy, Meyer's Rum, whatever you want—as much as you want. Piña colada?"

"Dad," she protested, "I'm not even seventeen yet."

A feral grin expanded across his face.

"That's the first big surprise," he said. "Tonight, you're not sixteen, you're twenty-one."

He pulled a packet from inside his suit jacket, extracted a driver's license and passed it over. The picture was a headshot she recognized from a BBQ a few months earlier. All the information was accurate, except for her date of birth.

"I spent a small fortune—this will pass any inspection, even the cops. You're twenty-one and I don't want to hear anything more about it. Tonight, you are a woman in every way. Because we're not driving, you can drink as much as you like. Martini or maybe just a Heineken to get warmed up?" He laughed. "Don't want you to pass out before the party gets really started, am I right? The martinis are pre-mixed, all we have to do is pour. If you want to wait, that's fine, but I'll take one now. Long day. Too much work. It's time to relax. I've been waiting for this night for so long, you have no idea."

Yes, actually, I do.

After filling two flared glasses and handing her one, he raised his for a toast.

"This is your night, Lacey. Congratulations on winning the student body presidency. This will be a night to remember forever."

She took a small sip. The ice-cold drink was bitter—the alcohol bit her tongue. As he finished his drink and turned away to pour himself a refill, she quickly dumped the remainder of her martini into the ice bucket.

Yes, Daddy, a night to remember.

Minnie and the Gift of the Corn

MINNIE WOKE WITH a start. She looked at her phone; it was 5:45, slightly before sunrise. From a lingering dream, a voice echoed in her head.

"Remember your promise, fish-girl..."

Fish-girl, fish-girl?

Where had THAT come from? Keela was still curled up next to her, all snug in her musky blankets. Minnie wiped the grit from her eyes and searched her memories for a promise made.

"Oh yahhhhh, Coranich in the corn field. I totally forgot about him. Now, where did I put that totem?"

After much quiet searching, Minnie found it behind a pile of books, wrapped securely in its scrap of tattered batik cloth. She picked it up; it hummed and pulsed in her hands. She ran her fingers down the tassel as if it were a field mouse curled up in her hand. When shook, it rattled with an odd sound, clicking with a plaintive echo.

"I'm sorry I forgot about you. I'll plant you today. I'll find a nice sunny place where you can grow undisturbed. At least, I assume you'll grow? I guess I don't really even know WHAT you are or what you'll do. But he said to plant you and I promised, so plant you I will."

Minnie carefully put the totem into a special hidden pocket in her backpack and snuggled up with Keela for a while longer.

As an oddity, the day turned out to be brilliantly sunny—it was cool, but not freezing. A few fluffy clouds floated by, enough to make Minnie look up to see if they would shift into familiar shapes. Bear, tiger and rabbit. Popcorn Majestic castle. As she ambled along, she kept her eyes open for the perfect spot to plant the totem.

"Nope, not private enough...nope, too shady...nope, too close to other plants...nope, those mushrooms are poisonous."

Her search went on and on and she became frustrated and cranky. After plopping on a rock, she closed her eyes.

"If I were a mysterious totem, where would I like to be planted?" she said.

"Over here," replied a small voice.

Minnie opened her eyes. Scanning her surroundings, she saw no one, human or creature. She closed her eyes again.

"It's not nice to ask a question and then close your eyes to the one who offers to help you. Some princess YOU are."

Minnie's eyes flew open. She'd not heard *princess* in way too long; she'd all but forgotten. Squinting her eyes, she couldn't see anything or anyone.

Maybe I need glasses.

"Ahhhh, your magical sight is fading. Forgive me, Princess. I've forgotten what is happening in this world. Here, let me climb up on your knee."

Minnie looked down and slowly, a forest gnome came into focus. He wasn't dressed gaily in a red cap and blue knickers, rather he wore the muted colors of the forest; a floppy brown cap, tan shirt and olive-green pants. With a tiny shovel in hand, he was ready to assist.

"Oh, hullo there, my fine sir. I'm sorry that I didn't see you earlier. Please forgive me."

"Oh, child, there is nothing to forgive. Magic flees from this world, fast and furious. We gnomes are the last to linger. I am here to help you plant your totem away from a proper trail, but not so far so you'll have to struggle to reach it."

Minnie nodded in agreement.

"What is your name?"

"I'll tell you when we get there. For now, there is no time to waste."

The trail blazed by the gnome led through swampy patch covered by dripping trees. After a few hundred yards, a meadow spread out under open sky. Turning, she scanned the area.

It was an unpleasant sight. Around the clearing, bare trees crowded around like an angry mob. Beyond the trees, rolling hills towered. The ground was covered with brambles and dried grass. She was reminded of what tricksters the gnomes could be. This was not a good place for planting corn.

"No," she said.

"It's just a little further, Princess."

"No," she repeated. "You are leading me astray."

Turning, she walked resolutely back toward the highway. The gnome did not follow—his protests faded into the background noise of the marsh.

By the highway, she found a rock. On the verge of bitter tears, she sat, spinning the totem in her dainty hands. Traffic streamed by, but an old Ford truck stopped and backed up along the shoulder. The passenger window rolled down and an old man's florid face looked down at her. The fat face was framed with long white hair, a white beard and bushy-white eyebrows. He wore a brown stocking hat. A deep scar crossed his cheek, left eye and forehead. Otherwise, he looked like a department store Santa.

"What's that you have there?" he said.

Minnie did not feel social. She waved him on.

"I prefer to be alone right now," she said.

The man opened the truck door and waved her in.

Right, like I am going to get in a stranger's truck and never be seen again.

"I'm no stranger."

She looked at him intently. Was he reading her mind?

"I've seen you in the café. I'm not a serial killer, I buy a pie now and then. I even know your name. Mona. No, Molly. No, that's not it either. Okay, I kind of know your name, it begins with *M* like mine. Martin. Martin Chambers. Come on, there's something I want to show you."

Ignoring him, she turned her back to face the drainage ditch and tangled underbrush that hugged the road. Watching with black, beady eyes and fighting against the wind, a crow held a death-grip on a telephone wire. She ignored the crow too.

The man leaned back into his truck and tossed something out—it landed beside Minnie. She took her time before glancing over.

It was an ear of corn—dried corn.

Trying to ignore it, a hint of smile hovered on her lips. She couldn't think of any reason a serial killer would have an ear of corn. Besides, the rock was chilly and sitting there was uncomfortable. After picking up the corn, she stood and smoothed her dress.

"Good, it's cold out here with the door open," the man said.

After climbing into the truck, she put on her seatbelt and pulled the door closed. He held his hand out for a shake.

"Let's make it formal so we're no longer strangers. I'm Martin and you're Merry, short for Meredith, I assume." Reaching, he said, "Show me what you have."

She lifted the totem, but held it out of his reach.

"I recognize the work," he said. The ink was splotchy. "Do you know the illustration?"

She studied the dried leather. The ink seemed shapeless—meaningless.

He continued, "Fish, trout. Ah, I got it. Minnie. They call you Minnie, a diminutive for Minnow."

"Short for Minerva."

"Hmmm," he mused.

"Where are we going?"

The question disrupted his reverie.

"Ah, right. There's something I want to show you."

He waited for a break in traffic, then pulled slowly onto the highway. The truck's engine labored and coughed as they gathered speed. They rumbled down the highway for several miles.

"The pagans believed in exchanges with the gods. If you made a proper offering, then you would get good things in return. When the world fell into chaos, it seemed like the gods had abandoned man. Christianity promised an eternal paradise to the poor and needy, which seemed like a fair bargain as the world fell into dark ages. You're carrying a pagan artifact, a tribute to fertility and harvest. Is that what you believe?"

"I'm too young to believe anything too strongly."

The man laughed.

"Hold that thought through all of your life and it will serve you well. Lammas was the corn king and his descendants live in the corn country. You met one of his sons."

She shrugged.

"I met someone. Where are we going?"

He turned the truck onto a gravel road.

"Along with European paganism, do you know about micro-climates?"

"I know nothing about any climates, big or small."

"That's good, because none of your science will explain what you're about to see."

After winding on a country road for more than two miles, they pulled up to an old farmhouse. Despite a trickle of smoke from a stone chimney, the place looked abandoned. The man pointed to a towering hill—a tumble of stones.

"See how the clouds skirt the hill and leave a path for sunlight?"

"No," Minnie said.

"I don't either, but it's my best guess." He stopped and studied her face. "It's either that or you believe those jumbled stones have a magical power to magnify sunlight and guard against the clouds and moisture that comes off the salt water to the west."

Without looking back, he walked down a gravel walkway and slowly, she followed. The path led through a stand of aspen and cottonwood trees and opened up on a field.

He raised his hands like a symphony conductor.

"Behold," he said with a grandiose tone.

The field was a few acres of emerald-green corn about five-feet tall. The wind rustled the leaves. In beams of sunlight, the glowing jade color was so bright, it was blinding. Minnie blinked, assuming the field would disappear when she reopened her eyes. Spinning like a top, she walked among the rows, trailing her hands through the leaves. On sturdy posts, the loose clothes of tattered scarecrows flapped in the breeze.

"I bought this farm for a hundred dollars an acre. No one knows it's here." He speared her chest with a stiff finger. "And don't you go telling anyone." Pointing, he added, "There's a perfect spot for you."

She followed the track of his gesture and walked until she stood before a space about eight-feet square. A trowel and wheelbarrow full of earth stood ready.

"Were you going to plant something here?"

"Don't worry about that," he said while taking a clump of dirt from the barrow and crumbling it. "Horse pucky. It works better if you work it into the earth with your bare hands. Have at it. When you're done, I'll run you home."

After dropping the totem, she picked up a handful of dirt and raised it to her nose.

Manure.

"Yuck," she mumbled.

But...if that's what it takes.

Careless of her dress, she dropped to her knees and started digging. To her right, she sensed movement and heard a thin voice. It was the forest gnome.

"Aenghus."

"What?" she said.

"You asked for my name and I am telling you. Aenghus, that's me. Though you are an ungrateful little girl, move over a little and I will help you."

She laughed.

"How did you get here?"

He pointed his shovel at a path winding around the stone hill. "Where did you think we were going? You chose the long way around, but got here just the same, didn't you? The meadow where you rudely turned your back and walked away is on the backside of the stone hill." He dropped to his knees. "Are we digging or yapping?"

They began to dig. She thought a small hole would be sufficient, but the gnome insisted on one much bigger. Regardless, it didn't take long—in a few minutes the totem was buried and the pungent earth was tamped down. With a mist of sweat on her forehead, she raised her head to the sun.

"This is a beautiful place."

The gnome stood and dusted off the knees of his trousers.

"It is, isn't it? My dear princess, the corn will grow big and strong. The roots will extend below and the stalk will grow taller than you. It's protected by Coranich, my fair one, and only a fool would counter his will and invoke his madness. Now, let's go."

In a very small voice, she whispered, "Thank you for helping me. I'm sorry I doubted."

The gnome shrugged.

"If doubt hurt me, I'd bear a thousand wounds."

They started toward the trail through the woods. Across the field, the old man waved.

"Hold on a minute," she said. She waved back and walked toward the house. The old man held out a gunnysack. She resisted the impulse to peek inside.

"What's this?" she asked.

Ignoring her question, he said, "It's only good for popping, so don't bother trying to boil and eat the kernels."

"Okay. I'm walking back, you don't need to give me a ride."

The man shielded his eyes with a palm and stared out over the field toward the jumbled stones.

"So I gathered," he said.

Back at the restaurant, Minnie walked in the side door and strolled toward their makeshift apartment. Fiona, chatting with Chet who sat at the kitchen table, glanced up from peeling apples and then looked again more closely.

"Baby, what did you do to your dress? What have you been doing? Rooting around in the mud with pigs?"

"Oh, not much, Mom, I was just out playing."

"What's in the bag?"

"I don't know, corn, I guess. I haven't looked yet."

She firmly pulled the apartment door closed behind her.

"Kids," Chet said. "They are an eternal mystery."

"Right you are," Fiona replied.

Sighing, she returned to paring apples—creating long, continuous peels collected in a pile for compost.

"Far too right," she muttered.

Lacey's Night to Remember—Part Two

SMOOTHLY, THE LIMO pulled into the Emerald Forest Casino valet parking area. With swift efficiency, the uniformed valet attendant opened her car door and held out his gloved hand. She took it and he gently aided her up and out of the car. His eyes locked onto hers and did not drift downward—she appreciated the extraordinary effort. It instantly occurred to her.

Not gay, just well-trained and disciplined.

"Welcome to the Forest," he said.

"Thank you," she replied.

Turning, she lifted her head. The casino was new. Against the darkness of night, the solid state lighting made everything all glittery and shiny—it was like being inside a snow globe. After taking it all in—the flashing lights, the totem poles that straddled the wide entry and the potted palms—she leaned over to speak to the valet attendant.

"Do you like working here?" she said.

As he pushed his lanky hair away from his face, she caught a glimpse of a tattoo on his forearm. She pushed up his sleeve to see. It was an attacking eagle with outstretched talons.

"Like all jobs, it has its good parts and bad parts." He pressed down the sleeve to cover the ink. "Eyes everywhere," he said while inclining his head upward.

"Is this a good place?"

He shrugged. "A fool and his money…"

"Got it," she said.

From a three-inch wad, her dad stripped off twenty-dollar-bills for everyone—it was magical how the bills—when received—were palmed and tucked quickly away. With rapid efficiency, their bags were pulled from the limo's trunk and loaded on the Bell Captain's cart. Attendants appeared from all directions, each making up a job or courtesy to earn a tip. The doorman tipped his top hat before throwing open the doors.

Already, her father was tipsy, his face was flushed and though the night was still young, he was unsteady on his feet. Folding bills into a bundle, he walked to the concierge—a tall, gaunt man wearing a black derby and pencil-thin mustache. His face betrayed no emotion. Her father addressed him.

"Get us checked in, will you?"

"Of course, Sir," the man responded. "We've been expecting you."

The room was cavernous and bustling. Lacey walked to the main entry and looked out over the gaming room where the air was filled with a cacophony of chirps, whistles, bells, tones, buzzers and snippets of blaring melodies. On an Indian reservation, indoor smoking was permitted, so the air was filled with dense tobacco smoke—she wrinkled her nose at the offensive odor. Most of the people did not seem to be enjoying themselves—they were mostly older folks, overweight and hunched over the machines where they staked their claims—guarding their game cards and pressing buttons over and over. The concierge gently took her arm.

"Let me escort you to the VIP complex," he said.

They walked along the wall past the cashier's cages where a set of double doors waited. The hardwood doors were eight feet tall and guarded by a pair of husky men in tuxedos. Inside it was far quieter. The domed ceiling was decorated like a night sky with wheeling constellations—a sliver of glowing moon hovered across the room. The room was huge, at least an acre. Around scattered tables, the players were more elegantly dressed, casually playing table games and appearing to enjoy life more. Here, the air was fresher. Waitresses bustled, carrying elaborate drink orders in tall glasses on silver platters.

The tall man handed her an engraved gold card.

"Show this and they will let you in. It's also your hallway pass and room key. I think your father wants you to go up to the suite to freshen up before your dinner and gaming experience begins."

Yes, I'm sure he does.

"Who will look after me while I'm here?"

A ghost of grin spread across his face, but only for an instant. Had she not been carefully watching, she would have missed it.

"Of course. Let me introduce you to the room manager."

He looked up and tipped his head toward her for a fraction of a second. Within ten seconds, as if from nowhere, a slim man approached.

"Thank you, Peter, I'll take it from here."

"Enjoy your evening," the concierge said before smoothly retreating from the room.

Lacey studied the man—he was an average-looking man of average height and weight, with average features on his round face. He was an anonymous man—she knew she would not be able to describe him if he was out of her sight. His shirt, under tailored jacket, was a muted pink and he wore a pearl-gray necktie. He seemed coiled like a spring under pressure.

The unbidden thought appeared in her mind.

Capable.

Despite his bland appearance, this man is capable.

"My name is Mr. Roderick and I will supervise your hosts for the evening."

"I'm not used to such fancy treatment."

The man shrugged.

"Your father made a remarkable deposit on account."

"Can I trust you, Mr. Roderick?" she said.

He was silent for a long stretch of time, as if considering the question as a life-or-death one.

"Okay, I'll choose," he finally said. "Yes, you can."

She laughed at his gravitas.

"Is this a good place?"

"It can be. It depends."

"Okay, fair enough," she said. "Regardless of what my father orders for me, I want ginger ale. Do you understand what I'm getting at?"

Again, amusement washed across his face, but only for an instant.

The staff must be trained not to smile.

"Yes, I believe I do understand," he said. "I will make sure everyone knows."

"And, tell me nothing but the truth, one-hundred-percent."

"Always."

She considered.

"Am I pretty?"

"Pretty does not capture your unique splendor, young lady. Will you be playing all of our table games or focusing on one?"

She smiled.

"I've been using the Internet to develop my blackjack skill."

"If you count cards, we'll take you out back and beat you bloody—then ban you from every casino on Earth for life." He hesitated, then continued, "That was a joke, not a lie."

"My friend Minnie and I came up with a plan for me to survive the night, and I need your help."

He turned toward her and studied her face.

"Is there, perhaps, more to you than meets the eye?"

Before she could answer, the big doors opened and her father rushed in. Out of breath, his shirt was mis-buttoned, as if he'd dressed in a hurry. He addressed Mr. Roderick.

"Send someone up to restock the minibar in the room," he said. "I had a few pops while I was waiting." He turned his head toward Lacey. "I thought we were meeting in the room before the evening got started."

"I'm sorry, Daddy. I couldn't wait. Would you show me how to play Blackjack?"

Suddenly distracted, her father turned and studied the room—there was a greedy look in his piggy eyes.

"Blackjack. Yes. Okay. We have plenty of time for everything." He turned back to Mr. Roderick. "If my princess wants to play Blackjack, then Blackjack it is."

"Yes, Sir," Mr. Roderick said while ushering them forward with his palm. "We have a table waiting for you."

For an instant, Lacey and Mr. Roderick's eyes met. His expression was completely passive and could not be read.

"Right this way, please," he said.

The dealer waited at their table with the cards fanned face-up on the table. Of medium height, she was a Native American, with dark skin and black hair pulled tightly away from her face. The casino uniform was tailored and the jacket covered her curves, if she had any to cover—it was impossible to tell. She wore no rings on her fingers, but her carefully trimmed nails on plump hands were painted an even pink and gleamed in the diffuse room lighting. Wearing no earrings, her ears were pierced multiple times on each side. Lacey read the nametag.

Stol'Tola.

Lacey stumbled through a pronouciation.

"Staul-taula."

The woman pointed at an English name in parenthesis on the nametag.

"Just call me Susan," she said.

To Lacey, the woman seemed exotic and mysterious.

I'll bet those long sleeves cover some interesting ink.

As if hearing this thought, the woman tugged outward at the white shirt's cuffs.

Lacey shook her head.

Impossible.

The woman's voice was quiet and melodious.

"Single-deck," she said, "with a twenty-five dollar minimum bet."

Impatient, Lacey's father looked around the room.

"Where's the cocktail-doll—who do I have to scalp to get a drink around here?"

Lacey winced and whispered 'sorry' to Susan.

Susan shrugged it off.

'It's okay," she whispered back.

Like magic, a long-legged waitress appeared. With her auburn hair wrapped up in an elaborate braid on top of her head, she wore impossibly high heels and a black, one-piece bathing suit fringed with white fur.

"What can I get you, sir?"

"Give me a J-D, twenty-seven-gold and Mexican Coke, make it a double, and the same for, my, uh, friend. Don't worry, she's legal, twenty-one. Does she need to show her I-D?"

"That won't be necessary, Sir," the waitress said.

"Then why are you standing around? I'm thirsty."

He reached out to pat the waitress's rear, but she skipped a half-step and he missed. Lacey was impressed—that was a ballet-worthy move on high-heels.

"Enough foreplay," he said, "let's play cards. Hit us with starting stakes of ten-thousand. Each." He turned to Lacey. "The point is to get closer to twenty-one than the dealer—without going over. Face cards count as ten and aces are eleven. Got it? Okay, let's play."

"Shall we keep the table private, Sir," Susan said, "or do you prefer company?"

"Bring them in and I'll show 'em what's what," he said.

Susan counted out the chips—including some brown, over-sized ones—$500 each—and pushed them across the table.

Where did he get this kind of money? She had heard the loud conversations at home. Sometimes he was late coming up with money for the mortgage payment.

Her thought was interrupted by the cocktail server, who

placed their drinks into inset holders on the table. Her father smacked his lips and took a big draught, then gestured with his glass.

Lacey studied the glasses and hoped her father would not notice their difference in tint. Both were amber in color, but his drink was much darker.

"Try it, angel," he said, "and send it back if it's not completely perfect. For the money I'm spending, I want everything wonderful for my princess on her special night."

Lacey took a sip—it wasn't cheap ginger ale, it had a crisp bite to it, more like a ginger beer or something else that was craft-brewed instead of the expected corn syrup and factory chemicals from a vat. However, it had none of the piercing fangs of alcohol—and that's what she cared about.

She pressed a $25 chip into the waitress's hand.

"It's faultless," Lacey said.

With an inscrutable expression, the waitress nodded.

On impulse, Lacey leaned over to peck the woman's cheek. The woman's initial impulse was to pull back, but she stifled it and allowed the kiss.

"Good luck," the waitress said.

As the night progressed, her father got drunker and drunker. With dismal etiquette, he made large bets on stupid hands, splitting tens, standing on soft-sixteens and doubling down—seemingly at random. Other players would join them, but they did not like his style of play, so they only lasted a few shuffles before wandering away, shaking their heads in wonder.

Lacey bet smaller amounts and was actually ahead, but only by a few hundred after covering reasonable tips her father should have been making for Susan and the waitress.

Just after two-AM, her father fell off his stool. Appearing instantly, security rovers lifted him back up, but, to them, he was done for the night.

"Perhaps you might try your luck again in the morning," one suggested.

Lacey thought he might argue, but she eased up the hem of her dress and the long, exposed expanse of her slender thigh caught his eye.

She thought it might.

"Right. Time to move this party to the suite." He stood and wobbled on his feet—holding out his hand. "Lacey? Shall we?"

"Please. Can I play just a little longer? Ten minutes? That will give you a chance to get ready."

His inebriated thoughts were jumbled. "Get ready?" he said. "Oh, right. Give the little blue pills a chance to work." He wondered if he said that last part out loud, but decided it did not matter. "I'll see you upstairs," he glanced at his watch, but there was no way he could read it, "in ten. Or twenty—take your time, sugar-plum, I'll be waiting." He pushed his small pile of chips toward hers. "Try not to lose it all," he said, laughing crassly.

The guards held his arms—he shook them off.

"I'm okay," he said. "I'll find my way."

Gently, the guards pointed him in the direction of the exit and, along with Lacey and Susan, watched him stumble away.

Lacey turned to Susan.

"We'll comp you a room," Susan said. "I doubt if he'll remember anything in the morning."

Lacey smiled.

"That's sweet," she said. "But, not good enough." She moved chips across the table. "One more hand, then color me up, and I'll cash out."

Susan studied the girl, then nodded. She dealt the cards—showing a Jack and an Ace in her hand. Lacey had 18, a big loser.

Susan shrugged.

"That's the way it goes sometimes," she said while scooping up the house's winnings.

"Tell me about it," Lacey replied.

Efficiently, Susan consolidated Lacey's remaining chips, twenty-one $500 chips and a handful of smaller ones.

"How much?" Lacey asked.

Susan knew the exact total.

"Eleven-thousand, four hundred and fifty."

Lacey pushed a big chip across the table. Susan nodded, tapped it on the table and dropped it into the tip box. Lacey poured the remaining chips into her handbag.

"Thank you," Susan said.

"Is Mr. Roderick still on shift?" Lacey said.

Susan pointed toward a lounge.

"After hitting the cashier's cage, wait over there. I'll find him."

In the mini-lounge, it was dark and quiet. Lacey sat at the bar and ordered the most exotic and weird drink she could think of—something she'd found on the Internet when she was learning to play Blackjack.

"Give me a Root to Longevity."

The bartender grinned.

"Could I have a hint, please?"

"Tanqueray and puréed beets."

"Coming right up," he said.

He placed a tall glass filled with ice before her and pulled a bottle of Blenheim Ginger Ale from the back of a cooler. With a nifty twist of his wrist, he popped open the top and poured. When he was done, she took the bottle from him and studied the label.

"I was wondering," she said.

"Do you like it?"

She took a sip.

"Not really."

The bartender laughed and cocked an eyebrow. Quietly, Mr. Roderick appeared at her side. The bartended moved down the bar and dried glasses he pulled from the dishwasher.

Mr. Roderick held out his hand.

"Can I show you something?"

He gently tugged her off the barstool and they walked to the doorway. He didn't want to point, so he stood behind her and steered her shoulders.

"Do you see the gentleman wearing the keffiyeh and kandora?"

She didn't know what those things were, but guessed he meant the man wearing a flowing white shirt and scarf on his head—surrounded on each side by two gorgeous women dressed to perfection in matching short, gold dresses. The man looked up at Lacey and smiled. His brilliant white teeth were as big as a horse's.

"Okay, yes, I think so. Why are you showing me?"

"I have an obligation. That is Ali Mohamed Al Eissa Abu Haliga. I'm not a hundred percent sure, but I think he's a sheik. Regardless, he's money. Big money. He booked the whole top floor of the hotel for a week. He's been watching you and expressed an interest, a serious interest, in you."

"Okay," Lacey said. "That's not something that happens every day, is it?"

"If you return his 'interest,' you'll be in Dubai tomorrow with a ring the size of an Easter egg on your finger. Wife number three, I think. That's not bad—worth a fortune and not a small one."

"You can't seriously think I would do it..."

"It's not my job to decide for you. I'm simply the go-between. I present the opportunity. You decide. I can tell you there are plenty of women who would give anything they had for a piece of that man's wealth."

She let herself be tempted for a few long seconds.

"Please pass my regards to the sheik, but I must respectfully decline. I can decline, can't I?"

"Good question, but we won't allow him to kidnap you—though, sadly, there are places where you would not get that option. You'd wake up with a screaming headache on a private jet in international airspace."

"A year ago," she mused, "I don't think I would have hesitated. I'd have taken the money and run away from home and never stopped running. But, I think I've changed. What happened to me? But, never mind that, let's go back to the bar, I need to talk with you."

They walked back and took a hidden table off to the side. She sat while he remained standing.

"Can you sit down for a minute?" she said.

He looked and his watch and then shrugged.

"Yes."

The bartender brought over her glass. She took a small sip.

"It grows on you. Like a fungus."

The bartender couldn't help himself, he grinned.

"Let me know when you're ready for another," he said before slowly backing up and then returning to the bar to leave them alone.

For a full, long minute, Mr. Roderick and Lacey looked at each other. Lacey reached in her bag and pulled out a handful of cash. Mr. Roderick held up his palm to stop her.

"House rules. I'm not allowed to accept gratuities."

"Okay," Lacey said. She dropped her bag on the table and took a deep breath. "Please don't insult me by pretending you don't know what I mean. I want a woman sent up to my father's room."

Quickly, he opened his mouth to respond, then thought better of it. Passively, he looked at her and remained silent.

She continued, "I want pictures. Compromising photographs. Are you with me so far?"

He nodded.

"Yes," he said. "I think I know where you're going with this."

"I would never have done this. I never would have even thought of it. My friend, Minnie, dreamed up this plan. I would never have the courage—or the grit—to follow through."

"Minnie sounds like an interesting person. Teacher?"

Lacey couldn't stifle a giggle.

"No," she said, "not exactly. She's just a kid."

"For this," he said, "I will need money to facilitate. A couple of thousand."

"Done," she said. "I'll give you an email address for the pictures."

Standing, he waited for her to fish out the money—which he

dropped in the pocket of his jacket.

"I suppose I'd better get busy," he said. "What are you going to do?"

Lacey made a funny grimace—twisting her pretty face and wrinkling her chin.

"Chill for a bit," she said, "then go home, I guess. What else can I do? Sit here and drink skunky ginger ale until dawn? I need some sleep. Look, I don't know why, but I don't want to walk out through the front door—can you show me a back way out of here?"

Standing over her, he said, "All of the taxis are out front."

She didn't respond, so he gave up.

"Yes, okay, I won't argue. Follow me."

They walked through the kitchen. At this time of night, most of the workers were cleaning—there wasn't much cooking going on. Walking past a huge pile, Mr. Roderick snagged a piece of bacon and chewed on it as they walked.

"Didn't get dinner," he said.

"You don't have to explain anything to me," she replied.

In the back, past the steam and heat of the Hobart dishwashers, Mr. Roderick stopped in front of an emergency exit. He pressed his badge against a reader.

"I can—you can't," he explained.

He pushed the door open and held it open for her.

"Stop by sometime and let me know how you're doing," he said.

"You got it," she responded.

Outside, it was cold and wet. The gusty wind tugged at the hem of her dress. Shivering, she hugged herself as the door closed behind her with an authoritative click. Across the loading dock, there were a small forest of propane heaters and she saw a figure hunched over a book.

Walking closer, she saw it was Susan.

Susan closed the book on her finger.

"Quieter out here," Susan said.

Lacey raised her arms to the radiant heat. It felt glorious.

"I suppose, as a dealer, you see all kinds of crazy things."

"Generally, things are the same-old, but some nights surprise us."

Lacey pressed down on Susan's book so she could read the title.

"The Red and the Black?"

Susan shrugged.

"Red represents the river spirits—black the sea. Our shamans, the wha-nanm, teach that there are five components to our spirit—the physical body, an inner soul, an outer soul, a central life force and its ghost."

"Does it all make sense to you?"

"Not always, but I know this much: we must believe in something or we're lost, hopeless souls."

"I don't think I *know* anything."

"The people who scare me are the people who are certain."

Lacey had the sense that Susan wanted to return her attention to her book.

"I guess I'll walk around front and grab a cab."

"There's no need for you to freeze. My boyfriend is in the taxi pack, he'd be happy to jump the line and get a fare. I'll call him."

Susan was right. In three minutes, a Yellow Cab swept around and skidded to a stop on the wet pavement in front of them. After getting up, Susan leaned into the driver's side window and kissed her boyfriend. He seemed young to Lacey, a teenager wearing his long hair in braids hanging like cables on the sides of his dusky face. His skin was raw and inflamed with acne, but he seemed like a pleasant sort with a cheerful disposition.

Turning to Lacey, Susan said, "He'll take care of you."

"Does he have a name I can pronounce?"

Susan laughed—a short snort of unrestrained glee.

"Yes, it's Jack. You can handle that."

Lacey slipped into the backseat. The cab was warm and she was instantly drowsy. After giving Jack the address, she was quickly asleep and stayed that way all the way home.

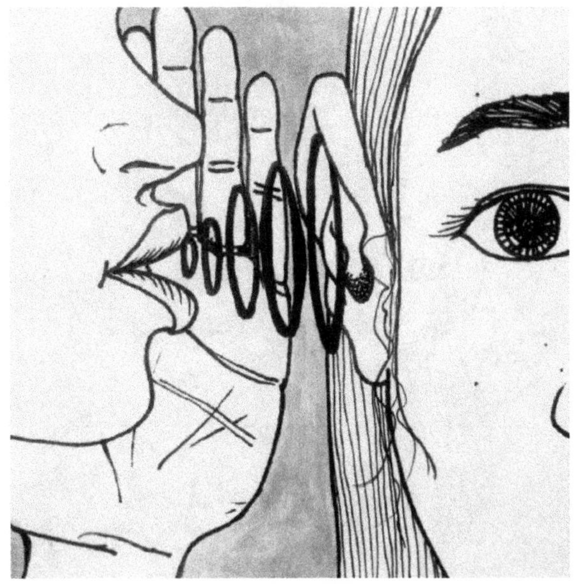

Lacey Tells All

THE NEXT DAY, Minnie was eager to hear about Lacey's date night, but Lacey was elusive. Finally, Minnie caught up and dragged Lacey to a seat in the library.

"I must know," Minnie said. "How did it go?"

Lacey shrugged.

"Pretty much the way we planned, give or take."

"Really? That's it—that's all I get?"

Lacey sighed.

"I met some cool people and had a memorable evening. We're not going to have any trouble getting my dad to help fund our carnival. Beyond that, let me have my private memories."

Minnie studied her friend's face for a long moment before speaking.

"Okay," she said.

Minnie and the Parking Lot Gang

UNDER THE DROOPING branches of a willow tree's massive canopy, a gurgling stream in an overgrown ditch was just a trickle. It was sad because, no matter how much debris Minnie picked up, the wind blew in fresh trash. However, this was a spot where she could be alone with her thoughts.

In the trash bin behind the school, she'd found a cracked plastic chair and a wooden crate to use as a side table. While reading a random poem from a book discarded by the town librarian, she ate her lunch—bottled water, Laughing Cow cheese and whole wheat crackers.

How fully I felt nature glued to me
And how my childish palate loved the taste
Half-fish, half-honey, of that golden paste

With no idea what the poet intended to convey, she loved the way the rhythmic words rattled around in her head. She'd been feeling low. The situation in Cement City was dismal; it was as if the soul of the town was drifting away in the wind, day by day. At her command, magic was fading away. It had to be, but what was left behind was gloomy and spiritless.

Chet had packed a leftover chunk of peach pie. She picked at it with a plastic fork, but the sweet mess was unappealing. Fiona made wonderful pies, but something was missing. Sighing, Minnie wrapped up the glop and stuffed it back in her paper lunch sack.

I'll eat it later.

Hidden behind the dangling branches, she had a good view of a far corner of the school's parking lot. There was continuous activity with people coming and going. In particular, there was a group of boys who had graduated years earlier, but, apparently, had nothing better to do than hang out by the school—on sunny days leaning against their old cars, some shiny and refurbished and some battered and barely hanging on, but none newer than twenty years old.

Kids from the school would come out during lunch and when they were skipping class—skulking across the parking lot like coyotes.

Coyotes.

Minnie did not care much for the skulking beasts and there seemed to be more of them around in the woods. And, they were getting bolder. According to one of Fiona's books, a repeating coyote dream might be preparing you for an illness or death, or some ugly, dramatic transition in your family.

She knew coyotes, like morticians, were important in nature's way for cleaning up cadavers, but she didn't have to like it.

There were crows around too, clinging to branches, devising dark plots and sarcastically commenting on the many flaws of human nature they observed. In fact, on the telephone wires hanging over the parking lot—she counted—there were thirteen crows, all facing the same direction and watching over the collected hoodlums smoking, cursing, spitting and throwing trash around.

She had her fill.

After packing away books and lunch bag into her knapsack, she shouldered the bag and emerged from the hideaway. It was a hundred yards to the collected cars. Along the way she gathered trash and had a large bundle of it by the time she reached the group. Punk rocker Jimmy was the first to spot her.

He stopped sucking hickeys on the freshman girl's neck, jumped off the hood of the car and pointed.

"It's the Mini," he said.

The other youngsters turned to look.

As she walked by the shiny Camaro driven by the leader, Zeke, she noticed the window was down. Feeling naughty, she pushed the bundle of trash through the window.

"I think you dropped this stuff," she said.

Zeke walked over, swaying like a sailor. He was an odd one, at least 22-years-old with lank black hair, so black it had to be dyed. Ezekiel Jones, they naturally called him Zeke. His loose skin had a yellow pallor—he'd had Hepatitis and had not fully recovered. With liver damage, maybe he would never fully heal. Clearly, he did not think he had anything to lose. This made him dangerous and with the pack behind him, very dangerous.

He glanced at the mess on the driver's seat of his car. Behind him, Albert Whinney started to speak.

"You want us to..."

Zeke raised his hand and Albert closed his mouth.

"She has a point. The garbage draws attention we don't need. We're sorry and we'll be neater—starting now."

From behind, there were muttered complaints and grunts. He turned and the group fell silent.

Zeke continued, "I've seen you around, but I don't think we've ever spoken."

His words were formed precisely. She realized that he might be trouble, nothing but big-t Trouble, but he was not stupid. This made him all the more dangerous. He smiled, but malice was part of him to the bone and every cell.

Her hand clenched. She wished for the little troll sword, but it was miles away. Besides, with magic fading away, the old sword was now just a cold piece of rusting iron. Still, it could poke or stab and that was better than being defenseless.

He continued, "Where did you come from?"

Turning, he scanned the parking lot and zeroed in on a path that had been cleaned up. This led his gaze to her tree.

"Lurking in the trees and watching, am I right?" Overhead, the crows chattered. "That's not very nice for such a sweet little girl, is it? Lurking and spying? Is that what you do?"

"You're right, we've never spoken. I would have remembered."

Zeke tilted his head back and laughed. It had been a while since he'd shaved. Curly black hair marched down his neck and under his grotesque Bad Brains t-shirt. His pimples were angry and swollen, like something inside was desperate to escape. He turned to address his followers.

"This little girl has spirit, I like that. Perhaps we'll be great friends." He turned back to Minnie. "Spend a little time with us and maybe your *perception* of us will change."

He emphasized the word 'perception' in an odd way. Her mind tripped over it.

Continuing, he said, "Do you sometimes feel like your observations don't do justice to reality? Of course you do, everyone does. I can help with that." He reached for her hand and she let him take it. Slowly, as if afraid she would bolt, he drew her into the center of the cars. "I like you. Let's have a little toke of my special stuff, you and me. And, don't worry, it's no charge. For you, it's free-gratis."

Grumbling, his followers did not like this. They had to pay.

He silenced them with a glance.

Her thoughts about marijuana were complex. It was a plant, an herb, a gift from the Earth Mother and people should be allowed to do what they want with their bodies. She objected to heavy-handed prohibition. On the other hand, she did not like anything that affected cognition or memory. All she had was her mind and it would be stupid to ruin her best tool.

Pushing her back against a 4x4 pickup splattered with mud,

the gang made a circle around Zeke and Minnie. They were big and small, male and female, all curious about what was going to happen. From above, the crows chattered with excitement.

She spoke.

"It seems odd that you keep coming back here to the high school. Don't you have a job and better things to do with your free time?"

Zeke laughed. He reached out his hand and one of the girls Minnie had seen in the hallway took it. She had long, henna-red hair and beyond-pale skin hidden behind a forest of freckles. Her name popped into Minnie's mind. *Aibrean*. It was Gaelic for April and she preferred to be called that. April was a lost soul, or nearly. She pleased Zeke for now, but not for long. Soon, she'd be discarded and taken up by one of the other boys, then another, but none who would fill the void inside her. The drugs helped mask the black hole in her belly. Minnie was sad, but couldn't blame the girl; we all did what we needed when faced with the unique path we followed. Minnie reached for her hands and held them.

This girl was sick. It didn't take magic to tell. A rotten odor came from her that was cloying and nauseating.

"Please, see a doctor," Minnie said.

The girl pulled her hands back.

"Fuck off, bitch," she said.

Zeke smiled.

"Now we're communicating, but it's time to get serious."

He fished around in an inside pocket of his overcoat, and drew out an old pipe. It looked like it was carved from gray stone and the bowl was black with tar. He produced a plastic box and popped the lid. Slowly and carefully, he filled the bowl from the box and tamped down buds.

Lifting the pipe to his lips, he said, "Torch."

With an anticipatory smile on her lips. April produced a butane lighter from her bag and triggered it. The flame was three blue inches. She applied it to the bowl and Zeke sucked in the aromatic smoke. He held it in for long seconds, then let it out slowly.

"There's nothing sweeter," he said with a dreamy tone.

"Me," April said.

Zeke nodded and let her take the pipe. She lit up the bowl and took a deep hit. With her eyes closed, she placed her hand on her belly and groaned with pleasure. "Ahhh..."

Jimmy-the-punk reached for the pipe, but Zeke swatted his hand away.

"Now the little angel," he said.

"No, thank you," Minnie whispered.

"Hold her and we'll do it the hard way," Zeke said. "Easy, like mouth-to-mouth CPR we learned in Health class. Chain of survival and all that."

Taking the torch from April, he flamed the bowl and sucked in a deep breath.

Her arms were gripped tightly with hands like vises. It didn't seem like a few hands, it seemed like a hundred. In an instant, she understood the crows. They talked among themselves about something coming, something dangerous and ugly.

Black Death.

She was not surrounded by kids, she was surrounded by wolves. Hungry wolves who wanted her to join their pack.

No magic.

She thought of Kurt in his hospital bed and the scared, dead look in his eyes.

No magic.

With a twisted grin on his face and a bleak coldness in his eyes, Zeke leaned in.

A Visit to the Broken City

TROLL SRENZO WAS unhappy. She stood before the curved driveway and watched Trevir settle into the back of their giant black Cadillac Escalade. Beside her, the troll standing guard at the entrance stood as still as a statue. It was early—the first rays of the eastern sun gleamed on the wide blade of the troll's sword.

"Where is he going?"

The guard-troll shrugged.

"I don't know," he said. "Ask him."

"I don't like him going to the city. He's young and his powers are not fully established. There's danger. His father was wiser."

"Shall I issue your command to him? Order him to stay here?"

Troll Srenzo turned her head to study the beast.

"You don't necessarily need a tongue to do your job, do you?"

The troll stood still, staring straight ahead. He said nothing.

Sighing, Troll Srenzo walked down the crumbling steps and climbed into the SUV.

As soon as the door was shut behind her, the vehicle started moving. Trevir was dressed in a black suit with a cream necktie.

In the dim light, his black, pointy boots gleamed. He lifted his fedora and scratched his head and patted his oily hair back into place.

"Where are we going?" she said.

Trevir looked at her.

"Out for a drive," he said. "We'll cruise Washington Street and see what's what. At lunchtime, maybe we'll go up into the city and get soft shell crabs at The Gallows. You have a problem with that?"

She almost complained, but clamped down on the impulse.

"Of course not," she said. "You want to cruise, we cruise. It's early, that's all. The streets don't get interesting until late at night."

Trevir looked at her but didn't speak.

It took over an hour to reach the outskirts of the city, then they were trapped in rush hour traffic. The massive SUV crawled along while Trevir and Troll Srenzo studied the city-cluster of tall buildings through the tinted windows as the sun climbed the sky. Aimlessly, they cruised the streets of the inner city until Trevir saw something he was looking for.

Leaning over the seat, he tapped the troll-driver on the shoulder and pointed at a loading zone.

"Pull in there," he said.

Before the truck was fully stopped, he slipped off his seatbelt, opened the door and climbed out. Making eye-contact with Troll-Srenzo, he reached back in for his walking stick.

Here we go, she thought.

Watching for traffic, she waited for a gap, then threw open her door. By the time she got to the sidewalk, Trevir was half a block away and moving fast. She spun on her heel to get a sense of things. They were on a busy, commercial street crowded with delivery trucks. On the corner was 24-hour liquor store that cashed checks. Irish pub. Dry cleaners. Newspaper/tobacco shop. A dark-skinned woman wearing hot pants and high heels leaned against a street sign. Her hair was tousled and her blouse was mis-buttoned and hanging open. She was too old for her job and the morning's early light was unkind.

Troll Srenzo studied the woman for a fraction of a second, then dismissed her. She was no one.

The Escalade was parked in a loading zone. An Office Depot truck driver honked and waved his hand to shoo them off. Ignoring him, she pointed to the troll in the front passenger seat.

"You. With me." To the driver, she said, "You stay with the car. Don't move, no matter what."

She caught a glimpse of Trevir as he turned to follow a side street.

To her companion, she said, "Hurry."

After turning the corner, a block down was a quarter-acre of dismal city park. Trash was strewn everywhere. By a metal bench, Trevir talked to a freckled man with vivid red hair. Every minute or so, the man would pick up his phone and scan a text, then with racing thumbs, type in a response. Across the park were a group of greasy refuse containers. There, kids, white, brown and black, after getting a message on their phones, caught bindles dropped from a third-story window and raced away on bicycles.

Scanning the area for trouble, Troll Srenzo finally caught up and could hear the conversation-in-progress.

"I'm not even vaguely aware of why I should be interested in where you have lunch."

Trevir laughed. Holding his stick in the crook of his arm, he pulled a bundle from his pocket.

"If you won't tell me your name, I'll call you Red. I have something wonderful for you, Red."

"The Mook Burger is a good one. They use balsamic aioli which, you ask me, is a nice touch. You wouldn't think it would fit, but it adds an irresistible tang. Tell them to throw on an over-easy egg. You'll thank me later, no question about it."

Trevir was amused.

"I like you, you're funny. You should have a primetime slot at The Comedy Vault." He took a plastic baggy from his overcoat pocket and waved it. "Does the streetwalker work for you? Call her, we'll give her a free sample and you can see for yourself."

"The pizza-fries are to die for."

"Who do you work for now that Gott is out of the picture?"

This comment captured the man's interest. He looked up at Trevir.

"We don't do business this way," he said.

"You're smart, Red, right? The phone is a throw-away. You don't touch the merch or the money. The po-po haul you in, they got nothing. But still, you got a boss and he has a boss."

"She."

"Ah, I've heard of Lady Katherine. Thank you for the correction. Now that Gott is gone, who does she work for?" To get some distance, the man scooted down the bench. Trevir continued, "Let's stop playing. Call someone and we'll show you what we have. Believe me, you want it. I'm not here to disrupt the food chain. Like everyone else, I just want to do business." Trevir put *push* into his voice. "Call someone expendable."

The man lifted his phone and spoke tersely.

"Send over Carter," he said.

Across the park, one of the kids pocketed his phone and walked to a bundle of rags. He kicked the heap and eventually a wooly head appeared. The kid pointed across the park. From the bundle, a gaunt man dressed in rags slowly stood, then shambled across the park.

It took a minute before the man stood before them. He blinked in the strong light. His red eyes were buried deep in his skull. His skin was a dark as an eggplant and was covered with black splotches. On his chin was an inch of tangled gray beard. He licked his purple lips and looked confused.

"Wassup?"

"Are you ready for the ride of your life, Mr. Carter?" Trevir said.

"I was in Vietnam," Carter said.

"No you weren't," Trevir said, "but, we're not quibbling about the fraudulent details of your deplorable history. You have your own pipe?"

Carter fished in his jacket and produced a glass pipe. Its well-used bowl was black with carbon soot. Trevir handed the bundle to Troll Srenzo. She tipped in a thumbnail of black crystals, then raised her torch. Without hesitation, Carter raised the pipe to his mouth and eagerly waited for the flame. After drawing in a lungful, his eyes rolled back in his head and he collapsed backwards on the ground. Blinking, he stared into the sky.

"Mr. Carter?" Trevir said. "Can you hear me? What is God telling you?"

"He's..."

"Yes?" Trevir said.

Carter started crying and his body trembled.

"He says, says, says...I'm chosen."

"He's calling you to glory?" Trevir said.

"My mistakes...all are forgiven."

Trevir shrugged and spoke to Red.

"It works differently for each person." Turning back to Carter, he said, "Mr. Carter? Tell me, what would you do to make this feeling last forever?"

"I'm a child, it *will* last forever. All my pain has been transformed...into...joy."

Trevir turned to Red.

"You could have picked a stronger test case. This one is not going to make it."

After staring at Carter for a moment, Red looked up. He reached out to take the bundle.

Trevir laughed while holding it out of reach.

"No, that's not the way this goes down. Tell Lady Katherine where we're having lunch. Tell her to bring her boss, whoever that is."

In salute, Trevir tapped the end of his stick on his forehead and turned away. While watching Trevir and his entourage walk away, Red raised his phone.

"Get some muscle to drag Carter to the Charles—we gotta get him out of here."

Then he switched phones and made the call to Lady Katherine.

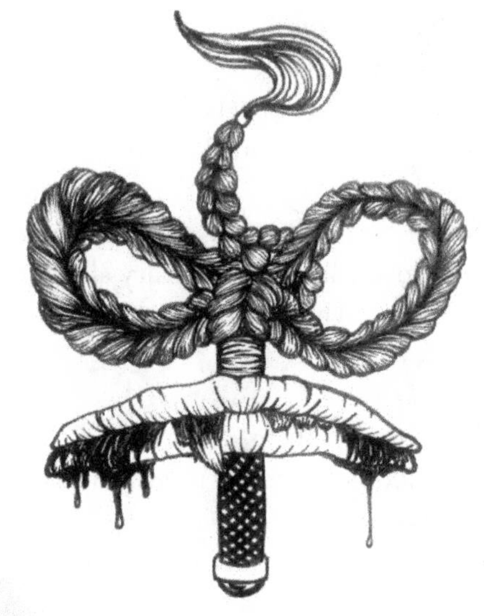

Soft Shell Crabs for Lunch

THE GALLOWS HAD a giant Ouija spirit board on the wall—this amused Trevir.

Why such a dangerous decoration used trivially like this?

He stood and studied the display. Before him, a group of college-aged young people sat at a table chatting and drinking beer from pitchers. It was noon, but they'd been at it a while. At first, they paid no attention to him as he spoke, nearly to himself.

"They call the movable piece a planchette. Its main character is low friction, so it readily slides across the talking board. It's an ideometer, which means it reacts to tiny muscle movements the players are unaware of. Most who study the board accept that the players control the movement—there is no outside influence. Of course, you have to believe the subconscious mind is autonomous and unconnected to an alternate world. Which is silly."

Troll Srenzo stood to his left and the guard troll stood to his right. Like all trolls, they reeked of rot and decay. Trevir was used to it and hardly noticed, but the students were not attuned to the odor. Deep inside, they might have felt distaste or discomfort, but it did not occupy the front line of their beer-sodden thoughts.

The nearest student was a meager yard away, but showed zero awareness of the aroma or spectacle. The trolls wore boiled leather, probably deer skins from the animals they hunted in the woods. The stained leather was only partially cured. Troll Srenzo was a sight. One of her yellow fangs was fractured as it splayed across her rubbery lower lip. She was hairy all over with a wisp of wiry beard on her chin. The hair on her head was twisted into an oily braid.

Did they ever bathe?

Trevir had never seen them do it. When the moon was full when they might wallow in swampy mud, but that was it.

"Excuse me," Trevir said.

The group of youngsters carried on with their chatter and ignored him. With his walking stick, he tapped the nearest on the shoulder.

"Pardon me, would you take a look at my companions and tell me what you see? Truly, I'm curious."

The nearest was a young man who wore a trendy, asymmetrical hairstyle—the right side of his head was shaved close and his long, lanky hair flopped over that side with the ends trimmed in a sawtooth pattern. His right ear bore four loop earrings and he had initials, PST, tattooed on the base of his neck. In the middle of an anecdote, the boy brushed off Trevir's hand.

"...the Black Justice League protested cultural imperialism—the hegemony of culture-asserting misappropriation. I helped with their manifesto." He proudly leaned back in his chair. "Twenty-nine pages, single-spaced."

Trevir turned his head partially toward Troll Srenzo.

"Can they hear even me?"

Troll Srenzo grabbed the boy's ear and twisted—hard.

"Hey," he protested.

He pushed his chair back and stood up. The trolls were stubby and short—their heads were just higher than the lad's waist.

Trevir pointed at his companions and put *push* into his voice.

"Tell me what you see."

"They only see what they want to see," Troll Srenzo said.

Trevir hushed her with an upraised palm. He addressed the boy.

"Speak," he said.

The boy looked left and right, then at Trevir.

"I can tell you are wealthy. Am I supposed to be impressed? And your mom and dad? Old. Old clothes and bad dentures. Blue hair and thin, almost skeletal bodies. Do you feed them?"

Trevir laughed. Troll Srenzo put her hand on the hilt of her sword. Trevir restrained her.

"You amuse me," he said. "But, I will have this table."

He turned back the college students and pointed.

"You'd all be happier with a table in the back."

"What?" the kid said.

"Now," Trevir commanded.

The boy shivered like a cold wind had passed through the room.

He turned back to his group.

"We'd be happier if we move," he said.

The group gathered their glasses and pitchers, then walked to the back of the restaurant where they continued with their conversation.

Trevir moved around the table so he was sitting under the Ouija lettering. The trolls arranged themselves across from him.

"Order crabs, I have a craving. And Scotch eggs, they're good."

After a few minutes, the waitress appeared. She was about forty and had massive breasts and stocky legs encased in white stockings under a black jumper. Her hair was pulled back in a French roll and she had a pen stuck in her hair over her ear. She addressed Trevir, but Trevir did not look at her. Troll Srenzo spoke.

"We'll have a couple of servings of soft crab, mix it up with sausage and the other stuff you do."

Startled, the waitress looked down at Troll Srenzo.

"Sorry, dear, I didn't see you. No crab, today's catch is

linguine with scallops—it's quite good and that's what I recommend."

"With the crab, put in calamari and lobster chunks, corn cobs, whatever else you have. Throw it all in."

The waitress grew huffy.

"As I said, we don't have crab today…"

Troll Srenzo spoke firmly.

"If you don't have it, then get it. And, no dawdling. Go. Now."

A puzzled expression settled on the waitress's face.

"I'll send a runner to the fish market."

To Troll Srenzo, Trevir whispered, "Get a pitcher of Wildfire and tell her not to skimp on the mescal. I'm in the mood for a celebration."

"We'll take a pitcher of Wildfire," Troll Srenzo said. "Double the mescal."

"That will be an extra ten dollars," the waitress said.

"We don't give a shit, make it twenty," Troll Srenzo said.

The waitress nodded and scurried away.

"She's cute," Trevir said. "Find out if she has a sister and we'll take them home."

It took an hour, but a steaming Dutch oven filled with mixed seafood and crab was placed on the table. Trevir leaned over to breathe in the aroma.

"Perfect," he said.

At that instant, the front door swung open and two large men entered, one after the other. They were large, tall and wide, like football linemen. They scanned the room, then one opened the glass door and, like royalty, *she* entered.

Lady Katherine was tall, thin and immaculately dressed in a black sheath dress. Gold watch, gold bracelet, gold necklace and a gold hairclip in her silver hair. She walked to the table and loomed over Trevir.

"I'll give you five minutes," she said, "then my guys fuck you up."

Trevir beamed.

"You're just in time."

He waved the guard troll to the side. With a scowl, the troll scooted over to make room for Lady Katherine.

"Take a seat and have a whiff, this crab bouillabaisse will make your tongue dance a devil's tango, I promise." He looked back toward the entrance. "Where's Mr. Big?"

"He sent me. Please state your business—I have things to do this afternoon."

Trevir leaned back.

"What's the best way for us to skip the preliminaries and get to know each other?" Musing, he tapped his teeth with a fingernail. "Let's do it this way. I'm going to kill your goons—then we'll talk. Don't worry, no one in this restaurant will lift a finger or say a word."

Katherine had a stoic, cold look on her face.

"You're mad. I don't have time for any of this."

He leaned over to whisper to Troll Srenzo.

"Drop her veil."

"You sure?" the troll said.

"Do it," he commanded.

Troll Srenzo clamped her eyes closed and whispered a few words—they were mostly inaudible, except for a few random words.

...briseadh...chnámha...

Lady Katherine's eyes went wide. She gasped, took a step backward and pointed with a painted fingernail.

"My God, what are these horrible creatures?"

Trevir inclined his head in a barely perceptible nod and the guard troll stood. In a flash, he drew his sword and lifted Katherine's gold necklace. With a flick of his wrist, he severed the chain—it fell into a gleaming heap on the floor.

Her two men stood a scant few yards away. Before they recognized any danger, both of their heads were severed. The trolls gathered them and placed them on the table, turning them so their startled eyes faced Lady Katherine. In a cascade, blood dripped off the edge of the table.

"Quick decision, m'Lady. Live or die, right here, right now?"

She closed her mouth and swallowed. She tried a smile, but it did not fit very well on her face. She sat down.

"Live."

Trevir grinned, arranged a colorful plastic bib around his neck, then reached over to caress her powdered cheek.

"Okay, beautiful. Wise decision. Dig in. We'll eat, then talk."

Minnie Discovers Dirt Logic

AS HE LEANED over, a trickle of smoke escaped from Zeke's mouth—the odor was sweet, but corrupt, like tired flowers at an overlong funeral. As bloodthirsty spectators, the agitated crows cawed. As Zeke's head grew closer, time slowed and stretched.

Every muscle in Minnie's body tensed against the strong, relentless hands gripping her. For an instant, she thought of letting go.

Why not?

She'd been feeling low: tired and depressed. What was wrong with feeling good for an hour? Hadn't she earned it? One kiss, one pull of the green-black smoke deep into her lungs. Clearly, she saw this path into the future. Losing her maidenhood to Zeke in a euphoric haze—becoming one with him. The delicious pain of needles in her flesh for her first tattoo: a crow with red eyes clinging to a wire. The first drag of a morning cigarette biting her lungs. Tequila, salt and lime late in the evening. Sleeping naked and unashamed with a boy's fluids drying on her skin. It was going to happen whether she wanted it or not, why not embrace the associated pleasures? They were not nothing, they were something. Her flesh craved the temporary release.

She gave in. Her body relaxed like water cascading into a pool. His face was inches away, so close she could see the animal desire in his eyes. There was nothing he wanted more in that instant than to corrupt her, to consume and trash her soul. It was her gift to give and who would care? She was ready. It was okay, she was no good, she deserved to be used and discarded.

Her body melted and she lifted her head to meet Zeke's.

After fighting the tension in her body, the hands gripping her rubbery arms loosened and she dropped like a stone to the pavement.

"Goddamn it, hold her, you assholes," Zeke hissed with smoke escaping through his gritted teeth.

She hit the parking lot hard. Gravel dug into the back of her head as it whiplashed over her backpack. The hovering faces were contorted and ugly as their hands reached down for her. The cacophony of the crows faded in and out while darkness made another effort to enter. She reached for it.

"I don't care, take me," she whispered.

Her legs disagreed and she scrabbled across the rocks like a crab. The jacked pickup was lifted far off the ground; far enough that she was able to scuttle underneath—even with the bulky backpack. From underneath, she read the brand of the shock absorbers. Dirt Logic.

Okay, she thought. Dirt Logic. She wasn't sure why, but this struck her as funny.

"Get her," Zeke hissed. "Drag her scrawny ass out of there."

Albert hauled the truck door open.

"Why don't I just move the truck?" he said.

"Do it," Zeke said.

A voice came from behind the group.

"Hello? What's up?"

As one, they turned. Halfway into the cab of the truck, Albert froze. It was Mr. Danvers. As if sensing that the show was over, all the crows all flew away.

Zeke was not afraid of Danvers. He was not his supplier, but he knew the shabby, long-haired teacher enjoyed a toke on the weekends.

"There's nothing going on. Why don't you wander back to the teacher's lounge for your afternoon tea—work on your memoirs like usual. That would be better for everyone."

Danvers cocked his head like a puppy, then shrugged.

"Sure, I guess. Take it easy out here, okay?"

Zeke laughed.

"You got it," he said. Turning, he muttered, "Move this fucking truck."

The pickup started with a rumble. Albert popped the clutch and moved forward a car's length. This exposed the view of Minnie a hundred feet away, arms pumping, backpack bobbing and skirt flying—running like the hounds of hell were on her heels.

"Shit," Zeke said.

The Magic of Fresh Water

WITH SHOULDERS SLUMPED, Minnie walked into their little apartment. She was weary and her legs could barely take another step. She dropped her backpack and went to the sink to pour a glass of water. The glass was old, an antique. Hand-blown, it was slightly asymmetrical and had air-bubbles captured in the glass.

One of a kind.

She raised the glass to the waning sunlight coming in the window and watched the rays diffract and diffuse. Tilted just right, a tiny rainbow appeared, but it winked out.

She tried, but could not recapture it.

Even simple things like cold, clean, fresh water, sunlight and glass were nature's miracles, but the magic seemed a million miles away and getting farther away with each passing minute. Without drinking, she put the glass down. She didn't feel like she deserved it.

Fiona breezed in and playfully pushed Minnie aside to wash

dried piecrust from her hands.

"I hope you had a great day at school," Fiona said. "You're my ray of sunshine—seeing you after a long day of work makes me feel young again, but I wish you wouldn't leave your backpack laying around for people to trip over."

Minnie walked to the kitchenette and dropped into a chair like a sack of rocks.

"We can't carry on like this," she said.

Drying her hands, Fiona looked up from the sink, glanced at the cup of water, then angled her head around to look at Minnie.

"Oh," she said. "What's wrong?" She walked to Minnie and ran her hand across the back of the tiny girl's head. With horror, she raised her palm to look at it. "Baby, you're bleeding and there's gravel in your pretty hair. What happened?"

"Can I just say I had a bad day and leave it at that?"

Fiona started to protest and demand information, but held her tongue.

"Okay, but let's get you cleaned up," she said.

She pulled the girl to her feet and ushered her to the sink. The first thing she did was lean Minnie over and pour the glass of water on the back of her head, then she reached over, turned on the faucet and waited for the water to warm up.

"Stay put, we'll do this here. I'll get a towel and the shampoo."

Leaning her elbows on the sink's rim, Minnie raised her head to stare through the window. Through water streaming over her face, she saw Luna sitting on a stump, staring back.

"We can't go on like this," Minnie whispered.

She could not tell if Luna agreed or disagreed, or even if he heard her. He slipped off the stump and disappeared into the brush of the surrounding forest.

"If I could disappear, I'd do it too," she muttered.

"What, baby?" Fiona said.

"Nothing," Minnie replied. "Magic is dangerous, but a world without it is cold and dark."

With a finger on the girl's chin, Fiona tilted her head to look into her eyes.

"It just takes getting used to, that's all. When I get you cleaned up, you'll feel like a million dollars. Look, I let Keela out, that should cheer you."

Keela glanced up, but waddled to the door and sniffed at it.

"She just wants out. Like me, like all of us, she's trapped and wants to be free."

"Hush now, let's get the grit out of your hair and talk no more about magic, okay? I don't want Chet to see you like this."

With the first rinse, the sink was stained with blood, dirt and twigs, but soon the water was all suds and clean foam. Gently, Fiona probed and examined Minnie's wounds while dabbing on fingertips of ointment.

"This is not bad. When you're ready, I'd love to know what happened. Did you fall off a skateboard? Those things are a nasty hazard."

Minnie's impulse was to tell the truth, but she didn't know how to explain what happened. If Fiona knew the facts, she'd come unglued and march to the police station or at least the Principal's Office. This would not lead to anything good.

Fiona wrapped a towel around the girl's head and rotated her shoulders until they were eye-to-eye.

"Can you talk to me, baby? Tell me what happened."

"No, Mom, it's nothing. Can I get to my homework? I have a ton."

Fiona studied the girl's eyes, searching for answers.

"Okay, when you're ready, you tell me, okay?"

"Yes, Mom, when I'm ready."

Which will be never.

Minnie scooped up Keela, who was mewling at the door. She buried her nose in her rank fur. The little skunk really didn't smell good, but they were all used to it.

In her cubbyhole bedroom, she gently pulled the door closed behind her.

Factory Tour

MISTER BIG, WHOSE real name was Fiorintino Riordan di Balistreri, arrived with an army. The odd collection of surnames came from a truce two generations earlier between rival Irish and Italian mobs—cemented with a forced marriage that flowered with three sons before Aoibheann Riordan had enough of Gaetano di Balistreri's catting around and threw his defenestrated body from the third floor balcony of their Somerville, Massachusetts mansion. Her body was found in a bathtub where she had overdosed on Percocet and a half-bottle of historic Pogue's Good News Kentucky Bourbon.

With a wry grin, Trevir, standing with Troll Srenzo and a welcoming party of trolls, watched the convoy of black limousines as they circled the parking lot and stopped before the factory's main entrance. The factory had been abandoned in the early 1970s and was unimpressive—with weeds sprouting through the crumbled pavement, arrays of broken windows and walls decorated with bulbous letters of colorful graffiti.

At the rear of the caravan came an old, white van with mud splattered on its sides. The lettering on the side said *Living Water Christian Ministry*. This van held the disposables—the test subjects. There were three, young Hispanic men looking around with suspicion. Gathered from a Home Depot parking lot, they were told there was day work waiting for them, work that paid cash. They expected to be hand-digging a swimming pool or repairing a roof, so the old factory confused them, but the ways of the white people were often a mystery to them.

In cream-colored, skin-tight jeans, a floral-silk, open-collared shirt unbuttoned over a heavy gold neck chain and Beluti sneakers worn on sockless feet, Di Balistreri was dressed casually—too casually for Trevir's taste. He seemed young, but Trevir knew he was thirty.

Old enough to know better and pay proper respect.

With a warm and open smile on his face, Trevir decided then and there to kill them.

Kill them all.

Except for Lady Katherine, who, as always, was dressed in a stylish manner. Gleaming Hermes Passion short boots, tasteful Camel-wool skirt, beige blazer with perfectly applied makeup on her face—her hair was pulled back in an elegant swirl.

Class, Trevir thought. *All class*.

Trevir took a step forward and stretched out his hand to shake Fiorintino's hand. The Don's handshake was weak, soft and perfunctory.

"Welcome," Trevir said. "Please go on in."

He ushered them in, but stayed behind to talk to Troll Srenzo who brought up the rear of the party.

"I changed my mind about the expendables. Make them rich."

Troll Srenzo, accustomed to his whims, hesitated only a fraction of a second before nodding in assent.

She turned and stopped the short, dark men, then twitched and finger at the closest troll-guard.

Get some sales packets, she whispered.

While looking over the men, she studied them. Short, stocky, with very weathered and dark skin. Guatemalans she decided. Very lucky Guatemalans.

"English?" she said.

The one in the middle nodded.

"Eduardo," he said. "I speak English."

"Okay, Eduardo. The boss decided to make you three very rich. How does that sound?"

Eduardo was puzzled.

"Señora?" he said.

The packets were brought; she took them from the stubby troll. They were black envelopes, each holding a bulky pound. She opened one to show the content...inside were fifty small, glassine bags filled with iridescent crystals.

"It's simple. Sell these for whatever you can get. When we come around, give us half of what you collected and we'll give you more. Give us nothing and we kill you. Painfully."

She studied their faces to see if they got it. Eduardo rattled off a quick burst of Spanish. After a moment of consideration, the men nodded.

"Don't ingest any of it."

"Señora?" Eduardo said.

"For your own good, don't smoke any yourself. Don't eat, don't snort, don't put any in your body in any way. Period."

"I understand, Señora," he said.

Quickly, he explained to his companions.

She wasn't sure how seriously they took the message, so she dropped their veils for a few short seconds. The men recoiled at her twisted visage and the snarling faces of the guard-trolls. Eduardo made the Catholic sign of the cross on his chest.

"*Madre de Dios*," he said.

"Follow our rules and you'll be rich in a couple of years. I don't mean BMW rich. I mean Rolls Royce and Gulfstream biz-jet rich. *Comprende?*"

"*Si, Señora*."

She dismissed them with a wave.

"Go."

With their packets held before them, they walked back to the dirty van and were soon headed back to the city.

Inside, Di Balistreri and his guards were already dead. One-by-one, the trolls gathered the bodies and hauled them to the factory floor to drop them in the Black Death vats.

"What did I miss?" she said.

Trevir shrugged.

"Not much."

He gestured at Di Balistreri's fancy leather sneakers lying on the dirty factory floor.

"They look like they might fit you, if you want them."

A quick look of distaste crossed Troll Srenzo's face. She shook her head.

"I'll pass," she said.

Trevir turned to Lady Katherine.

"This means you are in charge of the organization now."

Lady Katherine could not fully stifle a smile, but it was gone in a flash.

"I won't forget how I got here, sir," she said.

Trevir started at her feet, raised his eyes slowly and studied every inch of her carefully—stopping when he was looking into her eyes.

"No," he said. "Not enough. You will serve me with everything you have, fully, with nothing held back. You are mine."

Holding eye contact, she didn't flinch.

"Okay," she said.

Trevir felt a hormonal twitch and considered commanding her to disrobe, but he stifled the impulse. For a decade now, he preferred the rough-skinned, hairy trolls. He turned his head a few degrees toward Troll Srenzo and said, "Ring."

She had one in a leather pouch at her side. It was wrapped in leather. Supple, human leather, cured to soft perfection by the trolls.

Lady Katherine upended the sack and studied the ring. It was bulky gold carved into a troll, a gargoyle with blood-red ruby eyes.

She tried it on her wedding finger.

"It fits perfectly," she said.

"Of course it does," Trevir replied, while waving his hand to dismiss her.

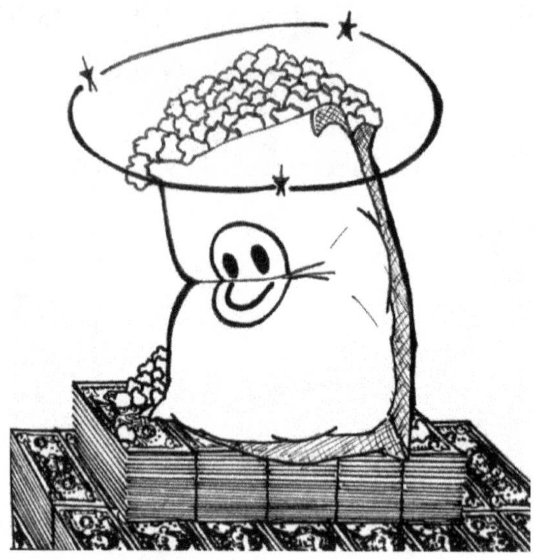

Popcorn

AFTER THE PARKING lot incident, Minnie went about her school and home life like usual. Homework, help around the diner, sleep, get up and go to school, repeat. So mundane. So boring. So very unfulfilling. She'd forgotten about the totem until one day on her way home a field mouse joined her on her walk. It would run in front of her, in and out of her feet and alongside her. Minnie had to watch her step lest she step on the little creature. Before long, the mouse had let her to where she and the gnome had buried the totem.

"Ohhh, I see. Thank you little one for reminding me to check on our plant. Creature. Totem. Thing."

Minnie pushed away the tall grass and to look at the mound. Only, it wasn't so much a plain mound anymore. Sprouted out of it was a tall, thick, purplish-greenish stalk. Out of the stalk were about a dozen or so long, floppy leaves. When Minnie touched them they were as soft as a lamb's ear, but unable to be ripped or torn.

"Strong," uttered Minnie to herself.

Growing from the base of each leaf was a sort of pod. It resembled corn, but not normal corn. Minnie could see multicolored kernels beginning to form. The smell coming from the plant was intoxicating. Earthy with a slightly floral scent. The bees were busy pollinating it and Minnie thought that they seemed happy, almost like they were smiling.

Odd. I didn't know bees smiled. Maybe I really DO need glasses.

Minnie introduced herself to the plant, told it how beautiful and strong it looked and said she'd be back in a few days to check on it again.

She could have sworn she heard the plant whisper "Thank you fish-girl," but she decided that it was a just a trick of the wind—though there wasn't any wind that day.

When Minnie went back a few days later, she was surprised to see that all the pods had grown ears that were falling to the ground. She scooped them up and tried to figure out what to do with them. By the time all was said and done she had a backpack overstuffed with deep-green ears.

She thanked the plant and said she'd be back in a few days. She hoped more would grow and hoped even more that she could figure out what to do with the ones she had. She brought her treasure back home and began to ponder.

Fiona and Chet were in the kitchen. Things weren't going well. The pies weren't selling. Fewer and fewer people came to the diner. They wracked their brains trying to figure out what changed, what had gone awry. It wasn't the ingredients, it wasn't the menu. Had highway traffic been re-routed? Were people sick of pie? There hadn't been any cases of food poisoning, so it wasn't that. Things had been going well, and now they just weren't.

Minnie knew why.

Magic was leaving their world. Magic is all that's good and pure. Magic helps those that need help, gives hope and guides when all feels lost. She breathed out a sigh, then returned her focus to the mound of kernels.

"Seed necklace? Nah, they're way too hard to poke with a needle. Mosaic? Meh, boring. Plant them and grow more plants?

Maybe, but let's see how much one stalk produces. Hmmmm, I wonder if I could pop them and make 'gourmet' popcorn to give to the misfits."

Minnie waited until Chet had gone for the night and Fiona was outside reading with her cup of tea. She grabbed a heavy iron Dutch Oven and oil and turned on the stove. She put a handful of kernels in and waited to see what would happen. Hopefully nothing would explode. Within moments the oil sizzled and she heard popping sounds from inside the pot. She shook the pot around on the burner and waited for the popping sounds to stop. When it did, she turned off the heat and carefully lifted off the lid. By this time Fiona had come in because she smelled popcorn.

"Whatcha doing, little one?" she asked Minnie.

Minnie was caught off guard so didn't have time to think of a good story.

"I gleaned this odd corn. I thought I'd try popping it to see how it tasted. Want some?"

Fiona raised an eyebrow. She looked inside the pot and saw the most beautiful array of colored popcorn. She was instantly intrigued.

"You're sure it's safe to eat?"

"Ugh, of course it is, Mom. Here, we'll try some together."

They both cautiously ate one kernel, and then another and before they knew it they were sitting on the kitchen floor laughing and giggling, savoring every bite.

"Oh, Minnie. That was perfect! You always know exactly what to do. Today was a tough day. Chet and I can't figure out why we're losing business all of a sudden. Sitting here on the floor eating popcorn with you giggling is just what I needed. Where would I be without you? You are such a love."

It seemed like popping it was all that could be done with it. Minnie decided to make bags up for Mr. Danvers and the misfits and bring it to school the next day. She cooked and bagged up six bags and put them near her backpack. She made one for Chet too, and drew a big smiley face on the bag—she hoped it would make him feel better, as it did for Fiona.

The next day Minnie left the popcorn in the Sanctuary for the misfits. It was her first time being back in there since Kurt had been possessed. It only seemed fitting that she return with a light-hearted gift for everyone.

As they sat and ate their snack, the air grew lighter. There was laughter and singing, jokes were told and everyone acted goofy. Mr. Danvers came in and enjoyed his bag of popcorn as well. Everyone felt very much at peace. It was as if the magic had returned to the sanctuary. Everything felt right, at least for the moment.

"Minnie, what *is* this stuff?" asked Mr. Danvers.

"Popcorn, of course."

"You didn't add anything to it? It's absolutely delicious—and so colorful."

"Nope, just kernels, sea salt and oil. I swear. I had a bag of the kernels I picked and I couldn't think of anything else to do with them."

Marcus piped up.

"You should sell this stuff, Minnie. People would totally buy it."

"You're crazy. Besides, I like to give stuff to people. I don't want to charge people for things. That seems so, just *so*—crass."

"Yah, but, didn't you say that Chet is having trouble with the diner? Money could help him, ya know. Just sayin."

Minnie looked down. Marcus was right. Chet had helped her and Fiona so much; really, he saved them. It might not be much but at this point, something was better than nothing.

Marcus could tell Minnie was thinking about it.

He said, "I'll help you, Minnie. I know what it's like to struggle. We can start spreading the word about your 'magic popcorn' and you could sell it for $5 a bag, easy. What do you say? For Chet and Fiona?"

Minnie thought $5 a bag was highway robbery but she guessed it was worth a shot. She nodded her head.

"I don't want to call it *magic popcorn* though. How's about *rainbow corn*? I don't want to call it magic because it's not. It doesn't do anything other than taste good."

"Ohhhh, I beg to differ there, Miss Minnie. It's certainly making me magically happy," chimed in Mr. Danvers.

"You can't be cranky while you're eating popcorn, Mr. Danvers. That's not magic. That's a universal law," smirked Minnie.

Thus, a small business was born in the sanctuary that day. Minnie soon found herself bringing ten bags of popcorn to school every day. Kids were more than willing to pay $5 a bag. When they ate the rainbow corn they felt relaxed and at peace; and some became downright giddy. The Principal, who at first seemed suspicious that it was laced with drugs, ended up trying some as well. Minnie gave him a bag at no charge. He smiled as he ate it and quickly gave it his stamp of approval. He felt that it was going to a worthy cause. Chet's diner had been a staple in the community. The food was always the best and Chet had a good heart and as gruff as he was, he meant well.

Minnie seemed to have an endless supply of kernels to pop. Chet didn't seem to mind if she used his pot and oil. Minnie didn't let on that she was collecting money for him. Instead, she popped him a bag every day, and that seemed like payment enough.

By the end of the month Minnie had collected $485. When she got home she put her stuff down, petted Keela and gave her some grapes. She then walked into the kitchen with an envelope. Chet looked worn. With a distant look, Fiona gazed out through the window.

"Hi, Pumpkin. How was school today?"

"It was good like always. Chet. Um, I have something for you. It's not much but I hope it will help."

Minnie handed the envelope to Chet. He opened it, started thumbing through the money and was utterly dumbfounded.

"How—why—what in the world?"

Minnie smiled hugely.

"I've been selling the rainbow corn. Everyone at school loves it, even the Principal. I've been collecting and saving the money to give to you. I know times are hard right now and you've been so kind and generous to us and well, I wanted to do something. I hope you're not mad?"

Chet looked from Fiona to Minnie to the envelope, back to Fiona and then to Minnie. He had a small tear in his eye.

"Miss Minnie, you are an absolute wonder. Thank you."

He scooped her up in a big ole bear hug and laughed and laughed. Minnie made him some popcorn and they all sat around, ate and celebrated.

In her head she heard the Coranich say, "Good job, fish-girl. Keep it up with the rainbow corn. All will be right soon enough…."

The Carnival

IN THEIR SECRET lair, sitting on a rickety chair that leaned to the right, Minnie was deep into her book, reading and trying to decipher the strange words of Huxley's *Brave New World*.

"It's wonderful, of course. And yet in a way," she had confessed to Fanny, "I feel as though I were getting something on false pretences. Because, of course, the first thing they all want to know is what it's like to make love to a Savage. And I have to say I don't know." She shook her head. "Most of the men don't believe me, of course. But it's true. I wish it weren't," she added sadly and sighed. "He's terribly good-looking; don't you think so?"

"But doesn't he like you?" asked Fanny.

"Sometimes I think he does and sometimes I think he doesn't. He always does his best to avoid me; goes out of the room when I come in; won't touch me; won't even look at me. But sometimes if I turn round suddenly, I catch him staring; and then—well, you know how men look when they like you."

Yes, Fanny knew.

Her eyes skipped ahead to a song.

Hug me till you drug me, honey;
Kiss me till I'm in a coma;
Hug me, honey, snuggly bunny;
Love's as good as soma.

This book was written in 1931. She thought of the gang that haunted the school parking lot in the afternoons.

Had things really changed so little?

There was a tap on the door. Wondering who it might be, she looked up.

"You may enter," she said.

It was Lacey. Memory flooded Minnie's thoughts. She'd sent a text message. Wearing a silk jumpsuit over lemon-yellow boots, Lacey was dressed to perfection, as always. Her bra, exposed at the sides of the loose-fitting top, was also a bright yellow. She wore her streaky hair pulled back in a ponytail to show off dangly turquoise earrings that glittered in the dim light.

"So, this is the mysterious hideout of the Minnie gang. I'm honored that you sent the map—how could I live without all this…uh, luxury? Can I get the password and learn the secret handshake?"

The room was clean, but all of the furniture was worn and threadbare. Books were piled everywhere. With a frayed power cord, the heater they used to boil water for tea was a fire hazard.

Minnie spun on her chair and turned on the heater.

"Sit down, I'll make you a nice cup of tea."

"No, thank you, let's get our business done and I'll get of here."

"You'll drink hot tea and love it."

Lacy flopped down on their lumpy couch.

"Tea, fine, whatever. Good goddess—this place is dead. A morgue has more life to it than this sorry excuse of a school. If I get any more bored, I'll die, I swear."

"That's why I wanted to talk to you," Minnie said. "But first, how did things go with your Dad?"

Lacey shrugged.

"You told me what to do. I did it. Everything worked out fine and he hasn't touched me since."

"I didn't tell you to do anything, I only made suggestions."

"Whatever. Look, I'm here, right? You sent me a strange text message and a map to your glory hole—I dropped everything and we're talking, so, let's talk. The thing with my dad is better left off rumor central, understand?"

Yes, Minnie knew.

Oh, how well I know things I wish I didn't.

The teapot just started its whistle—Minnie turned off the heater and studied the tea bags.

What would be perfect?

They had an assortment and Minnie picked white peach oolong. She dropped in a plastic spoon coated with a dollop of alfalfa honey and handed Lacey the steaming cup. The honey was from a local field—she knew the little clumps of purple alfalfa flowers, she knew the white boxes where the bees donated their honey, she knew the old woman who collected the sweet treasure, not all of it, leaving plenty for the bees. Alfalfa, Medicago sativa. She liked the Swiss name better. Lucerne. Alfalfa, from Arabic, *al-fisfisa.*

Minnie shook her head. If she wasn't careful, her mind would travel around the world and back—and maybe one day, it would not come back.

With a brisk click, Lacey snapped her fingers.

"Focus. Are you okay, Minnie?"

After taking a deep, shuddering breath, Minnie nodded.

"I'm fine," she said. "Lacey, we need to do something—something big. I feel like I'm suffocating."

"What do you want to do, squirt?"

Like an inquisitive puppy, Minnie cocked her head and looked at Lacey sideways.

"Really? Really? You call me 'squirt' after all we've been through?"

Lacey sighed.

"I'm sorry. You're right, that was rude. We're friends, we truly are, it just came out. Lemme try that again. What's your undeniably brilliant idea?"

"Okay, now you're teasing me."

"Good gawd, Minnie. Why are you so twitchy? What the hell do you want me to say? I'm sure you have some grandiose, but stupid, plan to cheer up your loser-clique, the school, our town, the whole dismal world, so get off your chump and blurt it so I can callously dismiss it and get on with my fabulous day."

Minnie smirked.

"Ah, there's the Lacey I know."

She waited for Lacey to blow on her tea and take a sip, then she spoke quietly—almost a whisper.

"How's about a faire, a carnival? We'll ask teachers and students to be in it—donate their talents or money or whatever. Have attractions like rides and games of chance and how's about a freak show? Maybe a small stage with live music where kids can showcase their out-of-tune garage-band songs. You KNOW your dad would help spring for it. To raise cheddar, we could do the obligatory bake sales and car washes. It just feels like we need to do something to infuse this wretched, gloomy place with some life, ya know? What do ya say?"

Lacey thought for a moment, then opened her mouth to speak, but hesitated. She dropped her eyes to the teacup. After leaning over, she stirred the golden fluid before taking another sip.

"I'm not really a tea person, but this is pretty good swig." With eyebrows scrunched up, she considered Minnie's idea. "A faire, you say? Tents in the parking lot. A couple of dollars for a ticket and the proceeds donated to the student activities committee?"

Minnie nodded.

Lacey continued, "I'm surprised, did you doctor my tea? Am I high? It sounds like a good idea—a really good idea. It's so good; I wonder why I didn't think of it."

Minnie shrugged.

"I don't care about the credit; let's tell everyone you dreamed it up."

Making a decision, Lacey lifted her teacup in salute.

"Yes, damn the torpedoes, whatever that means," she said, "let's do it. How shall we start?"

"Convince the student body council to endorse the idea. Use your charms to get them to draft a formal proposal and we'll present it to the principal. Is there a social committee thing? Whatever, draft up a plan, present it and get the bureaucratic buy-in. Once we do THAT we can attack the money part of it. Once we see how much your daddy-poo will kick in we'll know what to shake down the rest of the community for. Then we present the *fait accompli* to the entire student body and get THEIR buy in. Then, THEN my dear sweet Lacey, we are in the carnival business."

"The Student Counsel is easy; they'll do what I tell them to do. The teachers love you, that's your job, you work on them for support. Get Danvers' endorsement; he has sway with the Principal. With Danvers on board, I can handle the rest."

"Okay," Minnie said.

"Can I really say it was my idea? That would help win Daddy over."

"Sure, go for it, I don't really care about fame and publicity and all that. When shall we start working on the proposal?"

Leaning over, Lacey pulled her iMac from her backpack and flipped it open.

"Now's as good a time as any—it's not like we're doing anything else except sitting around and drinking fancy tea, am I right? Let's draft up notes and see what we get. Carnivals don't get up and invent themselves, ya know."

Bantering and tossing wilder and wilder ideas back and forth, Minnie and Lacey set to writing the proposal. After an hour, they proclaimed it 'good enough.'

Lacey slapped her laptop computer closed.

"Tomorrow," Lacey said, "I'll call for an emergency student council meeting and bend them to my will."

She finished the dregs of her tea.

"That was good, I'll have to get your recipe so I can make it at home."

"That was nothing. You want something special, come by the house and we'll raid my Mom's stash for something that will straighten your perm."

Lacey looked skeptical.

"You say that like it's a *good* thing," she said. "I don't know the protocol for co-conspirators. What do we do now? Hug?"

"No," Minnie said, "we can skip any artificial intimacy."

"Screw you, squirt." Lacey picked up the little girl, squeezed her close and planted a dry kiss on her neck. "After all we've gone through, we're homefries."

Minnie wriggled.

"I hate being picked up."

Gently, Lacey set Minnie back on her feet.

"Get used to it, Muppet. You're so cute, it's going to happen. See you on the flip side?"

"What does that mean?"

Lacey shrugged.

"I think it had something to do with the old-timey records that needed to be flipped over."

"That's weird, why did they do that?"

"Old people did all kinds of strange things. Look, I need to scoot. See ya."

Lacey disappeared in a flash, leaving only the scent of her perfume after the heavy door closed. Exhausted, Minnie sat back at the makeshift desk and eyed the book she had been reading. Sighing, she flopped it open and tried to recapture the thread of the story.

The scent organ was playing a delightfully refreshing Herbal Capriccio-

rippling arpeggios of thyme and lavender, of rosemary, basil, myrtle, tarragon; a series of daring modulations through the spice keys into ambergris; and a slow return through sandalwood, camphor, cedar and newmown hay (with occasional subtle touches of discord—a whiff of kidney pudding, the faintest suspicion of pig's dung) back to the simple aromatics with which the piece began.

Lacey's perfume was probably expensive and imported from France or Monaco. Minnie liked it and decided she'd ask Lacey to share a dab.

As expected, the proposal was met with rousing approval and immediately, many parties claimed to be originators. After unanimous acceptance by the student counsel, the next stop was the principal's desk. Principal Johnson, a tall, gangly man with slumped shoulders and a carefully arranged bald-spot comb-over was staid and did not like taking chances with anything. The students called him PJ, which he didn't much care for. Beyond authorial jackets with leather patches on the elbows, his one self-indulgent affectation was a pencil-thin mustache.

With Mr. Danvers in tow, Lacey breezed into the main office. She stood close and straightened PJ's bowtie and flattened his collar.

"You are such a handsome, dapper and intelligent man," Lacey said.

Principal Johnson tried to resist her charms, but it was impossible. He flushed from forehead to neck and touched his necktie to make sure it was in place.

"You think so?" he said. "No, never mind, you're here on business and I have a packed schedule. Let's see what you have."

Lacey and Mr. Danvers sat down across his desk and made their pitch. After many annoying questions about nit-picking details and negotiating irrelevant terms, he reluctantly agreed.

"You won't be sorry," sang Lacey as she trotted out of his office.

With a text message, Lacey let Minnie know the plan was a

go. Minnie texted back right away.

Next stop is getting your dad to throw down.

Quickly, Lacey responded.

Worry not, Sprout. I got this.

Lacey went home that night and approached her father with the proposal. He was in his La-Z-Boy recliner watching talking heads on the news while her mother drank white wine from a box in the kitchen, supposedly supervising a broiling pot roast. If it was overcooked, there would be hell to pay—if there was one thing her father hated, it was dried-out, stringy beef.

With clinical impassion, she laid out the plan—passing him handouts to illustrate the key points.

After she laid out her ideas he patted his knee and said, "Come here, Princess. Sit on my lap and let's talk about what you need, shall we?"

Feeling a shift in the power between them, she felt her insides lurch and roil. They needed his funding, but at what price? Since her birthday celebration, he'd been tentative around the house—as if walking on eggshells. His memories were fragmented—he didn't know what exactly had happened and her hinting that she had photographs on her iPhone made him cautious. Weighing the pluses and minuses, she decided to humor him, just a little.

With a little sway to her hips, she approached and settled on his lap like always. Wiser now, she felt movement under his trousers and fought back a gag-impulse.

"There's a good little lady. Such a beautiful daddy's girl. You have a great head for business; you know how to get things done. That school wouldn't be what it is without you, your great ideas and your guidance. I couldn't be prouder of my pretty little angel. Now, let's see. Every carnival needs rides. How's about I put out bids to locate a Carnival Ride vendor. No cost is too much and of course, safety first. Class the whole way—no scumbag carnies to gawk at my girl and her friends. Clowns, balloons, cotton candy, the whole nine yards. How's that sound, sweetie?"

"Sounds perfect, Daddy. Thank you so much."

"A kiss will seal the deal, Honey."

He puckered, but she leaned in and kissed him on his bristly cheek. She could tell he wanted more but she wasn't giving it to him; not today and not ever. He glanced toward the hallway to the kitchen, then wrapped his beefy arms around her.

"I'm glad we put your birthday—uh, events, behind us," he whispered. "Let's get out of town again for a special evening real soon, okay?"

Slippery as an eel, she bounced off his lap and hopped quickly until she was just beyond his reach.

"Sure, Daddy. I'd better help with dinner. If I don't get to the carrots now, they will be cold and undercooked."

"Wait, forget about the carrots, come back."

She blew him a kiss.

"Thank you so much, Daddy," she said.

Moving Up

IN THE BUILDING'S entryway, the lobby cop looked up from the guard station and held up his palm to stop Trevir and his entourage. He opened his mouth to speak. Troll Srenzo glared and the guard's mouth snapped shut. He didn't want to see Trevir and the trolls, so he didn't—he returned his focus to the sport section of the USA Today hidden behind his credenza.

For the third time, Trevir asked about his office. It irritated Troll Srenzo.

"Yes, it's ready—just like you asked. It's been ready for a week."

"Brazilian mahogany? A Murphy bed that pulls out of a wall? Single-sheet, Gorilla-glass window? Unobstructed view of Boston Common? Wide-plank Vermont cherry for the floors?"

"Yes, everything you asked for. Don't act so surprised that I got this done."

Trevir looked at her with a blank expression.

"I'll miss the old factory," he said.

"No, you won't."

He laughed.

"You're right, probably not."

The stainless steel doors of the elevator slid open. They crowded in—the elevator ascended quietly and smoothly to their floor.

"How did you find a building with a 13th floor?"

"I don't have time for stupid questions," she said.

He turned his head to look at her. He loved it when she was feisty. Not too spicy, just enough.

The elevator doors slipped open. They had the whole floor. Before them was a gleaming, tile-floored entry stretching out in front of a glass door.

He reached out to touch the lettering on the big windows, but pulled his hand back. The glass was clean and perfect—he didn't want fingerprints on it, even his own.

International Panda LLC—Commodities Trading

Though he dreamed up the innocuous name months before, it still amused him.

Our flagship product is Black Death.

Suicide in crystalline form.

International Panda.

He stopped and leaned over with tears of laughter streaming down his face. It took a full minute for him to regain composure.

Damn it, that's funny.

Troll Srenzo held the big door open and ushered him in.

The reception area was all in luscious cream with gleaming stainless surfaces and mahogany accents. Over the reception area was a giant mural of a panda holding bamboo shoots. It was beautiful—as beautiful as he imagined it would be.

His office would be straight back. He quickly marched to it, threw open the hardwood door and there it was, a thousand square feet of glass so clear it was invisible. On approach, the view of the Common unfurled before him.

"Oh, I like this very, very much. Point out the burying ground and prison. Oh, and the gallows. I need to know where the gallows were—where sweet Mary Dyer was hung by the puritans. Before I leave this Earth, the gallows will sprout again and claim many souls, I swear it. This is delicious, where was Mary's monster buried? Woman, fish, bird and beast, Mary's abomination must have been a glory to behold."

Troll Srenzo scowled.

"We don't have time for your nonsense," she said. "The Senator's man will be here in an hour."

"I'm surprised you got it done so quickly."

Troll Srenzo sighed.

"It wasn't magic. Bales of cash work wonders in a corrupt town like this."

Giddy, Trevir rotated in circles, taking it all in. He stopped with his hand on the massive, custom-built mahogany desk. Aligned perfectly, a blue-enamel David Oscarson Sankta Lucia fountain pen and a crystal vial of crimson blood, virgin blood. There was nothing magic about that either, but it amused Trevir to sign contracts that way.

A feeling of pride and accomplishment rushed in his veins.

"Show me the chute," he said.

Troll Srenzo led the way down the hallway outside his office, through the kitchen and into a utilitarian storage area. On the far wall, there was a large, black-rimmed hole covered by a hinged, silver cap. Engraved on the cap was a finely etched, detailed illustration of a man hanging from a gallows tree. Trevir lifted the cap. It was heavy, but counter-weighted so it lifted easily. He leaned over to look down into the inky darkness.

"Show me," he said.

Troll Szenzo sighed, then pulled her short sword from its sheath. Looking at the trolls, she pointed and picked one.

"You," she said.

"No," came the response. "Pick someone else."

She jerked her head toward the gaping hole. The other trolls grabbed the selected one and manhandled him toward the chute. He struggled, but in vain. With his legs flailing, he desperately held onto the lip. She leaned over and looked into his eyes.

"Goodbye," she said.

Until he let go, she rapped his knuckles with the flat part of her blade.

"Noooo," he said.

The sound echoed and faded into the distance. There was a muffled thud when he hit the bottom.

Troll Srenzo turned to Trevir.

"The trolls at the bottom will clean up the mess and dispose of him," she said.

"Whatever," Trevir said, while walking back toward his office. Standing in front of the wide expanse of glass, he said, "I am of a mind to try out the bed."

"There's no time—we can do it later."

He turned toward her.

"Are you denying me?"

There was defiant glow in her eyes.

"Yes."

"There's really no time?"

"That's what I said. We have an appointment with the Senator's factotum—it wouldn't do to keep him waiting, we need his support."

Trevir waved a finger at the trolls—they unsheathed their swords. Troll Srenzo still had her stubby blade in hand. She impaled the closest, but then the rest were quickly on her. Stepping over the body of the writhing troll, Trevir walked to the bed and examined an electronic panel mounted on the wall. After pressing a few keys, the bed slowly rotated out from the wall.

Vigorously, Troll Srenzo struggled against her captors.

"I will kill you," she said. "All of you."

Trevir grinned like a wolf.

"Tear off her clothes and hold her down," he said.

As the Carnival Day Approaches...

WHEN THE WORD spread about the carnival, the whole school was abuzz with excitement. Advance ticket sales were brisk. Students signed up to showcase their talents, teachers planned wholesome games and booths and parents orchestrated various fund-raising events. Solicitations were sent out to carnival ride vendors. What started out as just a tentative, nebulous idea suddenly grew beyond measure. It was just what was needed to bring life back to the school, and Minnie too. Instead of passively letting life happen, she was in the fray, planning and day dreaming. She realized she was happier with a mission. The coming event was even talked about at home.

Chet handed Fiona a flyer the kids were plastering around town.

Big Fun Carnival

The garish poster had elephants on it—lots of clip-art elephants the booster committee pasted in.

With mock sternness, Chet addressed Minnie.

"Is this false advertising? Where do you expect to get a herd of elephants?"

"Why are you asking me?" Minnie responded.

Fiona laughed.

"We know this was your idea, your doing, Minnie," Fiona said. "We're super proud of you, ya know."

"Lacey wrote up the proposal and ran with it, Mom," said Minnie. "It was all her and she's in charge of elephants."

Fiona winked at Chet.

"Right, Minnie. Whatever you say."

"I'm helping a little behind the scenes, that's all."

"You'll try to fool me? I know these things, Honey. You forget how much we've been through together. I may not be your birth mom, but our bond is strong. I know things."

Minnie hugged Fiona hard; harder than she ever had; harder than in a long time.

"I know I've been distant and unhappy, Fiona. I know I've been difficult. I'm sorry. I'm so sorry. It's just really hard sometimes and I feel so alone without Sean and the Fachan. I have you and Luna and Chet and Keela but still…"

"Shhhhhh, it's okay, Minnie. I understand. Truly I do. Let's just enjoy the here and now, shall we? All your hard work will come to fruition. Enjoy it. Relish it. Bask in it. Go and be with your friends. Feel the real world magic of the upcoming day. Most of the fun is in the anticipation, you know that. Don't get so lost in the details that you forget about the joy of anticipation."

"And you too, Mom. Most of the fun is in the surprise."

Again, Minnie hugged her hard, then scampered off for a planning committee meeting.

Fiona let out a sigh.

Standing by the big bay window and looking out over the forest and the star-studded sky, she whispered, "I miss you too, Sean. I wish you were here. You'd love this."

A tear trickled down her cheek—she quickly scooped it up.

No tears today, only laughter.

She turned to Chet.

"Can you believe this? A carnival, right here in Cement City?"

"I made a donation," Chet replied. "A hundred dollars I can hardly afford. If there are no elephants, I want my money back."

"It's crazy, right? But, if you know anything about Minnie, you know there will be elephants."

Chet took her hands and faced her.

"I'm joshing. I *do* know."

"I don't know how, but she'll do it. There will be elephants. If she fails, I'll make sure you get double your money back."

"Don't be silly," Chet said. "Look, wifey is opening a bottle of vino and serving left-over oyster chowder to the kids. You're alone tonight. Join us."

Chet's little one was two. Even she had heard of the carnival. In her highchair, she made a mess of her chowder, but managed to eat some of it.

"Daddy?"

"Yes, Sugar-pea?"

"What's a Car-val?"

Chet grinned.

Slowly and patiently, he said, "It's like a birthday party on the street where everyone can come. It will have games, clowns, balloons, food and music and maybe even wooden horses for you to ride on, around and around for as long as you like."

The baby liked the sound of all that—she squealed with delight.

"Horseys," she said.

"And elephants," Fiona added.

Chet looked at her, then shrugged before tilting his head back for a laugh.

"Ha, right, elephants, lots of elephants," he said.

The Senator

AT HIS DESK, Trevir read reports, endless reports. The news was all good, but there was *so* much of it coming in that he could hardly keep up. But, he had to manage the campaign properly or the inevitable ruination of the human race would be inefficient and slower.

That would be unacceptable.

There was risk, of course. If the magic world ever collected its strength and focused, the challenge would be orders of magnitude harder. But, so far, the resistance had been scattered and frankly, laughable. And, if there was one thing in life Trevir liked, it was laughing.

The Black Death program exceeded his expectations. Users would either join his movement to get more, or they would die. The recruiting and distribution network, based on the proven concepts of multi-level marketing, was a screaming success.

A *screaming* success. Trevir liked that.

In his world, there was a lot of screaming. And, people did not have to use his product to be affected; it touched families when their children succumbed, rich and poor, uptown or downtown. The system worked and was spreading. There were reports on his desk from Bangor, Maine, New York City, and everywhere in between.

I'm the Amway, the Mary Kay of death and destruction, he thought.

Restless, he got up and looked out over the Boston skyline. From his office on the 13th floor, the panorama was amazing. Off to the south, the Boston Neck Gallows was barely visible from his Park Street office. He enjoyed knowing it was there.

A 17th century Puritan law echoed in his head.

If any man or woman be a witch (that is hath or consulteth with a familiar spirit) they shall be put to death.

He thought of the first woman hanged there in 1648, Margaret Jones. She was guilty of making healthy and healing drinks from anise. Of course, she was a witch and very rightly hanged from the gallows tree. However, she died screaming in anger, which was not as satisfying to Trevir. He preferred people screaming in terror.

He sighed.

Can't have everything.

There was a pleasant church-bell-tone and a blue light flashed on a console on his desk. His visitor had arrived. He pressed the intercom button.

"Send him in," he said.

Trevir moved to the center of the large room and waited—it was few short seconds before the door opened. Studying the man, he extended his hand to shake.

Francis 'Frank' Dortmund was a tallish man, maybe an inch or two more than six feet. Wearing a sedate necktie, conservative glasses and a neatly trimmed beard, he had a studious demeanor. That made sense for his job as behind-the-scenes liaison, assistant, handler and factotum for Massachusetts's senior Senator Barkley Cassidy.

"It's a pleasure to meet you, sir," Trevir said. "Please, have a seat."

Troll Srenzo came in—carrying Frank's coffee in a steaming mug. The mug was decorated with an ancient quote, handwritten in Norse runes.

None refreshed me ever with food or drink,
I peered right down in the deep;
crying aloud I lifted the Runes
then back I fell from thence.

Frank took a sip and nodded in appreciation.

"Perfect," he said.

"Should be," Trevir said. "Sumatran. Brewed with French, ion-balanced spring water."

Trevir waved a finger and dismissed the troll. After she was gone, Trevir spoke. He was genuinely curious.

"What do you think of my secretary?"

"She's lovely," Frank said. "Beautiful figure, beautiful eyes. You're a lucky man."

Trevir smiled. He was never completely sure what others saw when the veils were in place—they see what they want to see. Frank wanted to see a beautiful, subservient woman. That was an insight into Frank's character.

He continued, "I hope you'll excuse the Senator for not coming in person…"

Trevir dismissed the apology with a wave.

"We recognize the endless demands on the Senator's time."

"Regardless, I can speak for him, one-hundred-percent."

"Of course," Trevir said.

"First of all, thank you for the generous donation to the Liberty Coalition Political Action Committee."

"Think nothing of it. We'll support the Senator and his initiatives to the best of our ability. We admire his accomplishments in governing our great state."

Frank raised his mug and waved it around.

"Can I ask? What exactly do you do here?"

"Oh, it's boring, really. A little of this and a little of that."

"I see."

"I suppose I should get to the point."

Frank took a sip and nodded.

"Go ahead," he said.

"The Senator has a tough fight coming this fall. To put it gently, the prevailing political winds are not blowing his way."

"I'm listening."

"We are prepared to contribute. When I say contribute, I mean really open the floodgates."

"Can I be crass and get an idea of how much?"

Trevir laughed.

"Let's say mid-six-figures for an initial offering and more after that. All on the quiet."

"There are limits, laws and election commission rules. The Senator comes from a wealthy family and will not embrace anything untoward. I don't want to offend—we really appreciate what you've done for our cause—but frankly, he doesn't need outside money and cannot be bought, sir. He will say no to anything that even smells slightly dodgy."

He stood and set the coffee mug on Trevir's desk. Not on a coaster, directly on the varnished hardwood.

Cute, Trevir thought.

Frank continued, "I wish you a good day, sir."

"Hold on," Trevir said. "We know the Senator has standards—a reputation to uphold and more money than God. I'm suggesting something different. Hypothetically speaking, suppose there was an ambitious man, a talented man, a man tired of working in his shadow, whom, with our unlimited backing, could challenge the Senator and take his seat at the big table. You've seen the polls. He's vulnerable. There are many who think he's outlived his usefulness and should retire to a well-earned life of leisure."

Retire, Trevir thought. *What an innocuous word.*

He could barely stifle a satisfied smile.

We're going to rip out his entrails and make him eat them.

Frank took a deep breath—and made a decision. He sat back down.

"Good," Trevir said. "Smart. To get started, would you do something for me, please?"

"Yes, of course," said Frank.

"Move your mug onto a coaster. It's the devil to remove a mark on this varnish."

Kissing Booth—Part One

AFTER COMMANDEERING A spare classroom, they transformed it into a carnival war room. There was no lack of volunteers and people, mostly girls, milled around all day, before, during and after school. The excitement was palpable. In a week, the show would start and the last-minute preparations were being carried out with haste.

Still, there was time for fun. Sunlight beamed through the windows and glitter drifted in the heated air—more of it seemed to go on the girls than on the posters they were decorating.

Into this cacophony, Kurt limped in. The room stilled. All the girls stared at him.

"You just got out of the hospital," Lacey said.

Not accustomed to the spotlight, he leaned on his crutches and looked around like he was lost.

"So?"

"So?" Minnie said. "So? You almost died. Do you know how long you were in a coma? Do you have any idea how close we came to losing you?"

"Well, I didn't die and I'm fully aware of what went on. I

heard everything you said." He looked at all the girls in turn. "I heard what everyone said."

Minnie blushed. So did Kelley.

Leaning over his crutches, Kurt put one hand on Kelley's cheek and the other on Minnie's. He looked deeply into Minnie's eyes.

"Deep down, now I know how you feel."

Minnie felt nauseous. She'd said lovey-dovey things to the sleeping Kurt because she wanted his brain filled with healing thoughts, but not in a romantic, boyfriend-girlfriend way. She had felt responsible for what happened—overcome with guilt and pity and many other emotions.

Ugh, this is not good, she thought.

Her mind raced.

How do I let him down easy?

"Don't let your hormones-in-overdrive lead you astray. You were floating around in the cosmos for a long time while we were worried sick about you."

"Nice try, Minnie. I know you love me. I know you want to be with me."

"No, no, no. Snap out of it, Casanova. I do love you, but like a brother. As a good friend. A dear, good friend."

"So you say, but I know better," replied Kurt.

Silence stretched, then Kurt leaned over, at the last second veering away from the shocked Minnie to kiss Kelley—just a quick touch on the lips.

"Oh, poor dear," he said, "did you think I was talking about you? I'm sorry, but Kelley is my girlfriend. "

Relief flooded Minnie's veins, then embarrassment.

"You, you, you…" she slapped at his hand, "pig."

The room filled with laughter.

After a few seconds of mortification, Minnie tilted her head back and joined in.

"Okay, you got me. Good one."

She looked between Kelley and Kurt.

"Yeah, good one," she whispered.

"So?" Kurt said. "I want to help. What is my assignment?"

"Are you sure you're strong enough? Healed enough?"

"There is nothing that heals more than being busy and getting things done."

Right, Minnie thought. *Right.*

Thinking furiously, she made a decision. If Kurt said he was ready, then he was ready.

"Fine, Mr. Joker, you can help me with the kissing booth. It's been neglected to the last. Are you game?"

"Anything for you, my princess."

"Oh, dear gawd, enough with the puppy-dog-eyes and sappy talk." She paused to take a breath. "Close your eyes. What do you see as the perfect, quintessential carnival kissing booth that won't cause trouble with the rowdy boys and busybody prudes and spinsters?"

Kurt closed his eyes. As soon as he did, he began describing the scene dancing before his eyes. Minnie furiously sketched the details as his words tumbled out.

"Hand-painted sign, of course. Two-dollar ticket. Blindfolded kissers. Boys and girls, let's not leave anyone out. Garlands of ribbons and flowers. Balloons. Donation box for tips. Hearts, lots of paper hearts. Picket fence enclosure. Counter. Everything painted white. A giant pair of red lips as decoration, like yours when you're pouting."

Minnie frowned at him, but kept writing.

"Big sign. Cement City Magical Kissing Booth. A hand-lettered sign that says *Experience a Kiss that will leave you Tingling with Delight.* A bell so the booth supervisor can move a bad egg along. We don't want to spread any herpes or other cooties."

"Okay," Minnie said, "I'm with you so far."

He took a deep breath before continuing.

"Dry kisses only. No tongues. And an automated boxing glove, like on a spring and triggered with a button, in case one of the bullies gets too familiar. Pow! Right in the kisser."

Minnie instinctively recoiled.

"What?" she said. "That sounds complicated. Who is going to

make it?"

"Don't worry about it," he said, "I have a plan."

"Okay, but what about this? What if someone kisses a girl and they don't get tingly and want their money back."

Kurt shrugged.

"Then we give them their money back. What's the big deal?"

That makes sense.

"Okay."

"Another sign that says *No Judgment, Just Kisses*."

"Inclusive and modern," Lacey said. "Fine. Whatever. Hey, people will bring their dogs to get a picture of a pretty girl kissing their pooch."

Minnie grinned.

"I don't care, I'll kiss a dog. Two dollars for a good cause—it's all good." She lightly slapped Kurt's face. "Open your eyes, love-bird, here's my sketch. What do you think?"

Lacey and Kurt, side-by-side, studied the crude drawing.

"Perfect. We make a good team, huh, Minnie?"

"Yes, Kurt, I'll give you that much."

"What do you say, Lacey? Work on this with me?"

She sprinkled a pinch of glitter on his head.

"Yes, when I'm done with my banner."

Kurt plucked the drawing out of Minnie's hand.

"Okay, now that I've done the hard part, I'd better get some rest. My mom is handy, she'll help throw this thing together."

Maneuvering on his crutches, he hobbled toward the door.

Sitting, Minnie thought about her sketch and visualized it in operation. In her vision, a boxing glove came out and popped a brat on the noggin. It was absurd, like a Saturday morning cartoon. She shook her head to clear away the silly vision.

Watching Kurt struggle off, she turned to look at Lacey. She could tell, those two had a long, happy future coming.

But, what about me?

In a sense, she was already spoken for. Betrothed. No one in this town or this school or on this planet could understand. Her life existed in another world. She shook her head as if shaking cobwebs from her hair.

That's quite enough of that, Minnie.

Magic doesn't exist anymore. That world is gone. Whatever betrothal pact made back at the Renaissance Faire is inevitably broken by now…

Time passed, magic died. Far away, her beloved must surely have moved on. Would she even recognize him if she passed him on the street?

She closed her sketch pad, put away her pencils and took in a deep breath of fresh, crisp rural air.

She thought of Kurt and Kelley.

Sometimes a kiss is not just a kiss.

She yearned for the magic world, but it was better put away, like a child's toys—outgrown and stored away forever.

The wind rustled at the rooms windows. There was evil out there, far away, but still too close.

She pushed the mood away and rejoined the girls and their cheerful decorations.

There was no time to waste.

They had a carnival to create.

Field Trip—Part One

TREVIR PUSHED AWAY the pile of paperwork on his desk.

"I'm sick of all these reports," he said. "I want to get out in the world and see how things are going—I want to smell the bodies in the street and hear the babies cry."

Troll Srenzo was unsympathetic as she scurried around capturing flying papers.

"The troops need orders. This war is waged, like all wars, with logistics. Cannon fodder belongs on the battlefield, Generals behind desks. That's the way it is and always will be. Besides, it's all in the field reports. Use your imagination. Or, failing that, do what the little people do and turn on the damned TV."

"I want to see for myself."

Troll Srenzo grunted with impatience. After walking around his desk, she tugged his arm.

"You want to see, then see. We spent a fortune on this crystal window, so look."

They stood looking out over the city. Outside, it was rainy

and gray—the low-hanging cloud cover was dense. In the park below, the pathways were wet and the wind whipped the trees. There were pedestrians, but they were hidden by umbrellas and did not linger—walking from point A to point B with brisk efficiency.

"How many fires do you see?"

Trevir scanned the horizon and counted.

"I see three."

"How many did you see a week ago?"

Trevir thought about it.

"I don't remember seeing any," he said.

"There's your status report. Now get back to work."

"We're going out," he said. "Get the car warmed up."

In the parking garage, the massive black Escalade idled. There was a minor tussle as Troll Srenzo bit the driver, set her claws into his arm and hauled him out from behind the steering wheel. Bleeding, he drew his stubby sword.

"I'm driving," she said.

He lunged at her, but his heart was not in it—his blade hissed through open air—no closer to her face than six inches.

"Get in the back or stay here, your choice," she said calmly.

The troll spit a writhing, gooey gob on the garage floor and stalked off.

Once Trevir was settled in the front seat and the trolls in the back, they sat for a moment waiting for instruction.

With eyes closed, he thought about where to go.

"Let's see what's cooking in Charlestown. Drive by Monument Square on High Street. We usually have people there—maybe Buddy Doe is hanging around."

On the street, the wind buffeted the big SUV. No one was on the street unless they needed to be, but there were eyes on them everywhere from groups of predators gathered on stoops and bus stops—all hiding behind sun glasses and sodden hoodies.

The neighborhood around Monument Park had been almost totally gentrified. The red-brick tenements had been converted to million-dollar condos with trendy bars and coffee shops on the ground floors. Still, there was plenty of street trash around—working girls trying to drum up enough drive-by business to finance a fix and punky teenagers on skateboards looking for purses left in cars. They found a ten-minute loading zone—Troll Srenzo pulled in. Through the leafless trees, they could see the Bunker Hill Obelisk.

"Bunker Hill," Trevir mused. "I love how the British General Howe allowed the revolutionary muskets time to reload between forays. The carnage on this mound must have been a wonder to behold. The Brits eventually took the hill, but at the expense of hundreds of dead and dying. Their blood is still soaked into that ground—on a day like this, we could probably smell it. Now young mothers bring their crawling vermin—along with strollers and pacifiers—for picnics. All the old ghosts are there. And, they are not happy. It's beautiful."

Troll Srenzo looked over at him.

"Sometimes I seriously worry about you," she said.

Trevir pushed the button and the dark-tinted window lowered smoothly and quietly.

Leaning against a barren trunk, peering out of the tree's shadow, a pair of hungry eyes.

Trevir gestured, waving the lost soul forward.

Sick, the figure didn't move very fast. It was a kid, maybe thirteen—all skin and bones and loose-limbs like an old scarecrow falling apart in the wind.

He stood a cautious foot away.

"Hey, Kid, what's up?" Trevir said.

"I'm Lee, " he said.

Trevir turned toward Troll Srenzo and laughed.

"This ragabond thinks we care about his name."

The kid took a breath and continued, "...my mum's in the hospice, inoperable, they say, and I don't have money for my little brother's medicine. The heat's out and he's been sick for a week—coughing—and I don't know what to do. Whatever you want, mister, I'll do it. Anything."

Trevir studied the kid carefully, then turned back to Troll Srenzo. His voice was filled with wonder.

"This kid is telling the truth. What are the odds of that?"

Troll Srenzo scowled.

"Zero," she said. "Can we go back to the office?"

Trevir turned back to the kid.

"I'm going to help you, okay?"

The kid's knees grew weak. He leaned against the Cadillac and looked at Trevir with a hope-filled, puppy-dog expression.

"Oh, Sir, thank you, thank you so very, very much."

"Do you know Buddy Doe?"

A wave of confusion washed across the kid's face.

"Uh, yeah, I think so."

"I want to talk to him. Find him and I'll give you a nice reward. Sound good?"

The kid did not respond—he was already gone, running up the street like his clothes were on fire.

Watching the kid disappear, Troll Srenzo spoke.

"What do you want with Buddy?"

For a few minutes, Trevir watched the few walkers on the street and in the park, then spoke.

"I have an idea," he said.

Field Trip—Part Two

TROLL SRENZO WAITED a few seconds to see if Trevir would continue without prompting, but he just sat there with a dreamy look in his eyes.

"Okay, don't leave us hanging, what is this idea?"

"You'll see. How quickly do you think you can get a bus? A school bus or Greyhound bus, something like that."

"What? I don't know anything about hiring a bus."

Impatient, Trevir spoke with command.

"Get me a bus, bring it here and I want it now."

Sitting beside him, Troll Srenzo looked at him for a few seconds, then got busy with her cell phone.

Patience was not a strength for Trevir—fidgeting, he sat in the SUV's cabin twiddling the radio dials until he found a news station he liked. It was reporting on the death toll overnight in the city. The mayor was becoming alarmed and suggested additional spending, which was no surprise, that's what mayors always suggest. But, seven people were killed in twelve hours. Trevir liked the sound of that—the sound of a city falling apart.

"Where is it?" he said.

"I told you the last six times you asked, it's coming."

From the back, a troll spoke.

"While we're waiting, maybe tell us what you are planning—so we can get all ready and stuff?"

Trevir twisted in his seat.

"You'll see."

After another ten minutes of waiting, Troll Srenzo sat up in her seat.

"Isn't that the kid?" she said.

It was, his loose-limbed walking-scarecrow gait was evident from a block away—plus he moved quickly, with urgency. Behind him, sauntering and taking his time, they could see Buddy Doe who stopped to shake hands with the locals and steal their fruit from their sidewalk crates. He'd take a bite, then discard it into the gutter.

Breathless, the kid stopped outside Trevir's window. Trevir pressed the button and the window slid down.

"Good job, kid," he said.

"You said something about a reward?"

Trevir turned to Troll Srenzo.

"I like a man who gets right to the point." Turning back to the window, he said, "Okay, no problem." He reached into his jacket and brought out a black sachet—the size of a sugar packet. "Here you go, kid, have fun."

The kid reached out, but didn't touch the packet.

"What am I supposed to do with this?"

Trevir shrugged.

"Eat it, snort it, smoke it, sell it. Whatever you want."

The kid recoiled.

"No, that stuff is poison—I've seen it. You said you would help me."

This interested Trevir.

"I *am* helping you. You could get two-hundred for that packet, easy. Maybe more if you can find someone hurting who has money." Laughing he turned to Troll Srenzo. "Though, we don't see that happen very often, do we?"

Unimpressed, Troll Srenzo shrugged. She kept her eyes on the approaching Buddy Doe.

"Smoke it yourself and forget about your troubles for an hour, that's a good deal, isn't it?"

"That doesn't help me or my brother."

"What's your name, kid?"

"Lee, Lee Crackstone. Crackstone's have been in this city since 1703. We're not trash, we're just having a temporary setback."

"*Touch* him and be done with this," Troll Srenzo said.

"No, a deal is a deal. Thieves' honor and all that."

"I'm no thief."

"Don't get your fruit-of-the-looms in a bunch, it was just a figure of speech. Temporary setback, eh? I see. Okay, how about a hundred dollars? How does that sound?"

Lee's heart lurched in his chest. He needed $105 to get the power turned back on in their apartment, but he had six grimy dollars tucked inside his sock.

"Sounds fair enough, sir," he said.

Trevir put the black packet back in his jacket pocket and snapped his fingers at Troll Srenzo.

She was unhappy, but produced a hundred-dollar-bill from a leather sack. She passed it to Trevir who in turn, held it out the window to Trevir, who snatched it.

"I'm curious, young man. When you look at us, what do you see?"

Lee took a step back. He pointed at Trevir.

"You're just bad, sir." He waved his finger at Troll Srenzo and the others in the truck. "I don't know what *they* are."

This irritated Troll Srenzo. She leaned over Trevir like she was going to grab the kid.

"Relax," Trevir said with a calm tone. Roughly, he pushed her back. "Money in the wrong hands can be just as dangerous as the

Black Death." To Lee, he said, "Run along, little man."

The kid turned on his heels and scurried off. He passed Buddy, who turned to watch him run, then slowly approached the Escalade.

"Who was that?" he said.

"No one," Trevir replied.

Buddy exchanged complex handshake gestures with Trevir, then taught him a new one with flapping fingers. Trevir giggled with delight. He loved the gangster and ethnic culture protocols.

Buddy spoke first.

"I hope you're here to give me good news. Increase my supply? I can't get enough."

"No, that's not it."

"If it's about the payments…"

"No, the money is flowing and you aren't stealing too much."

"Hey, fifty-fifty, I don't hold out on you."

"No, but some of your people do, but it's okay, that's not why we're here."

"Well, my friend, what is going on this fine morning?"

"That's what we've been asking," Troll Srenzo said.

By the time she stopped speaking, a giant yellow school bus rumbled up behind them—blocking traffic. Its giant diesel engine rattled and rumbled.

"Step one," Trevir said, "is to find a place to park that beast."

"Okay," Buddy said. "That's a can-do. What's step two?"

"Then we fill it up with troublemakers," Trevir said.

Lee Crackstone ran and ran. There were many places he could pay the Eversource power bill, but most charged a small fee, and he didn't have money for fees, all he had was the overdue amount and enough to cover the reconnection charge. Besides, at the main office, they could click-click-click on their computers and like magic, the heat would be back on.

He would harass them and look pathetic, whatever it took. His brother was barely hanging on and the cold was not helping.

It took hours, but Lee finally got the job done. He still had a dollar, so he bought two wrinkly apples. Exhausted, he trekked home and stood on the sidewalk looking up at their third-floor flat with an apple in each hand.

It was a miracle—the lights were on. For a minute, he admired this beautiful sight, gathering the energy to ascend the stairs.

Finally, he climbed and got to their door—to find a surprise waiting.

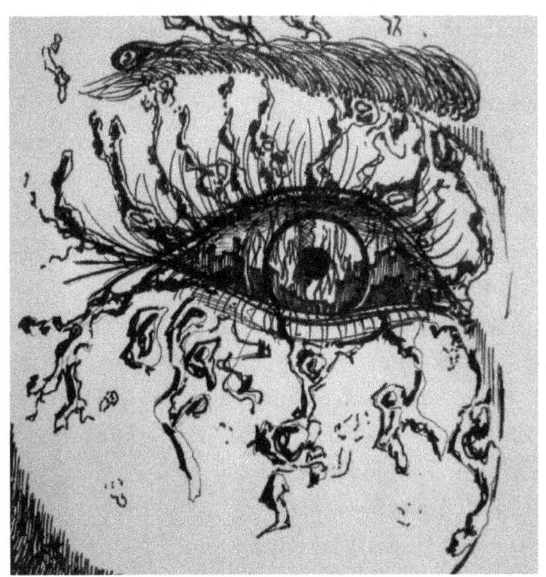

Field Trip—Part Three

STANDING ON A sidewalk by the park, Trevir and Buddy looked over the bus.

"How many do you figure it will hold?" Trevir said.

"I don't know. If we pack them in, a hundred?"

"If we offer free packets of Black Death?"

Buddy laughed.

"A hundred and fifty, easy."

Trevir looked deep into Buddy's eyes.

"Do it," he said.

After an hour, the bus was crammed and they were turning the disappointed away. Each rejected street-creep got a crisp one-hundred-dollar bill, so they didn't grumble too much as they hurried off for the package store in the middle of the block.

The driver was unhappy with the crowding and odor. When Trevir and Buddy were distracted, he simply walked away. Trevir laughed when they discovered he was missing.

"Smart man," Trevir said, grinning. He touched Buddy's arm,

then pointed at the group walking away. "See if one of them can drive a bus."

Trevir walked up and down, looking at the mass of humanity crammed in the yellow bus like sardines in a tin. One of them poked his head out of the window and vomited. The mess even smelled like sardines. Trevir skirted around the glob and carried on his inspection—after finding a driver, Buddy had reappeared and was trailing behind.

"Aren't they beautiful?" Trevir said. "We have brown bums, white bums, black bums, red buns, lady bums, kid bums." He pointed at a face squashed against a window. "Though I have no idea what that one is. Why don't I see any yellow bums?"

"I don't know," Buddy said.

"We'll have to work on that."

"We're ready, boss. Where to?"

Trevir thought for a few seconds.

"I was going to do Back Bay. The view from my office would be up-close and personal, but that's too urban. Can't get a good fire going. Let's do Dot."

"Okay, Dorchester it is, no problem. What then? What's the plan?"

"Do I have to think of everything? Take them to Beaumont Street or somewhere around there, give them their packets and set them loose."

"That's it?" Buddy said.

"That should do it," Trevir said.

As the bus fired up with a cloud of black-diesel smoke, Trevir spun on his heels and walked briskly toward the Escalade.

"Hurry, I don't want to miss a single minute of the show."

The Visitor—Part One

AFTER CLIMBING THE stairs to the apartment, Lee stood for a moment with his apples—admiring the glow coming from under the door.

Never take a fresh miracle for granted, he thought.

"Thank the Gods," he muttered.

As he turned the key, he heard bird-sounds coming from inside. Cawing, like a conversation.

Can't be.

After cracking open the door and peeking, he couldn't believe his eyes. His brother, Rufus, curled up on the couch under a mountain of blankets—asleep, with three crows standing along the back of the couch as if on watch. Rufus looked safe and comfortable, sleeping like a newborn. His coloring looked better than it had in days.

Lee looked over their coffee table, seeing a veritable feast laid out. One of those meals-to-go from Boston Market—a full chicken with all of the trimmings and even a dessert pie. Lee stood dumbfounded.

Where did THIS come from?

It couldn't be from that creepy Trevir guy. He might send poison, but not a meal.

"You have good instincts for a human," came a raspy voice from the largest crow.

With black, iridescent feathers, this giant bird commanded attention. Lee stood stock still.

Will this monster poke my eyes out and scavenge my scrawny body?

"No, human, I will not kill you. I've no appetite for human flesh; well, not now. Come closer and I'll reveal myself."

Lee blinked.

How could it possibly speak?

"I don't have all day, human. Come closer before I get annoyed."

Lee did as commanded. While walking across the room, a mist gathered around the crow's feathers—it changed its form. Lee rubbed his eyes.

Was this real?

Within moments, a tall woman stood before him, pale and lithe, but strong with long, flowing, jet-black hair and eyes that could pierce a stone.

"I am the Morrigan. Do you know of me?"

Lee shook his head.

She frowned.

"Humans, they forsake the gods and goddesses of olde, while we are the only ones left who can save them. I am the phantom queen and shape shifter from times long ago. I come in times of war and death. I am one with fate and destiny; yours and that of many others. Do you understand me?"

Lee shook his head again.

"You encountered a most vile creature named Trevir—the so-called King—and his consort, Troll Srenzo, did you not?"

Lee nodded.

"Yes, I saw them."

"He wants the human race to bow and pledge their souls to him. According to his plan, you will, or you'll be massacred, all of you. He must be stopped. While a rare few of you are brave and capable, you are blind and weak; unready for a heroic role. How did you let this happen? Never mind, I have a mission for you."

Lee looked over at his brother who still slept peacefully, being watched over by his new brethren.

She continued, "I can't go, we need to hide our alliance as long as possible. I need you to deliver *this* to Trevir."

She raised a jeweled talisman hanging on a chain.

"Don't stare at it too closely, it's a tricky one and this is no time for dreaming."

She placed it into Lee's upraised palm. It was warm to the touch, but not hot. It had a surprising heft and a glittery beauty. In fact, it was exquisite. It attracted his eye like a magnet. He turned it over and over, studying it, then pried away his eyes.

"It's a peace offering. We offer him one last chance to abandon his path of chaos and destruction. There will be a verbal message for you to convey as well—it must be memorized."

"As you wish, ma'am, I mean queen, your highness, I mean…"

"Morrigan will do, Lee, Morrigan will do. Close your eyes and say what I say."

The Morrigan recited words of olde as she circled Lee, around and around. The mist thickened while their repeated words became powerful. The chant entered his body and merged with his essence. He became the words. Eventually, he spoke them on his own and she nodded in approval. All the while, she wove a spell of protection about him, old, strong magick Trevir would struggle to undo.

When he opened his eyes, the Morrigan had changed back to crow form. The mist dissipated. The room was warm, brightly lighted and smelled of food. Rufus began to stir.

The Morrigan spoke.

"Rest now, Lee. Rest and eat and care for Rufus, then go to Trevir's office and deliver the message. This must be done before twilight. He will be unhappy, but you should be protected. Do NOT linger. Say your words, then leave. When you are done, come back here and pack your things. Later today, you and Rufus will leave for the desert."

"Desert? I don't know anything about any desert."

"That's where we make our last stand. It is written."

Lee puzzled over this.

"I know the city, I don't know about any desert. What happens there we can't do here?"

"It is written," the Morrigan repeated.

A thought flooded Lee's mind.

"But my mom, what about my mom?"

The Morrigan spoke with sadness.

"I'm sorry, my child, your mom will not make it. As we speak, Death is preparing to take her. She will go peacefully. After you eat, take Rufus and go and see her. Know it is your last time. Say all you need to say to her. She loves you and will always be with you. Her spirit will be well cared for. She will be with you in time of need; her strength and resolve runs through you. This journey, however, is only for you and Rufus."

Lee slumped. It was all too much. Too much for a young boy. Too much for him to take in. His head was spinning and he felt faint.

The Morrigan flapped her wings and perched upon his shoulder.

"This is your journey, Lee. This is why you are here. All things come to this. Be strong. You're not alone, you're not alone. You have our power on your side."

With that, the Morrigan and her followers flew out through the window. Outside, they vanished.

Rufus stirred.

"Food. We have food. I never lost faith in you, Lee. You're the best big brother ever."

Lee didn't know what to say or do. He willed his feet to move and joined Rufus on the couch. Rufus climbed onto him and gave him a huge hug. Lee clung to his little brother like a life raft.

"First things first, let's eat. Then we need to spend some time with mom. This might be the last time we see her so we need to say all we need to say. Understand?"

Rufus's little eyes welled.

He nodded.

"It will be okay, bub," Lee said. "We'll be okay."

I hope. I truly hope.

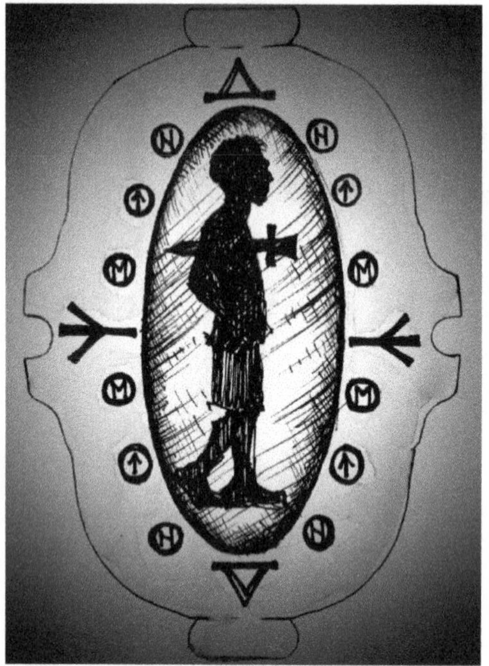

The Visitor—Part Two

TREVIR COULDN'T JUST have any TV, it had to be the biggest and the best. Technicians had installed a custom-built, two-hundred-inch Hisense screen that covered most of one wall of his office. For now, it was the biggest in the world, but soon every high-tech executive and Back Bay lawyer would have one and Trevir would have to find another way to symbolize his vast superiority over the rest of the world.

Watching nothing happening outside his crystal window grated on his nerves. On the TV, irrelevant talking heads endlessly ranted about equally irrelevant politicians.

"I have a half-acre screen and there's nothing on. Why isn't anything happening?"

At that instant, a news bulletin interrupted the regularly scheduled irrelevance.

"This just in, Dana. There is a disturbance in Dorchester. We have citizens calling in about shots fired and paramedics report stabbings, apparently from several locations. We don't have any indication this is terrorism, but after the Boston Marathon bombings, we will be excused for thinking that is possible. Hang on, we have another report, SWAT teams are being deployed."

Standing before the window, Troll Srenzo spoke.

"We have our first fire," she said.

Trevir joined her, raising a set of field glasses. She was right, in the distance, a column of black smoke speared the leaden sky.

"Finally," he said.

From behind, a troll spoke politely.

"Sir," he said.

Trevir elbowed Troll Srenzo.

"Shall we increase our wager? Do you still think more bums will be killed than civilians?"

Troll Srenzo shrugged.

"Increase it however you like. If the bums were good at anything, they wouldn't be bums."

A little stronger, the troll behind them spoke.

"Sir?"

"Okay, double it, the soft losers in Dot don't have a chance."

"Fine," Troll Srenzo said. "And double it again if you like."

With patience exhausted, the troll looked at Trevir's desk for something to throw. Trevir had a black and gold Ellepi Klizia stapler he hadn't used yet. The troll picked it up, weighed it, then threw it at the window. That got their attention. Troll Srenzo reached for her sword, but Trevir restrained her.

"What is it?" he said.

"You have a visitor," the troll said.

Trevir glanced at the broken stapler on the floor and took a deep breath.

"Fine," he said. "Show it in."

Outside, another fire had started and one breathless report after another on the TV. The talking heads were having trouble understanding and describing what was happening in the normally docile Dorchester.

When the troll returned with the visitor, Trevir and Troll Srenzo turned. It was the street kid.

"Ah," Trevir said, "it's you. Cruikshank."

Nervous, the kid's voice was broken and hesitant.

"Crackstone."

"Okay," Trevir said. "Whatever. You have my attention. What do you want?"

"I brought something. A message. An offer. One last chance for peace."

Troll Srenzo took a step forward, drawing her short, ugly sword.

Trevir took her arm in restraint.

"I suspect he did not come alone, or unprotected."

The kid swallowed.

"I don't know how any of this is supposed to work."

"Emissary?" Trevir said.

The kid nodded. Trevir dropped his hand from Troll Srenzo's arm.

"Okay, we can break that, but it's probably not worth the effort."

"This is bullshit," Troll Srenzo said.

"Go ahead," Trevir said. "See what happens."

She took another step forward, then quickly stabbed the kid in the chest. The sword went through, like he was made of mist. She dropped it—it clattered on the floor. Writhing in pain, she cupped her fist to her chest.

Pale-faced and shaking, the kid watched in wonder.

"That's what I thought," Trevir said. "Leave what you brought and say your piece, then begone. We're missing the show."

The kid wore an old Army jacket, olive drab. It was three sizes too large. From a side pocket, he brought out the talisman and offered it. Black, wrought iron. Old, very old. In the center, a blood-red ruby surrounded by gleaming green emeralds. Engraved with runes.

"There are words that go with this," Trevir said. "Go ahead

and say them."

The kid took a deep breath.

The power, the glory, the ancient's demise.
History recorded in dying men's eyes.

"Okay, that's enough," Trevir said while removing the talisman from the kid's hand. "Here's my answer. No. I will not stop until all of your kind are dead or serve me. You are losing. You are weak. Why would I stop now? We're just starting."

"I don't understand any of this," the kid said.

"Obviously," Trevir replied.

"As I heard it, they wanted to give you one last chance for redemption."

"Which I reject. I'll take the talisman as tribute and suggest you get out before I haul down the black book, break the silly spell and do what I will to you. Did they tell you emissary status can be dissolved, broken? Countered? Did they forget to mention that?"

The kid, scared to death, licked his lips.

"Can you tell me before I go? You said our *kind*. I don't know anything. What did you mean by that?"

Trevir stared at the kid for a few seconds before speaking.

"If you're still standing before me in five seconds, you will die today, screaming. Test me if you like."

It only took three seconds—the door slammed shut as the kid ran away.

"I think my arm is broken," Troll Srenzo said. "Why didn't you stop me?"

"Some lessons need to be learned the hard way."

He turned back to the window.

"Ah, look," he said. "Three new fires now."

Kissing Booth—Part Two

FINALLY, CARNIVAL DAY. Everyone from Cement City and the surrounding county wandered around the school parking lot, magically converted into a wonderland. The energy was felt miles away—all their senses were overloaded with electricity.

The air was filled with the aroma of grilled onions, hot dogs and burgers, deep-fried elephant ears and ice cream. All manner of carnival foods were on display and the cheerful, carb-overdosed lines were long. Rides galore; games of chance and games of skill. Rides that went upside down, sideways and all manner in-between. This event was good for the town—Cement City needed this revival of good cheer.

With parts cut up and painted by Kurt's mother, Minnie and the Misfits assembled the Kissing Booth exactly as Kurt had planned. It was ablaze with balloons, red and pink hearts and, to Minnie's mortification and good-natured embarrassment, a painted plywood version of her pouting lips. Stools were placed just so and a dozen tubes of ChapStick and Burt's Bees lip balm were close at hand.

Per a secret ballot, Minnie and Raven represented the girls, with Kurt and Marcus representing the boys. Each sat, awaiting their turn, blindfolded. Mr. Danvers oversaw the booth making sure no one lingered too long or got out of hand.

At two-dollars a ticket, they assumed the kissing booth would have a few customers and make a little money every day, but the booth was a huge hit with the teens. The lines were long with boys in particular, but many girls and even Stanley, who seemed confused about his sexuality, lined up for their turn.

Stanley bought two tickets, perhaps so he could see which kiss he liked best?

As promised, the boxing glove mechanism was handy. Of course, it wasn't really a mechanism; it was the football team center, Buster Cantwell, a huge young man, easily three-hundred pounds dressed in a silver jumpsuit and patiently waiting for someone to punch. Buster, none-too-bright, had a sweet nature and was perfect for the job of standing for the forty-minutes-per-hour the booth was open, all day long, waiting for someone to knock into next week.

With the nervous looks of even the parking lot gang, it seemed unlikely anyone would test Buster.

Long lines, kissing strangers, all day.

The kissers were nervous at first, but that wore off as the tedium of endless smooching set in. Some were pecks on the cheek from spinsters, some were lip kisses. Some whispered sweet nothings before moving on, some did a quick hit and ran away, embarrassed and laughing.

There were no judgments, just kissing and joy.

Toward the end of the first day, as they sat awaiting their next client, Minnie felt a change in the air. Her senses picked up a new vibration. It had to be close to break time; she began to squirm. The blindfold was tight and the self-imposed rules said they should not be removed. But, something was in the air, she could smell it. Her senses were ablaze and her skin tingled.

Moving lightly on his feet to hide his gait, the next kisser approached and placed both hands on Minnie's cheeks. He said not a word, then bent down to kiss her and in that moment they breathed as one. Minnie was lost. Her thoughts twirled and the world turned upside down and sideways. Before she could regain her senses the kiss was over and he was gone.

After a moment of wonder and inner turmoil, Minnie ripped off her blindfold. Leaning over, she frantically searched the crowd and saw no one moving away.

"Hey…" She looked left and right. "No fair."

Sensing trouble, Mr. Danvers ran over.

"Are you okay, Minnie? Was there a creep? What's wrong?"

"I, um, did you see who just kissed me? Where did he go? What was he wearing? I think I need to go to the bathroom. Will you be okay for a minute without me?"

Danvers laughed.

"You sound like someone who just kissed Prince Charming, Minnie. Yeah, it's a few minutes early, but take a break. Lacey will fill in. Come back for your last shift, the natives are restless and this kissing booth is a hit."

"Yeah…I'll—um, be right back. I just need to, yeah, I just need to go to the bathroom," she said in a dream-like state.

She started to walk and she heard Mr. Danvers shout, "It's the other way Minnie, the other way."

"Yeah, the other way, right. I'll go *that* way…."

All she did in the restroom was splash cold water on her cheeks. She didn't know how she made it there and back again, but she did. After wandering in a daze through the crowd, looking for the mysterious young man for twenty minutes, she found her way back to the stool and was blindfolded again—feeling and knowing her world had changed and there was no going back.

Betrothed.

She sent a heartfelt request for forgiveness to the east.

Surely Philip had forgotten about her and moved on.

The way she felt deep in her gut, maybe she was moving on too.

Carnival

MINNIE RUBBED HER lips…they were sore. She tried to estimate how many kisses she'd delivered. It was hundreds.

She wondered.

Is it harder to kiss or play a trumpet?

Right then and there she decided if she wanted to play music, she'd play guitar or accordion or triangle or something—anything that did not work the lips so hard.

Finally, she could walk around and get cotton candy or a hot dog. For her and the other organizers, everything was free, but truth-be-told, her stomach was unsettled and she really didn't want anything.

Well, a caramel apple couldn't hurt. It's fruit, right?

She munched and walked around. Everyone was happy and additionally, happy to see her. It was a nice feeling.

For the first time, she noticed the rides. Lacey and her dad had hired the equipment and the crew, Minnie had not paid any attention to their negotiations. The equipment and staff were nice, first class. It must have been very expensive to haul all this stuff in and pay everyone, but Lacey's dad was willing, even eager, to pay.

In particular, the Merry-Go-Round was beautiful, with freshly painted wooden horses twirling and swirling to the oom-pah carnival music.

And familiar.

And, it seemed that there were many eyes on her.

Watching, everyone seemed to be watching.

Sometimes a figure touched on a memory, but they quickly turned away and she lost sight of them.

Everybody looks like somebody, right?

It was weird, she could not remember ever going to a carnival—it was not something her mother could fit into their meager budget. It was okay, you can't miss something you never had.

She was at a beautiful carnival today and the weather was unseasonably nice. It was a blessing—clearly, the sun approved of their venture.

She stood in the middle of the school parking lot surrounded by people and rides and joy and spun in a circle.

There was something tickling at the back of her mind, something beyond the magical kiss from the mysterious stranger. Why did this equipment and some of the people seem so familiar?

It was a puzzle she intended to think on. But, for now, another apple called to her. She felt like it would be perfectly okay to have one more.

Kissing all day was hungry work.

Sunday, four o'clock. Finally, it was time for the parade. After months of preparation and the exhausting show itself, it was time for one last push. Parade. Finale. Fireworks. Then pack it up so the trash crews would clean up the parking lot.

Minnie was done, she wanted to disappear—hide for a week. Curl up in a corner and die. She gently probed her swollen lips. They hurt.

If we do this next year, I'm selling cotton candy.

The parade started with old cars and trucks plastered with banners advertising local businesses. They kicked in cash. They deserved their moment in the spotlight. From the middle school, the harvest king and queen waved from a Cadillac convertible. They were children, but looked elegant in their gown and tuxedo.

It made Minnie feel old.

Past her prime.

On a stake-bed truck, waiting for their moment to join the procession, the pep squad cheered and waved their pompoms. Lacey spotted Minnie and shouted.

"Get up here."

Minnie waved her away, but Lacey spotted Buster, leaned over and whispered in his ear. Like a retriever, Buster moved through the crowd. Minnie wanted to run, but could not assemble the energy. Buster picked her up like a sack of potatoes and ran back—then hoisted her onto the truck.

"I'm tired," Minnie complained.

"Smile and wave," Lacey hissed.

Horns tooted and loud speakers blared. It was an insane cacophony of fun and noise.

Summoning good sportsmanship, Minnie smiled…

…and waved.

The energy of the crowd reflected back and she felt energized.

Okay, I can do this.

The truck circled and stopped. The horns quieted and the loudspeakers were muted.

From around the corner of the gym, the marching band high-stepped. Mostly in tune, they made up for it by being loud. Following them came the elephants.

The crowd went crazy with cheers and jeers.

Elephants, there were three, were manned by the football team, two per elephant, one for the front and one for the back. Made of gray canvas for the hides, hunks of old firehose for the trunks and braided ropes for the tails, they danced and kicked and swayed and waved trunks and tail. It was a hilarious, ludicrous and silly scene and the kids ate it up.

And following, a team with shovels and garbage cans picking up what was dumped by the fake elephants.

It was funny, perhaps the funniest thing she'd ever seen.

They laughed so hard, their guts hurt.

Lacey shouted into Minnie's ear.

"The elephants are genius. Good one, Minnie."

When she finally made it to her bed, it was nearly midnight. Staring at the ceiling of her cubby, she heard an echo in her ringing ears.

Good one, Minnie.

In the history of mankind, there were many great days. Perfect days. Wonderful days. This one was in the running as the very greatest.

Good one, Minnie.

The Caravan

SINCE THE CARNIVAL, it was hard for Minnie to get back into her mundane school schedule; she was off her game. The energy around her was electric. Literally. She was shocked by everything she touched and her thoughts were scattered, but always seemed to return to that kiss.

What kiss?

That kiss.

Her friends were tired of her asking—and claimed to be clueless about what she went on and on about.

Who was the mysterious stranger?

What mysterious stranger?

Had she dreamed it all up? Could it all be imagined? Wishful thinking from a hormonal girl daydreaming about a proper suitor? The carnival experience was a whirlwind—who could tell what was real and what was imagined?

No one had seen a stranger and it seemed like big Buster looked at her differently now—morning and afternoon, he watched her from the corner of his eyes like she owed him something.

Oh, please, no, was it him who came around the booth and snagged a kiss?

Three days after the carnival, she grabbed his beefy arm in the hallway.

"Okay, what?" she said.

"It's just that..."

"Spit it out, I want to hear it."

"All that kissing and I got nothing."

Is that all it was?

Her relief was palpable.

"Lean over."

Slowly, from a great height, he stooped.

She planted a ripe one on his large, rubbery lips.

Nothing.

Thank the Gods.

"We good now?" she said.

Gently, he put a hand the size of a frying pan on her shoulder.

"You're a dear friend, Minnie. Thank you."

"You're welcome. You were there all day, surely you saw..."

"No," he interrupted, "I told you, I'm sorry, I didn't see nothing."

As days passed, she tried to forget all about the mystery man—kept brushing it off. She blamed static electricity or tiredness or being afflicted with the ladies' monthly curse.

Deep down, she knew there was more to the story, but she would just have to wait until it revealed itself.

She gave herself pep talks.

Magic may be dead to me but I know all things happen in their own time. So wait it out I will.

But, she could not deny the stray thoughts that wandered through her mind.

One day it occurred to her to ask about the carnival crew. Like a bloodhound, she tracked down Lacey who was holding court in the lunchroom—a meeting of the pep squad.

"Oh, Minnie, did you decide to join us?"

The girls did an impromptu cheer.

Oh, Minnie, oh, Minnie
You'd be easier to toss than Ginny
Yeah!

There was nothing wrong with Ginny, she was perfectly healthy, but was at least a muscular 110 pounds, while Minnie rarely touched 85. The pep squad was working hard on their pyramids and tosses.

Distracted, Minnie waved the girls away.

"No, sorry," she said, "not my thing, you know that."

She grabbed Lacey's hand and pulled her toward a wall. Putting her hands on Lacey's shoulders, she manhandled the girl so her back was against the concrete blocks. Face to face, Minnie looked up at Lacey.

"This better not be about your mystery kisser. No one saw anything, even me."

"No, Minnie said. "I'm curious about the carnival equipment. Where'd all that come from?"

"Oh," Lacey said. "We got a screaming deal—it was a Ren Faire outfit, we caught them before their season started. They were real happy to have the work. Didn't they do a great job? We got them for five thousand dollars and a percentage of sales. Truth-be-told, they made a fortune on their percentage, but that's faire isn't it? Get it? I said faire with an e, not fair like a county fair or something. That was funny, right?"

The word faire stuck in Minnie's mind.

"Where did this *faire* come from?"

Lacey thought about it.

"They move around, right? I don't think they come from anywhere. For now, they are still around, you know, but moving on today, I think. Why? What is on your mind?"

Minnie tugged on Lacey's shoulders, pulling her down so their faces were inches apart.

"Where are they?" Minnie said.

Lacey bobbed her head and planted a quick kiss on Minnie's lips.

"I don't know why I did that."

"Where. Are. They?" Minnie repeated.

"Oh," Lacey said, "I thought everyone knew. The big meadow by the gravel pit."

Thinking furiously, Minnie let go—then decided.

She ran down the hallway and crashed out through the doors. People milled around in the courtyard. She scanned the crowd and spotted Buster unlocking the security chain on his bicycle. Suiting Buster's size, the bike was huge, with giant, knobby tires. She ran over.

"Hey, Minnie," Buster said.

"I need to borrow your bike."

"Uh, what?" he said, but he was speaking to her receding back. In seconds, she was already thirty feet away.

Over her shoulder, she said, "I'll bring it back later."

The gravel pit was two miles away, to the south in a direction she rarely traveled. Pumping the heavy pedals furiously, she made the two miles in record time, not even ten minutes.

She rounded a corner and there they were, colorful trucks and collapsed equipment tied down as cargo—all lined up and ready to move out. The big diesel engines rumbled.

Standing beside the big bike and gasping from the exertion, she looked over the caravan. From the corner of her eye, she saw something arc from the sky. Without thinking, she reached out and caught it.

Perfect throw. Perfect catch.

She examined the object. It was an apple, a green, Granny Smith. This stirred a memory. These apples were a hybrid from Australia, named for the lady who accidentally bred them. Marla Anne Smith.

She had no idea how she knew this.

In her mind, she traced the apple's path through the sky and tracked back to the truck that held the elephant ear trailer. Pushing the bike, she walked toward it. As she passed the caravan, the diesel engines were revved with impatience. They were ready to pull out.

While approaching, she saw a dark, skinny figure climb up into the passenger side of the truck's cab. A young man. Slowly, he came into focus. With shaggy hair and wisps of spotty beard, she didn't recognize him.

After fumbling with the bike's kickstand and climbing onto the running board of the truck, she stared into his eyes.

"Roll down the window," she demanded.

He grinned, then slowly turned the crank.

Still no recognition. Then he spoke and her stopped-up mind broke like a dam.

"What can I do for you, m'lady?" he said.

She knew his voice, knew it better than her own.

Philip.

Grown up.

How? It hadn't even been a year.

But, he'd sprouted.

She was instantly livid.

"You were going to pass through and leave without saying hello?"

He grinned.

"Oh, I said hello, did I not, m'lady?"

"I don't know. Say it again."

It was impossible, but his grin grew bigger.

He leaned through the window and kissed her angry lips.

From behind, a truck's horn bellowed.

This kiss touched her everywhere, from bones to gristle to flesh to aura—an aura that expanded until it filled the field.

Not wanting this kiss to end, she waved a dismissive hand toward the rear of the convoy.

Philip pulled back.

"I have so many things I need to say to you," she said.

"Those words will have to wait."

"You can't leave me now."

"Like you couldn't leave me up east? Sorry. This is a dead place. We can't stay here—we're already gone."

"No. Please. When will I see you again?"

"I don't exactly know, but it will be in a dry, desolate place. That's what the cards say."

She looked out along the convoy under the gray, dismal sky. It was the six months of the year where rain continually threatened. It was hard for her to imagine anything dry.

"One more before you go."

He shrugged.

"It will have to wait—that's just the way of it."

The driver popped the clutch and the truck lurched.

She stepped down and moved back. In seconds the wagon train stated moving and in less than a minute turned the corner and left her alone, breathing acrid smoke and fuel fumes.

There were a lot of things she could feel.

Irate.

Forlorn.

Abandoned.

She wanted to stomp her feet and scream at the sky.

This is unfair and stupid.

She walked up to the bicycle, then stood still for a moment sorting though her emotions. Philip was right. This corner of the world was special and had many good things to offer, but without the sparkle of the magic world, it was soul-dead. However, that's the way it had to be with the Black Faerie Prince as their enemy.

If I use magic, he will find us.

A voice whispered in her head.

King.

Trevir is King now.

And he's coming.

Minnie shook off dread. Hidden in this remote corner, he would not find them.

There was the bright side of things. Philip was well and she would see him again. Not today, but some day.

But why would she meet Philip in a dry, barren place?

She couldn't even imagine it.

No longer in a hurry, she walked the bike along the highway back toward the school. By the time she arrived to return Buster's bike, the cold clouds let loose and soaked her—which was perfect for her mood.

She raised her face to the rain and let it immerse her.

Troll Carnival—Part One

IT WAS EARLY, so the vast field of rolling hills were mostly barren; populated only by clumps of workers assembling equipment and planting colorful banners that flapped in the wind. The massive stage and mountains of loudspeakers had been installed the day before and were ready. The sun was not yet visible on the eastern horizon, though the sky was brightening.

So far, foul weather had held off and it looked like an impending ice storm would come later in the week. A stroke of fortune. It would be cold and windy, but there were many bonfires being built like giant teepees with huge stacks of seasoned lumber and railroad ties. It would be warm enough.

Trevir, Troll Srenzo and his entourage toured and watched the concession trucks rolling in and setting up. In corrals far to the north, livestock was dropped by trucks and milled around. The meat for this faire would be fresh.

Along with nervous cattle, Trevir watched the abattoir being assembled. A dozen butchers sharpened their cleavers.

Very fresh.

There were corrals for humans too.

A runner approached and spoke with Troll Srenzo, then raced off.

"What?" Trevir said.

"Nothing," Troll Srenzo said, "the senior Senator wants to talk now."

Trevir grinned.

"I'm sure he does. Let's go see what is on his mind."

The Senator, standing straight with as much dignity as he could muster, stood with his hands on the wood slats of the largest human enclosure. This one was at least an acre and filled with groups of bodies huddled against the cold.

The Senator did not look very dignified with eyeglasses missing a lens and a bleeding wound dripping on the side of his head. He appeared very relieved to see Trevir and his entourage approaching.

"Sir," he said, "there has been a terrible misunderstanding. I am eager to hear your proposals and sign on to support your legislator-legislating-legister agenda."

There was something wrong with his head—he could not form the complex words accurately. He tried it slowly.

"Leg-is-la-tive…"

He seemed proud for getting the word out.

Trevir studied the man. His eyes were out of alignment, one was fully bloodshot and drifted left.

Trevir raised his voice.

"This man needs a doctor, right away."

Troll Srenzo scowled.

"The nearest doctor is twenty miles away."

Trevir leaned close to the Senator.

"Oops, sorry about that. No doctor for you."

"Please, sir, I'm sorry."

"I politely invited you to my office for a conference. Do you remember the message you sent back?"

"That was an error, I apologize. My chief of staff was not authoritied. Authorated. Au-thor-ized."

"Something along the line of 'I'll see the twerp when hell freezes over.' Does that sound familiar?"

"My chief, George..."

Trevir, buried deep in his greatcoat, laughed. The coat's collar was lined with the lush fur of a wolfhound.

"It's not quite hell-freezing-over freezing, but it's very cold, isn't it?"

"Sir..."

Troll Srenzo unsheathed her stubby sword.

"The King asked a question," she said.

The Senator looked around, confused.

"Yes," he said, "it's cold. Very cold. My chief of staff..."

Trevir looked around.

"Ah, George. He's here, isn't he?"

The Senator nodded eagerly.

"Yes."

Impatient, Trevir said, "Then get him."

The Senator turned and studied the assembled clumps of bodies. After spying George sprawled a dozen feet away—he walked over and grabbed the man's collar, dragging him to the barrier.

George's head lolled on his shoulders. He was barely conscious. Trevir reached through the slats, lifted George's head and looked into his unfocused eyes.

"This man is not doing well. I don't even think a doctor could first-aid him back to health at this point, poor man. What can I do to help?"

He looked around the field. Fifty feet away, a large, tall scaffold rose into the sky.

It looked like it was ready to go.

"Haul him out," Trevir said. "Let's test the equipment."

"What? No," the Senator said. "What is that thing? What are you doing?"

The trolls opened the heavy gate and hauled George out—

then hustled him to the tower.

Trevir twitched his finger.

"Do it," he said.

Raised by ropes, a gleaming blade was hoisted into the sky and George, who did not struggle, was placed on the bascule with his head in the lunette.

"During the French Revolution, it could have been as many as forty-thousand who took their last breath on *le machine*." Trevir turned to the Senator. "This wonderful thing was called the guillotine after an early advocate, a physician, Joseph Ignace Guillotin. He was unhappy about the association. After all, he didn't design it or build any, so it's unfair for this misnomer to carry on throughout history, right?"

"Sir, I don't understand," the Senator said.

Over his shoulder, Trevir waved his hand and the blade flashed in the dim morning light. He waved his hand again and a troll brought over George's head. Trevir pointed and the head was tossed into the human corral.

A wild look kindled in the Senator's eyes.

"You can't possibly think you can really do this?"

"I think I *am* doing it." To Troll Srenzo, he said, "What was the name of the newspaper guy? The Boston World guy."

She thought for a moment before speaking.

"Peters. Harvey Peters."

"Right," Trevir said. "Get him."

The trolls spread out through the enclosure and returned shortly with a tall, bald man. Other than a blaze of mud on his cheek, he looked unharmed. He glanced at George's bloody head and then looked away quickly.

Trevir moved until he was six-inches from the corral's slats.

"Peters. Think carefully." He waved to encompass the whole scene. "What is your newspaper going to say about all this death, destruction and mayhem?"

Peters swallowed.

"Uh, nothing? Or, we'll say whatever you want us to say?"

Trevir laughed.

"Two perfectly good answers."

He turned to Troll Srenzo.

"Let him go."

The Senator stood with his hands on the slats.

"What about me, sir? I've learned an important lesion. No, leisure." He tried it slowly. "Less-on. Lesson."

"This, my friend will seem like the longest day of your life. But, at the end, it will seem like it was not nearly long enough."

Trevir turned and watched the newspaper man walk toward the county road. The retreating man did not look left or right, just straight ahead.

"Shall we find someone to give him a ride?" Troll Srenzo said.

"No, let him walk," Trevir replied.

Troll Carnival—Part Two

TREVIR LIKED TO meander. The wind was bitter-cold, but the trolls were used to it. Unsurprisingly, the crowd was notoriously violent, filthy and disrespectful. Ale flowed and on huge cooking fires, cow carcasses turned on massive spits.

"How many do you figure?" Trevir said.

Troll Srenzo shrugged.

"Half a million? Give or take."

They stood on a knoll and looked out over the mob. A never-ending line of hunched figures urinated into a trench. Ten feet in front of them, a drunken female dropped her breeches, squatted and dropped a steaming pile of aromatic dung.

Troll Srenzo peeked out of the corner of her eyes to see how Trevir would take this.

He tilted his head back and laughed.

"When you gotta go, you gotta go," he said.

As Trevir's party wandered, the hundred-acre field was bedlam. Near the cattle pens, blood flowed as cows were slaughtered and hauled off on carts to the many cooking fires.

Hundreds of oak kegs of ale were in constant movement. When one was emptied, it was smashed and tossed onto the towering bonfires—which would not be lighted until dusk.

Overwhelmingly, the jostling crowd was composed of trolls, but there were ogres, ohrkks and other creatures in the mix too. A gangly, ten-foot-tall creature bit the head off a troll and gnawed on the body.

"What is that one?" Trevir said.

Troll Srenzo shrugged.

"I don't know. Mutant goblin? Who cares? Does it matter?"

Trevir raised his eyebrows.

"Just idle curiosity."

Turning, Trevir studied Troll Srenzo's face. She was large—he always suspected she was a half-breed, with black-ohrkk blood in her veins. Her face was lumpy and scarred. Broken tusk. Tufts of hair spouted like wild patches of crabgrass. In her own hideous way, she was beautiful. Energized by the horde milling around them, he felt an urge.

"Let's go to my tent. I will have you."

She pointed at the sun hovering on the smoky horizon.

"No time," she said. "You wanted the show to start at dusk, right?"

Trevir looked at her from muddy boots, stained leather pants, reeking vest and uncured sheepskin helmet. He sighed.

"I will have you every-which-way."

"Yes, but later," she said. "For now, you wanted to introduce the band and get the fires started."

The troop turned and moved through the crowd toward the massive stage where the towers of speakers loomed like skyscrapers. The troll-guards cleared the way. Along their path, they passed long lines of prisoners leading to the guillotines. The sight energized him. He had many enemies from the city and many of them would die tonight.

He pointed.

"I can't wait," he said. "Pick one."

Troll Srenzo reached out and grabbed a man by his collar,

pulled him to his feet and shoved him toward Trevir. Dressed casually in mud-caked Dockers khaki trousers and a Calvin Klein polo shirt, his arm was broken and hung at a disturbing angle.

"Thank God, sir, this is a horrible mistake. I have a family, kids, a dog. Let me go, please."

"Do you know why you are here?"

"Building permit. There were irregularities. I had to reject. It's the law, sir. I had to say no. Rules. Regulations."

Trevir looked deeply into his eyes.

"Your *rules* brought you here. Rules. Do you have any idea how much I hate rules?"

"From now on, no problem, I will approve everything. All of your projects, bang, right through, top of the stack, bingo, no problem, same-day service."

Trevir reached out and put his index finger on the man's neck—he could feel the frantic throbbing in the right carotid artery.

"Rubberstamp this," Trevir said.

Slowly, Troll Srenzo slipped the thin blade of her dagger in the man's neck by Trevir's finger. In seconds, the light in man's eyes died and he collapsed.

"Happy now?" she said.

"This will be the best evening ever," Trevir said.

The entourage moved through the crowd and slipped through burly guards to the backstage tent. Inside, the band was hyped up and ready. The singer and lead guitarist went by the stage name Melody Masher or Mel, but her given name was Michelle Smith. Her face was a forest of studs and piercings and every inch of her exposed skin was covered in tats in layers and layers. Her custom guitar dripped fake blood from the headstock—its body was shaped like a grinning skull. Her dreadlocks were oiled up and reeking.

Trevir loved death-metal; Melody Masher and the Soiled Virgins were the hottest act on the planet. They were really posers from Princeton, New Jersey, but their neu-industrial sound was loud, brutal and jagged.

On a satanic star stenciled on the tent's carpet, they gathered in a circle.

Mel pointed her guitar at Trevir.

"We dedicate tonight's performance to you."

Trevir grinned.

"Tonight," he said, "everyone bleeds."

The guard-trolls raised their swords and put ragged gashes into the musician's arms.

"Asshole," Mel said through gritted teeth.

"I will say a few words of introduction, then you rock as if your lives depend on it."

Their lives were already forfeit. Imagery filled Trevir's mind.

The trolls will tear you to pieces.

He pushed through heavy curtains and climbed up to the stage. It was impossible, but the crowd seemed to extend to the horizon. The blood-red sun, already occluded and sinking in the west, hovered over their heads. Guillotine towers dotted the landscape. The bonfire tenders were ready with their torches.

Trevir lifted his hands. From the loudspeakers, his voice boomed.

"Are you ready to raise some hell?" he shouted.

The crowd roared.

He dropped his hands.

Guillotine blades flashed. Blood flowed. The bonfires caught and instantly raged—pouring clouds of black, acrid smoke into the sky.

The mob's cacophony was split by squealing guitars. The drums thundered. Blood dripped down Mel's arm as she stabbed at the chords. It was an ungodly clamor.

Trevir walked to side-stage and watched the band for a minute before turning to Troll Srenzo and pointing at her.

"I will have you now," he commanded.

In all the noise, there was no way his voice could be heard.

But, she did not have to read his lips, she knew what he wanted.

"First," she said, "we see the troll-king."

Trevir grinned. Delaying the inevitable was fine with him.

Trolls did not like permanent structures. Nowhere in the world will you find a troll castle—castles are for elf-kings and human royalty. The troll-king's yurt was over a mile away. Too far to walk. They got in a Hummer and the giant tires chewed through the mud all the way to the rear fringe of the festival.

The troll-king's structure was made of large carpets—all sopping wet in the rain with thick smoke pouring from a hole in the center. There were guards standing by the entrance, who lifted the drapery. Trevir and Troll Srenzo ducked in.

Inside, it was hot, smoky and humid. The smell was a physical assault. In the back, barely visible, the troll-king, Ovard Skäld, sat on an ironwood throne gnawing on a human skull. He was squat, of course, all trolls were, wide and muscular with a broad face, wide gash of mouth and black, broken teeth arranged like old tombstones.

Trolls were not known for humor, but Ovard found the lighter side of almost everything. He waved them in and pushed his wives off the seats to his sides to make room.

"Bring glogg, bring mead, bring meat," he commanded.

"No, we won't be staying," Trevir said. "I just stopped by to thank you and wish you safe travels."

"A woman, a child? We get to keep the bodies? It's nothing. A week to travel, a day to get the job done. A week getting back. It's our honor to serve."

"Leaving tomorrow?" Trevir said.

Ovard leaned back and steepled his stubby fingers.

"Oh," he said. "All those kegs of ale you brought—I doubt if my troops will be in any shape to travel tomorrow. By the end of the week, for sure. No later than Saturday."

Trevir was unimpressed.

"No later than Saturday."

"Right, yes, I'm sure. Friday, Saturday or Sunday. We'll drink on it."

"No, we have a show to manage—need to be on our way."

"Nonsense, there's always time for one drink, always."

He waved his hand and mugs of frothy drinks were presented on a short plank. The misshapen mugs were made from clay—they appeared to be crudely fashioned from the same brown mud that filled them. Trevir took a whiff, but did not drink. He put it down. Troll Srenzo enjoyed the troll concoctions, downed half, took a breath, downed the other half, then sat and looked at Trevir's mug with open desire.

Ovard was puzzled.

"What's the problem? It's black and tan with a shot of Portmagee 9 and a dusting of ashes of my ancestors."

Trevir stood.

"We really must be off," he said.

Back in the Hummer, Troll Srenzo burped.

"Gross," Trevir said.

Troll Srenzo grinned. In the troll world, the louder the belch, the greater the compliment. While watching the reveling trolls through the window, she spoke.

"Why are you sending *all* the trolls instead of ten or a hundred?"

"Because I want to be sure, that's why. Those women vex me and I want them gone."

"They'll scurry—run and hide like roaches. It will be wasted effort. They are weak. You can't really be afraid of them."

Trevir's mouth twisted into an ugly curl.

"Who said anything about being afraid? Even if all the magic world united, which it won't, that would be an inconvenience, not a threat. Simply put, I prefer to get this done now rather than later when we're busy with other things."

Troll Srenzo studied his face.

"But you *are* afraid. Why deny it?"

Trevir dismissed her question by waving his hand—as if waving away gnats.

"Ovard said your drink was sprinkled with the ashes of his

ancestors. Was he being literal?"

Troll Srenzo studied his face.

"I don't really think you want to know," she said.

Crystal Ball

IN A DARK living room, Kurt and Kelley were snuggled on the couch watching an old movie, *Practical Magic*. It was a favorite of Kelley's and she never grew tired of watching it. She had memorized much of the dialog. She leaned away from Kurt and struck a dynamic, pouting pose.

"We're going to grow old together. It's gonna be you and me, living in a big house. These two old biddies with all these cats."

Kurt protested.

"Now I'm an old biddie?"

"Yes, you are," Kelley said, laughing. "I like that Gillian."

"Of course you do, my sweet. She's the rebel, the one who goes off course. The passionate one who finds herself in trouble again and again."

Kelley fake-frowned.

Kurt continued, "That's not a BAD thing, sweetie. I think it's awesome. That's what I love—uh, like, I like about you—you don't care. I mean, you *do* care but you're not like girls who live for what others think of them—living and breathing to be accepted and part of the 'in crowd.' You're different." He quoted from the movie. "...when are you going to realize that being normal is not necessarily a virtue? It rather denotes a lack of courage."

She tried to let his words through her armor—it took several minutes while the movie played out before she accepted Kurt's comment as intended, as a compliment.

"This movie makes me think of Minnie," she said. "Minnie is like Sally, the *good* one, the one who denies her magic. The one who likes to stay safe all the time."

Kurt nodded in agreement.

"I see that."

"Not that there is any *real* magic in the world," she said.

Kelley had not seen what Kurt had seen. He was uncomfortable. The mood needed to change.

He purred into her ear.

"What do you want to do tonight?"

Kelley giggled.

"I like what we're doing right now."

From above, there were footsteps on the stairs. Not covert ones, these were exaggerated, heavy footfalls announcing themselves. Kelley pushed Kurt away and checked to make sure her blouse was arranged and the buttons were all secure. The lights were switched on, flooding the room. Kelley and Kurt blinked while their eyes adjusted.

From behind, Kelley's mother, Yvette, spoke.

"Are you watching that old flick again, Kay? You've seen it at least seventeen times."

"Kurt has only seen it three times," Kelley explained. "He needs to catch up."

"I came down to get a glass of water."

Right, Kelley thought.

"You know," Yvette continued, "there is some of this witchery in our blood." She cupped her hand around her mouth and fake whispered to Kurt. "My mother was Roma."

"Mom," Kelley said while making a shooing motion. "Aren't you dying of thirst or something?"

"Okay. Look, seriously, did you tell him about the…"

"Yes, Mom, he knows about the cutting and the scars. I don't do that anymore. Get your water and go to bed. Don't worry about us; we're not making babies or anything down here."

"Okay, dear, I trust you."

She turned and walked back upstairs.

Kurt whispered.

"I guess she wasn't all that thirsty after all."

Kelley poked him in the ribs.

"Shut up," she said.

"We're not making babies?"

"Not today, we're not, and not ever if you don't shut your yap and watch the movie."

They settled themselves—skootching closer together as the footsteps ascended the stairs.

Kurt's eyes drifted around the room and landed on a sphere sitting on a bookcase, a milky orb perched upon an ornate wooden stand. Through a gap in the curtains, a moonbeam played on it.

"Look how the moon makes that globe glow," he said.

"What?" She glanced over. "Oh, that. It's from my grandmother. Crystal ball. Ravenscroft, whatever that means. It's old, really old. We're not supposed to touch it, but I play with it now and then. It's really heavy and sometimes it's like a TV. I see images in it, like a dream or something. Silly, right?"

At that instant, his crutches fell over with a clatter.

It reminded him of why he needed them—his belly filled with dread.

"After the movie, I will get it for you if you want to check it out. Here's the tequila scene, so shut up, this is really good."

Along with the ladies in the kitchen-tequila scene, Kelley raised her arms and wriggled.

"Do you think you can dance like that?" Kurt said.

"Like what? It's not that hard."

"I mean partially dressed."

She elbowed him in the ribs, hard.

"Pig," she said, laughing.

As the movie rolled along, Kurt's eyes were drawn over and over to the glowing orb—he had one eye on the ball and one eye on the screen. His injuries ached. Slowly his ebullient mood waned. His ears echoed with a message from somewhere and he felt an urge—an urge to cradle the ball in his hands and gaze into it.

With the credits rolling, Kelley hopped up and ran to the crystal ball—and stood before it for what felt like an eternity. She felt sneaky, knowing she was not allowed to touch it, but couldn't control herself. She reached out and touched it with a fingertip. It woke. Placing her hands on it, it was warm and got warmer. It vibrated and sang to her.

Hobbling on his crutches, Kurt approached from behind her—standing and watching. Kelley moved in a slinky, cat-like way—moving her shoulders and hips in a way that stirred his insides.

She shouldn't hold that thing, he thought.

He wanted to say it, but he couldn't.

A purple mist formed in the crystal ball, then changed to a white fog laced with coiling black swirls. Glowing red eyes appeared. Kelley gasped. While she stared into the ball, Kurt put his hands on her hips. Frozen, she was unable to move her hands, as if they were glued into place.

A voice echoed in the room.

"Well, well, well, who are you, precious young lady? And who is with you? Oh, if it isn't my old friend Kurt. Last time I saw you I was—I was *in* you. Swimming in your skin and looking out through your eyes. You survived, good for you. I'm surprised, but it just means I can kill you again. What fun. And here you are with a nubile young thing ripe for the picking. My, my, Kurt, who would have guessed a loser like you could attract such a wonderful specimen. She would be lovely to add to my collection. Shall I take her, Kurt? Shall I take her—till the fertile soil and prepare her for your evil seed?"

Wide-eyed, Kelley stared deeply into the ball. Couldn't move, couldn't talk. She could scarcely breathe. Kurt's hands gently pulled at Kelley's hips, trying to move her away. The voice filled him with dread, but he was powerless.

"Yes, Kurt, powerless like before. You couldn't stop me then and you can't stop me now. And, even sweeter, I smell the brat princess Minnie in the wind. She's close by. It won't be long and you will all be mine—you'll be mine or die. And you, my sweet girl, you will be mine as well; to do with as I please. I'm coming soon, coming for all of you."

The reflected moonbeam vectored back into Kelley's eyes.

"Oh, my favorite, a cutter. You hate yourself, but not enough yet to really do it, dear. I can help you and it will feel like justice. It will feel like everything you deserve—everything you earned, dirty girl. I feel it and it feels good. It's the only thing that feels good. Just a little deeper. Press just a little harder. Artery. A little pinch and it's over.

"No," Kurt said.

He couldn't save himself, but he found the strength to save Kelley. Leaning over his crutches, he slapped the ball. It landed on the carpet with a thud and then rolled. In a tangle, they fell backwards onto the floor, breathing fast and hard.

Kelley spoke in a rapid-fire staccato with eyes darting around the room.

"What, how, what WAS that ugly thing?"

"Nothing good," Kurt said. "Whatever happened to me and whatever nearly killed me—that was it."

"I need to put it back."

Kurt pulled her back, turned her shoulders and looked into her eyes.

"No, don't touch it. Leave it there—at least until morning, okay?"

She nodded.

"Do you think we should talk to someone about this? My mother? Mr. Danvers? Minnie? I feel like we should."

Kurt, with Kelley wrapped in his arms, felt her heart beat.

"Yes, talk, but not your mother."

An image flooded his mind. The crystal ball appeared to flinch and scoot across the floor a fraction of an inch.

"I know who."

Kelley felt her spirit returning. She elbowed his ribs.

"You going to tell me, or do I need to kill you first?"

"We'll wrap that ugly thing in a towel, then, tomorrow, after school, we'll show it to Fiona. She'll know what to do."

Kelley looked puzzled.

"I don't know Fiona very well. Why her?"

Kurt shrugged.

"I'm not sure I can explain."

"Try or die," she said.

"It's because she is our Queen."

Kelley unwrapped herself from Kurt's arms and turned toward him.

"Whatever are you going on about? Queen?"

Kurt shrugged.

"I told you I can't explain what I'm feeling. After school, we'll go see her and see what she says. Okay?"

Kelley studied his face for a long moment.

"Okay," she said.

A Meeting of the Minds

THE MUD ROOM broom fell over from its hallowed place by the back door. Fiona looked up...then came a tentative knock. As if blaming the broom, Fiona gave it a look.

"Who on Earth could be knocking around at this hour?"

After standing the broom back up, she turned on the back stoop's light and opened the door. Before her stood Kelley and Kurt. They had something in a bag, though what she knew not.

"Hi, kids. Ummm, Minnie's asleep already because she wasn't feeling well...." her voice trailed off as she looked at them.

Something was wrong—she could see it in their eyes and could smell it on their skin.

"Come in. Tell me, what brings you here? Are you and your families okay?"

No words were spoken. They looked like they didn't know why they were there or how their unruly feet got them there.

"Ohhhhhkay. Um, let's take a seat in the kitchen and I'll brew some tea."

Kurt and Kelley followed dutifully behind Fiona, as if being pulled along by an invisible string. They seated themselves on the high stools around the butcher block counter. They took off their jackets and stared from each other to Fiona and back again. Kurt put his hand over Kelley's. It was still warm to the touch and tender from having embraced the crystal ball for so long.

Fiona set about making a tea of chamomile, lavender and honeysuckle. She also lit a candle she'd made from pine sap from a hidden barren she'd stumbled upon one day when she was out for a walk. As she lit the candle she instinctively whispered an incantation for protection.

Misfortune and ill omens don't belong
Waft away like the whippoorwill's song

A little magic can't hurt, she thought.

I hope.

The flame danced and sparkled beneath her waves and words. She caught the eye of Kurt and winked.

"It's sparks from the pine resin. No need to be alarmed."

She placed the steaming cups before Kurt and Kelley, sipped her own tea and waited. The words would come out soon enough, she just had to be patient.

"My Queen," began Kurt.

Fiona choked on her tea. She wasn't expecting *that* as the reward for her patience.

"Why did you call me that, Kurt? You always call me *Fiona*."

"I, I, I don't know. It just came to me. Forgive me, my Quee—Fiona."

"Nothing to forgive, Kurt. Now, where were we? Why do you darken my doorstep at this hour?"

The floodgates opened.

Kelley began.

"You see, there was this ball, this crystal ball. It's been in my family for years. They always said *don't touch it* but we were watching *Practical Magic* and Kurt saw it and then my mom came down and then the movie ended and then we touched it. Or rather, I touched it and it was like my hands were glued to it."

Kelley fired off words without taking a breath with eyes darting left and right and waving her hands frantically. Fiona noticed it all, even the sparks that danced on Kelley's fingertips as they danced in the air. She sat and observed, not saying a word. When Kelley finished every detail, Fiona turned to Kurt.

"Do you have anything to add?"

Kurt's eyes locked onto Fiona's.

"That voice, Fiona. The voice I heard in me right before the *incident*. The voice that sent me to the hospital. The voice that renders me powerless. The voice that knows you and Minnie. He said he was coming. He said he was going to enslave us all. Worship him or be killed. That voice, Fiona..." his voice trailed off.

Fiona tried to hide her reaction. She knew that voice—knew of what Kurt spoke and knew a trail could lead Trevir and the trolls to where they were hiding.

Fiona blew on her tea.

How much to tell?

How much do they already know?

She should help them; they were Minnie's friends, but she had to protect Minnie. Her internal battle waged on as she silently sipped her tea.

Kelley spoke in a meek voice.

"Fiona? Where are you?"

Fiona raised her eyes to meet Kelley's.

"I'm right here honey, just processing all you two said. May I see your hands, Kelley?"

Kelley held out her hands, palms up. Fiona reached across to lay her hands on top of them. They were still warm to the touch. Trevir had imprinted on her, to track her across the miles. Fiona said a quiet incantation as her hands were on Kelley's and they began to cool and a "snap" was heard. The bond was broken, the chord had been cut.

They heard a disembodied voice.

Bitch resonated in the air.

Kurt and Kelley spoke simultaneously.

"Did you hear that?"

Fiona gazed at them.

"Hear what? The wind? It is gusty tonight. Is that what you heard?"

The kids looked puzzled. Fiona knew what they had heard. She'd heard it too.

"Now, kids. It always feels funny calling you 'kids' because you most assuredly are *not* kids anymore. Let's start over. Friends. Yes, that feels more right. Kelley, you know magic isn't to be trifled with. It's a powerful force that exists in all things. It's the energy found in rock and dirt, trees and flowers, water and sun, humans and animals."

She looked at them to see if they understood. Both Kurt and Kelley nodded.

"There are dark things happening in the world; there always are, I'm afraid. Such is the way of this life; light balances with dark. Whatever you put into words, whatever energy you put out to the universe, always comes back three-fold. Do you know what that means?"

Kelley spoke first.

"It means it can come back to you three times as bad or three times as good, right?"

"Yes, exactly. So while you two did nothing egregiously wrong, you touched a magic ball when you weren't supposed to. Humans have this innate ability to be so curious. By touching it, you tapped into something on the other side, the dark side. Now I don't mean Darth Vader's dark side, I simply mean the unknown. You opened a cosmic door, if you will. Does that make sense?"

They nodded.

"The question now is, what do we do now? Any ideas?"

Kurt and Kelley sat in silence, sipping their tea. Fiona pondered how far to go with explanation when Kelley piped up.

"In the movie, they buried the body, but it came back. Then the Aunties and all their friends fixed it and poured magical brew over it so the body went back into the Earth and stayed there."

"Go on..." urged Fiona.

"Couldn't we bury the crystal ball?"

"Wouldn't your mother notice it was gone?"

"Well, I could say that I felt it needed a cleansing so I buried it in the Earth to recharge."

"You could do that; it would only need to be buried for a few hours so your mum may not even notice. You could run it under pure and clean water, while visualizing the negative energy going down the drain. You could also pass it through sage smoke, or even pour holy water over it. Any or all of those would work."

"Do you want to seeeeeee it?" asked Kelley with a gleam in her eyes.

Instinctively, Fiona recoiled.

"No, no, I'm all set. I think there's been enough excitement for one evening. For now, leave it here with me. Are you two okay to walk yourselves home or would you like me to drive you?"

That was Fiona's less than gracious way of telling them it was time for them to go. Kurt spoke first.

"I think we'll be okay to walk. The night air feels good and it's not all that far. Are you okay with that, sweetie?"

Fiona smiled at the puppy love. Once upon a time she felt that flutter too; but it was long since gone.

Kelley spoke.

"Yah, I'm feeling better already. I'm glad you suggested coming here to Fiona's. You were right. She's awesome."

She jumped up and gave Fiona a hug.

Fiona almost fell over and giggled.

"Alright you two, get out of here. Be safe and I'll take care of the crystal ball for now. Enjoy your walk."

She walked to the edge of the driveway and watched them until they were no longer in sight. Luna joined her watched them as well. Fiona looked down at him and whispered.

"How much longer do we have, Luna? How much longer until we're found?"

Luna meowed and sauntered back inside. He was in no mood to have this conversation; not while he knew there was a saucer of room-temperature milk waiting inside with his name on it.

Fiona chided herself on the small magics she could not stop. They were instinctive and automatic.

They can only lead to trouble.

Inside, the ball was heavy in her hands…and warm. Its depths drew her eyes, but she resisted until it could be wrapped in an old towel. After donning an old sweater, she walked outside to the composting pile. With a trowel, she dug deep, then placed the ball and buried it.

Behind her, the wind whispered in the trees. She cocked her head and listened, but the voices were too far away to be understood.

Minnie, the Scold

STANDING IN FRONT of the stove's gas flame and waiting for the teapot's water to roll to a boil, Fiona studied the box for the new tea she was trying. Waykana Guayusa. Healthy coffee alternative, boost energy, performance and mental clarity, antioxidant tea, naturally sweet, no bitterness.

Feel the Jaguar Energy!

Shall we just see about that? she thought.

There was a wisp of airy melody in her head. Idly, she tried to track it down, but it was slippery.

Selkie unzips her skin…

The steam built and teapot wanted to sing—it was right on the edge of melody.

Loralie sings the song for lovers who were torn apart then left broken hearted…

With her index finger, she moved her hand around the teapot and marked index and compass points. She felt an urge to sprinkle salt. The only salt at hand was a PH-balanced salt from

Argentina...Chet's aquarium was long gone, but its crystal-salt lingered. She poured a heap in her palm, whispered secret words to it, then tossed it in the air—for an instant it caught the morning sunlight and made a million floating, kaleidoscopic, hypnotic prisms.

As vivid as the room, splayed pages appeared before her eyes. It was an unknown book, one she was sure she'd never read or even seen before, but here it was. An ancient book, a grimoire, *The Keys of Solomon.*

This will be tea for divination, she whispered. *Impart unto me thy knowledge—that which has been brought to thee on the four winds.*

She heard rustling from Minnie's nook. Turning, she admired Minnie's tousled hair and the shorts and ragged, over-sized t-shirt the waif wore as pajamas. The teenager looked like she was six.

Minnie pointed an accusing finger.

"What are you doing?" she said.

The spell Fiona was casting dissolved. At that instant, the teapot whistled like a siren—a disturbing sound in the quiet room.

Over her shoulder, Fiona said, "Have a seat...I'll pour your tea."

Hoping to lighten the mood, Fiona stood on her tip-toes and carefully brought down Minnie's favorite cup and saucer. It was something Minnie's mother had found in a thrift shop. Antique, a French mother holding a basket...escorted by her wily goose.

While pouring hot water over the teabags, Fiona absently recited a rhyme.

Sing a song of sixpence, a bag full of rye
Four and twenty naughty boys, baked in a pie

Minnie was unmollified. Her tone was troubled and harsh.

"Mom..."

Fiona interrupted.

"Hold on, Minnie, dear, I need to show you something."

She put her jacket on over her nightgown and slipped her feet into her boots.

"I'll be right back."

For the few minutes Fiona was gone, Minnie watched the steeping tea while the caramel-colored infusion swirled in the old china cup.

Fiona came back and she dropped the heavy, towel-wrapped ball on the table.

Minnie was afraid to ask.

"What is this?"

"Open it," Fiona said.

"No. When we left the sanctuary, you asked me to vow to never use magic. I skated around that promise, but you were right. Using magic comes to no good. The Black Faerie Prince will find us."

"King," Fiona said.

"What?"

"He's the young King now," Fiona said quietly.

"That's a meaningless distinction. King or prince, it doesn't matter, he's dangerous and his strength is growing. I can feel it. Weren't you paying attention to what happened to Kurt? He almost died."

"Ah," Fiona said. She pointed at the dirty bundle on the table. "I should have told you. Kurt came to visit. With Kelley. He brought that."

She loosened the towel and unwrapped the ball. Drawing light from the room, it glowed.

Tears filled Minnie's eyes.

"You asked me to give up the magic world. It took time, but I recognized the necessity. I did it. I closed off that part of me. But now, you make incantations over stupid stuff like tea. You'll get us all killed. We'll die. You have to stop, Mom."

Fiona was filled with an infinite sadness. They sat in silence while Minnie's words echoed—bouncing between them like ping pong balls. The crystal ball twitched, then rolled slowly and deliberately toward Minnie. She watched it with horror. Her teacup was in the way and was brusquely pushed aside. She barely saved the cup and saucer before they were smashed on the floor. Abruptly standing, her chair tipped over backwards. The ball reached the edge of the table and sat there, quivering.

Leaning over the table, Fiona's eyes were closed. Her concentration was complete, then she had a moment of perfect clarity.

"Oh, Minnie," she said. "Can you see what this means?"

Minnie could not lift her eyes from the vibrating ball—it drew her eyes like a magnet attracts steel.

While studying Minnie's face, Fiona continued.

"This means magic exists in the world whether we reject it or not. We can't push it away. No matter how much we might try, we can't kill the magic world. Kurt and Kelly brought this to me—thinking I would know what to do. I don't know what to do, but I was wrong to ask you to reject the other world, *our* other world."

The light from the ball grew more intense—like a tiny sun. Tears streamed down Minnie's tortured face.

"The King will come to us—and he will kill us."

Fiona placed the dirty towel across the ball and blocked its light. With the spell broken, Minnie took a deep breath and tried to shake off dread.

"You're right," Fiona said with strength growing in her voice, "he will come. But, can he kill us? We'll see about that."

She stood, reached over to place her hand on Minnie's shoulder and spoke quietly.

"I don't know what to do, but I was wrong to ask you to swear off magic. That said, until we have a plan, we have to keep a low profile—live quietly and hope he has other things on *his* mind for a while. He's far away. It will be a while before he gets to us. For now, get ready for school, dear."

Minnie nodded and walked back to her nook.

Fiona sipped her tea. It was cold.

Sighing and filled with infinite sadenss, she turned and poured it down the sink.

Fiona was pleased to have fresh, organic blueberries for Minnie's breakfast of Kashi multigrain cereal and clotty cream skimmed from the top of whole milk from a local dairy, but all this was lost on the young woman, who picked at her bowl and only ate half before giving up. Fiona felt bad for the girl and thought it was odd how they reversed positions back and forth.

Of course the girl was confused and frustrated. They grappled with big, important decisions. Was it right to run? Was it better to stand and fight, even if losing was inevitable? Life was filled with conflicting information and tough decisions. Standing at the sink washing Minnie's breakfast dishes, Fiona looked out through the window into the verdant, dripping woods. She thought about brewing another cup of tea, but decided to go for a walk instead.

It was an inhospitable day for a stroll, but that's what called her. She pulled on gloves, boots and a yellow slicker—tucking her wild hair into the hood. For a minute, she stood on the stoop and watched the rain ooze from the dark sky. The cloud cover was dense—like a dripping sponge. On impulse, she picked up the crystal ball.

Maybe I'll walk it home.

To take the first step, it took steeling her will, but once she moved, she trudged and kept trudging. Soon the woods enveloped her. For a while, the trail took her along the creek, which was swirling and angry, but she skipped over a slippery wooden bridge and went deeper and deeper.

To rest a minute, she leaned against an outcropping of cold granite and looked around. In the shelter of the rock, most of the rain poured all around her, but mostly missed her cooling body.

Life was everywhere, but it was the slow-life of moss, fungus, mushrooms, lichens and ferns. All around were the relentless agents of rot and mold—breaking down discarded wood, fallen leaves and lost animals whose spirits had transformed and left their body-shells.

She analyzed her mood, but could not figure it out—she was torn in a million directions. The scene before her eyes was gloomy, but filled with questing, striving life. Wrapped in its sodden towel, the ball vibrated. Sighing, she loosened the knot and unveiled the ball—holding it before her face and out in the rain where it was washed by the cleansing spirit of fresh water molecules and dissolved minerals. Trevir's handsome face floated before her, grinning with malice and glee. Surrounding him was firelight and milling bodies. The air was shredded with distorted guitars and a screaming singer, but Trevir's words came through clearly.

"Fiona, where's the sprout? I have things to show you. Beautiful, wonderful things, one after the other."

Instantly, she was angry.

"You can rot in hell, bastard."

Trevir laughed.

"That's what these losers said, each and every one of them."

The scene in the ball shifted to the fires which burned with evil intensity. Trolls pulled charred bodies from the flames and ate them just as they liked, burned on the outside and raw and bloody on the inside. The bones were tossed to the hounds.

The scene shifted. In the background, guillotine blades flashed, over and over. Severed heads were arranged in rows—one after the other displayed with horror written in half-lidded eyes peering out of mud and blood.

It was, by far, the most awful and terrifying thing Fiona had seen. Crying, her knees gave out and she collapsed.

"You—"

She couldn't speak.

"If you had more courage," Trevir said, "maybe you could have saved them. Queen. I spit on you, Queen. You are the Queen of nothing, the Queen of Filth. More likely, your head would be here in my beautiful collection. Yours and that loser-princess, side-by-side. What do you think of that?"

Fiona struggled to her feet.

Gathering her strength, she threw the ball as hard and as far as she could. As it arced in the sky, Trevir's face rotated and his laughter echoed in the trees. Again, she collapsed to her knees and covered her face with her hands. The faces of the doomed would haunt her dreams for a long time, she knew it.

What can I do?

Images flashed through her mind and settled on one, a dark and gloomy night in a shopping center parking lot, picking up loose change, penny-by-penny, nickel-by-nickel, dime-by-dime.

For some reason, it was important to get it all and into the hands of the sad woman who needed help.

Fiona remembered.

It was the first time she'd laid her eyes on the miniature Minnie.

It suddenly flooded her mind.

That was not the first time she'd seen Minnie.

There was a laughing little girl just north of Portsmouth at York's Wild Kingdom—feeding a kid-goat a handful of hay. Handsome father. Healthy mother. A sunny, perfect day.

There were dark days in the little girl's future, unbelievably hard days, but not this one, this one perfect one.

Why?

Why so many brutal days and so few heavenly, wonderful ones?

If it was possible to hide and be safe, she'd do it—do it for Minnie—in an instant without any thought.

But, was there any place in the world that was safe?

The remotest, hidden corner, anywhere?

The image of one final errant penny filled her mind. An insignificant, tiny and worthless coin hidden in the shadow of a tire and drowned in a puddle.

As close to invisible as anything could be.

But, Fiona found it and handed it over to Minnie's mom where it belonged.

As insignificant as it was, it was the last good thing that happened in Minnie's mom's life.

Please, what does this mean?

On the wind, the only answer was the faint echo of The Black Faerie King's laughter.

Filled with confusion and despair, she got up and walked back to their little home.

Lost and Found

THE END OF the school year was quickly coming into view and the big homecoming dance was on the horizon. All the students were abuzz with energy. They rented tuxedos and hemmed up and took in the seams of their gowns. It was all anyone could talk about for a week.

Everyone, except Minnie.

She was not in the mood and wanted no part of the social swirl. Wandering through the halls in a solemn daze and bubble of invisibility was generally working. She didn't want to be bothered. She didn't want to interact. Simply put, she wanted to be left alone.

The only student who could not accept *no* for an answer was the man-monster, Buster Cantwell.

"Who told you persistence is a virtue?" she said.

"Everyone knows that. Besides, you know my dad is a salesman, right? It's in my blood."

"The answer is still no. Thank you, I'm flattered, but no."

He pointed to their reflection in a plate glass window.

"We make the cutest couple ever."

"We look like an elephant and an ant."

This caused them to think of the antics of the carnival elephants—Buster was the rear end of one. He showed off his well-practiced backwards-elephant kick.

It was funny then and it was funny now.

Minnie laughed out loud.

"Tell me you're going with someone else and I will leave you alone."

He wasn't stupid, so she didn't want to talk down to him. Still, she wanted to be one-hundred-percent clear.

"I'm not going with you. I'm not going with anyone. I'm not going. Besides, you know my heart is..."

He interrupted.

"Yes, the mysterious stranger. We know. I still think it was the alpaca."

He referred to Eduardo, a South American camel brought in from a local farm for the petting zoo...it had escaped its tether and roamed the carnival until the ten-year-old llama-wrangler could catch up. Buster's irreverent theory was that the alpaca copped a kiss—which is why no one saw Minnie's mysterious stranger.

"No, it wasn't Eduardo," she said. "His breath did not smell anything like alfalfa, okay?"

"Come on, Minnie. It's a dance. Just for fun. I'm not suggesting we get married and I ruin you for Mister Mystery forever."

The class bell sounded.

"Gotta go," she said.

"Talk to you later, Minnie," he replied. "You'll change your mind."

"If I do, you'll be the first or second to know."

The day dragged on and on, but eventually the final bell sounded and the prisoners were freed for the weekend. Minnie raced home—evading Buster along the way.

While walking, Fiona's words filled her head.

"I was wrong to ask you to reject the other world, *our* other world."

The words rang true, but they stung like antiseptic alcohol poured on a fresh wound.

How could Fiona have been so hell-bent on hiding, and then with one visit from Kurt and Kelley, completely change her tune? How fair was that? Did she not see how much I gave up to be normal? Did she not see how dangerous it was to open the door and let magic back in? How could she be so flippant as to float from one end of the spectrum to the other?

Minnie shook her head. It was too much. She couldn't think. She needed space. She needed open space with no humans.

The forest. She needed the forest—its stillness and solitude. She needed peace and knowing only wild trees could provide. She needed it and she needed it now.

After making her way home, unseen and unheard, she dropped her pack in her room, put on warmer clothes and simply said to Fiona, "I'm going into the woods. I'll be back in a while."

Fiona understood—for she'd been there herself.

All she could think of to say was, "Be safe."

Minnie wandered down the road and turned where the trees told her to enter. She was tuning in, and it felt good. She'd missed this. This magical world that was such a part of her.

"I'm sorry I ever left you," she whispered to the air.

After walking on a pine needle laden trail for a bit she found a good sitting rock; a boulder left unceremoniously behind by a bygone glacier.

Fire.

"Yes, I need a fire. A small one."

She gathered dry bits of fallen branches and pine bark that had been shed—along with moss and paper skin from the birch trees that encircled her site. She made her pyre and whispered an incantation. The fire sprang to life. She looked around like a small child who had just stolen from a cookie jar.

"Just a few words and a small spell can't do that much harm. It's no more than Fiona did just this morning over tea."

She spat out the words like she'd just swallowed a mouthful of burdock.

An oily voice interrupted her spat.

"My, my, what's this? Is there a rift between you and your gracious queen?"

Minnie whipped around—expecting to see someone standing near, but there was no one.

She tuned in.

Crap. The Black Faerie—King.

Instinctively, she said, "Shove it, Trevir. There's no rift. Go. Away. Leave us alone."

"Oh, my sweet Minnie, I'll never leave you alone. I'll hunt you and Fiona down, find you and have my way with each of you. You'll rue the day you ever..."

"Oh, shut up, Trevir. Begone!"

She waved her hand in such a way that he truly was gone; for the short while anyway, then emitted a sigh. It felt as if all the trees and creatures sighed with her.

"This, Fiona," she muttered, "this is what you don't understand. Trevir found us. You opened the pathway. It's only a matter of time and he will be here."

Minnie sat on her log and hung her head.

"But, then again, we *are* magic. It's in our blood. We are powerful. If we don't use magic, then others will. Take Kurt and Kelley. They don't even know what they're doing and look what happened. Why does this have to be so hard? Why does it all have to be so confusing? Why us, Fiona, why?"

She closed her eyes and thought of Sean and the Fachan. They had been so happy in their magical home. Deep down, she longed for that life again. It was all so simple. It was both yesterday and a lifetime ago. Would she ever see them again?

Minnie stared at the fire, lost in her thoughts. First this way and then that. Magic, then no magic. Run away or stand your ground. Fight or cower. She sat forever it seemed, with her body present but her mind far, far away. Slowly, her mind sorted through things—and eased into a deeper perspective.

For the junior promenade dance, the gym was decorated with colorful crepe paper and balloons. The dance was well under way—the band played top-40 hits with ear-splitting enthusiasm and little skill, but it didn't matter—under the colorful lights and the rotating mirror ball, the evening served its purpose. With boutonnières, corsages, lipstick and fresh haircuts, the young, dressed in satin gowns and rented tuxedos, milled, gossiped and worked on their boogie. They were all excited about the nearing end of the school year, but also afraid of impeding high school life and adulthood.

The next year, it was inevitable that Lacey would be the Spring Queen, but this year she watched. To the backbeat, her body moved automatically, but she felt like something was missing. Something important.

On crutches, Kurt could move not much, but Kelley made up for it by energetically rotating and wriggling in circles around him. She was a sight—dressed in black from head to toe, from Dr. Martens boots to a black beret.

The religious fundamentalists would be horrified, but the young adults pirouetted in forgotten rites of Spring—the kiss of the Earth and the Sacrifice—celebrating fertility, the circle of life and the world's rebirth after the long, cold winter.

Across the room, Lacey's date, Art Paige poured punch for a cheerleader—he would not miss Lacey if she instantly dropped into the center of the Earth. There were people who cared about her, deeply cared, but the main and most important person was not present.

There was something wrong.

Instantly, Lacey felt guilty. Cheerful Minnie was troubled and sad about something, but Lacey was too consumed with planning her wardrobe to connect the dots.

Like a bull, Buster plowed through the crowd. Lacey had promised him a dance and he would not be deterred. The rental shop did not have a tux that was big enough; his wrists and white socks were exposed in several wide inches.

She stopped him with an index finger.

"We'll dance, but not here," she said.

A wave of confusion washed over his face.

"Then where?"

"Get Kelley and Kurt and I'll show you."

They slipped out a side door and stood in the parking lot looking up at the moon.

"Minnie needs us," Lacey said.

"How will we find her?" Kelley said.

Kurt, leaning on his crutches, pointed across the highway and into the dark woods.

"I can find her," he said.

Rejoining the world, Minnie looked around and was surprised to find the Misfits there with her.

"When did you get here?"

"A while ago," Kelley said. "The dance was no fun without you. Your fire drew us here. When we all got here you were in a trance state so we watched over you. We've been soul-searching with you."

Minnie hugged Kelley—the rest of the crowd gathered and joined in. They laughed and cried and began to feel better.

Buster tapped Lacey on the shoulder.

"Now?" he said.

Minnie jumped to her feet.

"No. Me first."

Buster tipped his head back and laughed. Basso profundo—his joy filled the clearing.

The ant and the elephant.

She reached up—he gently took her hands. The Misfits clapped and hovering over his crutches, Kurt clapped in rhythm while the giant and the minnow spun in circles around the fire and the fleeing moon chased the treetops.

While everyone danced with everyone, they were watched by

several pairs of eyes, and the number grew as the night proceeded. Wood elves. Pixies. Faeries. Word spread through the forest.

After everyone tired out and sat staring into the flames, Minnie realized that her band of Misfits would stand by her through anything—they'd be there when she called, when Fiona called. With her thoughts clear, with her path more known and the dawn sun a hint on the horizon, Minnie declared it was time to leave. They slowly and carefully tamped out the fire. Minnie wove her fingers in a spell to keep the area safe and sacred.

Things were beginning to change, and change was sometimes good.

Sometimes, very good.

The Watchers

AS THE MISFITS danced about the fire and their laughter and merriment filled the air, they were being watched. With every step they took, with every song they sang and with each and every breath, more and more magic was spun into the air.

It began with a Luna moth. She was quietly perched upon a thin vine wrapped around an elder oak tree on the outskirts of the glade. She watched, twitched her antennae and started to tap her delicate leg.

"It's starting," she whispered.

Her whisper grew inside of her until she could no longer contain it. She flew up and up, higher and higher—all the while yelling.

"It's starting!"

With her cry, birds emerged from their sleeping roosts, chipmunks came out from their hollows and red squirrels descended down the trunks.

"Could it be?"

"Could it really be?"

"Dare we hope Minnie is awakening?"

Unseen and unknown, they inched ever closer to the band. The laughter and singing was utterly contagious. No one but the forest dwellers seemed to notice delicate sparks of blue and purple arising from the fire. No one noticed that with each step Minnie took she nearly floated off the ground.

No one noticed, but the animals did.

"We must let the others know," whispered a gray squirrel. She turned to a fawn and her mother who were hidden amongst the growth, but watching with wide eyes.

"Go. Go and find Sebastian. You know where he's camped. He'll want to see this for himself. Fly like the wind."

As the revels carried on, wood elves and sprites appeared. Woodland faeries and pixies flew in and perched upon the branches. Delicate dryads swayed to the music. What to a mere mortal would appear as falling leaves and petals from flowering trees were really magical sparks and faeries upon the backs of swiftly flying dragonflies.

Eventually Sebastian appeared. He'd come with Ancamna.

Princess Ancamna lived in a castle and was accustomed to silk, satin and finery, but when faced with a hard choice between fleeing or fighting, she'd taken up a sword and leathers. Impatient with commonfolk and cowards, She was in no mood to venture out to see these pathetic humans, but for Sebastian she acquiesced. She'd given up on them; they'd always disappointed her.

From the underbrush, they stood watching; watching and taking it all in. Ancamna sniffed the air. Trevir had been here, but the Princess had sent him away.

"Interesting," was all she could bring herself to say.

"See, Ancamna, they're waking up. It began with Minnie. No, no, it began with Queen Fiona..."

Ancamna solemnly spoke and hung her head.

"No, Sebastian, it began with David dying. It began with something that never should have happened."

"Now see HERE, missy! I honor and respect you, but enough is enough. Yes, David should never have died. The world is a far less wonderful place without him in it. But, BUT, you have got to let it go; at least for now. David would NOT want his death to be the end of it all. He would want us all to go on and fight. Fight the darkness; not let it overtake us all. He KNEW, Ancamna. He KNEW the magic of our world. He preached it every single day; 'You are all beings of light, perfect in every way.' Humans are slow on the uptake sometimes; I'll give you that. But eventually they arrive. Fiona is waking. Minnie and her band are waking as we stand here. Our time draws nigh. We can't squelch this, Ancamna. We have to help it grow. We have to give it power. The ONLY way to do what needs to be done is to help them along. It's time you got out of your own way and helped."

Ancamna looked down on Sebastian who stood tall with his hands upon his hips. All the nearby creatures watched and held their breath. No one had stood up to Ancamna before. She was not one to be trifled with. A spitfire of a fae, her mood could turn on a dime.

She let out a sigh. She picked up Sebastian in her hand.

"Perhaps you are right, Sir Sebastian. Perhaps you are right. But, when I see Fiona, I'm sorry, she's acted weak and not as my queen. I will try, but I can't promise…"

She closed her eyes and worked her lithe fingers in such a way no one could accurately follow. As if conducting an invisible orchestra, she spoke the ancient fae words that would protect the hollow and allow magic to flourish. It would be a place where humans and non-humans alike could return to recharge. They wouldn't know why they were drawn here, but drawn there they would be. Drawn to heal, drawn to learn, drawn to grow stronger.

For their part, the misfits simply noticed that the glow of the fire suddenly began to burn more brightly. Minnie caught the most faint wisp of chamomile on the air and noticed that clovers were starting to spring up around the edge of the copse.

"They're watching and joining in," she whispered under her

breath.

She turned to where she sensed the watchers, gave a small bow and blew a kiss. Sebastian caught the kiss in his hand and emitted a very un-gnomelike giggle. Ancamna shook her head.

"Minnie is young, I forgive her, but Fiona should know better. Our people…" Ancamna choked off a sob. "Trevir and the Black Death is coming and our queen hides like a rat in a hole. We'll all be better off if I mount her head on a pole."

"You don't mean that," Sebastian said. "You sound like Trevir himself."

Ancamna flushed with rage. She glowed.

"I don't mean it? What I wouldn't give to NOT mean it. We're not going to beat him if we run and hide. We'll die. Everyone will die. Campfires and pies will not stop what's coming."

She drew her sword. It gleamed in the firelight.

"I don't mean it? She'll take her place and lead us, or, by the power of Lenus Mars, I will end her days, I swear it."

Solemn, Sebastian stared at the ground while the youngsters danced.

No Pie

BEING THURSDAY EVENING, Mr. Miller stopped in for Chet's meatloaf. It was a special, not-on-the-menu recipe with morel mushrooms, sundried tomatoes and almost, but not quite, too much fresh-shredded horseradish.

As he scooped up the last forkful, Fiona walked over and refreshed his iced tea.

"Saved room for pie?" she said. "Fresh Montmorency sour-cherry."

Mr. Miller grimaced.

"You changed something. The pies are not as good."

The last few months, pies had been unsold and were donated to the gleaners. This pained her, but she tilted her head back and laughed.

"No. Same recipe as always. Same fresh, local ingredients."

He pushed his plate away and patted his round belly.

"So you say. Sorry, Fiona. All filled up. No pie."

"I'll get your bill," she said.

She didn't lie; there was nothing different in the ingredients. However, other than a few random, minor spells, magic had been banished and it was true, the pies were not as good. However, this morning she had unleashed something in the kitchen—something missing for all of the dismal year.

She asked for a cottage-magic, green blessing from the kitchen witch…it was asked for and granted. The pies were fully wonderful—and the cherry pie was still warm from the oven. With a scary-sharp Santoko trimmer knife, she sliced an impossibly thin sliver and placed it in the center of her favorite—a large, scalloped, floral-decorated pioneer platter. She delicately added a thimble-sized serving of vanilla ice cream. It was absurd, but not yet perfect. After adding a spiral of cherry syrup and a dusting of powdered sugar, she looked around and added a serving fork that seemed to be designed for a giant.

Now it was perfect—hardly a mouthful, beautifully presented.

After easing out from the kitchen on floating feet and barely hesitating, she dropped the huge platter in front of Mr. Miller.

Complaining, he said, "I said I didn't want…"

She was already three steps away and grinning at him over her shoulder. His eyes drifted to the oversized platter and the microscopic morsel.

"This is an insult," he said while pushing the platter away. "No tip," he muttered.

He picked up the giant fork.

"Ran out of shovels, did they."

His impulse was to push the plate over the edge of the table just to hear it shatter, but instead he scooped up the ice cream and pie and jammed it in his mouth—just to get it out of his sight.

The taste was vivid and surprising.

Okay, he thought. *Okay*.

Slowly, she wandered back and dropped his check on the table.

"I will be your cashier when you're ready," she said.

"That wasn't a piece of pie," he said. "That was a flyspeck.

Where's the rest of it?"

Last week we were donating unsold pies to the homeless shelter, she thought.

"You said you didn't want any."

Mr. Miller glared at her.

"Don't test me, woman."

"I think I forgot to mention something…"

"What?"

"Whole pies went up five bucks," she said.

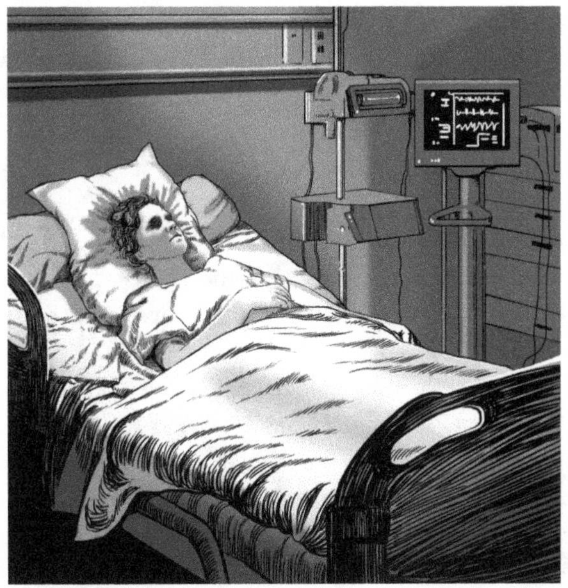

An Unexpected Message

CHET HAD GONE home for the night. Fiona was outside, composting the daily scraps, when he'd waved goodbye. She'd been humming as she overturned and mixed the soil with the new offerings. In her fingers, she felt the soil's energy and the Earth Mother's gratitude for the nourishment.

"Back to the Earth you go," she whispered.

Rising, she stretched her back, then walked toward the back door. Something was happening; she felt the downy hairs on her arm stand up. Spinning on her heels and studying the woods, she saw nothing.

Nothing. Just the cool evening air on my skin.

After rinsing out the bucket and leaving it outside to dry, she opened the backdoor and walked into the kitchen. In darkness, there was a figure sitting on the counter with dangling legs. She flipped on the light.

It was Sebastian, the field gnome from faraway Maine. The tiny gnome was old and weathered and his tunic and trousers were stained and dusty. He looked weary, weary beyond any human weariness. Towering over the slight Sebastian was the militant Ancamna. No longer draped in fine, red ribbons, she had donned war attire with a longsword in a leather sheath. With a displeased look on her face, she stood stiff as a statue with her arms crossed.

Fiona flashed back to the last time she'd seen them. It was a lifetime past and she instantly thought of her dear friends and neighbors: David and Elizabeth. Fiona fired off questions as quickly as they entered her mind.

"What, how, when?" sputtered Fiona like a boiling tea kettle. "How did you know where I was? How did you find me? When did you get here? Did anyone see you?"

Ancamna's face took on an impatient expression. Sebastian placed his hand on hers, cupping it as it rested on the pommel of her sword. He gave her a look of warning.

"Of course we knew where you were, we've known all along, Fiona. We knew you and Minnie found a safe haven. We traveled from the East upon the backs of the migrating geese. We came undetected. All is still safe..."

Ancamna stamped her feet and growled.

"No, it's not," she said through gritted teeth.

Sebastian gave her another look, one of warm, fatherly kindness.

"Let's simmer down and be patient," he said.

Fiona sat on a stool and pondered what to say next.

"So, how is home? How's David and Elizabeth? How's your family, Sebastian? How's, um, Sean and the Fachan and the house? Is it all still safe and sound?"

Sebastian smiled.

"Ah, Fiona, my family is well, thank you for asking. As promised, we've been keeping an eye on your old homestead. Every once in a while we sense darkness, but when we go to investigate, there's nothing to be found. Sean and the Fachan are..."

Ancamna could take no more. Glaring at Fiona, she had

nothing but bitterness and disdain in her green, gleaming eyes. The blade of her sword shone brightly in its sheath, hungry for retribution.

"No! Enough! This is not some friendly get-together where we sit around sipping tea, eating cookies, telling stories and exchanging pleasantries! I won't stand for it. Not now!"

"Ancamna, that is not how you speak to Queen Fiona."

"Queen? What sort of Queen lets her world sink into the black ooze while she bakes pies? What sort of Queen looks the other way, abandoning her friends and loved ones to evil? What kind of Queen refuses to step up and do what must be done? What kind of Queen ignores her daughter and her plights? Tell me Sebastian, what kind of Queen do we have?"

Sebastian bowed his head. Though the delivery was harsh, her words rang true. He could not bring himself to look at Fiona—who hung her head as reality came crashing down upon her.

She let out a sigh; a sigh the whole world could feel. The sigh of one laying at the bottom of a ravine at night, knowing no one would come to help and the only way to save herself was to start climbing. The sigh of one no longer willing to run from fate. The sigh lasted and lasted and lingered longer than the air in her lungs.

She steeled her will and asked a simple question of Ancamna.

"So tell me, what happened?"

Ancamna bowed her head.

"It's David. He's dead."

Fiona felt her world spin. She tried to stand and slowly fell to the floor instead.

"Fiona," cried Sebastian. To Ancamna, he said, "Did you have to blurt it out it like that?"

"Yes, yes, I did," she replied coldly.

As Fiona lay on the floor, Ancamna dropped to her knees and pinched Fiona's arm with such force, with such anger—to Fiona, it felt like a burning poker shooting straight through.

"Ow," she screeched.

"Are you okay, my Queen?" said Sebastian while running toward her.

"Oh, no, you don't get to act that way this time, Fiona," spat Ancamna. "No, no, NO! You don't get to lie around and drift through the various stages of grief, only to run away like a dog with its tail between its legs. Oh, no, Fiona. Not. This. Time. You did that with Llwyd. We all turned the other way and let you wallow in your cowardice and see how it felt to grieve. We all hoped you would rise from the ashes but noooo, you ran across the whole country only to land here and bake pies! Pies?? PIES?!? You left us to our own defenses, never looking back. You care nothing for this world, Fiona. Magic is leaving; or have you even noticed? Your daughter Minnie has abandoned her path. She is being influenced by those who do not have her best interests at heart. Did you even notice?? Do you even notice ANYTHING anymore, Fiona? Tell me. What are you doing to save this world?"

Ancamna backed away and spoke rapidly quickly in Fae, waving her arms madly about and turning various shades of green. Sebastian made his way to Fiona and sat on the floor next to her, his hand upon hers. He had a worried look about him, one that scared Fiona. She knew Ancamna was right, and she also knew the faerie wasn't done.

Ancamna came back, looking more composed—composed like a dangerous pot of simmering water. One wrong word from Fiona and she would boil over. Fiona knew she had to take whatever came next.

"David. He and Elizabeth had been out gardening. I was helping them. I'd been staying close because I'd felt a darkness as of late—a mist that had begun showing itself here and there. David climbed a ladder to clean out a gutter. There was a bird's nest in there and he wanted to relocate it so it would be safe. Before I could get to him, the mist appeared and David was on the ground. The police report—useless— says it was a freak accident whereby the ladder shifted, but that is not the case. David was transported to the hospital where he was in a coma for twenty-four hours. When he awoke, Elizabeth had to tell him that he was paralyzed. This, on top of his other ailments as of late, led to a discussion. Would he survive? Yes. Would his life be what it was?

No. Elizabeth made sure he understood everything, all of his options, all of his future challenges. David indicated he did not want to live that way. With his beloved by his side, David asked Elizabeth to pull the plug. Life support was removed and David took his last breath while Elizabeth held him close and sang into his ear."

They all bowed their heads. Fiona began weeping.

"I should have been there. I could have helped...I could have prevented...poor Elizabeth...what will she do?"

"Yes, Fiona, you should have been there and yes, you could have prevented this from happening. But instead, you were here, baking pies. We lost Llwyd. Now we've lost David. Both because of you, Fiona."

Those words hovered in the air, filling the space between them. Ancamna slowly and deliberately spoke.

"So, Fiona, the question is: what will you do now? Will you rise as Queen or will you continue to hide until everyone and everything you cherish in this world is slowly and tortuously destroyed by the evil faerie king Trevir and his odious trolls?"

Sebastian looked up at Fiona. Ancamna refused to avert her glare. Scarcely a breath was taken.

Fiona slowly raised her head with a steely gaze.

"It is time," was all she said. "It. Is. Time."

The Halifax Gibbet

TREVIR'S TROLLSTOCK HAD been filmed by roving camera crews who captured endless scenes of violence and mayhem. It pleased Trevir; the file server in his computer system was filled with hours and hours of video. On his flatscreen wall, the images were huge and vivid—it was like he was there once again. Better than there. *Everywhere* in high-definition with great audio.

The idea of missing something troubled him.

I can't be everywhere at once, he thought.

Using the remote control, he ran scenes back and forth—studying the faces of the doomed. Like cattle, they lined up for the guillotines. Even with nothing to lose; they didn't scream, cry or run away.

It was a mystery.

In particular, there was one young woman. Small and skinny, she reminded him of the evil princess Minnie. Through the mud, she marched along with the rest of the losers, taking a step forward a couple of times per minute as heads were severed and bodies were thrown onto the blazing fires.

What was she thinking with the end of her life so near?

Her face filled the camera's lens with a resigned and hopeless expression. It hit Trevir like a fist to the gut. He wanted to be the one who flipped the wooden lever, pulled the retainer pin and ended this waif's sorry misery.

There was no expression on her face. It was like she was waiting in an endless line for a vaccination. No hurry, but not lagging behind or making any effort to escape.

Inside, did she beg her god for mercy? Was her life so dismal, she ready to leave it and be done with its misery? Was she simply stupid with a foggy mind shut down and incurious?

In slow motion, he watched her head drop into the basket while her sopping dress flopped around her filthy legs. It made something stir in his gut. Again and again he watched and wondered. The power of life and death filled him with energy. It was not enough. It was never enough.

After putting the image on hold, he stood by the window looking out at the fires of the city, then turned and commanded the guard-troll standing at his office entry.

"Get me Srenzo," he said.

She kept him waiting twenty minutes. Her insolence filled him with even more rage and desire.

It was given; she would pay tribute to his needs or pay with her life, like the youngster in the video. The image of the friction-free, blood-streaked blade filled his mind.

It was beautiful.

Finally, Troll Srenzo entered the room. Trevir turned to study her.

She was a sight—dressed from boots to collar in stained leather, tall for a troll, hairy and covered in scars. She was not all troll, she was a mutated mix with troll and ohrkk blood and maybe something even uglier farther up the family tree. Yellow fangs, asymmetrical, with the broken one catching at her rubbery lip.

She was also a princess—Trevir strained to remember her husband's name. It came to him.

Kelpht.

A huge, lumbering ohrkk with craggy brows and a nasty temper.

Trevir decided to play nice.

"While you are undressing, tell me of news of your husband and child."

"Now?" she said.

He gestured.

"Take it all off."

"They grow weary of waiting for their turn," she said, while unlacing her jerkin.

"It won't be long," he said. "I'm sending all the trolls to the west to deal with the so-called Queen."

She hesitated with her fingers on the jerkin's lacing.

"All of them? Really? Is that wise?"

"I'm not ready to go yet and I want to be sure. So, they all go."

She worked on the laces of her breeches.

"As you wish, Master."

Trevir studied her.

"No, I want you to fight a little. Think of how your husband feels."

"My husband feels nothing about this."

"Okay, imagine your son, right here, watching your humiliation." He grabbed the wiry hair at the back of her neck. "Imagine him seeing what you're doing, right now, serving me."

With blazing eyes, she snarled. With her strong jaws, she could take easily his hand off at the wrist.

He imagined it happening and it made him mad with passion. Impatient, her tore at her trousers. In the background, on the video screen, repeated over and over, the girl was marched to the platform, her neck was pressed into the lunette and her head fell into the oilcloth-lined basket.

This one was not really a guillotine; it was shorter, more like an earlier, historic version, the Halifax Gibbet, the bloodthirsty Scottish Maiden of Yorkshire. Crude, it used an old axe head for a blade and the cuts were ragged, not as surgical and precise. Trevir could not decide if that made things better or worse. The razor-sharp mouton blade was quicker and more precise, but there was something pleasing and wonderful about the more ragged stump of neck and the blossom-fountain of blood from The Maiden.

His blood raged as he satisfied himself with Troll Srenzo's body and her degradation. It was quick, a few minutes, then he rested while she pulled her clothing back into place.

Feeling mellow, he clicked the remote and froze the video image on a close-up of the doomed girl's face. There was no light in her eyes; it was as if she was already dead. This pleased Trevir.

Thinking, he spoke hesitantly.

"I think—I would like to talk to a banker. Yes, a powerful one from one of the big banks. The biggest bank."

She pulled tight a leather lace on her vest.

"Do you have someone in mind?"

Trevir grinned.

"Start at the top with the CEO and work down through the corporate food chain until someone agrees to meet with me. Whoever it is, we'll make him or her happy, very happy."

Trevir laughed.

"Or, regret the day they were born, either way."

He dismissed her with a wave of his hand.

"Be gone," he said. "Get it done now."

Fire

AT NEARLY THE end of the school year, Zeke and the Parking Lot Gang, idling away a Saturday morning hour at the Big-D coffee shop, were restless. Most people loved the leisurely summers, but the Gang did not work and were at loose ends in the hot months when the other kids traveled, goofed off and worked their summer gigs.

Zeke was all twisted up inside and the Black Death, even in all-day maintenance doses, did not satisfy. In April's place, Cheryl served him, but she was passive and had a bland personality. She did not fight like April—who drove him crazy. April made him work for it. When she let go and submitted, it was a pure dose of nirvana. Cheryl was a slow-witted and dim. She was no challenge.

April was in the hospital and her situation was not good. Zeke did not understand much of what the doctor said, but it was written in his eyes. April was in bad shape and her prognosis was poor. Zeke flashed back a few months to a comment Minnie made to April when they had the little girl jammed up in the parking lot.

Please see a doctor.

Minnie was right, April had been sick, very sick and kept getting worse until she fell into a coma at home. Her parents claimed they never saw it coming; but the signs were there. An ambulance rushed her to the hospital, but hopes weren't high—she was rotting from the inside out and no amount of hydration, antibiotics or modern medicines helped.

It was caused by the drugs she'd taken with Zeke, but more than that, her disease was caused by the corrupt life she led and the guilt and perversion of her spirit. It was caused by doing anything to keep the dope coming. It was drinking, smoking and shameful, humiliating hours captured on camera phones and uploaded to dark net websites in exchange for a few advertising dollars.

As her body failed, Zeke spent less time with her and more time out and with other girls. This is what she expected from life—pain, sorrow and ending up feeling lost and alone.

Zeke felt vaguely bad, but only for brief moments—he was a surface dweller clinging to his own selfish needs and wants, resentments and grudges. Deep down, he knew right from wrong, but he didn't dwell in the deep down—the fun was in the here and now.

"Eh, she had it coming. She smoked so much more than her share. What did she do to earn everything I did for her? Serves her right."

Looking across their breakfast table, he looked over his entourage. They needed a mission.

But what?

An image flooded his mind.

"Cornfield," he said.

Puzzled, the gang looked at each other.

"What?" Jimmy said.

"Let's go to the cornfield. The one we heard about. You know, where the *magic* corn grows on the other side of town."

The way he said *magic*, the word dripped with sarcasm.

He continued, "The rainbow popcorn the slippery bug, Minnie, grows, pops and sells."

"That stuff is really good," Cheryl said.

Zeke glared.

"Just sayin'," Cheryl said.

After Chet's morning rush, Minnie put away the dishes she washed. Leaning over the sink and catching her breath, she craved fresh air and open spaces.

Coming from the dining room, Fiona pushed a strand of hair behind her ear.

"Finally, tea time," Fiona said.

"Popcorn," Minnie said.

"Excuse me?"

"I'm going to check on my corn," Minnie said.

"Tea first?" Fiona said.

Minnie did not answer.

The little girl went to her nook, pulled on her jacket and on impulse, slipped her sword under her arm. The sword was dead, rusty iron.

Useless.

But, she walked out of the diner with it anyway.

At the corn field, the sun, hovering over the trees, was only a bright spot in the cloud cover. It had rained a few days before, so the ground was soft and damp. From walking in tall grass, her blue jeans were wet up to her knees and she was cold. Though late in the spring, the field was brown and dead except for the wonderful, emerald-green patch of corn.

Divided by the wind, sunlight infused the field—coming from the sky like an open eye. It wasn't the season for corn, but there it was, pressing out ears of hard-shelled kernels that were dried and shucked for popping. It was impossible, but here it was before her.

She raised her sword to the sky and sliced it through the air.

Nothing.

Dead metal.

It made her sad.

What am I supposed to do? A life without magic is miserable, but the King will come if he finds us.

The blade of her troll-sword was pitted and dull; the iron was rotten.

Worthless, like me.

As a weapon, a serving spoon would be better.

I should just bury it and be done with it.

Darkness pressed on her from all directions. She felt weak and helpless. Hopeless and insubstantial, like a gentle breeze could carry her away into nothing where she belonged.

Behind her, she heard commotion.

She turned.

It was the Parking Lot Gang.

There were six of them. She felt an impulse to run, but staved it off. There was bloodthirsty eagerness in their eyes.

"Cute sword," Zeke said. "How does it work? Scratch your enemy and they get tetanus and die?"

She held out her arm and dropped the sword—it stabbed into the ground like a tilted cross.

"Build a fire," he growled to his entourage.

They got busy with the tasks of gathering wood, kindling and tinder.

He held his wrist before her face. On it, he had a large metal bracelet with a marijuana leaf embossed on it. In the center, it said BD in gothic letters.

Black Death.

The design, blackened by fire, was a branding iron.

She had a vivid imagination and could already feel her flesh burning—and the smell.

"We'll mark each other," he said while pointing at his inner arm—already twisted with scars. "Then, forever, you will be mine and I will be yours."

A thought roared through her mind, but she did not speak it.

How did that work out for April?

He continued, "In all of your life, Minnie, you have barely made a dent—like a gobbet of spit in a thunderstorm. However, this mystical popcorn intrigues me—is it really magic? What's your secret? You're making money with it and I want in. Bearing each other's marks, we'll team up. I'll sell the weed and the black meth and you'll sell the munchies. Fifty-fifty. What do you say? We'll seal the deal with a celebratory toke."

"Over my dead body," Minnie said.

"Oh, Minnie, you shouldn't say such things. That would be too easy."

He gave the boys and Cheryl a quick look and before Minnie knew it, they had pinned her to the ground. It took four of them to hold her. Two held her arms and two held her legs. Minnie suddenly felt fear, but wouldn't let it show.

Zeke strutted like a wolf circling a trapped rabbit with delicious thoughts and images rolling before his eyes.

"This little cherry is ripe for the picking…I could claim her in more than one way."

A flood of anger flowed through Minnie's body, but she pressed it away and accepted her fate. She could hurt them and they could hurt her.

What would that do for anyone?

It was just her body. No one could touch her soul. She would retreat—leave and come back when this was all done. Her eyes were open, but she saw nothing as she let her body relax into the cold weeds. No bones.

Ragdoll.

Zeke stopped and leaned over.

"Playing dead? No more fight? Where's the fun in that?"

From the woods, alert pairs of eyes watched. Owners of three of the pairs were warrior princess Ancamna, field gnome Sebastian and Linnaeus, the wood elf.

"This is what you get," Ancamna said. "She doesn't know who she is…she can't be trusted."

"She's asleep," Linnaeus said. "But we've seen it—she's waking up."

Bitterness filled Ancamna's voice.

"Look at your princess. She has the power to lay waste, but she takes this abuse. They will mark her, then rape her. She should die fighting. I can't watch."

Linnaeus's face twisted with determination.

"I will not allow it," he said.

Ancamna took a few steps away, then stopped. She pulled her sword from its leather sheath.

"Okay," she said.

Linnaeus nocked an arrow.

"No," Sebastian said. "Let's go another way."

From inside his vest, he pulled out a snakeskin pouch.

The bracelet, heated by the fire, glowed orange. Zeke worked it away from the flames with a stick, then picked it up with a shirt wound around his hand for protection. Except for her eyes following the brand, Minnie did not move.

"It hurts less if we do this quick."

From a foot away, she could feel the intense heat. Inside, she braced herself for the pain.

There was a rustling in the corn—like a rat in a cellar.

Zeke glanced up. It was just a snake, a little emerald one no more than a foot long.

Nothing, he thought.

But, there were more.

Five, ten, twenty.

Cheryl did not like snakes. She jumped up—freeing one of Minnie's arms. With eyes locked on the steaming brand, Minnie did not move.

"Keep them away from me," Cheryl said.

"Get back here," Zeke commanded.

In seconds, she was halfway across the field.

Fifty snakes, all wriggling and coming from every corner of the corn field. They were brown, black and silver, some as fat as fire hoses and seven feet long.

100.

They rustled and hissed—the noise grew louder and louder.

Zeke dropped the brand—it lay steaming in the grass. He leaned over the passive Minnie.

"Snakes?" he said.

She shrugged.

"I don't know anything about them," she said.

Closer and closer came the scaly wave.

Jimmy and the others stood. Minnie was free.

"I don't like this," Jimmy said.

"We don't have venom-snakes around here," Zeke said. "But, maybe it would be better to do this later."

He refused to run, but walked more quickly than they arrived. Still, his gang raced ahead.

With a loose, rubbery body, Minnie felt as if she was melting into the Earth. The snakes overran her and wove all around her body. They were cold and smelled really bad, but she refused to react as they piled on, deeper and deeper.

Then, as soon as they had arrived, they rustled off—leaving her freezing and staring at writhing coils of clouds in the sky. After a few shivering minutes of allowing the cold to enter her body, she sat up and looked around. There were eyes in the woods, she could feel them, but it was as if the show was over and they were drifting away.

The brand lying in the weeds caught her eye. She picked it up and studied it—it was still warm to the touch. She pressed it to the skin of her arm—pressed hard, then pulled it off. The red mark on her skin was vivid, but quickly faded—she imagined being marked like that forever. BD. It was an ugly thing, but she felt an odd fondness for it—she raised it to her lips and kissed the now-cold metal before stuffing it in her jacket pocket.

She turned over onto her knees, then stood up and towered over the stubby sword—the sword that watched and did not help. She felt like there was a lesson she should have learned, but could not pinpoint it. She plucked the sword from the Earth, stored it under her jacket, then turned. The fire was still hot; she walked over and let it warm her. Holding her hands as close as she could, she felt the pain of circulation restarting. After a few minutes, she glanced to the left.

It was her old friend, Linnaeus, the wood elf.

"Snakes?" she said.

Linnaeus shrugged.

"Sebastian's doing," he said. "Gnomes are weird."

She gestured toward the corn field.

"Were they real? I would not have guessed there were so many close by."

Linnaeus's face twisted into a wry grin.

"There are a lot of surprising things in the world. Look at your sword."

Puzzled, she looked at him, then pulled the sword from under her jacket.

It gleamed as if freshly forged. The edge looked wicked-sharp. Instinctively, she reached out to test it with her thumb. Linnaeus shook his head.

"I wouldn't," he said.

She nodded.

"Yes, I think you're right," she said.

When Minnie saw Jimmy in class later that week, they locked eyes but no words were spoken. She wiggled her finger like a baby snake.

He formed his lips, but did not utter the word

She knew what he meant to say.

Bitch.

It didn't offend her; in fact, she didn't know exactly how she felt about it. Before she could pinpoint the emotion, the bell rang and her mind was filled with other, more important things.

The Banker—Part One

THE BIG BANK they chose was the Bank of North America, a gleaming, glass-sided skyscraper in the beating heart of Manhattan. By making phone calls, one-after-the-other, Troll Srenzo worked her way down the org chart from the CEO, the COO and through various division presidents and vice presidents.

If needed, she would go all the way to the bottom—to janitors and mail clerks. She would eventually find someone. After a total of nineteen phone calls, she got a response from the office of Daniel Gottleib, Assistant Chief Marketing Officer for Crypto Currencies. After his assistant checked his schedule, Daniel agreed to meet Trevir face-to-face.

Daniel had a squeaky voice and seemed very young. They learned differently by assembling a database on him. It was surprising how much could be learned from the common public databases, but Trevir had subscriptions that went deeper, far deeper. In a half-hour, they knew him better than he knew himself.

With thinning, sandy hair, Daniel was in his mid-forties and enjoyed an hour-plus daily commute on the train to and from South Norwalk, Connecticut to Harlem. From the Harlem station, rain or shine, he walked to his office with an umbrella and half-read Wall Street Journal—he read the second half on his return trip. Married for twelve years, his wife, Olivia, and eight-year-old son, Edward, appeared wholesome and charming. She drove a two-year-old Nissan minivan, ferried Edward to soccer and violin practice and taught twice-a-week Zumba classes at the Norwalk YMCA. She made a grand total of $2,294 the previous year.

Pocket change.

Daniel made $219,000 and took home about 60% after taxes and deductions. He seemed like a responsible father—enjoyed three beers at O'Rafferty's on Friday nights and bought an occasional lottery ticket, otherwise, it appeared he had no other bad habits. With his year-end bonus, they paid off their minivan. No car payments. They put twenty-percent down on a house a block from the river reach and were paying down a fifteen-year mortgage. His credit score was 837. They vacationed in the Hamptons on the cheap and had fully funded retirement and other savings accounts. Dutifully, he put 10% of his net income into tithes for their church and 5% into gold coins hidden in a safe embedded in concrete in their pantry.

They attended the Christian Deliverance Foursquare Pentecostal Church and once a year, Edward gave a lecture to teens called *Endtimes Bible Prophecy*.

"Read some of it to me," Trevir said.

Troll Srenzo looked up at him with the question on her face.

"Go," he said.

She shrugged and started reading.

"Do we love each other? Do we love those who are different? Do we love and welcome visitors, strangers, no matter who they are? Do we know them and try to learn their ways, so we can love them? Do we put their comfort above our own?"

Trevir interrupted.

"Okay, that's enough. I get it."

Daniel was on the board of directors of a group called Blessed Earth Northeast and contributed healthy amounts to *Médecins Sans Frontières* and Greenpeace.

"What's a crypto-currency?" Troll Srenzo said. "Does it have anything to do with his biblical end times?"

Trevir thought about it for a few seconds.

"I don't know, but I like the sound of it."

Troll Srenzo had printed a glossy portrait of the family from their Facebook page. Trevir rotated it in the light and studied their expressions.

He was delighted.

"Aren't they cute?" he said. He tapped the picture with a long fingernail. "That's America right there. It's beautiful."

Expressionless, Troll Srenzo studied his face.

He continued, "This is perfect. A man with everything to lose. Let's wager. I can break him in twenty minutes or less."

Troll Srenzo shook her head.

"He's religious. It will take an hour, easy."

Trevir grinned.

"Twenty dollars says I can do it," he said.

She nodded.

"You're on," she said.

After dropping the portrait on his desk, he stood up, put his hands on her shoulders, stared deeply in her eyes and explained carefully and in detail what he wanted her to do.

Damn it, she thought.

Her twenty dollars was as good as gone.

The Banker—Part Two

TREVIR SUBSCRIBED TO the philosophy that if you're on time, you're late, so they appeared twenty minutes early at Daniel Gottlieb's office on the 42nd floor of the big-bank building. The building had 80 stories, so Daniel was not high on the corporate food chain; he was a mid-level bureaucrat in the monstrous organization.

After Trevir's entourage—Troll Srenzo and two guard trolls—left the elevator, they walked down a hallway and pressed a button at the door of the reception area. They were buzzed in. Trevir smiled and politely announced that they were there to see Mr. Gottlieb.

There was a question in the receptionist's eyes.

"Yes," Trevir said with an expansive toothy grin, "we have an appointment at ten o'clock."

The receptionist glanced at a hidden clock.

"Mr. Gottlieb will be right with you, sir," she said. "Can I get you water, coffee or tea?"

Trevir knew. When someone makes an offer like this, politeness dictates one to accept.

"Yes, please. A black coffee and a hot cup of peppermint tea." He leaned over and whispered intimately, "The last thing my assistant needs is more caffeine, if you catch my drift."

The receptionist picked up her phone.

"Of course, sir. It will be here right away."

In minutes, the drinks were delivered on a silver tray by a pimply intern. The trolls wanted coffee, but it did not show in their eyes as the refreshments were served. Troll Srenzo looked at her cup with distain and refused to touch it. She hated peppermint tea.

At 9:59, the receptionist caught Trevir's eye.

"Mr. Gottlieb will see you now," she said. "I will show you the way."

The coffee was good, so Trevir pointed and a troll picked up the cup and saucer. They trooped through an open-office space where fashionably dressed workers clicked on computers and talked on headsets. Then came to a long hallway with endless mahogany doors, all closed. Finally they stood before a corner office.

"Please go right in," the receptionist said before quietly leaving them.

Troll Srenzo pushed in and held the door open for Trevir.

Daniel was a little taller than they imagined—and a little older. He ushered them in.

"Please, sit. I apologize for only having a few minutes for you—my morning is jam-packed."

Troll Srenzo pointed to a satellite clock on the wall…showing calibrated time from a satellite. Trevir grinned. Message received.

The twenty-minute count-down clock of their wager had started.

Trevir ignored Daniel's hand held out for a handshake and walked to the plate glass window.

"Your view is wonderful," he said.

Troll Srenzo grinned.

Maybe he'll waste time and I will win after all, she thought.

"Busy-busy," Daniel said. "Busy day."

Trevir turned.

"Gottlieb. A grand, historic name predating the German form. God's Love. A religious name, from the obsolete gothic language. As recorded in the *Codex Argenteus*, the Silver Codex—an early translation of the Holy Bible, *Gudilub*. Do you think God's love will play a role in the next life-changing—" he glanced at the wall clock—"seventeen minutes of your life?"

"Excuse me, sir?"

Trevir switched topics.

"I'm curious. Tell me about this crypto-money thing. Just the elevator pitch."

A puzzled look washed over Daniel's face. His speech was well-rehearsed and he started it automatically.

"Depending on which numbers you use, the accumulated wealth of the world is something like a hundred trillion, maybe half, maybe double, who knows? We'll use the round number for talking sake. Crypto currencies are a spanking new, up-and-coming, computerized asset with distinct advantages over traditional stores of value, like precious metals and gemstones. And don't get me started talking about the madness of fiat currencies. For those who understand global monetary theory, crypto currencies will disrupt and realign the established forces and wielders of wealth and power. Imagine private ownership of capital protected from plunder. Even if only five-percent of the world's wealth flows by means of crypto, imagine how rich will be those with the foresight to get in early. To get in now."

10:06. Fourteen minutes left in the wager.

"Not bad," Trevir said. "A bit verbose, though. Isn't the average elevator pitch supposed to be done in eleven seconds? You're long-winded, but okay, I am intrigued. I like what I hear. You're busy, I'm busy, so I'll get right to my problem."

He snapped his fingers and Troll Srenzo spread a sheaf of photographs across Daniel's desk. The photos showed money, literal tons of it wrapped and packed onto pallets—then onto trucks. A hundred trucks. An unbelievable amount of money.

Daniel could not form any words.

"Uh—," he said.

"Carrot and stick," Trevir said. "Let's talk about carrots, bushels and bushels of beautiful carrots. For example, how would you like to be the president—the big cheese, head kahuna, el Jefe—of this bank with more money than you could keep track of? Stretch limousine money? Chauffeur money? Private jet money. Chalet in Switzerland money? Vacations in Monaco money? Mistress in Singapore money? All that sounds wonderful, doesn't it?"

Daniel's mind was not processing—he glanced at the clock.

10:09. One minute left in the scheduled appointment. His mind grasped at the minute. One minute, then he could usher these lunatics out of his office and get on with his hectic day.

He took a deep breath.

I can do this.

"Sir, I'm sure you know, all deposits over five-thousand-dollars are logged and recorded, particularly cash. There are rules, regulations, forms and intense governmental oversight."

He stood.

"I'm sorry," he said. "I can't help you."

10:10.

I made it.

"Now for the stick," Trevir said.

With his index finger, he tapped a spot Daniel's desk.

One of the guard trolls stepped forward and carefully placed a tablet computer—on the screen was a live image.

10:11.

Two boys on the screen—bound onto chairs with silver duct tape. Two scared boys with their eyes flicking left and right.

"What is this?" Daniel said.

"The picture quality is good, isn't it? You recognize them, of course?

"My son. Edward. And his friend, Peyton. What is this?"

You can talk to them."

Daniel leaned over the desk.

"Edward, where are you? What is happening?"

"Daddy, I'm scared. They took us from school."

Trevir glanced at the clock.

10:13.

"I can give you a minute to decide. If you don't pick, then both."

"Both what?"

Trevir smiled, then leaned over the screen himself.

"Show him," he said.

A guard troll walked in from the left. He drew his stubby sword and displayed it for the camera. It was rusty and dirty, but the edge gleamed like a razor.

"You wouldn't," Daniel said.

"Oh, how we'll get to know each other," Trevir said. "You'll find out how serious I am in about forty seconds. Choose."

Daniel's face twisted in torture.

"I don't understand what is happening."

"Busy, busy," Trevir said. "Pick a boy or test me. It's not that big a deal, you and your wife can make another. If you have a wife by then, of course. Ten seconds."

Daniel dropped to his knees.

"Please, sir. I beg of you."

"Choose now."

"God forgive me, take my son. Take him."

Trevir looked surprised.

"That was an interesting choice. What were you thinking?"

Daniel spoke so quietly that his voice was barely audible.

"I'm not sure why God put me here and now in this position, but I can't do this to Peyton's mother and father. If one must pay for my sins, then it should be mine, Lord help me."

Trevir walked around the desk and tilted Daniel's head back.

"To make sure you got the message, I was going to take both heads, regardless of whether you chose or not. My escalation plan was making you choose between your wife or your mother."

Thinking, he rubbed his chin.

"There's no hurry, but I want you to create a plan for converting billions in pallets of cash into the fancy crypto money. Hidden from prying eyes. Untraceable. Tax-free. Can you do it? Will you?"

Daniel couldn't speak, but he nodded his head.

Vigorously.

"Okay, I believe you," Trevir said. He decided. "Both boys can go."

Turning to Troll Srenzo, he pointed at the clock.

10:19.

Troll Srenzo scowled, then nodded.

Son of a bitch, she thought. *He did it.*

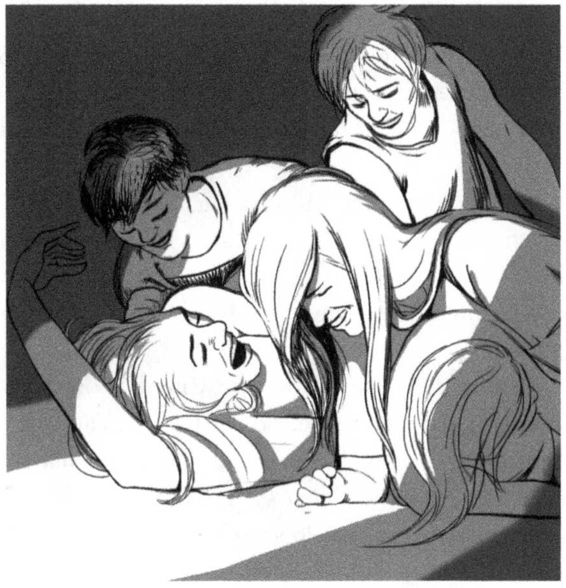

The Last Day

THE LAST DAY of school had finally arrived and the school was abuzz with energy and kids making plans for the school break—going to Indian-themed summer camps or on family road trips. No real work was getting done in the classrooms; final tests had already been administered and graded, text books were turned in and after the bell, tardy clumps of students lingered in the hallways talking about the year behind and their plans for the years ahead.

The teachers played nice to top off their student evaluations. Surveys were dispersed about the year—what kids wanted changed for the next year and commentary about the pros and cons of their teachers and their social and academic experience. All sorts of obligatory red tape was thrown in to the mix of classroom celebrations for a job well done and *bon voyage*.

However, Minnie, feeling the heavy weight of the world on her young shoulders, was not in a mood to celebrate. Melancholy beyond words, she wanted no more than to float through the day, unnoticed. More than anything else, she felt dread and doom, like the last day of this school year was a permanent goodbye. She wasn't ready for that. Not knowing exactly what was coming or what would happen made things worse—she felt profoundly sad and wanted to be alone.

As she walked down the hallway, Lacey bounded up.

"Hey, there. Who peed in your Wheaties? Why all wet-blanket like?"

Minnie let out a sigh. She could barely look up at Lacey-who was undaunted.

"Hey, stop walking and talk to me, Minnie. What's going on?"

Minnie stopped, then turned so her back was against the wall. She looked down at her Converse sneakers, one black and one red. She hadn't even noticed that she put on two different ones.

Random fragments of an old song echoed in her head.

Red and Black, it's their color scheme

Hornswoop me bungo pony, on dogsled, on ice…

She didn't remember what song it was or where she might have heard it.

Hornswoop me?

Whatever does that mean?

She frowned at her mismatched shoes. People would think she was making a statement about conformity.

Her elevated mood quickly faded.

"I don't know, Lacey. I just feel, well, I don't know, sad, I guess. I feel like this is all going to end and I'm never going to see anyone again."

Lacey picked up Minnie and spun her around.

"Don't be silly, Minnie! We're besties, remember? We have all summer to hang out and do fun stuff. You, me and the rest of the gang. No one is going anywhere. You'll see, we'll have so much fun. I'm already planning all sorts of adventures. It's going to be an absolutely EPIC, capital E, capital P and capital all the rest, summer."

"You can put me down anytime, you know."

"Only if you promise to come to the sanctuary after school.

Mr. Danvers said we need to tidy up before we vacate the space for the summer. Work-work-work. He said nothing will happen to the space and we can have it again next year, but we need to clean it up a bit. No dodging. Right after school. It won't take long. Many hands make light work, and all that. Get it? Deal?"

"I suppose," sighed Minnie.

Lacey put her down.

"Suhweet," she said. "Okay, Eeyore, see ya then."

She blew Minnie a kiss and scampered down the hallway.

Eeyore, huh? Wonder if Eeyore would have worn mis-matched shoes too. Clean up duty after school. Guess it has to be done. Then I can escape to home and hide from the world.

After suffering through several classes with zero information registering in her brain, Minnie, trudging, walked in the secret door, down the abandoned hallway and approached the Misfit sanctuary.

Dead silence.

Am I the first to show up?

Is this a trick to get me to do all the work?

I hope so, that's what I deserve.

With her hand on the doorknob, she hesitated.

People were inside. It was a trap. Her mind filled with the vision of the parking lot gang waiting—waiting to beat her to pulp and drug her.

Yes, that's what should happen.

Steeling her nerve and preparing for vicious blows, she opened up the door and flipped on the lights. All at once there was a cacophony of whoops and hollers.

"Surprise!"

It took a few moments to loosen up and expand her senses. She stood dumbfounded, with absolutely no words. It was as if her feet were stuck in cement and she was frozen.

After an eternity of seconds, she was able to speak.

"Huh? What? Why?"

It wasn't Lacey who approached—it was Mr. Danvers. He put his arm around her shoulders and the warmth and weight of his arm instantly soothed the little girl. She let out a breath and looked up at him as he spoke.

"Sorry, Minnie, but I have a speech."

With his free hand, he pulled a wad of papers from his jacket pocket and started to read in a magisterial voice.

"Dear Minnie, you have done SO much for this school. You brought your magic to us and we all responded to you. You gave us hope when we had none. You showed us new worlds we never knew existed. You gave this school and town a new life with the Carnival. You changed the course of our lives, Minnie. This party is in your honor. You're not your right self today and that's okay. As you have held the space for us this year, today is the day we hold it for you. Today is a celebration of *you* and how awesome you are."

If I'm so awesome, why am I always running away like a coward, she thought.

Running away. Her mind filled with the vision of running away again. She did not want to face it. She pressed the image away.

He squeezed her shoulders and the Misfits attacked with hugs and kisses aplenty. Overwhelmed, her knees gave way and she crumpled to the floor.

"Dog pile," Kurt shouted.

Everyone, laughing, rolled on the floor, barking like a pack of puppies.

For that moment, Minnie forgot all of her troubles. She let go of the weight on her shoulders and embraced the joy and happiness of the moment. Were her tears of sorrow or of something else? Tears of letting go and going into the unknown; tears of innocence lost and trouble to come; tears of release and acceptance? Whatever they were, they ran freely down Minnie's face. She realized then that she'd never lose her friends. Her pack, complete with Mr. Danvers, would always be there; constant like the North Star. She would call on them and they would come; steadfast and true.

In the midst of the laughter and rejoicing Minnie heard a faint whisper circle around the room.

"Enjoy your time, Princess, for these golden days will quickly come to an end."

Like someone swatting away an annoying gnat, Minnie waved her hand dismissively and muttered, "Fek off, Trevir. You're unwanted here."

"I may be unwanted, but I am here, Minnie. Trust me, I am here...."

Minnie tuned him out and extricated herself from the roiling bodies. While she watched, they carried on with their nonsense.

She clapped her hands and scolded.

"Enough of this twaddle," she ordered. "This is undignified. Untoward. Get up, all of you. Get up."

Kelley wormed out of the mêlêe and jumped to her feet.

"You're right, Minnie. It's not twaddle-time."

Minnie caught Kelley's eye and nodded in approval. She squared her shoulders and used her most mature voice.

"Thank, you, Kelley."

Kelly grinned.

"It's cake-time. My mom baked all night."

Minnie sighed and rolled her eyes.

There was no hope for this motley group of miscreants.

The cake was good. Fluffy white, with buttercream frosting.

And rainbow sprinkles.

It had been a long time since Minnie was happier.

Trolls

HIDDEN BY THEIR veils, they could spend the night in town, even in a cozy motel, but they were more comfortable in the woods. Lost in thought, Ancamna and Sebastian sat and stared into their flickering campfire.

"It's starting," Ancamna said.

Blinking, Sebastian looked up.

"Trolls gathering in the woods? I sensed them. I hoped we'd have more time. How many?"

Ancamna turned to him.

"I think it's all of them."

Sebastian tossed a twig on the fire.

"Oh, my," he said.

All the Trolls

THE TROLLS KNEW many old trails over the Rocky Mountains, but it was still hard going. The oxen strained and the wagons creaked. Rivers were forded. The half-million stretched out miles—weaving through the plains and farms of the flat lands, over the permanent snows of the Continental Divide, across the salt flat desert, the wheat fields, over the Cascade Mountains and then into the verdant rain forest. It took ten days, all on foot and wagon, but they eventually arrived at their last campsite.

There, fires raged and venison stews cooked in black-iron pots. Deep in the woods, the veil settled around them, masking their smoke and clamor from the real world.

Though smelly and dirty like all trolls, Ovard Skäld liked to keep his sword clean and sharp. For hours he sharpened the edge so the surface gleamed like a mirror and the edges were as sharp as razors. It wanted to cut something—it craved the taste of blood.

He whispered to it.

Soon enough, my sweet. Tomorrow you will have your fill.

With a half-million trolls against two human women and a scattering of their supporters, the battle would be quick—maybe only an hour or a day, then they would make the trek backwards the way they came. But, maybe a feast first.

A victory feast.

Ovard liked the sound of that.

He could have mead and grog brought to his yurt, but he liked to mingle with the soldiers. After pulling on his boots and leathers, he slipped the sword into its sheath where it would sleep until it was time to fight.

The fires glowed red like dying suns and the smoke was thick—thick enough to chew. With a horn of ale, Ovard wandered—stopping only at a latrine trench to pee. He traded the mug for a haunch. A haunch of what? Deer? Elk? Rangy cow? Dog? He didn't care, meat was meat. He chewed down to the bone, then tossed the remnant to their hungry hounds.

"You'll have plenty of bones to gnaw tomorrow," he murmured.

They didn't care about tomorrow. They wanted their feast today. Ovard laughed. He didn't care what they wanted; they would get what they get.

Like all of us.

Old women tended the stews—chewing tobacco leaves by the bushel and spitting out brown saliva by the gallon.

There were few women in the army, maybe only a few thousand young enough for rutting. This made them very popular. They all had blades hidden in their skirts; maybe dozens of dirks and daggers, but the trolls did not mind getting cut—as long as the cuts were symbolic and not serious. The young ones were chased by suitors…only the toughest could claim them. Ovard stared into the eyes of one pressed back against a tree with her arms pulled by brutes while their captain had his turn.

What was written in her eyes?

Lust, of course. But what else? Pride for being wanted. The captain would kill for her. That gave her power and power was an addiction. With a whisper, a soldier who annoyed her would be gutted and tossed on the fire. Her eyes teased Ovard. She licked her thin lips.

Did she think she would join his harem? He already had a dozen to serve his needs. He studied her dirty face.

No, her skin was too soft. Her hair too lush. Her eyes too innocent and clear. Squat and fleshy like all trolls, but too pretty.

Ovard liked hard women with inky tattoos, deep scars and a murderous glint in their eyes.

Those were real women—real warriors worthy of his attention.

He continued his stroll.

All around him, the orders were clear and repeated over and over. The little girl, Minerva, was for Trevir, alive, but trolls could have the entourage on a first-come, first-served basis, but the woman…

The woman was his.

Fiona.

The things he would do.

It was hard to decide what to do first.

Of course, she would be bloody and screaming when he raped her, that was given. But, how much would she be hurt?

How much of her should be left whole? Was it better for her to have eyes to see or better for her to be blind and terrified—not knowing what was happening and what was coming her way?

He decided.

It was better for her to see, but without arms.

Just stubs.

The image pleased him. She could beat her bloody stumps on his back. Under his belt, he felt the twitch.

Tomorrow would not come soon enough.

Something is Coming

EARLY IN THE evening, Fiona stood at the kitchen sink gazing out through the kitchen window toward the woods.

Sometimes it seems that all I DO is wash dishes. Morning, noon and night. All the world's dishes.

She smirked while a vision of Cinderella filled her mind.

No way would I wear a glass slipper. I'd be more like Snow White maybe, barefoot and in the woods with all my furry woodland friends about me.

She let her mind drift to the home she had with Sean and the Fachan; woven and built with love and magic.

"It would have been so perfect, our happily-ever-after…" she mused.

While scrubbing and daydreaming, her eyes drifted to the deep, black forest that embraced the diner. Her love-filled thoughts of Sean and their fantasy life grew dark. It was on her. They weren't together because she'd left. Like the biggest coward ever, she'd gathered Minnie and ran away. Though planted and happy in Cement City, she was still running.

On a china serving platter, there was a speck. Tiny, but thoroughly baked on. A thumbnail did nothing. Scrubbing with soapy steel wool did nothing. How long had it been there?

Years?

No one else would notice it, but it vexed her. There was nothing more important in the world. It was a flaw on the broad expanse of the cream-white platter. Maybe it was a birthmark, like Marilyn Monroe's mole...there from birth. Placed there by God to accent the platter's perfection.

The Spanish word occurred to her.

Chiqueador.

Originally, these beauty spots would be artificially applied to cover smallpox scars, but later became fashionable.

Obsessed, she flicked at the nearly invisible spot with a butcher knife.

Nothing.

She pressed harder. After stubborn reluctance, the fleck flew off. It was gone. In its place there was a pit. A small gouge. A nick.

That's better.

She looked up.

Before her eyes, the forest changed. Its edges blurred and darkness edged in. Soon, she saw nothing but darkness. The world turned black. Her ears filled with screams—her skin turned clammy and cold. Though she saw nothing but endless darkness, she couldn't turn her eyes away from the forest. Her hands were immersed in a sink full of hot, foamy water, but she felt naked and submerged in ice water. Paralyzed and helpless, her arms began to ache and felt as if they were no longer part of her.

What is going on?

The veil isolating humans from the magic world was not blindness; it was focused concentration on the day-to-day ordinary. When the mind was filled with the routine, it had no room for the alternate. The secret world was not hidden, but unobserved.

We don't see what we are not looking at.

There could be an army in front of us, but we don't notice because we're consumed by...

By what?

By things like flecks of irrelevant imperfection on a platter.

She projected her mind into the forest.

What is out there?

Like an owl, she flew over the trees...over brook and dale and hill and meadow. Swamp. Crags of raw rock reaching for the sky.

There was something in the forest. Staring, she couldn't turn away. It did not approach; it was already there, though she knew not what. Something formless, but dangerous and evil. The hairs stood up on the back of her neck.

An army.

"Trolls, demons, black death," she whispered.

They weren't safe here.

But, doesn't that mean we will never be safe anywhere?

Her knees grew weak.

They were out there. A million, or more.

Trolls.

How many?

The thought entered her mind like an echo.

All of them.

Minnie. Minnie has got to go. She must be kept safe and that could only be far, far away.

Like a child woken from a nap rubbing sleepies from her eyes, Minnie's voice sounded small and fragile.

"Fiona? Mom? What is it? What's going on? What's wrong?"

Fiona shook her head to dispel the vision and returned to the steamy kitchen. Beside her, Minnie looked up with a puzzled expression.

Fiona turned toward the waif and kneeled.

"Did I wake you, dear? Were you dreaming?"

"I was in a desolate place. Those weird cactuses—the ones with the arms—dancing in the moonlight like they were on crazy-brain drugs. I didn't like it, Mom. It was a dead place and I was alone with the hot wind and dust. Dry. Stuck. The chain on my bicycle all tangled around the axle. It wasn't a dream. It was real. What does it mean?"

"I don't know, Minnie." She pointed over her shoulder at the dark forest. "Something is out there and it's coming. It's coming for us. What does your gut tell you?"

Standing on tippy-toes, Minnie looked at the forest and soaked in what Fiona had experienced. Absorbing the wicked energy, she began to shake uncontrollably. With knees like jelly, she broke her gaze and dropped to the floor. There were tears in her eyes as she looked up.

"We have to go, Fiona, but I can't see you. Where are you? I have to go. I have to. But I can't see you."

"So young you are; so brave and so strong. So much has happened in your years on this planet already; too much. Trouble has come to our doorstep, Minnie, and we don't have much time..."

In her head the thought was altered.

I don't have much time.

Hippies

THERE WAS NO plan. At two o'clock in the middle of the night, Minnie had bundled her clothes and treasures and stood by the restaurant entrance. She was a sad sight with her worldly possessions stuffed into black-plastic trash bags.

"What now, Mom?" she said.

At the frazzled end of her wits, Fiona shook her head.

"I don't know, baby."

At that instant, headlights swept across the parking lot. A thought flashed through Fiona's mind.

Creeps.

She pushed the thought away, then walked by Minnie and out through the door. Then another thought filled her mind.

Hippies.

The vehicle was a mud-splattered, 1960's Volkswagen van all covered with psychedelic paint—faded by the sun. With effort, the driver rolled down the stubborn window. He was an old man, at least eighty, with white hair and a long, scraggly beard. His companion was younger, a woman, maybe fifty, with long, straight, gray-streaked hair and a crooked smile.

"Tor Forrest," he said. "My old lady here is Gretchen."

Fiona shrugged. She took another step forward, then wrinkled her noise at the odor pouring out of the window. This couple was no stranger to marijuana.

"Fiona," she said.

"Seems like we took a wrong turn coming off the mountain. Camping. Hiking. Picking mushrooms. Playing my guitar and groovin' with nature. We're lost. Give us a hint?"

"Just keep on, you'll hit the freeway."

Tor looked around.

"Thanks."

He started to roll up his window, then changed his mind.

"Clem's," he said. "Seems like I've heard of this place. The place with the pies?"

"Where are you going?" Fiona said.

"Drifting down the coast. No hurry. We got a job waiting in the desert. Ren Faire, biggest in the west. We're silversmiths. Canada. U-S. Here and there, that's where we live. Making jewelry and selling it hither and yon to discerning folks who have taste. Good taste and cash money."

One word jumped out at Fiona.

Desert.

Bleak and dry.

It broke her heart, but she knew what she had to do.

"This will sound weird, but we have a bad situation here and you need to take my daughter." She gestured at the cargo space which was crammed tight. "You have room."

Gretchen laughed.

"I read the tarot, but I didn't see that coming," she said.

Her charming accent was European, either German or Dutch.

With her hands on the side of the van, Fiona leaned in.

"We're desperate," Fiona said.

"We don't want to get in the middle of something ugly," Tor

said.

"You have to help us."

Tor turned to look at Gretchen, who shrugged.

"Okay," Tor said. "Give us a pie and we'll take your daughter and keep her safe for a few weeks until you come get her."

There *was* a pie. One. Apple with cinnamon crumbles baked on top. It was possibly the most perfect pie she'd made. It was possible it was the best pie ever baked—one where everything came together, the dough, the oven temperature, the apples, the spices. Everything. Her mind was focused on the pie, excluding everything else—excluding things she could not face.

Until the rest of his words hit like a hammer.

Until I come get her.

She couldn't see it.

Once these two drive off with her Minnie, that might be it.

She turned and looked beyond the restaurant into the woods where there were fires burning and drums pounding. Maybe no one else could hear them, but they were there.

Thousands. Many thousands all thirsty for blood.

She gestured to Minnie. Slowly, the little girl approached with her bags thrown over her shoulder. It was surely the saddest, most pathetic sight Fiona had ever seen.

I'm not going to cry. Not now.

She stooped and looked at Minnie, eye-to-eye.

"You have to," Fiona said. She waved a hand toward the woods. "You can't stay here."

She stood.

"Tor and Gretchen, please let me introduce you to my Minnie. You have to protect her—she's the very most important thing in the world."

Tor opened his door, eased out, then slid open the cargo door of the van. It was packed, but he moved things around until there was room, almost. He tossed in Minnie's bags, then gestured in welcome.

"I don't think anything will fall over and kill you."

He helped Minnie with her seatbelt.

"I love you, baby," Fiona said.

"I love you too, Mom."

With finality, Tor slid the door closed, then turned.

"Time waits for no one," he said. "What kind of pie is it?"

Five minutes later, Fiona watched as the van disappeared. The dark sky pressed on her shoulders and threatened to crush her. She fell to her knees.

What have I done?

She struggled to her feet. On loose legs, she walked back to the restaurant.

From the forest, fires flared, black smoke obliterated the stars and the drums pounded in a deafening roar. A feeling filled her from head to toe.

This is my last day on Earth.

The Angry Elf

STANDING IN THE kitchen looking out into the woods, Fiona did not sleep for the rest of the night, not a wink or blink. Overloaded, her brain had shut down. She was not thinking. She was not feeling. She was nowhere and felt nothing.

That's exactly what she felt. Nothing.

An emptiness that filled everything.

Dawn did not bring peace. Dawn brought more nothing until she felt a sharp prick in her thigh.

"Ow," she mumbled.

She pressed her hand to her leg, then raised it before her face. It showed a streak of blood.

What the…

It was Ancamna. As usual, her face was twisted with anger.

"It lives," Ancamna said.

"You poked me," Fiona said. "That was rude."

"Rude? Rude is standing around doing nothing while danger

brews. Rude is calling yourself Queen when you refuse to do anything for your people. Rude is—"

"I've never called myself Queen of anything. I don't even know what it means. It's not something I asked for. It's not something I deserve or earned."

"Finally we agree about something," Ancamna said. "We need a plan. We need to gather the clans and make a stand."

"I don't know what is out there."

Ancamna exploded. Raising her sword, she slashed it in front of Fiona.

"Don't hide behind ignorance. You're weak, we all get that, but don't pretend you don't know. You know perfectly what is out there and what will happen if we don't gather strength and devise a plan of attack. Trolls. A lot of them—maybe all of them from what I hear. Filthy, flesh-eating trolls."

As always, Sebastian was the peace-maker.

"Okay, Ancamna, you made your point. Let's put on our thinking caps and reason our way through this."

Ancamna turned on him.

"I'll skewer you and roast you over a fire," she said. "We need a strong Queen of action and war, not a cowardly Queen of indecision and confusion. If she won't, I'll be the Queen and lead."

Fiona had never felt so small.

"Yes," Fiona said. "Please, take it. I don't want it. Take it all."

"I will start by contacting the wolves. I think I can draw them to our side."

"I hate the wolves," Sebastian said.

"Everyone hates the wolves, that's irrelevant," Ancamna said. "What matters is if they will join us to fight a common enemy."

"Wait," Sebastian said.

With eyes blazing hellfire, Ancamna shouted down at him.

"The time for waiting is over. Now it's time to act."

"No," he said. "Where did Fiona go?"

Ancamna spun around. Sebastian was right, in all the shouting, Fiona was gone.

"Never mind," Ancamna said. "She's useless, less than worthless. We don't need her. It's time for a warrior to lead."

"I'd feel better if I knew where she went."

Through the kitchen window, Ancamna caught a glimpse.

"There she goes."

"Where?"

"Into the woods. What does it matter? You'd feel better knowing? Now you know. Feel better."

"I'd feel better if I knew what she intends to do."

Ancamna stomped in anger.

"She's running away. She always runs away. I'm the Queen now. Forget about her and help me call the wolves to counsel. It's our only chance."

In the woods, the path was muddy. The sky was clear, but it had rained overnight, so everything was wet. Ferns dripped and spider webs caught the morning sun and gleamed like strings of icy diamonds.

The bridge over the river was a deadfall, a huge Douglas Fir, slippery with bare wood and loose bark. Fiona nearly fell in and it would have been welcome to let the rapids take her away and drown her sorrows. Gasping, she wrapped her arms around a branch and stared down at the roiling water.

From nowhere, she heard a voice.

That's not how this story ends.

Right, she thought. *But I do not survive this day, so, what does it matter?*

She pressed the branch into her cheek, then for no reason, bit off a chunk of bark and chewed it. Mossy and pitchy, it was bitter and dirty, but she did not spit it out.

This tree in now part of me.

Everything is part of me.

The river, the trees, the crows, the weevils, fungi and ants.

The wind. The sun. The Earth.

All are part of me, always were and always will be.

This tree stood tall and reached for the sun, but now it's fallen and rots away, piece by piece, washed away by the river.

The river that flows to the sea, then evaporates into the clouds, drifts again and falls on the snowy mountains to complete the endless cycle.

There was no comfort in this train of thought.

She kicked off a swath of bark and watched the river wash it away. In seconds, it was out of sight and gone.

I don't know what I am doing.

A minute later, she realized she did know.

She was walking.

Deep in the woods at the end of their watch, Troll Earwin and Troll Xythe argued about whether slugs were edible. Xythe had one speared and was about to taste it when Earwin spoke.

"I hear something," he said.

Xythe shook off the slimly slug and raised his spear.

"Is it a fawn? Fawns are tender until the cook chars them into leather. Wave bloody chunks over the fire twice and they are done enough for me."

"No," Earwin said. "Look."

It was a muddy and exhausted Fiona, lost in the woods.

Xythe took a stance and prepared to throw his spear.

"Hold on," Earwin said. "That's the woman, right? The one Skäld wants for himself?"

"We're alone. We kill her, no one knows. I get the feet. City folk have beautiful feet. Soft and chewy."

Earwin shoved his companion.

"Idiot. Skäld will find out and he'll roast us slow. He wants her, so he gets her, but he'll give us something. You want the feet? Maybe Skäld will save one for you."

Earwin stepped into a patch of sunlight, then shouted.

"Stand where you are—and don't run."

Fiona was exhausted and beyond caring.

Run?

Her mind was a jumble.

I'm never running anywhere ever again.

Fiona and the Troll King—Part One

FIONA WAS NOT thinking, she was not observing, she was nowhere. Following a faint game trail, she and her guards stomped through marsh and stands of crooked, dripping trees. When she stumbled or slowed, the shorter troll poked her back and she could feel trickles of blood dripping down her back. It hurt, but it seemed like what she deserved.

At the edge of the forest veil, she stopped. The veil was invisible, but she could see it and feel it. One step away, there were evil things, thousands and thousands of odious creatures all soulless with cold-stone hearts.

What am I doing?

"Move it," one of the trolls said.

She turned.

"I'm moving," she said. "Stop poking me."

"Or what?" the shorter troll said.

The taller troll spoke.

"We have her, Xythe. Leave her be."

The troll's name sounded like 'scythe,' but the proper spelling appeared in her mind.

Xythe.

Knowing his name triggered something in her. It gave her power. He jabbed at her with his spear and cut her belly. Not deep, just a scratch.

"Or what?" he repeated.

I'm not here to fight, I'm here to surrender.

"Or nothing," she said.

But that was not it. Out of nothing, her mind filled with a vision of vines.

Xythe looked down. His muddy boots were covered in green, coiling vines and they grew, wrapping around his legs. He lunged with the spear, but she dodged.

"Stop it," he said.

"I'm not doing anything."

The vines coiled around his waist.

"I don't like this," he said.

In a few seconds, he was completely obscured and frozen like a statue. She reached out and pulled the spear from his grasp. It was heavy, with a crooked hickory shaft and black-iron tip with a drop of her blood on it. She studied it for a second, stabbed it into the ground like a marker, then looked into Earwin's eyes.

"I'm not going to poke you," he said.

Fiona shrugged, then turned and stepped through the veil. In an instant the noise and odor was overwhelming. It seemed as if the fires and huts covered many square miles—her mind could not grasp the scale. In the center was a giant yurt with banners flying. With his spear, Earwin pointed.

"It it pleases m'lady," he said with exaggerated politeness.

There is nothing about this that pleases me.

Onward like a doomed soul, she put one foot in front of another. It was impossible, but each troll they passed seemed uglier than the one before and there were thousands all shouting at each other, pissing, gnawing bones, drinking from gourds and smoking stubby pipes filled with blackweed and rock lichens. Under thick, boney brows, their snake eyes stared at her as they passed and each pair of eyes seemed to take a bite from her. She was mostly unaware of the old tattoos on her body, the mermaids, moons, stars and runes, but they were crawling. Under the glares of the endless trolls, it seemed as if the ancient ink moved across her body. A thought echoed in her mind—over and over.

What am I doing?

But, she knew.

I am trying to save Minnie.

But, she knew there was nothing she could do. She was doomed. In the middle of this stinking, endless hoard, there was no hope. But, vividly, the taste of the deadfall bark came back to her. There was no reason and it made no sense.

Bark, wood, roots, water and Earth—these things were part of her body now. Decay, rise and fall, birth and death, the cycles of orbits, seasons and life. While following twists and turns through the troll camp, an image of a church spire filled her mind. How she wished she could take the leap of faith and embrace the one benevolent God who ruled over all. What a great comfort that would be, but she could not do it.

What did that leave?

The common magic of stones, mountains and seas and the teeming miracle of life everywhere from the bottom of the deepest ocean to the pinnacle of the tallest peak.

What did that leave?

In an instant, her mind filled with images of green, coiling vines, but it was funny. There was nothing vines could do to defeat these million trolls.

She tilted her head back and laughed.

Miles and miles of trolls with a million spears and I have vines.

It wasn't funny. There wasn't anything funny about it, but she laughed anyway.

It won't be long before all of my troubles are over.

While, on and on, through the smoke and raucous clamor, they walked.

Getting to Know You

THE TIRED OLD VW van could barely do 60 MPH on a flat road and much less on inclines, so their southward progress was slow, but steady. After a full day of driving, they had traveled just over 300 miles, but that was enough to weave through bumper-to-bumper traffic in Portland, Oregon. As traffic eased, Tor took a deep breath and visibly relaxed.

Daydreaming in the back, Minnie had no concept of time or location, and she wasn't sure Tor or Gretchen did either. She seemed to be immune to the marijuana they were smoking, or perhaps she was already just too numb to care. A day earlier, she never would have guessed she'd be in an overstuffed van driven by a man older than dirt and with a woman passenger with kind eyes and an old soul. She didn't know them, but she liked them—she felt safe, but lonely—she pined for Fiona and Sean.

She'd give anything to see the Fachan hop up on his one foot with the absurd red bow in his hair. She wanted to snuggle with

Keela and forget the cold world existed. Hell, right now, she'd even take Lacey and her trivial rambling. She wanted nothing more than to fade away into the ether.

Yet here she sat.

The van had an eight-track player and it was Gretchen's task to swap the tapes in and out and keep the music playing.

There is a road, no simple highway
Between the dawn and the dark of night
And if you go no one may follow
That path is for your steps alone

While Tor tonelessly sang along with The Grateful Dead's staticky, lo-fi recording, Gretchen turned back to study Minnie with knowing and love in her eyes. Minnie guessed she'd been in similar shoes once or twice in her life. Gretchen reached back and touched Minnie's knee.

"It will be okay, honey. We'll protect you like our own. Mama wolves can't always stay with their pups, but the rest of the pack helps out. We're your pack until your mama comes for you. She will come little one, she will come..."

Minnie mustered a smile but no words. She closed her eyes for a spell and drifted off into a dark, dreamless state.

When she awoke, she sensed they'd been stopped for a while. Tor and Gretchen were off only a little ways away and had started a camp fire. It was big enough to keep them warm, but small enough to remain undetected. They'd parked the van so Minnie could see them; the van's door was ajar so she could enjoy the fresh air.

After extricating herself from the van's mess, she rubbed her eyes and walked sleepily toward her new companions.

Tor spoke.

"Well, hello there, Sprout. We let you sleep; you seemed awfully tired. We lit this here fire to keep us warm and keep the wild critters away..."

"They won't approach; they'll just keep a watchful eye over

us," whispered Minnie.

Gretchen looked from Minnie to Tor.

"She's right, you know. She's like me, or I'm like her. There are just things we know..."

Tor rolled his eyes.

"Oh, great. Another witch. Welcome to the club, Sprout. Tell us about yourself. As my old lady said, we'll protect you like our own until your mama comes. We'll do you no harm. We may be old, but we been around some. Nothing will get by us to you. Understand?"

Minnie let out a huge sigh and the world sighed with her; she nodded and whispered, "Thank you."

"Here, honey, have some tea. It's boiled it over the fire and I added lavender and fresh honey."

Minnie took the warm tin cup in her hands and drank down the sweet elixir—she'd never tasted anything so good. She looked at Gretchen who had a twinkle in her eyes.

"There ya go, darlin'. Have another cup. It will make you feel better."

No wasn't an option; Gretchen took Minnie's cup, refilled it and handed it back. Minnie cupped it in her hands and stared into the fire. Fire. Fire was coming to Fiona. Fire and blackness, charred Earth and creatures of doom. Minnie shook her head to dispel the vision.

"Where are we anyways?"

Tor grinned.

"Somewhere between here and there, Sprout. Safe and sound in the darkness. Off the grid. We'll get to the desert in a couple days or so."

"Tor knows all the good places. We're by one of the Oregon Vortexes. Can you feel it?"

Minnie shook her head, but realized it was a lie. She felt something. She tried to think of a description.

A channel of energy.

"Nikola Tesla, you know him?" Tor said. Without waiting for a reply, he continued, "He said we live in an electric universe.

Magnetic flux. Oscillators. Electric fields. That's everything. We can break particles apart all we like and see what flies out, but without a proper level of abstraction, we understand nothing. What does cellular biology tell you about your soul?" He answered his own question. "Nothing, that's what."

"Please forgive the old man. He was a physics professor before he retired. Don't listen to him."

Minnie patted Gretchen's knee to quiet her.

"Tor, what's a vortex?"

Gretchen grinned.

"I warned you," she said. "Once he starts, he won't stop."

Rudely, Tor stuck out his tongue.

"You know what they are—you just don't know you know. Ever seen a swirl of cream in a cup of coffee? Ever seen a smoke ring?" He puffed one out. "Of course you have. What about a whirlpool, a dust devil or a satellite photo of a hurricane? Vortexes come from fluid dynamics, where a liquid rapidly revolves around an axis, but the velocity is slower the farther from the center. Nothing is uniform, there are peaks and valleys, places of rarefaction and focus. As an example, the Vortex near us—one I call Tor's Secret Yellow Vortex—is a focused convergence of the Earth's magnetic field and electrostatic fields from the sun."

"He names everything after himself," Gretchen interjected.

"Hush, woman," Tor said. "I have a captive audience."

"And, there's nothing he likes better," Gretchen whispered. "Fresh ears for his old stories."

"You are magnetic," Tor said. "I mean literally. The iron in your blood and the oh-two oxygen in your veins. Oxygen is paramagnetic, but it works the same. You're electric, too. Synapses building charge and arcing and muscles twitching."

Minnie spoke quietly.

"Paramagnetic means the molecules align in the presence of an applied field."

Tor sat back with a surprised look.

"How old are you, dear?"

Minnie had to think for a second.

"Fourteen," she finally said.

"Oh," Tor said, "I thought you were younger. Sorry about that. I have to calibrate my explanations."

Minnie shrugged.

"No big deal."

Gretchen spoke.

"Tell us about yourself."

"My name is Minerva, but people call me Minnie. I like 'Sprout' though, or, at least when you two say it, I do. I lost my real mom when I was very young, and then Fiona became my mom. We lived in an enchanted forest with her boyfriend, Sean, and other magical creatures but we had to flee because evil chased us. So we ran and hid and started a new life at Chet's Diner. Now the evil has found us again. I think Fiona may try to face it alone, to save me. I don't know what will happen. I don't know anything anymore."

"Enchanted forest, creatures, evil? What sort of hogwash..."

"Tor, shush, she's telling the truth, her truth. It's okay, Minnie. You're safe here. Fiona will come," cooed Gretchen.

Tor opened his mouth to continue his lecture, but Gretchen raised a hand to stop him.

"Enough," she said.

Rummaging around in her knapsack, she found her handmade clay flute and handed Tor his bongos. With fingertips, he tapped the paired drums in a tentative polyrhythm. The silence was filled with music; the rhythm became the heartbeat of Mother Earth while the flute wrapped them in a mystical sphere of protection.

Yes, for now, they were safe.

Minnie's eyes drifted and Tor smiled—she stared into the center of his vortex. She was tuned in and could sense it. He looked at it himself—it shimmered and the mix of fields and flux were faintly golden. Some vortexes were violet, blue, green or red. This one was yellow, a fluorescent lemon yellow. It warbled with drifting frequencies. Tor noticed Minnie humming along with the pitch. His mind drifted back over the prior 24 hours—

the twists and turns and timing that put them at the restaurant exactly in time to load Minnie up and carry her away.

All that was no accident.

Who is this child? he thought.

Their improvised song took them deep into the night, then Tor's playing slowed and stopped. He poked Gretchen's shoulder.

"What is it?" she said.

"It's time to serve up that pie," he said.

Fiona and the Troll King—Part Two

WITH A MILE left to walk, Fiona closed her eyes and let the troll guide her. Her legs were leaden and did not want to move, but she kept on, step-by-exhausted-step until, gently, the troll tugged her jacket collar and stopped her.

She opened her eyes and raised her face to the sky.

Built on raw, stacked logs, the Troll King's crooked iron and leather throne towered high above them. With grit and a swath of leather, he polished his longsword—its blade gleamed with a hungry sheen. Earwin tapped her shoulder.

"Kneel before your King," he whispered.

She collapsed to her knees. Ovard Skäld leaned forward to look down on them.

"She came alone?" he said.

"Yes, your Majesty," Earwin replied.

"Unarmed?"

"Yes."

"Did you search her? Tear off her shirt."

Seven trolls stepped forward, but the King waved them back.

"He's earned the right."

Earwin grinned. He pulled his longknife from his belt. In a second, her blouse and foundation garments were puddled around her feet. Instinctively, she raised her hand to cover herself, then stopped and allowed her arms to drop by her sides.

Ovard Skäld leaned further forward.

"Interesting," he said.

To see what he saw, she looked down. It had not been her imagination, her tattoos *had* moved; they had migrated across her body. Not all of them, but the runes from her shoulders and thighs were now arranged around her heart dead in the center of her chest. They weren't the same, either, there was added a sea dragon and the Earth-tree.

"Do you think *Askr Yggdrasils* will protect you?"

She almost said she did not know what *Askr Yggdrasils* was, but realized she *did* know. It was the tree of life, the guardian tree of the nine worlds. How the elaborate design got on her skin, she had no idea.

Absurdly, a fragment of Jimmy Buffet's song flooded her mind.

A Mexican cutie, how it got here—I haven't a clue…

She shook off the image.

"I'm not here to be saved," she said. "I am here to trade myself for the protection of my daughter, Minerva."

Ovard Skäld leaned even further forward as if he could not believe what he had heard. Then he leaned back and laughed with a throaty rumble.

"Look around. There is no saving yourself. You are mine. The little girl belongs to King Trevir."

He pointed his sword downward and flicked at the center of her chest. From her breastbone—and the center of the tree—a trickle of blood flowed.

"I wish to see the rest of her," he said.

Earwin was happy to use his knife again—even the rubber and

canvas of her shoes were easily sheared and in a few seconds she kneeled naked before the King. He shook his head.

"All this soft, white flesh. You are like maggots." He considered for a moment before continuing. "Not that there is anything wrong with maggots—they have their place."

He stabbed his sword into the log platform where it quivered and waved in the wind.

"If you are here to bargain, then let's bargain. I was going to take your arms and cauterize the stubs to keep you from bleeding out. To reward Earwin's loyal service, I'll grant him one of your arms to use as he pleases."

Nencee, the lead concubine in his harem tapped him on the shoulder and whispered in his ear. A thunderous anger flowed through him, but he shook it off.

"Fine, when I'm done, Earwin can have a foot, no, both of them, after I've had you in every way possible, including ways you can't imagine—ways I promise you will not enjoy. Then we go after the girl and believe me, we will find her. However, if you deliver the girl here, just like you are in front of me right now, naked, then I will not take your arms. You'll die, but in one piece. We won't dismember you until you are beyond pain—after your worldly suffering is done. You'll not get a better deal. What do you say?"

With eyes clamped shut, she struggled to her feet and slowly raised her arms. Terrified, her naked body vibrated in the breeze—her only solace was the thought that it would all be over soon.

"No," she said.

Ovard Skäld nodded his head.

"So be it," he said. "Bring torches to seal the stumps."

To Earwin, he said, "Your choice, right or left. We'll do it together."

Earwin grinned and moved behind to her left. Ovard Skäld raised his blade over her other arm and they impatiently waited for the torches to get closer. Earwin's arm moved a fraction of an inch.

"Wait for my signal," Ovard Skäld said.

The wind stilled and the Earth moved, just a twitch. Watching the torches come closer, the King paid no attention. Five more seconds and the Woman's blood geysers would erupt. Then the rumble grew in strength and could not be ignored. There was a grinding and a roar. Boulders rose and fell like giant teeth.

Fiona did not care. Her life was over. With eyes clenched shut, she stood, waiting for the swords with her arms outstretched. The sound was like a brutal, physical pressure.

I am not doing this.

But, she realized *something* was coming from her—coming out of her. Coming through her. It was a feeling she could not describe, like her atoms were fusing and energy was being created and channeled. It was not something she wanted, but, at the same time, it was not something she could stop. Her hair was on fire. Her soul shouted in despair.

I'm already dead. I could not save Minnie. What does it matter? I'm just a regular person, why is this happening?

The grinding and rending was deafening and continued for a few minutes or an hour or a year, she couldn't tell. The trolls screamed, then they were quiet.

I don't want to know.

She opened her eyes anyway.

Grinding stones, stained with rivers of blood, sank back into the Earth. The landscape was raw and chewed up. Standing high above the vast field on a pedestal of rock and mud, she was alone.

I didn't do this.

That was true, but she was used as a conduit for a tremendous energy from the Earth.

But, there was a price. Her bones turned into water and her blood turned into air. Like a stranded, naked jellyfish, she collapsed into a loose-limbed heap and the old, carefree Fiona died.

I am nothing.

Lights out.

Piercing the Veil

AFTER MILES OF following Fiona's winding trail through the woods, Ancamna and Sebastian stood before the veil, catching their breath. Neither would admit it, but they were afraid of what waited on the other side of the gray curtain. They heard muffled sounds, but they couldn't see anything.

With little hope, Sebastian took a few steps left and right to see if Fiona's trail led elsewhere, but no, if they were to follow her, they would have to enter. There was no other way.

Ancamna poked the veil with the tip of her sword. Like fog, it was insubstantial. The sword did nothing. Filling their lungs with air, they looked at each other, steeled their nerves and prepared to take the next step.

The path vibrated. Heavy footfalls approached. They raised their swords and took a step back. A troll burst through. He stopped, gasping, then fell to his knees.

"Don't kill me, I didn't do anything."

Confused, Sebastian looked up at Ancamna. She twisted her face into an exaggerated frown and shrugged.

"Who are you?" she said with her gruffest voice.

"No one, I collect firewood. Please, let me go. Not all trolls are the same."

Ancamna shouted.

"Name!"

Like a whipped cur, the troll shrank even further, drawing back. He opened his mouth, but couldn't speak. It was as if he did not know his name.

"Please. I had nothing to do with what's happening."

Ancamna and Sebastian looked at each other. He raised his palms in wonder.

"Hell if I know," he mouthed.

"Algyre," the troll said.

"What!" Ancamna realized she was still shouting. She took a breath and quietly repeated, "What?"

"My name is Algyre. Take me prisoner, do whatever you want, but don't send me back."

Sebastian jumped up on the troll's knee. Algyre's eyes were locked on Sebastian's blade. He slid it into its sheath.

"All we care about is Queen Fiona. Is she in there?"

"The King has her. He's mean—will bite your face off if his gruel gets cold. Firewood. The camp needs a lot of firewood. That's what I do—that's all. Please. You need wood? No one can find dry wood better than me. I'll feed your fire day and night."

Ancamna was not noted for patience. She raised her sword and put the point under Algyre's chin.

"I'll split your gizzard. Tell us what is happening inside. All we care about is Fiona." Her face clouded over as is if the next words were painful. "*Queen* Fiona."

"I'm sorry. She's..."

"She's what?" Sebastian said with a gentle tone.

Before Algyre could speak, there were more footfalls from the mist—like a herd of elephants was thundering toward them. Sebastian jumped to the left side of the trail—Ancamna pulled

Algyre's collar and they collapsed on the other side. One-by-one, heavy figures raced by, then, tumbling over each other, slid to a stop. There were eight, all carrying crude weapons, mauls, clubs, and crude axes.

They dropped their weapons and fell to their knees.

"I surrender," one said.

Then the others took up the words.

"We surrender. Please don't kill us."

Ancamna pointed her sword at the closest.

"You, speak." She scanned the crowd. "Everyone else shut their grog-holes. What is happening under the veil?"

The troll did not get a chance to answer. The Earth shook like a million herds of elephants approached. There was tearing and rending and thunder rumbled—this went on for a few minutes, then silence. Ancamna's face was pallid. She tried to think of a time that she'd been more scared, but abandoned the useless thought. With no further hesitation, she took three steps forward and entered the veil.

Inside, it was a wasteland. Under the relentless sun, steam rose from the fractured landscape. Square miles were flattened.

Sebastian stood beside her. He kicked a rock and a clump of dirt—nothing living could be seen, no brush, no trees, no flowers, nothing but raw, tortured Earth. Ancamna shielded her eyes from the sun and pointed.

"Can you see that?" she said.

"I don't see anything."

She lifted him and placed him on her shoulder.

In the distance, over a mile away, an earthen pedestal projected out of the landscape. Twenty feet tall, it was a flash of green against the far edge of the gray veil. Slowly, the crowd of trolls gathered around them.

"Where are our brothers and sisters?" Algyre said.

Ancamna shook her head.

"I don't know," she said.

Hope

TO REACH THE pedestal, it took a quarter-hour and along the way, they found bits of bone and fluttering fragments of leather and slowly accepted walking on a quiet field of death. Other than the whispering wind, it was completely silent. The lush forest had turned into a giant cemetery.

Ancamna hated trolls more than anything, but she felt sorrow for their lost souls. One of the trolls, a young female, did not get it. The whole way, she wailed.

"Where is my family?"

Ancamna had enough. She turned and slapped the girl's hairy ear.

"You'll join your dead family if you don't shut up."

"Dead?" the girl whispered.

Ancamna leaned over and picked up a twisted fragment of an iron spear's pointed head.

"This is all that is left of your family!"

The girl amped her wailing.

"Oh, for the love of the Queen," Ancamna muttered.

Giving up, she turned on her heel and walked the last dozen yards to approach the towering pedestal. There was a figure on top—sleeping or unconscious.

Walking around the heap of Earth and looking up, she said, "Now what? How are we going to get her down?"

One thing trolls are really good at is digging. They briefly studied the situation, then started clawing out mounds of dirt.

"What are they doing?" Ancamna said.

Sebastian shrugged.

"Beats me."

In twenty seconds, the pedestal stood on a narrow column. The column collapsed; Ancamna and Sebastian jumped back. The pedestal was now four feet shorter. It swayed, but stood.

After looking it over and talking amongst themselves, the trolls started in again. In minutes, the column had collapsed three more times and Fiona lay before them, as if displayed on a table.

Sebastian and Ancamna looked at each other.

"Well, now," Sebastian said. "That was well done."

With their heads drooping in submission, the trolls nodded and stepped backward. The crying troll still sobbed, but more quietly.

Ancamna reached over to put her fingers on Fiona's neck.

"She's alive," Ancamna said. "Sleeping?"

She gently shook Fiona's shoulder. There was no response. With aggravated roughness, she gave Fiona a vigorous shake.

Fiona opened her eyes, but did not appear to see—she was unaware. Before her nose, Sebastian snapped his fingers.

Nothing.

Ancamna looked back at the trolls.

"Help me with her," she said.

The trolls gathered and sat Fiona up—she followed their guidance, but stared straight ahead, unseeing.

"What are we going to do with her?" Sebastian said.

"Trevir will come. We have to get her out of here—to somewhere safe. I know a way, a way to send her home, maybe she will get better there before we have to move her again. Then, we hope."

"Hope for what?" Sebastian said.

Ancamna shrugged.

"Hope she wakes up."

Ancamna's power came from the woods. She turned and found a dark place barely visible.

"There," she said.

Ancamna and Sebastian tugged at Fiona's arms—on legs that moved slowly and automatically, she followed compliantly. After they had traveled thirty feet, the trolls began to follow.

Ancamna stopped, but gestured for Sebastian to continue.

"Where are you going?"

Algyre spoke.

"We don't have anywhere else to go. We're coming with."

Ancamna scowled and ground her teeth.

"No, you're not."

The crying troll caught up.

"She's going to leave us here to die."

Algyre walked up to Ancamna and stood before her, nose-to-nose.

"The only way you will stop us is to kill us," he said.

She hated trolls and was sorely tempted. The crying troll dropped to her knees and stretched out her neck.

"Just make it quick. I'm ready to go and join my family."

With fists clenched at her hips, Ancamna raised her face to the sky and howled. In the woods, the sound was echoed and magnified. Soon it seemed like the whole world was howling. She turned on her heels and took long strides to catch up to Fiona and Sebastian.

Following her, the rag-tag team started moving in a single-file line—with the crying troll trailing far behind.

Sebastian looked up.

"I guess they are coming with us?"

"Shut up," Ancamna said.

It took 45 minutes, but they eventually arrived at the edge of the desolation. Standing, they looked up at the towering trees. A figure came out and stood before them.

Troll. Female. Young.

"Great," Ancamna said. "Now we have another one."

She had a wide face with tiny eyes buried deep in brown flesh. With dirt-caked hands, the troll raised a large rat by its tail.

"No one makes a better stew than me. The secret is in the roots. Boil them good for the flavor. Hours and hours. Holly, blackberry and cedar. No one believes it, but cedar roots work good. Gaile, that's me, just get an iron pot and build a fire, I'm not good at fires and I don't like gutting the animals, but I'll chop them up once they've been cleaned. I don't care, I can use squirrel, possum, prairie dog, any kind of mouse or rat, but it takes a lot of mice to make a stew. Lucky, right? There *are* lots of mice."

Ancamna raised her hands and shouted.

"For the love of the Queen, close your flopping mouth!"

The troll was silent, but for only a second.

"I talk, I know, but that's me and that's what I do. I talk and I cook, but once you taste my stew, all will be forgiven. I've seen it again and again. No one complains when their mouth is full of tasty stew. It's that good. No one makes a better batch. Once you try it, you'll see."

Ancamna tugged Fiona's arm and pulled the compliant woman into the trees. Under the arboreal canopy, it was dark. Weaving around deadfalls and skirting a dank pool, Ancamna found a power spot and prepared the spell.

Gaile caught up.

"Black iron makes the best pot and it doesn't do to clean it too much. It's a secret to flavor. Not the only trick, but an important one. Leave a little from the old batch for the new."

With a face twisted with frustration, Ancamna said the words and the portal opened. Gently, she and Sebastian pushed Fiona through and then followed. Then, one-by-one, the trolls followed too.

Homecoming

IT WAS AN odd place. The sun sat at one spot just off the noon center, so there were places in permanent shadow where the mushrooms grew. This magical place had day and night, of course, but only because the intensity of the stationary sun increased and decreased. It was completely black at night. Sean did not know how this could be, but he did not agonize over it—trying to imagine how the Earth turned to keep the sun in one place gave him a headache.

Stretching his sore back, he leaned on a hoe and looked over the farm—at the rows and rows of vegetables, zucchini, cucumbers, carrots, sweet peas, leafy lettuce and tall corn stalks that waved in the breeze. Far across the field were the tall trees, almonds, pecans, walnuts, peach, apple and apricot.

Mucking about in the herb garden, he took a deep lungful of mint and parsley leaves and muttered to the useless Fachan who hopped around nibbling on a radish.

"At least you could brush the dirt off," he said.

The Fachan scowled.

"That's the best part."

"Comfrey. So much comfrey. I always forget how much this spreads. It has a mind of its own. What are we to do with it all?"

The Fachan and Sean had become inseparable since Fiona and Minnie fled in the middle of the night. They were quite the pair of forlorn males; Sean pining for Fiona and the Fachan pining for Minnie. Yes, yes, there were other magical creatures about to be sure, but still, their hearts ached with loss.

The creatures gave them time to grieve in the beginning; a wide berth as it were. The Fachan would wail long into the night, and could only be consoled by hopping up on the couch next to Sean. Sean would simply stare out the window, hoping and waiting. As time went on, the pain became less. Or perhaps it transformed into acceptance. Either way, life went on; but differently and with less joy.

On this day in the garden, the Fachan stomped seeds into the freshly tilled earth. There were no stores around to gather supplies, so they relied on what they could grow and mill themselves.

"No, no, just the seeds NOT the seedlings; watch out for the new shoots," yelled Sean from across the yard.

The Fachan looked up with big watery eyes.

Sean came running.

"I'm sorry, I didn't mean to yell. Just watch out for the little guys, okay? They're starting to peek through the soil and we need to give them a chance."

Sean rested his arm on the Fachan's shoulder. He always forgot that underneath the grotesque exterior, a sensitive soul lived. Minnie had found that part and nurtured it. Within moments the Fachan was back in form and stomping away, his red bow bouncing up and down wearing his ever present goofy grin back on his face. Sean couldn't help but laugh.

Sean said quietly to himself as he slowly began to walk back across the yard.

"We're quite the team, you and I. I daresay I'd be lost

without you."

The sun was out and the sky was a brilliant blue.

Perfect day to be outside tending to the Earth, Sean thought.

He hummed a little tune, nothing of specific nature. He hummed when he was happy. It made the work feel lighter and go faster. As he bent down to inspect the comfrey a flock of crows flew out of the forest. He looked up.

Odd.

He shrugged and got back to work. Ravens followed the crows, and then he heard a familiar *hoot* in the distance.

"Selene? Could that be you? No, you've been gone so long."

He stood and listened intently. Something approached; something that spooked both crow and raven. The Fachan noticed it too and quickly hopped to Sean's side. They looked quizzically at each other and then turned their eyes upon an opening in the trees. Selene came down and alighted on Sean's shoulder.

"Well, hello there, old friend. So that WAS you I heard. Welcome home. I hope you bring tidings and news of peace, or at least not of darkness and despair."

Selene bowed her head in acknowledgment and then raised it so her eyes were piercingly set on the opening in the trees.

Two trolls emerged, looking lost and confused in the sunlight. Sean slowly pulled an arrow from the quiver he dutifully kept upon his back when he worked outside. Slowly, he reached for his bow that leaned against a stump.

"I'll send a warning shot to scare them away," he said.

As he pulled, Ancamna emerged from the woods.

"Don't SHOOT!" she bellowed.

Sean was so startled that he dropped his bow.

"What the…?" he said.

As he and the Fachan stood still but ready, he noticed additional trolls carried a platform of sorts, like a makeshift cot—birch trunks with rawhide. On it was a body.

"Oh-my-goddess. Fiona!"

Sean sprinted toward them. The Fachan hopped as fast as his leg could go. All manner of creatures came out of the house and gardens. When Sean finally reached them he was completely out of breath.

Sebastian sat next to Fiona's ear, keeping a watchful eye on his queen. Sean's words poured out like river rapids over stones.

"Sebastian. Anacamna. Fiona. Is she dead? Where did these trolls come from? Why are they carrying her?"

Ancamna opened her mouth to speak and Sebastian silenced her.

"I'll do the talking now. No, Sean, she's not dead. She's away. Far away. She can take care of herself if you help her. Eating, dressing, cleaning up, but she's not here. She's somewhere else. We don't know what happened. These dozen trolls are among the few survivors. Trevir is still afoot. We came through the veil and followed a most secret path. I don't trust trolls. I will never trust trolls, but they will have no memory of our journey. We believe we are safe here, but as you know, not forever. We would like to take this time to rest and recover if we may. It is our hope that with you by Fiona's side, in this most magical and sacred place, she will come back to us."

"And Minnie? Where is Minnie? Is she safe? Is she alive?"

Sebastian and Ancamna looked at each other. This time it was Ancamna who spoke.

"We have no knowledge of Minnie. The one who knows is Fiona and well, you see what state SHE is in..."

"Yes, yes, come into the house. What's ours is yours. Let's get Fiona into an herbal bath and fresh clothes. We'll lay her in bed and go from there. It's a start, anyways."

The trolls carried Fiona to the house and then Sean picked up and cradled his queen and carried her inside.

"You're home my love," he whispered to her, "you're home. You must come back to us; you simply must."

"Ugh, humans and their sentimentality," sneered Ancamna.

"You would to do well to learn some of that," uttered Sebastian.

"You are a peculiar little gnome, Sebastian."

Sebastian smiled. Perched on her shoulder, he studied the

trolls. They were the last of their kind as far as he knew unless there was another army lurking elsewhere. He motioned with his eyes and Ancamna knew what he was thinking. He spoke in an ancient language to avoid being understood by the trolls.

"Show them mercy. They helped us immeasurably on our journey; we truly couldn't have made it without them."

Ancamna nodded in agreement. She ever so quietly began to weave a spell. The first troll turned and before he could say a word, he was turned into a flowering magnolia.

"Now they will be forever beautiful. They won't bear poisonous fruit. They won't kill us in our sleep. Does that please you, Sir Sebastian?"

"No, it doesn't seem fair, really. What did they do to us? Nothing."

"I hate trolls," Ancamna said.

Gaile had been exploring.

"Plenty of good roots here. I make do with what I have, that's what I do." She spotted the new magnolia. "What did you do? Magnolia roots are bitter, no good. You changed Boyle. You're going to change us all."

The crying troll screamed.

"I knew it. We're betrayed."

"An hour ago she was ready to die," Ancamna said.

She raised her sword to cast a spell.

"Wait," Gaile said. "You want to know what happened? I saw the whole thing, clear as day. I'll tell you all you want to know and more."

"And more is right," Ancamna muttered. "Very well, gather your damnable roots and you'll tell us your story."

Gaile tugged at the shoulders of the crying troll.

"Come and help," she said.

Ancamna watched them walk away, chattering, then she, Sean, Sebastian and the Fachan carried Fiona inside for a bath and a stein of cold mead.

Gaile's Story

EVEN ANCAMNA WAS forced to admit the stew was good, but she dared not think about the meat—the tender flesh in a rich broth. Now, if only the cook would shut up. Even when no one listened, Gaile maintained a steady, unbroken chatter.

Fiona could eat if the food was chopped up and held to her lips. Unconsciously, she chewed and swallowed, chewed and swallowed. After they'd eaten their fill and more, they gathered in the cabin's main room. Sean stoked the fireplace—against the cold night, it emitted welcome heat in waves.

Sean brushed Fiona's tangled hair and kissed her lips, hoping that would break the spell.

Nothing.

"Okay," Ancamna said to Gaile. "Tell your tale and tell it well."

Standing in front of the gathered group, the squat troll licked her lips.

"A touch of something would lubricate the vocal chords."

Ancamna scowled, then reached out to pour a cup of gooseberry wine.

"There's ale, I can smell it. Wine is fine when there's naught else, but ale is better for loosening the throat for a story." Recognizing the murder in Ancamna's eyes, her words tumbled. "A long story with endless details, I was there, I saw it all and I can account everything and answer all of your questions."

"Endless I can believe," Ancamna said.

She nodded to Sean who got up and walked to the stairs leading to the cool cellar where the crocks of ale were stored. He returned with a two-gallon clay jug.

"Don't bother to pour," Gaile said. "I can sip from the flagon. Thirsty after a long journey and gathering roots to cook the best stew you ever ate. That's enough to loosen the tongue. Barely, but I will make-do. Grateful, I am, thank you sir and lady."

"Get on with it," Ancamna said.

The troll drank deeply—she must have drained half before catching her breath. Ale cascaded down her chin, her coarse whiskers and onto the front of her leather jerkin. Finally, she was ready and began to speak.

"The King, Ovard Skäld, could not have been happier. There she was standing in front of him—he didn't have to search the town to find her. It was the little one the Black Faerie King wanted, Ovard could do with the older one as he wished and there was a lot he wished." Gaile licked her lips. "A lot."

"Get on with it," Ancamna said.

"All the way from the East, he talked about what he would do. His sword, he sharpened it every day, it could split a crow's whisker."

"Crows don't have whiskers," Sebastian said.

"Right," Gaile responded. "That's how sharp that blade was. It could split a hair so fine, it doesn't even exist. He was going to rape her and with no arms, what could she do? She might bite off his nose, but he would be wary of her teeth. I'd seen it before, there was no need to watch. To feed a thousand? That takes a lot of rodents and roots. So I gathered my baskets and walked in the forest. The rain forest. There are mushrooms there, lots of them. There's nothing like a field toadstool or coral fungi to flavor the broth. Beautiful mushrooms, I gathered as much as I could carry."

Ancamna drew her sword and in the firelight, started sharpening it with a whetstone from her bindle.

"Right," Gaile said. "Getting to it, I'm getting to it. The Earth was alive, rumbling and shaking. The air was electric, I could tell something was happening. Stones, boulders, they were shaking. Then, as I watched, the Earth opened and rocks came up from the ground, chewing like giant teeth. Everything eaten, trees, bushes, brambles and my brother and sister trolls, chewed up and dragged down toward the center of the Earth. And the sound, it was horrible, a grinding and growling roar, like the Earth gods, the stone gods were angry. No mercy, there was no mercy. Granite teeth grinding and drawing the dead souls down into the deep."

"Trolls don't have souls," Ancamna said.

"We do, not like you, maybe, but we do. We're not all the same. Some are good."

"Most are bad."

"Okay, most, but not all." She pointed at them, one by one. "Tell me *all* forest elves are good. All dwarves. All humans."

The Fachan laughed.

"Maybe all the Fachans are good, but everyone else? There are good and bad. Wholesome and tainted. Tell me true."

Ancamna stood and sheathed her sword.

"That was it? That was your grand tale? The Earth opened and chewed up all the trolls? We already knew that. You should get changed into a flower, but not a magnolia. Better yet—a mushroom. You'd make a good mushroom to be plucked and thrown into a pot." Whimpering in her sleep, the crying girl stirred. "I've heard enough." Ancamna pointed. "Go. Sleep in the woods and we'll decide what to do with you tomorrow."

Gaile picked up the ale jug.

"I'm taking this. I'll be back in the morning. Reheated stew is good for breakfast with black bread and duck's eggs. Don't tell me there is no bread and no goose eggs, I can smell them. As sure as I am standing, I can smell them. Ale is good for breakfast, too."

"Go," Ancamna commanded.

The remaining night was filled storytelling and filling in the blanks. It was a night of sleep and restlessness. It was a night of hope and love returned; all the while troubled by what was to come and how briefly they would enjoy peace.

At midnight, Ancamna finished a dram of blackberry cordial and spoke to Sean.

"We can't keep her here forever," she said. "Days, not weeks. It's not safe."

Unhappy, Sean nodded.

"I know," he said. "Where will she be safe?"

Ancamna considered.

"I have a vision. A hot place. Desert land. I don't know what it means, but that's what drifts through my mind."

She tipped her glass to avoid wasting drop, then stood.

"Tomorrow is soon enough to decide," she said.

On the Road

ON THEIR RIGHT, the sun kissed the horizon. The sunset was spectacular, brilliant crimsons and oranges in tie-dyed splendor. On rises, where the trees and landscape allowed, a huge, snow-capped mountain could be seen.

"Tor, where are we? What's that mountain?"

In the rearview mirror, Tor locked eyes with Minnie.

"You can't see the mountain from here," he said. "There's too much in the way. We're somewhere between where we were and where we're goin'."

Minnie complained.

"I don't know how I can't see the mountain when I saw it. Big peak. Little peak. Where are we?"

"Why do you wanna know?"

Minnie let out a sigh. She never got straight answers from Tor; banter and obfuscation was expected.

Gretchen swatted Tor's arm.

"Ouch."

"That didn't hurt, you big baby," chided Gretchen. "Be nice to our guest."

Minnie giggled.

"Give her a straight answer for once. If I were her I'd want to know. In fact, I have no idea. Tell me. Where exactly are we?"

Tor gruffled.

"The indigenous people called the mountain Waka-nunee-Tuki-wuki and we just crossed the border into Nevada. We'll stop soon to set up camp. Is that okay with you, mistress travel director?"

"Waka-what?"

"We pale faces call it Mount Shasta," Gretchen said.

"Okay, thank you, Gretchen. That's in California. Why are we in Nevada? We missed California. How could we miss a whole state?"

"Guess we up and drove right around it," said Tor.

Minnie let her mind drift to visions of sunny Cali.

"But why? It would be nice to see the ocean; the *other* ocean. Feel the warm sun, put my feet in the sand and eyeball the cute surfer boys. Maybe we'd see seals and dolphins and otters swimming in the waves...."

"Things ain't always what they seem, Sprout," Tor said. "Some places are best left to the imagination and bypassed in reality. Too many bums. Too many cops. Too many rules. Catch my drift?"

"According to the dictionary, *you're* a bum," Gretchen said. "You ain't had a real job in decades." To Minnie, she said, "What he really means is there is a police warrant for his arrest in California, so he stays away."

"Damned fascists," Tor mumbled.

Minnie sighed and sang a fragment.

"We'll do the Surfer's Stomp, it's the latest dance craze..."

Again, Tor caught her eye in the rearview mirror.

"You're too young to know anything about the Beach Boys."

"Leave her alone, ya bully." Along with Minnie, Gretchen sang the chorus, "We're going surfing, bom-bom-dip-di-dit, surfing."

The landscape had flattened and grew more desolate and arid.

Soon enough Tor pulled over and drove a mile on a rut that was barely a road. He stopped on a ridge overlooking a dry riverbed.

"This is the spot," he proclaimed. "Campsite."

He stopped the van and got out for a walk—peeing on the ground as if to mark his territory. Gretchen called this his "cock walk." She looked back at Minnie and they giggled.

"Here we go again," Minnie said.

Stumbling in the dark with a battery lantern, Minnie gathered armloads of dried mesquite branches and twigs. Stirred by a breeze, a tumbleweed rolled by. By the van's headlights, Gretchen assembled a campfire in a circle of rocks already burned by previous flames.

Within moments, the fire sprang to life. It felt warm and life-giving. Gretchen prepared an iron pot of venison stew and brewed her tea elixir, complete with lavender, chamomile and a touch of catnip. She added wildflower honey and a "smidge of something special." Minnie didn't know what the "something special" was, but she loved that elixir—its warmth coursed through every inch of her body, calming and reviving. Gretchen smiled in a motherly, all-knowing way.

After they ate, Minnie asked if it was okay to go down to the riverbed.

Tor looked up at the sky.

"Nope, no flash floods. The rains are all to the east, far away. They're gittin' the rain, not us; not for a while." He pulled a flashlight from one of the many pockets of his overalls. He flicked it on—it emitted a deep red light. "Use this one, it won't ruin your night vision. Scamper along, Sprout. Holler if you need us, otherwise we'll leave you to your peace. There's a vortex out there, see if you can find it."

"Hold on," Gretchen said. She fished around in a canvas bag and found a spritzer bottle. "The bugs will eat you alive."

While Gretchen sprayed, Minnie wrinkled her nose at the odor.

"Smells like dead skunk."

"Old family recipe. Works great."

"If you say so," Minnie said.

Picking her way, she wandered through scrub junipers and sage.

Behind, while the flames licked the sky, Gretchen whispered.

"Well, I'll be. She's growing on you, isn't she? You ole' softy."

"Oh, pish-posh. Hush yourself. Just lookin' out for the chickadee is all. She's been through enough, and you and I both know there's more to come..."

Tor stuffed his custom blend of Captain Black Royal tobacco and BC bud in his corncob pipe. Flicking a wooden match with his thumb, he lit up, then passed the pipe to Gretchen. Warmed by the fire, they sat and smoked in comfortable silence.

"Is she going to be okay out there?" Gretchen said.

Tor considered.

"If she's not back in a bit, I'll go out and check on her."

Picking her way over the rough landscape, Minnie wandered. Standing with her arms raised and eyes closed, she reached out to Fiona, but got nothing but silence in return. After a futile minute, she gave up and continued her exploration.

Vortex?

She wasn't sure she believed in them—they seemed like something Tor made up for his own amusement. It was hard to know when to take him seriously. After tripping down a rutted motorcycle trail, she arrived at the streambed and plopped down on her butt.

Surrounded by oval, loaf-sized stones that had been smoothed over the course of time, she put her hands out, palms down, and felt energy gathering under her skin—hum and residual warmth from the sun. She heard the fire ants talking and snakes slithering about looking for field mice. She saw lizards running amuck, cautiously hiding from the hungry, watchful eyes of the owls. One with the high desert, she heard and felt it all. She closed her eyes and let it all enter into her soul. For a time she was quiet, weightless and limitless. When she opened her eyes, she found a stone in her hand.

"Well, hello there. I don't recall picking you up. You fit nicely into my hand though..."

"Maybe you didn't pick me up at all. Perhaps I aimlessly wandered here. Did you notice I'm perfect for your hand? I roll right into your lifeline crease and into your palm's dents and dimples."

Minnie let out a sigh and the desert responded with a cool breeze.

"You remind me of another rock I met long ago when Fiona and I traveled to the square city. That seems like a lifetime ago."

"You've changed much since then, little one. You met my brother on that trip, though he would be displeased to hear you call him a 'rock' when he's really a boulder. For now, anyway. All rocks are boulders and all boulders are rock. And sand. And Earth. And dust. In their time."

"Yes, I have changed a lot since then. I guess you can't go back to what you were, huh? Can't go back to simpler times when the sky was blue and the grass was green and that was all I needed to know. Go back to before the pain and the hurt, the sorrow and darkness. You just can't go back."

"And why would you want to go back, Minnie? Look how much you've grown. Yes, you've experienced pain and sorrow and loss—just like all of us. But there are lessons on the other side of that; there always are and there always will be. You wouldn't be *you* without what you went through."

"I know. I know. But still. Would you like to accompany me on the rest of my journey, whatever that may be? Or shall I leave you here in the riverbed with your family and friends?"

There was silence. Perhaps she'd just dreamed the conversation. Perhaps it was the tea or the dizzy delirium of travel.

"I shall like to go along with you if that's okay," replied the stone. "I like how I feel in your hand. We could keep each other company."

Minnie smiled and hugged the stone to her cheek.

"Thank you. I had to leave Fiona and Keela at home. Lacey and the others have no idea about me. I welcome the company more than you know. What shall I call you? Do you have a name?"

"My name is unpronounceable in your tongue. You may simply call me River."

"River it is. Shall we go? I'm getting cold and would like to join Gretchen and Tor by the fire."

"Onward, fair Minnie."

On the way back, she saw the red glow of Tor's pipe—and smelled the aromatic flavor of his smoke. He sat on a toppled deadfall.

"Did you find my vortex?"

"I'm not sure I believe in them."

Tor tipped his head back and laughed.

"I'll tell you what. Take my lantern. Go back down and keep going upstream a hundred yards, give or take, then climb the far bank. Once you find the spot, look up."

Minnie shrugged.

"Okay."

Leaving Tor behind, she extended the lantern and traipsed up the riverbed. He called after her.

"When you get there, turn off the light."

"Whatever," Minnie mumbled.

She spoke to her stone.

"We'll humor the old guy and go up a ways, then tell him we didn't find anything—didn't *feel* anything."

She didn't walk a hundred yards; she walked twenty-five, then stopped and turned around to go back.

However…

Something tickled. A hint of an electrical charge stirred the back of her neck's tiny hairs.

"Nope," Minnie whispered.

She turned and walked further upstream. At a bend to the east, she stopped, then climbed the sandy bank. There was rustling in the dry brush, but she ignored it. A bat whizzed by. A trail weaved, she followed it. In a few minutes, she found the spot. She wasn't sure what she was feeling. There was a glow, but invisible. Something flowed up from the Earth, through her body and into the dark sky. She raised the flashlight and looked around and saw nothing remarkable.

It was a patch of dry desert. Lumpy. Rolling hills. Everything sun-bleached and gray. She felt her cells, one-by-one, rotate and align with rays that sprayed upward from the Earth like a fountain. She moved six inches and the force increased.

This is the spot.

With her thumb, she clicked off the light and the sky exploded. The stars were invisible with the lamp on, but they were blinding with the light off. The cloudy Milky Way spread across the sky, vivid and awesome. There were more stars that there should be. Millions. Billions. While soaking in the immensity of the scene, she shrank and shrank until she didn't exist as a single unit, she was part of the cosmic fabric, a tiny spot of light among the uncountable.

She disappeared. It was more than the most beautiful thing she'd ever seen. It was far more wonderful than anything she could imagine. She raised her arms and twirled, faster and faster until she was dizzy and could not stand. Giggling, she collapsed with the lamp and her stone by her side.

I am aligned.

I am not atoms and molecules, I am energy. Weightless. In this body for a while, then something else.

What's next?

It does not matter.

There was a fluttering and a black shape assembled before her eyes. She knew it was her imagination, but it seemed like the figure had assembled out of the thin air.

It spoke.

"It's not safe out here for little girls."

A pair of red, glowing eyes appeared at his side. Coyote. Not a huge one, it stood about a foot tall at the shoulder. It was an unfriendly spirit, all teeth and desperate with hunger.

"I don't think something that small could hurt me," she said.

The black figure laughed.

"Pack animals."

In an instant there were more eyes—and more teeth. She was quickly surrounded.

"One will go for your hamstring, another will knock you over. Once you're down, all of your soft spots will be theirs."

There was a hot spot of fear deep in her belly, but she pushed it away. The eyes and teeth grew closer.

"No," she said. "They won't hurt me."

"You seem very sure of yourself. If I snap my fingers, you will be dead in seconds."

"Go ahead," Minnie said. She raised her hands and let the power of the Earth flow through her. "Do it and we'll see."

The man laughed.

"Okay, you live to annoy others on other days."

His coat rustled in the wind—as if it was made from black leaves.

She realized there was no wind. She reached out.

"What are you wearing?"

In an instant, the fluttering became a cauldron of bats—who scattered. Just as quickly, the coyotes were gone, too.

It had been a warm day, but at this altitude, it cooled off at night. Soon, she was chilled and craved the warmth of the campfire. She stood and stepped away from the vortex. Diffuse energy. She stepped back in. Focused energy. A tingling at her fingertips. It was thrilling.

She knew this was a small one. A baby. She could feel it, a big one, a mainline one out there somewhere. She placed the stone dead in the vortex center and moved it around to settle it into the sand and dust.

"I prefer to travel with you, Moon Maiden."

Moon Maiden.

She did not know what that meant.

"What's a *Moon Maiden?*" she said.

"Take me with and I will tell you about that and more."

Minnie laughed.

After switching her lantern back on, she turned and skipped away.

Over her shoulder, she said, "Tell your brother I said 'hello.'

In ten minutes, she was back at the fire and greeted by Tor's twinkling eyes.

"Did you find it?"

Minnie smiled back, "Maybe a baby one."

"I call it…"

"…I know," Minnie interrupted. "Tor's Baby Vortex."

"Did you see anything else?"

She shrugged.

"Just a quadrillion stars, the batman and some feral, starving coyotes." Quickly changing the subject, she said, "I'll bet the Baby Vortex has a song."

Tor and Gretchen exchanged knowing glances and took out their instruments—banjo and mandolin. Set to tinkly chords, Tor made up nonsense verses while Gretchen wordlessly harmonized.

Flowing around an invisible burning
Baby Vortex learning and turning
Bats in the air, they push and they pull
Coyotes hungry even when they're full.

Softly, he repeated the last line and their voices echoed in the wind. After putting the instruments away, they settled in their blankets and fell asleep one by one, with Tor being the last.

Drowsy, he whispered a prayer.

"Watch over us, Great Spirit. We've many miles to go and we need your protection…especially this lil' Sprout over here. Keep us safe."

In the far, far distance, bats squeaked, fluttered and hunted.

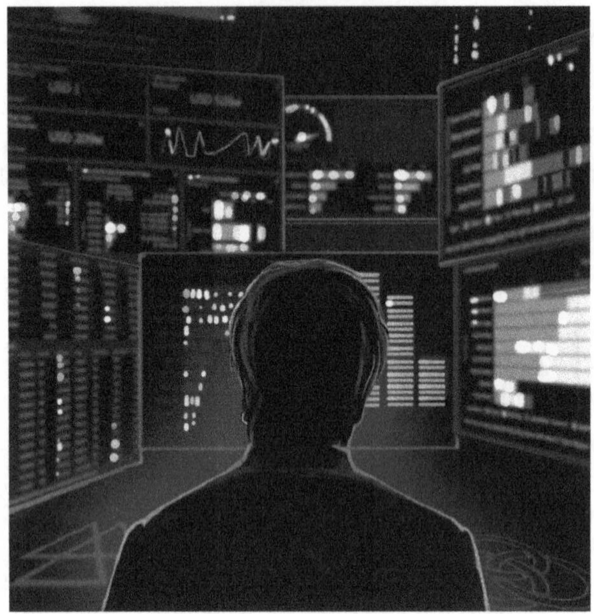

Dashboards

LIKE ALL CORPORATE dictators, Trevir was in love with dashboards. Page-after-page on his computer screens, with a glance, he could see trends and who was making their numbers—who should be rewarded and who should be punished. Baltimore, Providence and Manchester were rock stars. They were doing fine. But, the Charlotte performance was dismal.

What's with those losers in North Carolina?

Trevir had called for the North Carolina regional director to fly up for a business review. The man stood at ease before Trevir's desk. With cropped black hair and a short, dark beard, the man was dressed in khaki trousers and a starched white shirt with a wide tie loose around his neck. He did not appear afraid, or even concerned. Trevir made eye-contact with Troll Szenzo—he didn't have to say it out loud.

What's with this guy?

"You're not moving the needle, Chatsworth. Are you

following our solution-selling platform? It's not rocket science—we're not trying to boil the ocean here. When I drill into the numbers and peel the onion, I don't see robust performance with leveraged impact. I'm tempted to flush the buffer with your whole team and start over. Convince me otherwise."

Chatsworth polished his front teeth with his index finger, then looked to see if anything dislodged.

"Convince yourself or not, it's no matter to me."

The man's voice was unexpected…heavy and thick with a Russian accent.

Trevir was surprised.

"You're not English," he said.

"The name is a convenience—you couldn't pronounce our family name. In the south, an English name raises no eyebrows. That's how you say it, right? You raise your eyebrows at the unexpected? Also, you probably don't know my father—or worse, my brothers. We're happy to have the Black Death, but we'll sell it our way and you'll get what you get."

No, not Russian, Trevir thought. *Albanian.*

Interesting.

It amused Trevir that the man was so clueless. He motioned for Troll Srenzo to drop her veil, but at that moment there was a commotion in the main office. The door flew open. It was Troll Srenzo's husband, Kelpht, the ohrkk.

"There's news from the west," he shouted.

"Can it wait five minutes?" Trevir said. "Troll Srenzo is about to have Albanian fingers for dinner."

"It's the trolls. The Earth opened up and ate them."

"But the bitch-women are dead? That's a fair trade."

"No, you don't understand. The trolls are defeated and the women have fled."

"The trolls…"

"Gone. All of them."

"This can't be," Trevir whispered.

Like a whirlwind, he raged around the room, breaking everything that could be broken. In minutes, the floor was strewn with broken glass. In the rampage, the forgotten Chatsworth slipped out and away. With his heavy desk chair raised over his head to smash the skyscraper's sapphire window, Trevir stopped and caught his breath. Gently, he lowered the chair, then fell into it.

"Gather the wolves," he said. "I will go to the Pacific Northwest and finish this myself."

"We don't know where yet, sir, but the woman disappeared. The girl is headed south. To the desert, it is said."

Breathing hard, Trevir relaxed and spread his mind. His brain filled with an image of a desolate land that stretched from horizon to horizon.

"Gather the wolves," he said. "Gather everyone. We're leaving now."

The Moon Maiden